GOLGOTHA FALLS

An Assault
on the
Fourth
Dimension

by
FRANK
DeFELITTA

Simon and Schuster
New York

Designed by
Irving Perkins

Manufactured in the United States of America

1 3 5 7 9 10 8 6 4 2

Library of Congress Cataloging in Publication Data
De Felitta, Frank.
    Golgotha Falls, an assault on the fourth
    dimension.
    I. Title.
PS3554.E35G6   1984   813'.54   84-5626

ISBN: 0-671-50775-3
ISBN: 0-671-50776-1 (Pbk)

TO THE MEMORY OF
JENNY,
PAT,
RAY
and
JACK

And He bearing His cross went forth into a place called the place of a skull, which is called in the Hebrew Golgotha: where they crucified Him. . . .

John 19:17

I assert that the cosmic religious experience is the strongest and the noblest driving force behind scientific research.

Albert Einstein
(Recalled in reports
of his death, April
19, 1955)

P R O L O G U E

GOLGOTHA FALLS, 1890, north Massachusetts. The town lay in a hollow of hard, obdurate terrain where the stagnant ponds bred crawling mites on browned, drooping reeds. Siloam Creek choked on detritus from the woolen mill and there, on the clay bank, the Catholic merchants from the nearby town of Lawrence decided to build their church.

The ground when broken was sandy. Indians, long dead and disinterred from the loose soil, had to be carted away in skeletal heaps. Workmen finally hit bedrock and put cloth over their mouths and noses. The granite was deeply fissured and it issued a stench like soured milk. When the rock fractured, four workmen died under collapsing timbers. Two more paled and wasted from diphtheria. A subcontractor fell delirious with malaria. By the time the iron gate was erected, seven fresh graves rose from the poorly drained church-yard.

Yet it was a delicate, white-steepled edifice that rose from the miasma. Lilacs rustled and bees murmured at the small Gothic windows. Traceries of light shifted like butterfly wings over the varnished wood floor. Paintings of the Passion hung at regular intervals on the white interior walls. Over the church rose the bell tower, and its deep, reverberating hollow-voiced iron rang a new presence over Golgotha Falls.

Old men of the grist mill and canal locks, veterans of the Civil War, peered into the outpost of the Church of Rome, named the Church of Eternal Sorrows. Behind the ruby-red and viridian stained-glass windows, the priest, Bernard K. Lovell, carefully prepared the chalice, pyx, and vestments from the sacristy. Lawrence money saw to it that walnut carvings elaborated the pews. Angels were embossed on transept pillars and the cornice molding undulated like white ribbon around the interior. It was too resplendent, too exotic for Golgotha Falls. The veterans shook their heads and predicted the crass display of wealth would lead to ruin.

Father Lovell dutifully laid the heavily ornamented Gospel on the altar. Behind him the embroidered roodscreen caught the reflections of brass candlesticks and censers. The entire chancel bathed in the eastern sun. Over the altar, visible sign of the presence of Christ, a brass and consecrated lamp burned steadily, a warm ruby glow in the birdsong of morning.

Lovell was a shy man, barely past thirty. A slight diminution of his left leg gave him a limp. He was blond, with eyes pink and watery, like a rabbit's. It was his first church and he had the air of one striving to bury ancient humiliations.

The Lawrence Catholics rode into Golgotha Falls, uncomfortably, ostentatiously, in their black cabriolets. The Irish farmhands and loom girls milled into the plain, unpillowed pews, gossiping in a low brogue. Lovell envied the merchants their prestige. The loom girls upset him with their calloused hands and unclean English. His reedy, fluted tenor proclaimed the service of God. When it was over, the merchants left, vaguely disappointed.

The winter was harsh, unimaginably harsh. The Lawrence merchants, protected by their wealth, still did not believe such a harsh winter was possible for them. For Golgotha Falls, it was catastrophic, for the town lay in the track of every major storm that crossed the continent. The Siloam blocked with unpassable ridges of saw-toothed

8

ice. Bridges grew treacherous. Needles of ice slammed down savagely on cattle huddled under dead oaks. The populace shivered in their furs and not the largest coal footwarmers kept the dank chill from their bodies. By the time the winter was over, twelve families had contracted pleurisy.

Came spring, and the mud outside the church abounded with insects crawling, slithering, and brown toads leaping up into the sills of the Gothic windows. White cabbage butterflies hovered over the graves. Father Lovell trapped a nest of six garden snakes within the sacristy. In the evenings, low clouds of dense, boglike vapor hugged the clay banks of the creek and seeped into the church foundations, leaving dark stains on the interior floors.

The summer wore on, and the Sunday masses were dank with human perspiration. Mosquitoes hovered in clouds and lit on unprotected hands and faces. Mold infected the paint of the exterior walls. The mill folk of Golgotha Falls refused to assist, so the Lawrence merchants privately contributed yet more sums to the white church.

Gradually, the fine ladies refused to leave Lawrence. Even the simple textile mill girls and stolid Irish farmhands began to loathe the incessant badgering of Lovell for more contributions. For, by accident or design, and Lovell thought by covert persuasion on the part of the Lawrence merchants, communication with the Boston archdiocese had dried up. Lovell cursed them all for abandoning the church, and with new vigor continued sermonizing those stalwarts who still came. But as he looked out on the aged men trembling in their denims, at the large empty spaces in the pews, he knew that his was a dying congregation.

As the years passed, an economic depression devastated the mill towns and the Lawrence merchants refused further investment. The looms fell silent. The once-busy canal fed by Siloam Creek was filled with stinking algae and wild irises. Infuriated, Golgotha Falls found its scapegoat, the crumbling Catholic Church of Eternal Sorrows.

Lovell disdained the town's bigotry, its obsession with money. He retired to his small room in the adjacent rectory, his books of etymology, the portrait of his mother on a black marble-topped dresser. He wrote elegant letters to the Holy See in Rome, describing a bustling congregation in a growing town. In truth, Golgotha Falls too had begun to die.

In the rectory, the silence grew. The amber of the night lamp shone over the unkempt quarters. Requests for funds lay on his desk,

9

refused by the merchants. Out of bitter pride, Lovell continued to lie to his ecclesiastical superiors. Drinking red burgundy, he stared through his reflection at the dark hills of the Massachusetts interior. His mission was as obscure and bleak as the Siloam sucking at the church's cornerstone.

One wintry day, Lovell, his hair wispy and gray, hacked alone at the rock-hard earth and then with frayed rope tried to lower the casket of the last parishioner. The weight was too much for his frail arms. It tumbled in sideways. He had to step down into the open grave and wrestle the casket upright.

After that winter, no new gravestones appeared by the banks of the creek. The incoming mist discolored the clapboard walls, and Lovell let the iron gate rust shut. Property adjacent to the church fell into disrepair. Weeds grew between the church and the town. Nobody heard the priest's lusty, reedy voice, not on the calmest, most silent black summer night.

In the tenth hard winter, Lovell allowed himself to be captivated by the strange traceries of frost against the stained-glass windows. Silvered and amethyst light-flickers touched the abused music of his soul. Distracted, unshaven, he mumbled a litany to empty pews. There was solace in the reflections of light that shifted of their own accord on the damp floors. The paintings of the Passion, abused by mold, made a humpback of the Man of Sorrows. Lovell found amusement in the delicate light and shade of the walls, and he prayed to the great indifference outside the hollow.

For something had entered the church. Subtle as windblown seeds on a spring afternoon. As immaterial as the onset of disease. It was an absence, come floating into the interior of the ruined varnish and spore-spotted walls. It was nothingness, and yet it was palpable.

It came in the manner of a shadow drifting over the hills.

Unredeemably drunk, Lovell held midnight mass in fevered, devotional ecstasy to rid his mouth of the foul taste that intoxicated him to the marrow. The organ thundered, the stained walls signified, and the flickering tapers seemed on the verge of voice. Lovell's vestments glittered in vibrant splendor, his cheeks flushed in an uncertain light. Degree by degree, unknowing, he drifted to a pact so subtle it was as gossamer. Yet so strong, it broke the man.

Over the altar, unnoticed in the paroxysm of a new service, the red glow of Christ's lamp gasped for oil, flared wildly, creating shadows, and died.

Golgotha Falls, culpable through ignorance, absorbed in its economic woes, abjured the church, and saw nothing, heard nothing, as though Lovell too were dead.

In 1913, the archdiocese of Massachusetts began the laborious procedures of restructuring their parish jurisdictions. A committee of Boston clerics, examining records of the interior, discovered an inconsistency in the communication from a small congregation near the New Hampshire border. Inquiries produced no replies. An envoy was sent.

It was hot, early summer. The dust clung over the yellow roads as the envoy advanced on horseback toward Golgotha Falls. The Siloam Creek was clogged with reeds and logs, and the bullfrogs echoed raucously through the hollow. Shocked, the envoy stopped and looked down at the church.

The walls were cracked, blistered, and stained with mud that, in the muggy distance, resembled dried blood. Ragweed and scrub brush infested the churchyard. The once-erect gate hung at an oblique angle into the yellowed grass.

The envoy dismounted. He peered into the rectory windows. Nobody was home. Yet piles of clothing proved it was inhabited. Cautiously, he stepped over the uneven ground and looked into the dark church interior. The envoy called, pounded, and shouted, but the heavy door was fused shut on rusted hinges.

He wiped the sweat from his neck. A stench emanated from the church. With a violent cry, he launched himself at a side door and tumbled inside. Seconds later, sickly and white as salt, he stumbled back into the hot sun. He screeched for the police.

Farm boys heard the cries and dragged the envoy to the shade of the elm trees. Others stepped slowly into the church. There, in the gloom, they saw the distraught and emaciated Lovell, mucus running from his nostrils, a crucifix smeared in beeswax, incoherent at the pulpit. Then, very slowly, they turned to look at the pews.

Corpses embalmed in varnish, ragged flesh stuffed in tweeds, gloves, and millinery, grinned stiffly at the service through a cloud of black flies.

Lovell was wrestled to the floor. That night, the police transported him by wagon through the humid, gnat-hung midnight to Boston. The envoy observed a reburial of the dead. Even the furthest lilac and forsythia were filled with a rank, nauseating stink of decayed flesh.

Vandals now ripped through the rectory looking for macabre mementos. Under the rectory was found a one-armed choirboy, halfway prepared by Lovell's varnish into a gesture of benediction. It was one of the McAliskey twins, missing since the previous year. No amount of digging uncovered the second twin.

But the odor filtered down through the cracks in the bedrock and reemerged under the center of Golgotha Falls. Before a rain, as the atmospheric pressure grew, a thick stench rose in the brambles. Passersby were obliged to cover their faces. The church became known as the Church of Eternal Damnation and was shunned.

The Boston archdiocese let it decay untended. Ivy worked into the wall cracks. Tendrils twisted in the warping sacristy. Rats left fecal material in the clothes of Lovell's grotesque "congregation" under the pews. Fragments of stained glass fell onto the buckled floors, and the weather blew unresisted into the interior.

During long autumn sunrises, the entering rays of the sun illumined the broken brass candlesticks and bits of glass until they gleamed with an alien, triumphant power.

Orange mushrooms grew on the stone steps of the church path. Spores flourished on the remnants of flocked ecclesiastical garments dumped in the chancel. Dead leaves piled in the southwest corner of the interior. Slowly, slowly, the long strings of cobwebs moved over the darkened debris.

In November 1914, Bernard K. Lovell, en route to a smaller and better-equipped asylum, escaped from his orderlies. The defrocked priest committed suicide under the wheels of a beer transport wagon on the cobblestones of Boston.

The same night at Golgotha Falls, two male goats burst into the church door, rampaged through the clothing mildewed on the floor, and mounted one another in furious bouts of copulation.

Two nights later, November 23, 1914, the English instructor of Golgotha Valley Elementary School, a Robert Wharton, saw two illumined blue globes move slowly over the west wall of the church.

November 24, and no fewer than twenty townspeople swore before a notary public that they had heard choral music echo in the dark and empty church.

The next morning, Silas E. Gutman, owner of the adjacent property, slit the throats of his two prize heifers because of their low, voicelike gutturals after grazing among the tombstones.

On November 25, the wife of the real estate agent, a Mrs. Gerald T. K. Hodges, complained to her husband that she heard the untended bell slowly tolling in the vapory hollow. Two hours later, she was dead of a cerebral hemorrhage.

Thus began the legend of Golgotha Falls. The events continued, in memory and fear, in the collective imaginations of the dying valley. Blue luminescences, disembodied voices at night, and animals gone mad from grazing too near the church were observed well into the next generation.

Parapsychology then was in its infancy. Records were few and scantily documented. But the data available indicated that during November 1914, a cyclic increase in sightings of the paranormal had occurred far from Golgotha Falls. A threefold increase in the manifestations of apparitions was plainly observed in the British Isles. Five archeological expeditions to the Mideast documented glowing winds and maddened animals circling the ancient tombs of Jerusalem.

The Catholic Church's archives were swamped with parish priests claiming visitations, stigmata, and miracles in Guatemala, Brazil, and France.

Indeed, veterans of the Battle of the Marne in the First World War released incomprehensible stories of entire battalions panicked by ethereal visions sweeping close over the blasted trenches.

Deeper in the Church's archives, hidden from laic eyes, lay the unnerving spectacle of Pope Pius X, the "blessed shepherd of souls," who fell into catatonia during a consistory of cardinals and whose writhing feet and wrists fibrillated in horror, a crude mockery of the Crucifixion.

And in more recent Vatican memory, noted in the records of the Holy See and buried in secrecy, lingered the bizarre events surrounding the election of incumbent Pope Francis Xavier.

Rome was wild with rumors. The cameras of the world were perched over the heads of one hundred thousand faithful packed in St. Peter's Square to view the pomp and splendor of the gathering College of Cardinals. The College had assembled from around the world to elect a new Pope under the guidance of the Holy Spirit. It was a grave occasion. It was a joyous occasion. The tension ran high among the journalists, religious orders, and the staff of the curia and foreign archbishops.

The visiting cardinals had split into two camps. One was the conservative Roman curia. The other was a new movement of ecstatic preparation for the second millennium—Christ's long-prophesied Second Coming upon earth—a group called the "millennialists." The

College was deadlocked between the two groups, with a vast number of undecided votes.

On the twenty-first day of balloting, the ninety-two-year-old archbishop of Genoa suddenly rose in the Sistine Chapel and wandered away from his chair with its tasseled canopy, called the *baldachino*. The entire College of Cardinals, over one hundred men in crimson robes, stared thunderstruck as the old man staggered across the marble floor, gazing upward at Michelangelo's magnificent ceiling.

Suddenly he pointed upward at the finger of God awakening Adam.

"It is chosen—It is chosen—It is chosen—" he whispered.

The cardinals gasped at the violation of the rule of silence. But, transfixed, they watched as his hand tremblingly moved from the frescoed divine finger, across the vaulted ceiling, down, down the wall. Involuntarily, over one hundred pairs of eyes followed that rigid, bony finger.

The archbishop pointed at the shock-white face of the barely known Sicilian, Giacomo Baldoni.

"It is you— It is you—" he rasped, and collapsed into the arms of two frightened chamberlains.

That night the Borgia Apartments, divided into simple cells like a huge dormitory of cots for the attending cardinals, was awash with rumor and passionate argument. The Roman curia tried desperately to restore a sense of logic and pragmatism. But the millennialists, sensing an intervention of the Holy Spirit, fiercely converted the undecided votes.

The next morning at breakfast, the Nuncio Cardinal Bellocchi walked behind the pale Giacomo Baldoni and whispered in Latin, "He whom the Holy Spirit elects, to him the Holy Spirit gives strength."

But the ruggedly handsome Sicilian, the strangely bright gray eyes at odds with his complexion, looked back as out of a deep tunnel of apprehension.

"But *is* it the Holy Spirit?" he whispered in agony.

Startled, the Nuncio could find no answer.

That morning Giacomo Baldoni of Sicily received well over two-thirds of the votes. An aura of silence filled the Sistine Chapel. Into the Sicilian's hands, for good or evil, the College of Cardinals placed the entire Roman Catholic Church, all its souls, its wealth, its very historical mission as the second millennium approached. On the basis of the mystical vision of the archbishop of Genoa.

The president of the College hesitantly crossed the marble floor, sweating heavily in the tense atmosphere.

"Dost thou accept the election of the College of Cardinals?" he asked, the prescribed question.

In the deep-set, intelligent eyes the Nuncio Bellocchi saw again the profound doubt, amounting almost to horror, and the Sicilian's hand trembled violently on the armrests of his chair.

Disturbed, the president repeated the question, looking nervously at the assembled cardinals, as though for assistance.

The Sicilian, in an agony of indecision, tried to rise, looked as though he wished to warn the assembled of a grave danger, but found no words. Instead, he stared mutely at the president.

"Dost thou accept the election of the College of Cardinals?" he asked for the third time, his voice barely steady.

The Sicilian's face changed. He settled in the chair, an internal battle decided. Victorious or defeated, the Nuncio could not decipher it on that handsome, ambiguous, passionate face.

"I do," said the Sicilian clearly. It was as though Baldoni had almost known it was going to happen.

"By what name shalt thou be called?" asked the president, the second prescribed question.

"Francis Xavier," came the immediate answer.

Murmurs of approval and applause came from the millennialists. Francis, as in Francis of Assisi, the mystic and compassionate saint. Xavier, the name of the Lord. The name indicated allegiance to the cause of the Second Coming in all its significance. Under Francis Xavier and the spirit that guided him, the Church was taking a decisive new turn.

The chamberlains lowered the *baldachinos* from every chair except Baldoni's, signifying his enthronement. In less than ten minutes it was done. The Roman Catholic Church, the chair of Saint Peter, had passed into the care of the unknown and volatile temperament of Francis Xavier.

That night after private devotions the spiral candles outside the papal chapel dripped perfumed wax red as blood. Frightened, the chamberlain destroyed the candles and replaced them before the new Pontiff emerged from prayer.

Down the marbled corridors of the Borgia Apartments two Jesuits saw blue luminescent globes passing silently over the magnificent paintings on the long walls.

Francis Xavier dreamed of a congregation, its pews filled with goats, donkeys, and horses. Did it refer to Saint Francis of Assisi? he wondered as he slept. Or was it a vision from somewhere beyond the far side of grace?

That night in Golgotha Falls, after a storm, a dead sheep washed up on the grassy banks opposite the church. By coincidence a torn, tasseled fabric had been caught on the brambles of a shrub behind it, forming a canopy over the sheep. Opposite the dead and broken animal was a semicircle of over twenty dead roosters, crimson with blood still, washed down from the farms when the Siloam broke through the coops.

The inhabitants of the town and the farmers gazed at the spectacle of the orderly death and could not decipher it. It was a new kind of sign. It was as though death created form now at Golgotha Falls.

The town retreated to a terrified secrecy. And waited.

CHAPTER
ONE

DUST SWIRLED down Boylston Street in the September heat and disgorged clouds of grit, bits of dead leaves, amber pollen, and winged
seeds. It came down from the north. A dry, sulfurous heat rose from
the drought there and sent great semicircles of haze as far south as
Cambridge.

The Harvard campus, silhouetted in the warped air, was covered
in a thin scum of dust.

Within a conference room, Mario Gilbert lectured. The red-brick
and ivy-strangled Georgian walls stood as bulwarks against the heat
wave and it was dark and still among the red plush chairs, the portraits on the wall, and the mahogany lectern.

Seven men of the Harvard faculty, dressed in light summer suits,
listened.

At the leaded-glass windows, almost white with the morning glare, between the long vermilion curtains, the dust specks glittered, suspended in a Brownian motion. It was as though tiny flecks of matter were being strangled and shivered to nonexistence in the oblong heat of the hedge-shrouded window.

Mario Gilbert turned the pages of his lecture and tried to keep his mind focused on his speech.

"Lateral research into the Golgotha Falls site," he continued, "uncovered clues from the aboriginal tribes. The Algonquin word for the hollow in which the church is found must be rendered as *where the smoke rises*. But the word is not exactly *smoke*, nor is it *fog*, or *mist*. Dr. Wilkes of the Department of Anthropology, an expert in Algonquin dialects, determined that the word is at best a derivative of the root for *steam* or *vapor*. And, in fact, the granitic limestone of the church foundations exudes a visible vapor in early spring and autumn."

Mario felt sweat forming on the back of his neck. The green wool tie he felt obliged to wear stifled him and his fingers played uncomfortably at its knot. He turned to pick up a glass of lukewarm water.

Behind the slide carousel and folders of documentation, his colleague, Anita Wagner, sat, impassive as an ivory statue. She wore beige linen and small gold bracelets that tinkled with each movement of her slender wrist. She had the long, black hair that matched her startling black eyes, but the pale skin seemed to belong to someone else, to some ethereal being from a distant and superior world.

Mario turned back to the impassive committee on interdisciplinary studies.

"Thus we know that the Algonquin knew the place, gave it a name, and migrated carefully around it."

The portraits on the wall irritated Mario. They were dead men from a dead, liberal world, and like the faculty before him, they smiled, benign, complacent, insipid.

Mario squared his stocky shoulders and leaned forward for emphasis.

"*They avoided it*," he declared. "From archeologists and anthropologists, we know that there were no slash-and-burn cleared forests, no fish-fertilized crop areas, no charred organic materials that would indicate fires, no lodge-poles, no animal-skin or tooth remains, and no pottery fragments. Whether en route to shamanistic conclaves or migrating for the berry season, the Algonquin systematically circumvented the hollow by at least five miles."

The men sat like stones.

"We know, too," Mario continued, turning another page, "that the first settlers, the English Separatists, avoided the area, though this is probably due to the disease potential of the Siloam Creek where it runs into the bog. Nevertheless, they practiced a primitive form of mining by dredging the nearby lake bottoms for deposits of iron ore, which they smelted in wood-fed furnaces on shore. Perhaps these fires, blazing into the night for material gain, originated many of the tales that subsequently came out of the area—tales that normally had a satanic or Christian-demonic quality."

Still, the men sat without a flicker of emotion. Mario felt a subtle cynicism behind their bland expressions. It made his skin crawl. The historical presentation was complete. It was Anita's role to bring them up to date. Mario sat down, exchanging glances with her, and Anita smiled reassuringly. She calmly opened her folder on the lectern and leaned forward slightly.

"The church itself," she began, while Mario reached behind and closed the shade, then turned on the slide carousel, "the Church of Eternal Sorrows, was virtually abandoned by the Boston archdiocese. It has never been reconsecrated. This is most unusual for an area that retains a high Catholic population."

The first slide appeared. In the gloomy room the men squinted dutifully at the image: a picturesque, run-down white wood-frame church in a New England winterscape.

"The cause of the neglect must relate to the mental breakdown, around 1913, of its first parish priest," Anita continued, "Bernard K. Lovell."

Mario pressed a button and a vaguely focused, sepia-toned photograph, enlarged from a class graduation photograph near the turn of the century, appeared. The men in the room stirred uncomfortably. On the white screen the piercing eyes of a disturbed personality regarded them with an unnatural, almost catatonic rigidity.

"Lovell was declared insane by the Municipal Court of Boston after a three-day hearing with no defense by the Roman Catholic Church," Anita continued. "Details are still not available from the archives of the archdiocese. But it appears from folklore and legend that the unfortunate seminarian was seized by a mania for dressing dogs and goats and seating them in the pews as parishioners."

Anita watched the men look at the slide of Lovell, then slowly back at her.

"Some versions have it that he dug up cadavers from the church grounds. And similarly dressed them as parishioners."

The case was beginning to bite. After the dull and lengthy exposition of the geographical and historical background, Mario felt the men fall under Anita's persuasive spell. Even Dean Harvey Osborne, Mario's nemesis, the most senior of the faculty men, chuckled as though embarrassed by his rising interest in the case.

Mario pressed a button. A bluish copy of a bad photograph appeared, with white arrows superimposed. The men were rapt.

"Father Lovell committed suicide while he was incarcerated," Anita said. "This photograph, taken by an amateur astronomer from the valley ridge two weeks later, was but one of thirteen sightings of luminescent globes during the subsequent year."

Several more images followed, some merely sketches by feverish observers, others taken from cracked photographic plates and barely discernible. Still, it was clear that various kinds of brightnesses seemed to hover at the church roof and walls.

"Local inhabitants have reported shaking of the church's structural supports and shadowy motions within the nave. But the crucial thing is this," Anita said, pausing dramatically.

She looked each professor in the eye, directly challenging his disbelief, yet smiling softly and without rancor.

"*The sightings have begun again.*"

It worked. The old, the young, the cynical, and the suggestible—each member of the faculty was hooked.

"*Something* exists there, gentlemen," Anita concluded. "*Something* has caused the inhabitants of a dying town to experience sensations in and around a deserted church."

Dean Osborne took the moment to tap the contents of his pipe bowl against the lower leg of his chair. A thin, black residue of burned tobacco fell to the floor. The mood was broken. Sucking wetly, Dean Osborne relit his pipe.

Anita immediately changed her voice to a matter-of-fact tone, closing the folder. Things were objective now. Everyday. Scientific.

"As scientists of the paranormal," she said gently, but insistently, "it is our duty to strip away the horror and the fear, the legend and the folklore, and to penetrate into whatever *is* there. Our job is to chart its existence by measurement or, without prejudice, to dismiss the previous documentation and the site as nothing more than a fraud."

Dean Osborne yawned ostentatiously. Yet the rest of the faculty found the raven-haired woman reasonable. Dean Osborne slumped a bit in his chair. Mario hid a smile.

Anita turned directly to Dean Osborne.

"By so doing," she said, "we can add our input to one of the most potent and universal elements of man's life on earth: the belief in the paranormal."

Mario switched off the slide projector, opened the curtains, and stood to face the men blinking from the sudden infusion of bright light.

"Any questions?" he asked.

Mario waited a second, several more seconds, but the faculty sat in the gloomy, dank conference room like living sculpture. Mario shielded his eyes against the brilliance of the September weather beyond the portraits, the stained wall, the abused coffee urn disgorging brown drops onto a paper towel under the spigot.

"Any questions?" he repeated.

Mario's palm had left an oval of sweat on the lectern's edge. Distantly, in a classroom, a clock bonged feebly. It stirred the men, who now coughed, and chatted among themselves as they rose in a body and moved toward the door. Anita stood at the table behind Mario.

"What's going on?" she whispered.

"I don't know—they're acting weird—"

Mario walked after them and cornered Dean Osborne in the corridor. At the end of the corridor, the door opened, the rest of the faculty was engulfed in the furnace of day, the brilliance of the atmosphere slowly receded, and the door closed again. It was quiet.

"Is that it?" Mario demanded. "Is it yes or is it no?"

Dean Osborne, in a striped seersucker suit, looked down the several inches to Mario. Both their faces were lined deeply in sweat. The dry, energy-absorbing dust and pollen gilded the air around them in a miasma of stuffy heat.

Dean Osborne saw Anita emerge from the conference room with the slide carousels under her arm. He admired her tall, sleek form, the elegant carriage of her head and the long legs in the linen skirt. Anita had the stance of a distant bird, Osborne thought, bold, lovely, and proud.

"I guess you pulled it off, Mario," he said. "I would have bet my tenure against it."

Mario grinned.

"The budget? Everything? Just as presented?"

"Hell, it's less than the coffee budget for the anthropology department. Don't go thinking it's the Nobel Prize."

Mario's grin transformed into subtle defiance. The black eyes glinted.

"All in due time, Dean Osborne."

"I'm going to give you some advice, Mario."

Now all that was left on Mario's face was a hard, jutting suspicion. He felt Anita's calming hand gently brush his elbow.

"Yes, sir?"

"The interdisciplinary budget for these experimental classes is going to dry up. By spring term, I'd say."

"I appreciate the tip."

"Mario, how will you finance these, er, expeditions?"

"I'll sell heroin to the preppies."

Dean Osborne winced in spite of himself. He maintained his calm with difficulty.

"Attach yourself to a department, Mario," he advised.

"Why?"

"Because there are going to be some drastic cutbacks in every budget. And anything without important protection is liable to be eliminated."

"I'll survive."

"No, you won't, Mario. It doesn't matter what department— zoology, psychology, or what. Just get under somebody's umbrella before the spring term."

Mario's fingers began to play nervously against the edge of the file folder, belying his sardonic smile. Dean Osborne's calm, penetrating stare made him uneasy.

Anita stepped forward.

"Whose decision was this?" she asked.

Her voice was cool, businesslike, faintly suave, the kind of voice that echoes of private girls' schools, of established society, of family that wields influence when it needs to.

"The board's," Dean Osborne said, modulating his voice respectfully. "I had nothing to do with it."

"I'm sure you didn't," Mario said testily.

"Look, Mario. Harvard is a billion-dollar corporation. Money is very tight now. The feeling is that there must be no inefficiency. And experimental classes and laboratories like yours are not efficient. So take my advice and integrate yourself into a large department."

"I'm not giving up any independence," Mario said instantly.

"Explain it to him, Anita," Dean Osborne said, frustrated. "It's for your own good and his."

Dean Osborne walked away. The exterior door received him, a glare of yellow-white flooded the corridor. Mario and Anita were left alone.

Mario savagely ripped the wool tie from around his neck as they quickly crossed the Yard.

"If I presented Jesus *Christ*," he shouted, "Ecce Homo himself— it wouldn't fit their curriculum—"

Several undergraduates, forced onto the grass by Mario's furious pace, stared backward. Anita had to double-step to keep up with him.

"They're *dead!*" he said. "Up here. Between the ears. They can't see—they can't believe—!"

Mario kicked a stone into the road. It careened into a metal garbage can. A cat leaped out of the debris and hurled itself up a fire escape.

"Mario—we got the grant," Anita said, as soothingly as she could.

"Yeah—the last few crumbs before they close the store on us!"

Mario walked, slower now, disconsolate, toward the Charles River. A faint odor of creosote, gasoline, and ragweed hung in the air. A fine, yellow powder carried down from the north enveloped the student housing.

The university at his back was an almost palpable presence, a physical pressure of stone buildings and dead history. He stared ahead at the glare of the river. Small boats went by in a slithering reflection of the midday heat. It was all the difference between slavery and liberty—and yet he needed Harvard.

Anita put her slender hand in his pocket, keeping pace with his silence as together they crossed the Anderson Bridge.

Mario unlocked the white, slightly tilted door to their apartment. Inside, the bed was crumpled with fresh laundry. The two closet doors were open. One was filled with work shirts, jeans, and boots. Anita's more expensive dresses and tweed suits bulged out from the other. The window was open, and beside it was Anita's print of a Matisse, her favorite composition of the Fauvist days, but incomprehensible to Mario.

From the low factory roofs far in the west came the tantalizing fragrance of drifting milkweed and the river past Cambridge.

On shelves braced to the walls, immaculate and precisely organized, were hundreds of dossiers of field investigations, reference works, case histories, and volumes of bound journals from the University of Utrecht, the Rhine Institute at Duke University, the Stanford Research Institute, and the Frankfurt Institute.

Anita settled herself on the bed, and Mario brought her a cold beer from the refrigerator.

"Is the van loaded?" she asked.

He nodded, and settled by the open window, putting on his heavy work shoes.

"All the wiring?" she asked. "The sensors and gauges?"

"All there."

Mario slipped into his beaten brown leather jacket. Despite the heat, it relaxed him. It was virtually his alter ego. Days on the barricades, nights in strange terrain, and his first afternoons with Anita, seven years ago—now the sheepskin lining was spilling out of the collar, but it was still a prized possession. Mario relaxed at the window and put his feet up on the sill.

"So get changed," he said, sipping his beer. "I'd like to arrive there before dark."

He noted the boxes of notes and correspondence, neatly folded reference charts, statistical graphs, and catalogues from electronics firms, all arranged under the red-checkered-clothed kitchen table.

Over his desk was a long shelf of their own field investigations. Tidewater Basin, Virginia: luminescences reported by illiterate shack dwellers, descendants of runaway slaves. Five months of time-lapse photography, interviews, temperature gauges embedded in the sandy dunes and low-lying flat basins of reeds and swamp growth. Result: two rolls of questionable incandescent billows over the eastern edge of the sea, with a vague correlation to the erratic tides of late autumn. Nothing more. Except a bad case of swamp fever that still made him anemic.

Atlanta, Georgia: an odor of decay in an abandoned railway terminal. Several derelicts had disappeared and others mumbled incoherently about a "something" that came out of the clapboards of the ruined switching shed. Research revealed it as the site of a former slaughterhouse, now covered by weed-grown rails. Three months of all-night vigils with infrared cameras and ultrasensitive sound recorders, of digging through dead cats, spiders, and rich detritus under the switching shed, and all they got was a brief correlation between the growth of the odor and some static pick-up from the sound microphones. That and copious police harassment. The net result was a single article in *Modern Parapsychology*.

There were dozens more field investigations, each in its separate dossier. Ball lightning, immunity of ecstatic snake-handlers during gospel service in Appalachia, a comparison of ESP among IBM executives and unemployed Italian dockworkers. Probability studies. A paradigmatic outline of the observer-experiment problem. A refutation of particle-wave theory as an explanation of dream transference. Notes toward the study of organized religion as a monopoly of suggestibility. All dead ends.

"Something's eating you," Anita said, interrupting his thoughts, "more than Osborne."

Mario slipped a folded letter from his pocket and handed it to her.

"What is it?" she asked.

"Read it."

As she read, Mario went to the refrigerator, brought back two more beers, and popped them open. Anita read the letter with a sense of impending disaster.

"It came this morning," he said. "I didn't want to show it to you before the presentation."

Anita shook her head, disbelieving.

"This is incredible," she said softly. "Herbert Broudermann is the top man on the West Coast."

"Was. They just took his lab from him."

Anita reread the letter. The handwriting was tiny, cramped and filled to the margins, an ironic but desperate warning from a distant colleague. The letter ended with several feeble jokes, but pain was evident in every line.

Mario sat heavily in the chair beside the window. He wiped a fleck of beer from his upper lip.

"In April it was Charles Simpson," Anita said soberly.

"At Tulane."

"And in January, it was Jessup and Weinstein at the University of Chicago."

"Refused tenure. That was a real blow."

"Mario—what's going on?"

"I don't know—I just don't know—some kind of witch hunt—"

Out from the kitchen came Anita's cat, a female amber named Dr. Lao, and it leaped onto the desk and slithered around a sugar-and-sand model of Golgotha Falls.

"And now today," Mario confessed. "I mean, the dean—it hit me like a bombshell—Anita, we could lose the whole lab!"

"Nonsense. My mother knows the chairman of the anthropology department. They're tennis partners."

"Good. We'll put our lab on your mother's tennis court."

"Believe in me, Mario. We haven't lost a damn thing."

Mario lit a cigarette. Dr. Lao leaped into his lap. He stroked the cat's ears as he stared out at the violent cascades of dust brewing in the north.

"Hell," Anita offered. "Maybe it's more than campus politics."

"It's the new materialism. We're on the outs now."

Mario swiveled in the chair, as Anita slipped on her work shoes, and his eyes examined the scale model of Golgotha Falls. Three feet in diameter, it rested on a plaster base, and tiny wooden blocks among twigs simulated the ruined Catholic edifice on the banks of the Siloam Creek, the Church of Eternal Sorrows.

The laboratory was Anita's. Originally she had been assigned space in the behavioral psychology department. As her research moved away from behavioralism and into belief systems, and then into receptivity to ESP and other forms of suggestion, she inveigled Dean Osborne into giving her a place near the physics department so she could use its more powerful computers in statistical work. There she met Mario Gilbert.

Aggressive, uncouth, deliberately offensive when he wanted to be, he was driven into the sciences by some personal demon.

The young man's energy, his determination, were extraordinary. It was as though he wanted to strip away everything, destroying as he went, trying to find out what animated the universe. His genius for electronics dovetailed neatly with Anita's more cautious examination of the subliminal. Mario became her technical assistant and soon the laboratory was as much his as hers. Night after night he stayed late, recalculating, devising new experiments, reading the professional journals. Whether he desperately needed to destroy his intuitive belief in the paranormal, Anita did not know. Lately she wondered if Mario himself knew.

Mario first embarrassed her when he exposed thirteen Boston mediums, engendering five lawsuits against the university. Undaunted, he rooted out two bogus mind-readers in Albany, and a notorious metal-bender giving exhibits in Manhattan. Then he assailed the claims of a wealthy yogi from Bombay and brought down on Anita's laboratory the wrath of an influential religious community based in Boston.

Anita's contacts protected the laboratory. The professors admired her as much as they universally loathed Mario. But Mario was secretly hurt by his abrasive contact with charlatans and professors alike. He disdained the unqualified need to believe, and just as fiercely ridiculed the obstinate refusal to accept quantified evidence of the paranormal. He threw himself into the development of electronic sensors.

ESP studies proliferated when Mario found how to use the massive capability of the physics computer for probability analyses. He also found means of adapting the latest microtechnology from the medical school to help measure the brain during altered states of consciousness. An extraordinary force propelled him into components, transistors, and lenses, as though the inanimate tools would provide some sort of personal transfiguration.

Probably Anita knew by the second week that they would become lovers. Probably Mario knew it right away. But they delayed, they moved slowly, warily, toward that commitment of the body, sensing that in each other they had found their equal.

Anita yielded in Mario's apartment, as a willow bends to the unstoppable flood of a river, overwhelmed, drowned, but not broken. The experience transformed her. For there was a violence, even a savagery in Mario's physicality that shocked her, then raised in her an entirely different, suppressed aspect of her nature. The sensual in her blossomed. It disturbed her at times. The crudity of Mario repeatedly embarrassed her. In his arms, though, she dived deeply into an ocean where she and Mario ecstatically drowned.

But Mario was changing. He was approaching forty. The promise of his undeniable gifts was receding. The field investigations had yielded virtually nothing. His lack of manners had alienated him from everyone who should have been able to promote his career. And now universities throughout the country were clamping down on parapsychology itself. For Mario, time was running out. He was growing tense, bitter, less stable.

For Mario's self-esteem, Anita desperately wanted some tangible success at Golgotha Falls.

Mario stood and closed the window. The cat leaped to the floor. Distant shouts of children died.

"Bill and Dede promised to look after the cat," Anita said.

"She's a scrounger. Don't worry about her."

Mario picked up a canvas bag of film, spare lenses, and light meters. Something in the apartment seemed unsettled, but he did not know what. He looked at her and he seemed nervous. There was always anxiety before a project.

"Let's move," he said, forcing a smile.

Outside, the white Volkswagen van stood brilliant in the midday heat.

Mario had reworked the van's interior. It was now fitted with shelves, straps, and small enclosed built-in metal boxes. The electronic sensors were neatly aligned within the padded boxes according to size, and three temperature gauges were also buckled within felt-lined boxes against the walls. Super-sensitive sonic microphones rested in heavy wooden cases. On racks were rolls of red wiring, black electrician's tape, and a dented tool chest including soldering materials, needle-nose pliers, wire strippers, and a motley assortment of screws, templates, glues, and small crystals. Mario had converted two small computers from Navy parts, bought through Harvard's liaison with MIT, and they lay, with spare parts for the tiny solid-state circuitry, in specially buttressed caskets, lined with folded blankets, behind the sleeping bags.

Next to the sleeping bags was a long canvas bag of clean clothes, and on hooks were yellow oilskins and rubber boots. A Coleman lantern was nailed to a projecting wooden shelf. A small butane heater was behind the passenger seat. Various metal eating utensils, canteens, and emergency foodstuffs were crammed neatly under the canvas clothes bag.

Anita checked off the items, one by one, on three pages attached to a clipboard.

Small rolling drums, equipped with reams of graph paper, pen-needles, and spare black ink, were secured under a tiny red fire extinguisher behind the driver's seat. A camera tripod was strapped longitudinally where the wall curved to become the roof. On a built-in shelf over a rear wheel were logbooks, clipboards, and a few reference works on similar sites.

A dozen battery packs and a heavy green generator, badly rusted and smelling of gasoline, occupied the space at the rear. It was covered by an Army blanket. Behind it, thickly wrapped in towels and tough canvas, was a thermovision camera with video screen, snug in the shadows of the van.

By the sleeping bags Mario had put an entire case of Italian dry white wine. Two large pillows occupied the space behind the front seats, and even with a full load of equipment there was now room for both sleeping bags to be unrolled completely on a small but thick carpet that ran the length of the van.

Anita found the glove compartment in the front heavily equipped with knives, small batteries, work gloves, lighter fluid, and county and surveyor's maps of the Golgotha Falls area. Under the van, secured with sturdy wire and bolted to plates, were long-handled spades, a shovel, and a multipurpose pole for probing sensors into areas too slender for the human hand. Rope, wire, and a small hatchet hung from the driver's door. Concealed in the map compartment, a black revolver, unlicensed.

"It's all here," she said finally. "Except my sunglasses."

"On the sunshade."

"Oh."

Mario closed the van doors and got into the front seat beside her. The vinyl upholstery was hot and sticky, and the sunlight glittered glassily on the road.

Mario started the engine. He looked up the road and then eased the van forward. The Volkswagen was underpowered, and the full load made it sluggish. As he drove, he listened for anything sliding loose behind him, but it was all strapped down tightly. All he could hear was the gentle sloshing of the water and extra gasoline in two separate tanks under the front seats.

To go north, the van had to recross the Anderson Bridge and pass the university. Anita watched the massive red brick and strangling ivy roll by, and, behind the ancient Yard, the more modern steel-and-glass facilities. It was like a fortress in the center of a medieval town.

"Mario," she said softly, her eyes closing against the warmth of the sun.

"What?"

"This site—Golgotha Falls. We might find nothing at all."

Mario's jaw clenched but he said nothing, just shrugged with feigned indifference. Her eyes opened, the deep black eyes that contrasted so startlingly with the pale, lovely angular face.

"It could be a documentation of delusions," she said. "Architectural stress and wind that farmers hear as ghosts. Spooks among the tombstones that are really just rabbits jumping in the moonlight."

Mario grinned as the van cleared the north end of campus, and he drove into the shabby, dusty streets north of Cambridge. His optimism—or was it his necessity?—overrode his worries. He reached for his sunglasses and slipped them on.

"Could be, love," he said brightly. "It wouldn't be the first time."

"No," she said. "That's the trouble. It wouldn't."

Though Mario seemed relaxed, his mind was churning. What indeed *did* he expect to discover this time? He considered the many places in North America and Europe where sites, usually abandoned, yielded small findings of the paranormal. Occasionally, blue luminescences were reported, as at Golgotha Falls. Quite often minute changes of inertial states—stationary objects set in motion, moving objects that veered—were reported. Almost always the native inhabitants, whether American, Irish, or Yugoslav, incorporated these aberrant events into their mythologies.

In addition to small physical events, there was often reported a kind of "mental atmosphere" or suggestibility that at some sites remained active. It was this that Mario hoped to document and correlate. Golgotha Falls would depend to some extent on the people who lived nearby, on their abnormalities, their obsessions, for such emotions fed the physical events.

Indeed, several theories worked on the assumption that highly charged individuals, driven to commit acts of murder, incest, or suicide, could project sufficient psychic energy to inaugurate paranormal events that might outlive the individual who was their catalyst.

Mario shifted into top gear and pulled out from behind a truck laden with long, black pipes. He leaned closer to Anita and shouted over the roar of the Volkswagen churning into the open highway.

"Negative findings," he yelled. "Just as valuable as positive findings."

"If we could just—get our hands for once—on something—something tangible. Too tangible for them to dismiss."

Mario squeezed her knee affectionately.

"I'll have a ghost on Osborne's desk by Christmas," he chuckled, but deep within him the dread of failure assailed his flagging confidence. This would be it, he knew. No more reprieves. This time it truly was publish or perish.

The highway flew by. Anita grew drowsy and settled back, arms folded, and closed her eyes. He looked at her from time to time as he drove. She had made him complex. Her inbred refinement, the inexplicable and abrupt brilliance of her research—it all transformed him. Once the strident Marxist on the barricades, he now was complicated, almost too complicated, as though her more socialized personality had invaded his and not all his rough defensiveness could ever drive her out again.

The hills twisted, and from time to time small factory roofs were visible among clusters of dusty trees. Mario smiled as Anita, asleep, slid gracefully onto his shoulder.

The heat was intense and small beads of perspiration glistened on her forehead, under the paisley bandanna that kept the silky black hair straight. She jerked awake.

"What's wrong with the countryside?" she asked. "It looks dead."

"Summer heat. Drought, really."

Anita wet a tissue with water from Mario's Army canteen and daubed her face, neck, and upper chest. She dropped the crumpled tissue into a bag hanging from the dashboard. She leaned back against the warm upholstery.

"How far are we from Golgotha Falls?" she asked.

"About an hour."

She watched the gray, weather-beaten farms roll by, farms and fences that would have looked pretty in early spring or in autumn, but now an arthritic dehydration seemed to have sucked them dry. Several bay horses ran magnificently through the tall grass and disappeared into a wooded valley.

Anita rubbed her eyes and had another drink of water.

"God, I had the worst dream," she shuddered.

"What was it?"

"I was crawling in the fissured bedrock of the Golgotha Falls church," she said. "It was full of red lava and hair. It was repulsive."

Mario looked ahead at the unwinding curves of the asphalt highway. Some small rodents scampered across into the rough grass.

"Do you ever have dreams like that?" Anita asked. "Images that are foul?"

"Hell, yes. Worse."

Anita turned around in her seat, then unbuckled the seat belt and got on her knees to fish for something in the van. She finally found two plastic cups and a bottle of the white wine. Mario admiringly patted her derriere before she sat back down.

"It was like the Church of Eternal Sorrows—was reaching out to me—" she said, laboriously uncorking the bottle. "Like a message. It had that flavor."

She handed Mario a cup of wine, which he drank, looking over the rim onto the highway. He held out the cup for more. Anita held the green bottle over it and half-filled it a second time.

"You know what it is," Mario said. "It's your own sexual nature. Your conscience is warning you—"

"Knock it off."

"It's true. A family background like yours—"

"I don't buy that Freudian line."

Mario smiled and finished the wine. With a slight shake of his

31

head, he declined more. Anita put the bottle on the dark vinyl floor and pressed the cork back in.

They left the coastal plain and entered the Massachusetts interior. Subtle valleys rose slowly toward the Berkshires in the west. It was as though a blunt pitchfork had once been dragged over the stony soil, leaving shallow, infertile ridges.

Anita referred to a map on her knees. The towns they were heading for had names like Kidron, Zion Hill, Golgotha Falls, New Jerusalem, and Dowson's Repentance. Bridges crossed the Siloam Creek at a juncture still called Sinai Crossing. As the heat of the dying sun blasted inward through the windshield, Anita watched the brooding, sun-burned farms roll by in a heated haze of sulfur-yellow, violently twisting fields.

No one worked the fields. There were no horses, no cattle under the trees.

"People here came to accept the Bible in its most literal sense," Mario said. "And these are their monuments. Broken barns and debris."

"What's wrong with that?" Anita observed. "Wasn't Bethlehem just a poor, dirty town in a desolate country?"

"Nothing wrong with it. If you don't mind living in illusion."

A pile of broken stones and a rusted crank marked the well that once had been the center of Kidron. Mario stopped the van. The weather-beaten boards of a nearby mound had sunk into a decay so complete it was almost loam and the ragweed grew from it in dense profusion.

Mario took several photographs with his thirty-five-millimeter Leica. The heat was overwhelming. Nothing moved but undulations of rising air. It was a messianic landscape. As a wilderness, it had been peopled by Christ-seekers, patient and fanatic, but the millennium had never come.

"Saddest landscape I've ever seen," Mario murmured.

The van began to climb the last ridge and the asphalt gave way in patches to a fine, powdery dust. The tires lost traction. Mario tensed. The steel radial Pirellis whined, the van swerved, and Anita's hand rested gently on his arm.

"It's okay. It's okay," Mario said. "We won't get stuck."

But the van slipped sideways, and only then caught traction. Mario drove the oblique road up the long slope, half on the shoulder, half in the field.

Anita rolled up her window, but the choking, pink-brown dust sifted through, hanging in the sun-brought reflections of the dashboard.

Abruptly, the van went into the deep shade of a stand of birch trees. The white, mottled bark stood out abruptly from the night-dark depths of the woods. Caterpillars hung from silk threads, twirling, and as the Volkswagen passed by, the pale green segmented bodies smeared over the windshield.

"God," Mario swore, "I'm blinded."

The spray nozzles under the wipers were clotted with arcs of wriggling, crushed bodies.

The Volkswagen shuddered out from the woods. Mario stopped. Anita stepped out with a thermos of water and a paper towel. It was quiet. The sun was down. Vermilion clouds covered the west and an amber glow seemed to rise from the fields of the ridges. A mournful owl cry echoed through the darkness on the valley floor below them.

A mauve-brown smoke curled along the dark, serpentine Siloam. Night was settled in the ruined shacks and from the clay and limestone hollow, through the moving smoke, rose the derelict steeple of the Church of Eternal Sorrows under the evening star.

Mario climbed from the van and looked down into the valley, but save for the steeple, the smoke obscured everything. Distraught, restless, he paced the edge of the ridge, looking through binoculars, but saw nothing but broken silhouettes.

Down in the hollow, where there should have been the town's lights, there was nothing but an oval of even darker blackness. An odor of unclean water rose to the Volkswagen. The blackness was overwhelming. Through the broken branches over him, Mario could see the cold stars. But down beyond the dried, cooling fields, there was not even the vaguest rectilinear form that could have been a street, a building, or even a rock. There was nothing visible at all.

Anita came to his side.

"Welcome to Golgotha Falls," he murmured.

C H A P T E R
T W O

GOLGOTHA FALLS in the morning steamed with a heated white mist that rose from the clay and spread out to the yellow fields.

Anita boiled water over the propane stove for coffee while Mario went again to the last row of trees and stared down at the miasmic valley floor.

The church, on the right, rested in a gray hollow where the Siloam behind it was bright and restless. On the left, where the creek became a muddy, bramble-infested bog, were the remnants of the town. In between was nearly an acre of dessicated thistles and broken ground. It was difficult to escape the impression that the town had crawled from the church and had died in the process.

Anita came slowly, carrying two cups top-heavy with coffee.

"Thanks, honey," he said, kissing her.

"You didn't sleep, either, did you?"

"I had the same kind of dreams you did. Broken rocks, filled with blood, or lava, or something."

"The caterpillars kept dropping on the roof. I could hear them wriggling."

Mario handed her his cup and raised the binoculars. The white clapboards of the church were oddly bright behind the haze. The Gothic windows were devoid of glass, black shapes in the heated brightness. Behind the ruined ornamental gate Mario saw the Siloam rise and fall, as though it were breathing.

Closer to the birch woods, nearly lost in the yellow grass, were twelve gravestones, leaning down toward the hollow. Some of them still had crosses, but all were badly marred by fungus and brown lichen.

Like a psychiatrist who needs to pinpoint why a patient is unpleasant in order to remain objective, Anita studied the site in front of her. The more she looked, the less she liked it.

From the birch woods a red-brown dirt road made a long loop past the graveyard and went into the town of Golgotha Falls.

It was not yet hot, but the atmosphere had a humid, cloying quality that sucked the energy from them. In the shadows of collapsing buildings, the dogs moved as though underwater, with a lolling, doll-like swaying of the heads.

The shadows of the storefronts hung down. A grocery store sign obliquely touched the chipped white-painted clapboards. Everywhere the town was striated by conflicting angles of black shade against the sunlit morning of bright wood and milk-white air.

Off the main street, Canaan Street, they saw early Victorian houses, many with newspapers covering broken windows. The town was calm, too calm, and the morning glories had the enervated stare of the dogs whose vitality had been totally depleted.

"Not a very healthy-looking place, is it?" Mario said.

"It looks terminal."

Canaan Street led into the field that intervened between Golgotha Falls and the Catholic church. Mario parked the van where the road disappeared into the tall brush and thistles.

When they stepped out, the full force of the humid, acrid air curled around them. It was clear, from the rising steeple out of the hollow in front of them, how the church still dominated the town.

They crossed to the edge of Siloam Creek, between the hollow and the town. There the water had backed up and silted into a dense, gray, heaving bog. June bugs in massive invasions covered the muddy, glistening reeds, streaming out from the church grounds.

The heat was now beginning to rise. It breathed up out of the bog, until the bramble thorns and humpbacked branches wavered in the rising waves.

Mario stripped off his shirt. The subtle muscles interplayed along the forearms, shoulder, and strong neck, as he wiped the sweat from his face. Mario had a physical presence that no one missed. His students called him "Mr. Cambridge."

"Weird, isn't it?" Mario said. "An atheist like me—and my professional career depends on a nineteenth-century Catholic church."

The church door was wooden, cut in a Gothic shape. The paint had peeled badly in the sun, leaving the oak panels bare.

"Do you suppose it's still sanctified?" Anita asked, as they approached it.

Mario shook his head. "A church that suffers a defamation—and this one certainly has—loses the presence of Christ." He turned to Anita, grinning broadly. "Well, I *was* a Catholic once . . ."

He sized up the door, calculating its probable strength, then, suddenly and violently, smashed his boot heel against it. It sprang back on its hinges, revealing a drafty, black interior.

". . . so I know what I'm up against," he said, his smile less droll.

Inside, it took many seconds for their eyes to adjust. When they did, Mario and Anita saw a jumble of pews broken on a spider-active hardwood floor, and hanging debris of curtains where the altar should have been.

"God, it smells awful," Anita muttered.

"I suppose every animal in the countryside has stopped here to pay its respects."

Mario put on his shirt against the damp chill.

The door of the church, now that it had been opened, sent a strong, Gothic-shaped wedge of sunlight streaking to the altar. At the far end of the church was the ruined rood screen, and a rat's nest of wood and fabric, and brass candle-holders jammed and fallen against the floor. It was all barely perceptible in the gloom.

There were no side chapels. Against the opposite wall, and facing the graveyard, was a single confessional booth. The black curtain had fallen and now housed bits of straw and, strikingly, the remains of a woman's high-heeled slipper.

The pews also contained remnants of women's clothing. A piece

36

of feathered hat and curved velvet, a bit of a mink collar, tatters of yellowed lace, cotton prints smudged by dirty rain falling through the room, now lay in piles or trapped under the collapsed benches.

Mario picked up a piece of an old-fashioned corset, the eyeholes still in place, the hooks dangling by threads.

"A bit kinky, our celibate priest," he said.

The pulpit, carved from wood and with a short spiral staircase, ornamented with scenes of the Passion, was now completely gray. The damp had rotted off the paint, leaving a sick, colorless hulk.

A wooden angel, wings partly upraised, gazed down from the pillar closest to the chancel. The bolt holding it had partially given way, so that its face was downcast in defeat. It, too, was uniformly gray, and small white insects crawled over the dry wood.

The gold-embroidered cloth on which was designed IHS, the name of Christ, had fallen from the choir loft and, with repeated storms blowing through the church, tangled among the rotted kneeling bars and bits of Gothic Revival wood decoration fallen from the roof.

Behind the chancel was a roseate window. The glass was littered in shards over the interior. Only a few sharp razorlike fragments remained in the frame. Mario looked up at the sky through the window. Instead of a stained-glass image of Christ, there was a twisted, dead tree branch against the sickly white haze.

"See?" Mario said, nudging a pile of rubble with his boot. "Christ is not present."

"What do you mean?" Anita asked.

She came closer. Among the brown, grossly moldered cloth and wood splinters was the brass chain of a lamp. The lamp itself was small and flattened on the bottom, like a small bowl. The red glass that would have made the lamp glow ruby was shattered, with only slivers remaining.

"This lamp," Mario said. "It's supposed to be over the altar. When lit, it signifies Christ's presence."

Anita turned to examine the remnants of the twelve paintings of the Passion along the walls. Nine of the paintings miraculously held, while three had tumbled to the baseboard debris. A minor artisan had dutifully painted an uninspired series of scenes, and the scenes now were dark and warped. An oval, spreading stain had transformed the Man of Sorrows into a hunchback.

When she turned around, Mario had placed himself at the altar, arms outspread in a mockery of the Crucifixion, grinning.

37

"Oh, Mario—" she laughed, "cut it out."

Mario grinned and rolled his eyes.

"You have no idea," he said, "no *idea* what the nuns and priests do to you as a kid."

"I'm surprised you let them."

"They scare hell out of you. They heap you with guilt and shove God and the devil down your throat until you want to vomit."

"A lot of people seem to get something out of it."

Mario noted the dead ivy that had twisted its way in from the graveyard and then died in the church.

"Yes, and they pay a bloody fortune for it, too," Mario said.

He held down the altar cloth with one boot and with the other tested the strength of the fungus-dappled velvet. It shredded without resistance.

"The Roman Catholic Church is the largest private property owner in the world," he said, fingering the debris at his feet. "Did you know that? Assets in the billions." Various bits of brass and mahogany wood came up in his hands. He threw them into the chancel.

"It owns gold bullion, silver, jet aircraft, real estate, art treasures, not to mention diplomatic privileges that it abuses."

A small gargoyle head, a grimace of a wood face, appeared on the floorboards. Mario smiled and put the head on a tilted pew. The face seemed forlorn, as though overwhelmed by whatever had thrown it down from the high ceiling.

"And it's all based on belief," he said sadly. "Which means gullibility."

The sacristy was ruined. A hole in the roof had let in generations of water, grime, and leafy detritus. Pieces of ornate yellow robes had turned brown and stiff. A hymnal had reverted to an organic heap in a wet stain.

Anita scraped the wood along the Gothic window frames with her jacknife. The wood on the sunny south side was brittle and flaked easily. On the north windows the wood was fibrous and moist from the vapors of the Siloam.

Wooden stairs led up toward the steeple, but the supports had given way and weeds grew at the joints.

Mario scraped through the dirt at the baseboard and studied the uniform gray clay that united the clay ground to the foundation stones.

"The church is in contact with the bedrock," he announced. "Anything going by on the dirt road, even a passing tractor, would send tremors right up to the bell tower."

"And that's what the people heard?" Anita asked.

"Afraid so. That's probably all it was."

Disappointed, Mario walked the north aisle, measuring the church. It was modest, dark, and something in it was unresolved. Mario felt a kind of anxiety in the jumble of debris and religious artifacts. Something was uneasy.

"The priest must have gone mad slowly," he said. "Maybe it took years. Degree by degree."

On the confessional booth was a small crucifix. The top screw had fallen off, so it had fallen upside-down and backward. Mario reached for it.

"Mario—"

Mario turned, his face obliquely hit by the long, hard shadow cut by the brilliant south windows.

"What is it?"

"Nothing. I don't know."

Mario turned the crucifix right side up and began to screw the brass screw into the top hole.

The low, groaning echo of the bell filled the church and gradually died away. Mario grinned.

"Never touch an upside-down crucifix," he said. "That's what the nuns told us."

Now the atmosphere of the church interior changed. Anita stood rooted. "Do you sense it?" she whispered.

"What?"

She shook her head. "An ambience. Almost an intelligence. As if the church knows we're here."

Mario shrugged and muttered, "Let's bring in the equipment."

They carried in several heavy consoles from the Volkswagen, a box of delicate sensors, rolls of red wiring, braided black cable, and the Coleman lantern.

"Let's put the sensors along the north and south walls," Anita said. "And one under the altar."

Mario unrolled slender green, yellow, and white braided wires from a leather case. These he attached to four ultrasensitive microphones. He laid out the microphones and wires along the baseboards. Then he set the built-in limiters to protect the delicate, almost fibrous wires within. The microphones could pick up mice running at fifteen feet.

Every building has its own distinct characteristics of ambient sound, tremor, and temperature variation. It would be crucial to know those characteristics in order to detect any departure from them. It might take weeks, even months, but it was absolutely vital to any accurate experiment.

Mario connected the microphones to a digital system assembled from medical equipment components. The system kept a steady time record for all sound below that limiter threshold.

"'Where should I put the temperature gauges?" Mario asked.

Anita studied the dark, jumbled mountains of wood and cloth among the pews. The temperature gauges were extremely sensitive but had very short ranges. Placing them correctly was a matter of intuition as well as experience.

"One behind the altar, near the sacristy," she said. "The other at the northwest corner. The corner full of clay."

Mario joined the two gauges to a linear graph-analysis with a self-contained power source. Referenced against time, the countless minute changes of temperature in the daily cycle to night and back would begin to show characteristic patterns. Patterns that would then reveal deviations.

Mario stretched his back, relieving the strain of bending and uncoiling the yards of wire. Anita's blouse was covered with dropped twigs and curled leaves from the roof.

"Let's take a break, please," Anita called, brushing off her sleeve.

They stepped over fallen debris, past the clotted basin for holy water, and bathed their faces in the heat of the open sun. It was a relief after the claustrophobic, dank chill of the interior.

"What about the seismograph?" Anita asked.

"After dark."

Mario stretched, flexing his back and neck, and looked back at the church.

It had once been pretty. Most of the clapboard was still white and brilliant. The steeple rose picturesquely over the Siloam and the low scrub on the opposite bank. But in the heat of the late afternoon, there was a glimpse of something unnatural about it, as though reality had become disoriented in a vain attempt to conceal the horror of a previous age.

"That priest," Mario said, shaking his head. "He left his mark on this town."

Anita collapsed on a tuft of mossy ground, gazed balefully back toward the church and the black void beyond the shattered door.

"What do you think actually happened in there?"

"Who knows?" Mario shrugged. "While the myths proliferate, no one's ever been able to ferret out exactly what did go on here."

They had both researched the church's history thoroughly, but had little to show for their efforts save that in 1921 a secondary school teacher from Providence came on his own funding to study the violent folklore emanating from Golgotha Falls. The result, two years later, was a comprehensive collection of original observations. There had been three cases in which the priest's silhouette had been observed along the walls, one case of his insane choral music emanating from the destroyed loft, and several cases of disease or even death associated with proximity to the church.

Next, during the Depression, came the Olgivy Report. It included Golgotha in its purview of northern Massachusetts phenomenology. Olgivy was spiritualist and had attempted communication with the suicidal priest. He also tried to photograph the luminescence he saw climbing the north wall. All he achieved were badly overexposed plates. Two months later, he suffered a bleeding disease of the ears and died.

Then, just before the Second World War, a well-funded excursion sponsored by a Boston theosophy organization came with electric probes and infrared cameras. Prayers failed to raise the priest. Surrounding the graveyard with the black lights failed to produce the slightest responses. But the cattle, maddened by the eerie lights, stampeded and trampled the generators into the sandy soil. The theosophists never returned but wrote to the town, asking it to burn the church to the ground.

It all belonged to the ludicrous, gullible days of early parapsychology. No more than witchcraft, Mario thought. Yet they all, intuitively, had searched for the priest. Something of the priest's passion. Something unresolved among the desecrated dead. Was it all folklore?

Mario turned back from the church. Ahead, the long, yellow grass rustled among the stone crosses and fungus-stained stone angels in the graveyard.

Almost all the stones were effaced by decades of rain, but two bore the date 1897. One showed a faint name, Clare or O'Clare. Thrown dirt from two burial sites had formed a mound from which a rose bush grew without a single bloom.

Two stones were roughly Gothic in shape, one was square-topped, and the rest were crosses, now toppled on their sides in the dirt. A few of the pedestals had ornamental scrolls worked into the vertical lines. Mario dug at the base of a standing stone. The initials of the stonecutter appeared clearly in the daylight.

"These two look more recent," Anita said, pointing to the two Gothic stones.

"Maybe those are the twins. The priest is supposed to have murdered twin boys."

Anita shuddered.

"Let's check the rectory," Mario said. "Before the sun goes down."

The rectory lay behind the east wall of the church, under the broken roseate window from which the stained-glass image of the Savior had collapsed decades ago. It was a small stone structure with a low, wooden roof. A dead apple tree hung over the ruined chimney.

Mario stepped on a rock and peered into the window. An oval mahogany table had tilted over and was now splinters over the remnants of a small blue rug. A basin and pitcher lay on the floor, badly chipped.

"It's amazing that the townspeople have left this place alone," Anita whispered. "Some of this stuff looks valuable."

"Bad reputation," Mario grinned.

Anita tried the door. It bulged fast against the jambs. Mario put his shoulder to the rotting wood. It gave like papier-mâché.

In the shadows of the interior, the bookshelves, denuded now except for gray sawdust eaten from the ceiling by insects, lined the wall over the bed. The bed itself had utterly dissolved under a leaking roof. Only the crude, rusted springs remained in disarray over the floor among tatters of mattress stuffing. The headboard and footboard lay savagely warped among dead leaves.

There was no evidence of a crucifix on the wall. An armoire with an inlaid scrolling along its bottom strip and along the vertical doors stood against a wall. Rat droppings were visible under it, among rotted galoshes and some fallen strips of fabric.

"It's the most uneasy place I've ever seen," Anita said.

"Something about the decay here," Mario suggested. "The ants. The spiders. The bog heaving up and down. It's too alive to be so dead. We'd better put a sensor here. Just in case."

Mario brushed the red soil from Anita's jeans. He put an arm over her shoulder.

"Are you ready for supper?" he asked.

"I sure am."

"Then let's go into town and see what we can scare up. There's no hurry about the seismograph."

She put her arm around his waist, her slender hand in his rear pocket, and leaned against him as they walked to the Volkswagen among the rubbish mounds where Canaan Street died.

Inside, they changed quickly, Mario smiling at the delicacy of Anita's movements, her graceful modesty despite all the years together. Then Mario closed the van doors behind them and secured the locks.

Golgotha Falls had only seven active buildings, yet it sufficed to service the local farmers and the few remaining inhabitants. Besides the tavern, grocery store, and real estate office, there were a small hardware store, an all-purpose dry-goods shop, a garage with functioning air pump and diesel pump, and a men's clothing store. Other houses occupied Canaan Street, but they were either boarded up or collapsed into timbers and concrete supports.

They walked slowly onto Canaan Street. The street itself was empty. Only one pickup truck and a farmer's vehicle stood in front of the grocery store.

At the far end of the road sat a squat building with a red neon light in the shape of a martini glass. As they neared the building, a low grumble of voices drifted over the parked pickup. An old man emerged from the screen door and hobbled away on a knobbed wooden cane.

Mario tucked in his shirt and tried to smooth down his unruly hair. Anita combed down her long, silky black hair.

"You look lovely," he said, smiling.

"I feel like a horse blanket."

Mario pushed open the screen door.

Inside, a jukebox stood on a wooden platform, and a pool table with red bumpers, its green baize badly warped, indifferent to players. Two farmers on chairs sat at a black-painted door laid over two heavy crates. That was the bar. In the far end of the long, narrow room were piles of broken chairs and pool cues, a vending machine, and the men's-room door under a naked bulb.

It smelled like the church. Dank, closeted, and full of the fine-sifted powder blown up from the drying Siloam.

"Evening," said the bartender.

"Evening," Mario replied. "Two draft beers, please."

The bartender had a round, pinkish face, and when the floodlights over the single tap hit him, he looked vaguely piggish. The rosebud mouth opened in a tuneless whistle as the beer slid into the two glasses.

The two farmers in dirt-encrusted overalls gazed shamelessly at Anita.

Anita stepped to the bar, slightly behind Mario. She kept her eyes on the single tap, from which a translucent hose led directly to the keg on wooden blocks.

"Where you from?" the bartender asked.

"Cambridge," Mario said politely.

There was a long silence. The farmers turned back to their musings, fingering their beer glasses. The first of the farmers was so skinny his elbows bulged.

Mario ordered two ham and cheese sandwiches, potato chips, and two more beers.

"You got enough electric equipment in your van to sink a submarine," the bartender said suddenly, looking directly at Mario. "What do you need it for?"

The farmers gazed ahead moodily, but they were clearly listening.

"We're parapsychologists," Anita said boldly. "We've come to investigate the church."

A nervous chain-reaction went through the men. They looked at one another.

"Ghost-hunters," spat one of the men in derision.

The bartender turned away from Mario and began to wash beer glasses in a frenzy of anxiety.

"We should've burned that goddamn church down, Frank," said the skinny man. "Like them theoso-people wanted us to."

The bartender shook his head vigorously. "It's property of the Catholic Church. Nobody wants trouble out of Boston."

The skinny farmer tapped his glass. Quickly, the bartender placed it under the tap and the amber beer began to flow into it with excruciating slowness.

"People is a little upset," the bartender explained to Mario. "Being made fun of."

"Nobody's making fun of anybody," Anita said.

"Not at all," Mario said. "Things have been happening. We want to find out why, that's all."

The farmers and the bartender now studied Anita and Mario with surprisingly frank stares. The bartender leaned forward.

"Can you get rid of what's there?" he asked quietly.

"What *is* there?" Mario asked.

The men drew into a sullen, conspiratorial silence. Outside, the headlights of trucks and battered cars retreated up Canaan Street toward the farms on distant ridges. The headlights sent long searching brightnesses into the tavern.

The men seemed unresolved, silently trying to make up their minds about the two interlopers.

"Can you get rid of things?" the bartender said.

Mario leaned forward to include them all in a confident, friendly masculine camaraderie in which there was no pretense, no shyness.

"Depends," Mario said. "What have you seen?"

The bartender looked positively frightened. He glanced down to the dark corner of the tavern as though a sensibility there listened to his every word.

"Oh, hell, tell him," said the skinny farmer.

"I never seen a damn thing," the bartender mumbled.

The skinny farmer wheezed an abrupt laugh and slapped the black-painted bar so that the glasses shook.

"You hairy-assed liar!" he exploded. "You seen the altar boy with no arm!"

"You said he come down out of the graveyard and headed for the church," solemnly added his companion, staring at the bartender.

The skinny man could only shake his hawk-nosed face back and forth, wheezing with laughter.

"I had these dreams," the bartender said, blushing, to Mario. "And one day I got really pissed and sort of saw one of my dreams."

The skinny man leaned closer to Mario.

"He dragged us all out to the church," he said. "But we didn't find a damn thing."

"I gave up drinking for a year, too," the bartender added.

"Do you still have these dreams?"

"No."

Anita saw the bartender gaze into the suds of the interior of the glass, blankly, as though remembering something else, something revived on a frosty morning in a late December he could not forget.

"They found a one-armed altar boy, you know," he said to Anita. "One year after."

"After what?"

The farmers now looked darkly away, at the black windows. There

45

were no lights on in Golgotha Falls outside the tavern. The red martini neon tubing cast its glow out onto the cracked asphalt.

"You know about the priest?" he asked.

"Yes," Mario said.

"They found out about him in 1914. Well, one year later, the man who owned this here bar found the remains of an altar boy under the rectory."

"The priest had this mixture of beeswax and varnish," the skinny farmer confided to Mario. "To preserve the flesh."

Mario nodded, encouragingly.

"They thought it was one of the McAliskey twins," the other man said, swiveling in his seat to face Anita and Mario. "But a lot of the face flesh was gone. Nobody could tell which one."

"Never found the other twin," the skinny man said softly, moodily.

"Nope," the bartender added. "But they put two headstones in the ground anyway."

There was a reflective silence. The bartender's face was softer, revealing a deep-felt sadness. "There's a legend in Golgotha Falls," he said. "That rose bush in the graveyard—it won't bloom until the other twin is buried next to his brother."

Mario lit a cigarette and exhaled away from the men. It was the only movement in the room.

"People seen flashing lights," the skinny man said to the darkness. "Sometimes they move like they was looking for something."

"Harriet—she runs the grocery store—seen the priest's shadow," the bartender added. "When she was a girl. Tried to rape her. "

The skinny man nodded and leaned back in the broken chair. "My mother saw thistles in the churchyard change into birds," he said in a faraway, flat voice. "Black birds with scarlet throats. They flew into the steeple."

Mario let the smoke issue from his mouth and float upward toward the ceiling, where it moved in sluggish currents.

"Why do these things happen?" he asked softly.

It seemed to break the spell. The farmers finished their drinks and pushed them toward the wash basin.

"Oh, hell, everybody knows," the skinny farmer said, wiping his lips with the back of his hand.

"I don't."

"Figure it out, mister," said his companion, rising and walking toward the door.

The skinny farmer waved grandly to the bartender and also went out the screen door into the night. Outside the dark window the headlights of a pickup truck flared into Mario's eyes. The engine revved, and the shock absorbers rattled over the rutted road out of Golgotha Falls.

The bartender flicked a switch on a white cord. The red martini sign went off.

"Why do they happen?" Anita persisted in a silky, persuasive voice.

The bartender smiled.

"It's only a story," he said, embarrassed. "Some people here aren't too educated, you know."

"That's exactly what we're interested in," Anita said. "The full story."

The bartender blushed, stacked the dirty plates into the wash basin, and turned off the floodlights.

"Closing hour," the bartender whispered politely.

"Yes, but why do they happen?" Mario insisted.

"Let me escort you to the door."

As they went to the screen door, where the grasshoppers threw themselves raucously against it, the bartender studied Mario openly.

"The priest," the bartender said quietly. "He perverted the dead."

"I see."

"Do you understand what I mean? He perverted them. After he dug them up."

Mario nodded encouragingly.

"You see, even the dead have to have their revenge," the bartender said.

The bartender had opened the door for them, and now they stood, all three, on the cracked sidewalk where the weeds grew at the curb. The crickets in the fields screamed under the stars, and the smell of the sediment was thick in their nostrils.

"That's the story," the bartender said. "You can believe it or not."

"Well, I appreciate your telling us," Mario said.

"That's quite all right. Good night."

The bartender went back into the tavern, looking up and down the street as he did so.

Mario and Anita walked hand in hand up the deserted, dry, dust-polluted Canaan Street. Their reflections dimly followed them in the dead, dark store windows.

"What do you think?" she whispered.

"I think we should finish our work in the rectory."

Mario opened the van doors. He slung yellow loops of low-amperage wiring over his elbow and lifted the delicate seismograph to his chest. Anita turned on the small light on the van wall and took up the metal box of pens, inks, and the graph paper in rolling drums.

Slight tremors ran along Mario's neck as they carefully picked their way back to the rectory.

"Don't trip on the gravestones," he grunted.

Anita's flashlight played over the thistle scrub that led to the open, dark doorway of the church.

It was hollow-sounding inside. The Coleman lantern had been stationed at the head of the altar. Now it rested on top of the broken pews. Who had moved it?

Anita played the flashlight beam slowly over the church interior. The shadows elongated, merged, and elongated again as the yellow beam moved down over the stained walls.

"Turn the light off," he whispered.

She flicked the switch. After a few seconds, they could see the stars through the Gothic windows and in the cracks of the roof. The pale moonlight bathed the church floor in a barely perceptible glow.

Waves of heat came in from the graveyard, and with them a steady stream of white insects in the currents of heated air.

They heard the sound of restless birds in the steeple, the soft wings rattling against the fallen iron bell.

"*Mario*—" Anita whispered.

Even with the flashlight turned off, the fragments of stained glass in the roseate frame behind the altar shifted abruptly and glittered.

Mario turned his head, listening.

"*Anita*—" he whispered tensely. "*Come away from the door!*"

Around the southwest corner of the church, a figure appeared—a tall, slim silhouette of a man wearing the flowing, flapping robes of a Catholic priest.

C H A P T E R
T H R E E

MARIO FLUNG himself past Anita, over the fallen church door, into the brambles of the church path.

The silhouette moved at the rectory entrance.

"*Mario*—" Anita's trembling whisper cut through the darkness.

But Mario already was running along the south wall, its heat still palpable along the path. His boots dug up the gravel on the edge of the cemetery. Anita moved quickly after him.

"*Mario!* Wait for me!"

Mario leaped into the shadows, caught hold of black cloth fluttering there, whirled it around. Anita's lantern caught the pale face of a tall Catholic priest.

The priest writhed, ducked, and twisted, but Mario's arm pinned him against the rectory wall.

Gradually, the priest subsided, head back against the stone, eyes

49

like pinpoints in Anita's lantern, staring at Mario. The priest was blond, and his hair trembled in the night breeze while the crickets screamed an abominable and indifferent derision.

Mario's hand dropped to his side. "A priest," he whispered, disgusted. "A real live Holy Roman cassocked priest!"

The priest licked his lips and straightened his robe. He tried to avoid the paralyzing beam of light. "What are you doing here?" he demanded. "Who are you?"

"Us? What are *you* doing here?"

"I have a right to be here," the priest said. "My name is Eamon James Malcolm. I am a Jesuit."

Mario leaned against the wall on his left arm.

"Great," Mario said slowly. "A Jesuit. Wonderful."

Anita moved the beam to the side of Malcolm's face. The pale eyes went from her to Mario, back and forth, glistening with anger.

"When did you arrive?" Anita asked quietly. "You weren't here an hour ago."

"I just came. I drove up in that Oldsmobile. When I saw the church door had been broken down—" Father Malcolm hesitated. "I was afraid. I thought of vandals."

"Vandals!" Mario howled without warmth. "For Christ's sake! Didn't you see the cables? Our electronics components?"

Father Malcolm shifted from the wall. He smoothed his hair down. "If I misjudged you," he said, "please forgive me."

There was a long impasse. Mario became aware of the night chill at the base of his neck.

"Please let us go inside the rectory," Father Malcolm offered. "We can speak there."

Mario and Anita followed the dark figure toward the rectory door. Twice Father Malcolm turned to observe them as he stepped through the dark debris to a lantern by the armoire.

The rectory stank as before of decayed organic dust, and Anita remembered the wax and varnish mixture that the priest Lovell had concocted in this very room so many years ago.

The priest bent over the lantern. He adjusted the alcohol knob and Anita and Mario saw the strong contours of an intelligent face.

"Tell me who you are," the Jesuit said, "and what you are doing here."

The voice had the familiar authority of the Church. Mario bristled.

"I am Anita Wagner," Anita said evenly. "This is Mario Gilbert. We are parapsychologists."

The Jesuit raised an eyebrow. He glanced from Anita to Mario, the anger modified by curiosity.

"Parapsychologists?" he murmured. "ESP? Clairvoyance? Things like that?"

"We're from Harvard University," Mario said. "We've come to investigate the church."

The Jesuit looked back at Anita. She flicked the raven-black hair off her forehead and her smile, though polite, was also defiant. The lantern burned behind her. It made her silhouette firm and full underneath the cotton blouse. The Jesuit turned away.

"Harvard University," he repeated with respect.

"Yes."

The Jesuit toyed with the top of a coffee pot still in a cardboard box.

"Well," he conceded, "ESP has been proved, hasn't it? Everybody experiences it to some degree."

He stared at the parapsychologists. They did not budge. The woman had an almost preternatural confidence that worried him.

"And clairvoyance," he added, "I suppose the mystics of the Church experienced something very much like it."

The parapsychologists made no effort at finding common ground. Father Malcolm thought he detected a derisory smile on Mario's lips. He changed his stratagem.

The Jesuit leaned forward on the kitchen table. "And you've come to conduct experiments in my church?" he asked.

Mario and Anita exchanged glances.

"*Your* church?" Mario said. "You left it derelict for sixty years. You hardly have a right to it now."

"The taxes are paid, the title kept. It belongs to the Holy See of the Roman Catholic Church and is administered by the bishop of the Boston archdiocese."

"Look at it!" Mario said, gesturing at the brooding black absence of stars beyond the doorway. "Is that a Roman Catholic church? It's a pile of shit!"

The Jesuit winced at the profanity. He drew back from the kitchen table.

"It suffered a terrible profanation, Mr. Gilbert," he said. "Unsanctified, it fell under the influence of—another power."

Even as Mario stared angrily at the Jesuit, the man intrigued him. Father Malcolm had a quiet, obsessive quality that threatened to disrupt Mario's intellectual control.

51

"May I ask, Father," Anita said after a long silence, "just why you are here?"

Now the twin poles of Father Malcolm's nature produced a nervous confusion. He did not know whether to trust Anita and Mario. He could not size them up, for all his study. The Jesuit stood rooted among the bright lantern beams and chasm-dark shadows.

"I've come," he said hesitantly, "to reconsecrate the church, and return it to Christ."

Mario's thumb involuntarily jerked across the palm. Anita sensed the entire tensing of his body, but Mario only gazed shamelessly up and down the Jesuit.

"You mean you've come to exorcise it?" Mario said incredulously.

"Yes. I have an authorization from Bishop Lyons."

Mario held a lit cigarette. Spiders crawled out along the rectory wall, feeling their way past the oval bright spot under the window. For a long time, Mario simply watched the spiders, then the priest.

"Strange, isn't it?" Father Malcolm said.

"What?"

"That you and I have come to the Church almost at the same hour."

"Coincidence."

"Perhaps. One never knows how these calls are sent."

Mario repressed a smile at the archaic language.

The priest suddenly brushed a hand through his hair, and the ring glittered violently like a flame.

"How long do you need to be here, Mr. Gilbert?"

"Two months. Maybe three."

"Not possible. I need only a few days to prepare the church. Once it is cleansed, it will resume as a functioning holy edifice."

Mario calmly smoked, but Anita saw the dark, dangerous spark growing in the depths of his eyes.

In the long confrontation, neither man spoke, each accustomed to the twisted and necessary conduits of political power.

"Well, I'm not moving, Father," Mario said finally, flicking ash out the rectory window.

"And yet you have no rights, have you?"

"I have all kinds of rights."

Surprised, Father Malcolm settled back against the far window-sill, half out of shadow, so that his blond hair contrasted vividly with the dark night of the fields.

"What rights are those, Mr. Gilbert?"

"For two thousand years, the Roman Catholic Church has obstructed every avenue of scientific inquiry. I'd say you owe us three months."

"A bit overstated, don't you think?"

"Religion is organized monopoly of the paranormal," Mario said quickly. "But now, here in Golgotha Falls, the monopoly is being broken."

The Jesuit merely clasped and unclasped his hands as though they caused him pain. "It's true," he conceded. "The Roman Catholic Church has never denied the existence of the supernatural." He folded his arms, looking altogether uncomfortable, even unable to collect his thoughts. "The very core of the Church, the abiding presence of Jesus Christ that occurs when the bread and wine change to the Body and Blood of the Savior, is perhaps the greatest example of this."

Mario groaned. "Spare me! I was inoculated with that as a child. So I'm immune."

"I see. And now you are an atheist."

"I am a scientist. I believe in what I can measure."

"Then I cannot allow you in the church."

Mario's eyes went dangerously deep and dark.

"Why not?" Anita asked gently.

"Because the mysteries of the Church must not be analyzed by the instruments of science. It would be a further profanation."

"Bullshit," Mario countered. "Science abounds in the Vatican. The Pope gives televised masses. The place is filled with computers. It's a new day, Father Malcolm."

"Perhaps," Father Malcolm said quietly, "but the Pope experiences the interior act of grace. As do all priests. In any case, the truths of science and the truths of the Church can never be compatible."

"If what the Church believes is true, you shouldn't fear the analysis of science."

Anita crossed her legs. The movement broke the rising argument.

"Father Malcolm," she said carefully, "we have no desire to interfere in your services. As far as we're concerned, we're looking for frequencies or wave patterns in the extreme range of the human response. What the Roman Catholic Church interprets that to be, or how it wishes to treat them, is of no concern to us."

The Jesuit smiled.

"I do understand your position," he said. "But this church was so grossly defiled, and to be able to celebrate the Eucharist in it once again—why—this is the sole purpose of my mission here. It is hardly a Petri dish designed for your study."

"Try to understand," she said persuasively, "we have risked much to be here."

The Jesuit tried to read the depths of her eyes, and thought he found sincerity there. His manner softened.

"I believe I understand, Miss Wagner," he said. "I know what universities are like and I know Harvard. They can hardly be supportive of your presence here."

"There is a very mixed feeling," she conceded.

"Look, neither of us wishes to disturb the hierarchies that have allowed us to come here," he said carefully. "Is this true?"

"Yes," Anita replied.

"Then perhaps we can work out a compromise."

Mario looked at him with suspicion. "What kind of compromise?"

"Perhaps we might work together," the Jesuit offered naively. "At least through the exorcism."

Mario slowly shook his head. "I don't know what you mean by 'work together.' And I don't know if I'm willing to risk a half a million dollars of equipment on whatever mumbo-jumbo you're planning!"

Mario watched the Jesuit's pale face grow paler and the delicate eyes darken. A savage thrill surged briefly through Mario. Grinning, he turned to share the feeling with Anita. To his surprise and dismay she looked back with a cautious glance, a look of sympathy on her face that meant she had sided with the priest.

"Mario," Anita leaned forward, out of the shadow, her angular face pale as a satin pillow. "We have to talk this over."

"What the hell—"

But something had sparked Anita's imagination. Some vague plan, some improvisation, some mental manipulation that would exploit the Jesuit.

"Mario. Let's talk it through tonight."

Mario wondered what had occurred to her so swiftly. He knew better than to dismiss it out of hand. But the Jesuit's presence rankled. It rankled Mario even more now that the Jesuit was agreeing to a compromise. Priestly goodness always smelled impure, like sour milk in his nostrils.

Mario relented grudgingly with an almost imperceptible shrug of the shoulders. He gestured to Anita that they should go.

"Good night, then," Father Malcolm said hopefully, coming to the door with them.

Anita nodded with a friendly smile, but Mario stalked off into the tall grass without looking back, hands jammed in his pockets.

"A priest!" he whispered. "I can't believe it! A Satan-hating Catholic priest! And a Jesuit to boot! Those bastards love nothing better than to argue! And we don't have the *time!*"

Anita caught up to him at the side of the Volkswagen.

"Mario—please listen to me—"

Mario slumped against the side door, running both hands into his hair, and then, in a frenzy, threw open the door and reached for a bottle of the Italian wine.

"God's punishment for becoming an atheist," he quipped, drinking straight from the bottle.

Mario saw the determined look in her eye.

"Okay, lady," he said. "What bright idea came to you in there?"

"Mario. *Let* him do the exorcism."

Mario drank deeply from the green wine bottle, shaking his head.

"Let's make *him* the object of measurement. Let's record what we've never recorded before, a believer in the midst of a passionate ritual."

"We didn't come here to record an exorcism," Mario said with distaste.

Anita came very close to him.

"There's an opportunity here, Mario. Granted, it's not what we planned. But it's good. It's very good for us. Let's make the most of it."

Mario briefly considered the mass of equipment in the church and still in the van, waiting to be assembled. He felt the uniqueness of the opportunity like a dread weight in his heart. As a scientist, he knew Anita was right. It was an unprecedented situation for field research. But the whole notion of a practicing Jesuit made him sick.

"Please. Anita! The man's got a messiah complex! He's preparing to wage a battle with Satan and his fucking minions! It's mythological bullshit! There's nothing real in it!"

Anita gently put a slender hand on his arm, calming him down.

"It's real to him," she reminded Mario. "Unless you have some private reason to avoid watching an exorcism?"

Mario looked away.

"No. Of course not," he mumbled evasively. "But, shit, Anita, this stuff makes my skin crawl, this sanctimonious—"

Anita walked in front of him and looked directly into his eyes. Mario did have an ancient score to settle against the Catholic Church, she knew. But she had never seen him frightened before. The Jesuit had triggered deep memories, memories that began long before she ever met him.

"Agreed?" she insisted.

But Mario only dug his toe into the clay, reluctant to concede.

"Mario. We can't *fight* him. The church belongs to the archdiocese. All the Jesuit has to do is contact his bishop and have him complain to Harvard. Dean Osborne would shut us down in a single afternoon!"

Mario miserably gulped more wine. He offered the bottle to Anita. She gently pushed it aside.

"This could be our last project with a functioning lab, Mario," she said persuasively. "Don't destroy it by being obstinate about the priest."

Mario grinned charmingly. The grin wavered, revealing a strange, powerful sense of despair. He tried putting an arm around her waist. She softly pushed his hand away.

"Agreed?" she repeated.

Mario nodded. "Agreed."

Depressed, Mario followed her into the van. They undressed. From the slats in the small side windows, they saw the light in the rectory. A silhouette moved back and forth between the door and the old American car parked under the apple tree. The priest was bringing box after box into the rectory.

Mario moaned and sank softly onto the towels rolled up into a pillow. The sight of the cassocked priest had succeeded in stirring up the ashes of the past, rekindling scenes of his lonely youth, so carefully repressed. Try as he now did to quell their stabbing insistence, the miserable years he had spent in Our Lady of the Precious Blood Home for Wayward Boys sparked full-blown back to life.

It had been a tough school in which to acquire a sentimental education. The boys had been rough, moody, and violent, and by the ninth grade fully a third of them had seen the inside of reform school.

Mario would stare out at the tenements of Boston. He knew no other world. He knew only that his mother had given him three times to the home and taken him back twice. After that, according to Father Pronteus, she was barely subsisting on welfare and didn't have the heart even to visit him.

The institution was the poorest in Boston. The floors were so warped, grown men tripped on them. The toilets reeked. A pervasive odor of sweat and mold lingered in the shower stalls and locker rooms, and in the tiled halls as well.

And in those halls, among the black lockers and black benches, it was reputed that half the Fathers were homosexual. It resulted, Mario gradually realized, from the abnormal imperative for celibacy.

A vague homoeroticism was the medium of all relationships in Our Lady of the Precious Blood. Mario, even at the age of seven, was fascinated by the nuns who floated, so strangely impassioned, past the Virgin Mary. His own ambiguous mother—the Virgin Mother on an azure field with painted stars—and the nuns, whose most casual motions revealed layers of starched cloth, all fused into a vague yet powerful ambience. It was a moody, almost erotic atmosphere that weighed on his heart and first taught him desire.

The principal and Father Superior, Father Pronteus, was an opponent of that atmosphere. He was a large, handsome, charismatic man in whose bright eyes Mario detected a fierce spirituality, a burning idealism, that raised him above the dreary claustrophobia of the orphanage.

Mario served as Father Pronteus's altar boy. Mario excelled in Father Pronteus's Latin class. The early history of the Church, with its subtle distinctions of matter and essence, transformation and existence, fascinated Mario. Often he stayed late after class listening to Father Pronteus. The Church taught that beyond the flesh, even though it animated the flesh, lay a sphere of idealization and spirituality, where Christ reigned supreme.

Mario discussed with Father Pronteus the possibility of becoming a priest.

Mario was fifteen when Father Pronteus caught him masturbating in the locker room. The older man brought him immediately into the administration office. There was a rambling, awkward discussion of the distinction between the flesh and the spirit. Father Pronteus drew closer to Mario, paternally.

Father Pronteus laid a hand on Mario's shoulder, down the arm, and on the thigh, even as he spoke of St. Augustine and the temptations of the flesh. Mario saw Father Pronteus's face become flushed, his breathing harder. It was like razors sliding into their idealized world, tearing everything to shreds.

Suddenly Mario struggled against his mentor. He felt the massive,

57

warm weight over him. Somewhere, Father Pronteus succeeded with his hands, strong and yet subtle and sure.

In that vile instant the entire superstructure of Platonic and Thomistic thought crashed into disintegration. Father Pronteus had used his idealism to mask a desperate genital need—to seduce Mario. Mario saw in a flash that the entire belief structure of the Church was built upon repression, sublimation, and glorification of sexual deprivation.

Something worse: the incredible, repugnant thrill of being handled by another man.

The Pope says, give me the child until he's seven and I'll have him the rest of his life, Mario thought bitterly, recalling the old epigram. Well, the Pope had me until I was fifteen. And that's long enough for him to regret it.

Beside him, Anita stirred.

"What is it?" she whispered.

"Can't sleep."

Anita lay against him, stroking his dark curled hair. The nightmare of the past receded in her warmth. Mario reached for her body with a strange desperation.

Inside the rectory, Father Malcolm paused in his labors. Sitting on a ruined cane chair, he thought about the parapsychologists. He wondered if he had already been indiscreet, had compromised too much. True, the bishop had finally authorized the exorcism, but the price had been high; the meeting painful and abrasive.

White-haired, with tiny blue veins in the nose and cheeks, Bishop Edward Lyons had regarded with a long, silent stare the new exorcist.

"It is because of the great tragedy that befell your uncle that I'm allowing this," he said. "I know what Golgotha Falls means to you."

"Thank you, Your Grace."

Bishop Lyons looked annoyed.

"I'm trying to tell you, I have real misgivings about this adventure."

"The church is defiled, Your Grace. It wants acceptance into the bosom of Christ."

"There are many lost churches whose deeds are in our possession."

Father Malcolm found the crude directness irritating. The bishop motioned to an antique chair, one gleaned from a Venetian estate upon its foreclosure.

"Father Malcolm," he confided. "I know *of* your uncle more than I knew him. Yet I loved him even so. What happened to him at Golgotha Falls was a tragedy for me personally as much as for you and the Church."

Father Malcolm stirred uncomfortably.

"Thank you, Your Grace."

The bishop's thick white eyebrows lifted. The clever dog's eyes regarded the young Jesuit.

"But—" he shrugged his shoulders "—an exorcism?"

"Why not?" Father Malcolm snapped. "The nature of his death—"

The bishop held up a ringed finger for silence.

"It was a scandal for the Church. And for me personally. And you must learn to avoid scandals."

"I have no intention of publicizing the rite."

Bishop Lyons studied him carefully. He smiled, but it chilled the young Jesuit.

"No. *You* don't. But you don't understand the secular world. You rush headlong into things. You forget that the baser world watches us, judges us, and accuses us."

"Yes, Your Grace."

"I ask you to remember what I've said."

"I will, Your Grace."

Father Malcolm wondered now if the parapsychologists would publish their research. But then, who reads obscure journals? Still, he had received an injunction. The Jesuit combed back his blond hair with his fingers and sank into troubled reverie.

It was broken by the sudden rush of an animal in the bushes. A bold, heavy, insistent pushing of the body, cracking branches. He stood and walked to the open window. He could see nothing beyond the Oldsmobile in the weeds. The hooves struck out from the rectory and thundered into the fields, into the dark, the mare pursued by the stallion.

A woman's laughter floated like a silvered butterfly out from the Volkswagen.

Owls hooted in the apple tree. Heifers moved among the tombstones, throat bells clanking, great flanks passing. The Siloam made voices behind the church. A comprehensive force seemed to animate the valley, a bizarre communion between the church, the van, and the animals and birds. The rhythms passed from one to the other, through the Siloam, and back again. They were all part of an ecology of the damned.

59

CHAPTER
FOUR

THE JESUIT drank bitter coffee.

Outside, the Oldsmobile was laden with heavy crates in the trunk and on the roof. Crossing through the weeds, his black trousers were stuck full of nettles. Winged beetles clung to his plaid shirt. Sweating, he lifted a long crate from the rear.

Anita Wagner and Mario Gilbert swam nude under the willows. They were in the Siloam, in a clear, cool pool only fifteen feet from the north wall of the church. Their arms were muscular and with assured strokes they pulled through the blue water.

The sight of a nude woman reminded the Jesuit, paradoxically, of his uncle, Father James Farrell Malcolm. He had been an expert on Renaissance painting, particularly the Venetians, and the heavy volumes of Titian were replete with white, well-rounded womanly forms. Titian had a thorough view of women. To him they were complex, intelligent, and ideal creations, in every way man's equal.

It was after his uncle's death that Father Malcolm, in searching for an explanation, had been obliged to study the psychopathology of sex. It repulsed him.

Father Malcolm carried a wooden crate on his shoulder from the Oldsmobile to the rectory. Through the willows he saw Anita reclining in the sun and Mario, the broad shoulders and heavily bunched genitals, climbing from the pool.

In the rectory, the Jesuit heard the woman's playful calls.

The Garden of Eden might have had such inhabitants, he mused. Such frankness of the body, an ease with bodily love. His own upbringing had been a labyrinth of disguising the natural functions, modesty raised to an absolute imperative. Yet it was not without envy that the image of Mario's shamelessly physical attributes came back to the Jesuit.

But the Garden of Eden suffered the Fall of man. He acquired the consciousness of sin and shame. Therefore, the Church endeavored to direct that awareness and turn it to a praise of God. Therefore, also, the new generation, which rejected the notion of sexual inhibition, was an affront to the Church. For the new generation proclaimed that fulfillment could be found in the life on earth. Which, of course, was not true.

A memory of the Potomac flickered quickly through his mind. Of a place, hot and humid, as at Golgotha Falls; of a hotel where elegant men took their women for pleasure. On the balcony, confused and unable to think—for one single afternoon he had stood not alone on this earth.

Surprised by the vehemence of the memory, the Jesuit went back to the Oldsmobile. Apparently, it would take a good deal more time than he had thought to eliminate, or at least neutralize that scene. Involuntarily, he leaned to look at the willow banks.

Mario and Anita were gone. Had they seen him watching? Would they have cared? Beyond the church and river rose the fields of the farms, too dry for this season, and over them the celestial white of swiftly moving clouds.

The Jesuit wiped the perspiration from his eyes. The hot miasma rising from the bog recalled the same lethargy, the same sensual abandon, as had the roiling Potomac. That memory, and his uncle, were why he had come to Golgotha Falls.

He walked into the church.

61

Anita had set up the seismograph beyond the crypt door. Her hair was still wet from swimming. The cotton blouse was soaked at the collar. Her slender fingers worked effortlessly over the slowly turning drum and the fine black line coming from the inked scribe. She turned to smile at the Jesuit.

"I picked up your footsteps in the rectory," she said.

"Did you?" Father Malcolm said, uncomfortable. "Are all these instruments so precise?"

"Yes. We work in very small increments, Father Malcolm."

Father Malcolm stepped away. To hide his awkwardness, he surveyed the rotted debris on the floor.

"I see real possibility for renewal," he said. "Not so vile as it looked last night."

Mario came into the church, forearms bulging, teeth gritted from the weight of a black metal box against his bare chest. He pushed past the Jesuit and maneuvered down the aisle toward Anita.

Mario unscrewed the top bolts. Carefully, he lifted out components of optical equipment from the thick lining. To Father Malcolm, the pieces rested like an alien presence on the church floor.

Mario swung a dark red piece, a ruby laser, gently onto its grooves. He examined the beam-splitter and reference beam mirror, then replaced the plastic housing. It was a double-pulsed laser for which he had augmented the amplifier to provide an expanded viewing image.

The Jesuit, transfixed, advanced closer to the camera. His shadow fell over Mario. Mario stopped working and looked up.

"What's the matter, Father Malcolm?"

"All this equipment and miles of cables, too."

"So?"

"Well, it is, after all, a church."

"It is, after all, a scientific investigation."

"One must render unto Harvard that which is due Harvard, Mr. Gilbert. But unto Christ—"

"I know. Ten percent."

At a signal from Anita, Mario sank into silence.

The Jesuit began shoveling the debris of rubble and pieces of women's clothing into cardboard boxes. Anita leaned over toward Mario.

"Let me handle him," she whispered.

"Why?"

"Because you piss him off."

62

"Well, that makes two of us. The smug hypocritical bastard."

The morning proceeded in silence.

Mario's concentration on testing the laser camera was broken by the Jesuit's incessant movements through the church as he carried out the broken pews and debris fallen from the ceiling. Finally, in the empty church, Mario watched the priest sweep the accumulated black grit of a century from the hardwood floor.

Suddenly, Mario's eyes became fixed on the viewing box of the laser camera. He made a sound of surprise.

"What's the matter, Mr. Gilbert?"

"The laser camera is picking up architectural stress. Behind you."

Father Malcolm looked up at the rafters. Only the northwest corner looked in disrepair. "I had thought the stucture was still basically sound."

"So did I."

The priest swept the black debris into a box and took it into the hot sun. In the laser camera viewing box, the stress of the church reduced, and the curled patterns straightened to normal cross-ended beams.

The priest came back in with a bucket of steaming soapy water. The stress followed him around the church.

"You look really disturbed, Mr. Gilbert," Father Malcolm said, mopping the floor.

"Something is unstable," Mario admitted.

Father Malcolm swabbed the floor vigorously. Now the stress was greatest where the priest scrubbed the baseboards. When he paused, the stress continued to show up on the laser screen.

"Anita," Mario whispered. "Trade places with the priest."

Anita went to Father Malcolm and spoke briefly. Puzzled, he gave her the bucket and mop, but the stress now showed incongruent undulated lines over the door, away from Anita and over Father Malcolm.

"What is it?" he asked.

"I don't know," Mario replied. "Something is following you around in here." He looked up with a sly grin. "Looks like we're not alone."

Anita suddenly shivered as a frigid chill wafted through the church, followed by a pervasive odor, rank and foul. They all sensed it, but none spoke of it. Then it was gone, as were the stress lines.

For the rest of the afternoon, despite Mario's vigilance, no further chills, odors, or stress patterns were experienced.

By early evening, the rubble mounds beyond the church yard were smoking thickly.

Father Malcolm poked a dead branch into the blue rising smoke, which exuded a sickly, sweet odor, like decaying flesh. Gathered around the mounds of ragweed and broken brick, some of the towns-people of Golgotha Falls watched, mesmerized, hostile. The priest saw the expressions on their faces change with every puff of smoke from the filthy, burning cloth, as though they were trying to deter-mine whether the intruders were for good, or for evil.

The flames ate into the discarded clothing, hissing and snapping, through rotted church vestments, curling black through molded altar cloths. Red ants fled the heat, like animated drops of blood fleeing into the soil. Malcolm covered his face with a handkerchief.

"The smoke!" cried an elderly woman. "It has the face of the first priest."

The Jesuit spun on his heel, but saw only the heavy particulate fumes flowing down low into the hollow.

"Don't mind her none, pastor," cautioned the bartender. "Her right mind has left her."

But the woman was insistent.

"It was there for a second," she screamed, "and I seen it!"

"I did, too!" echoed a short boy.

Others laughed nervously. The old woman took the boy home.

Mario came up from the church, loops of slender wire over his shoulder. He stopped to look at the fire. Its stench almost made him gag.

The Jesuit stirred the black and rotted cloth where the buttons melted down to a liquid morass. "Sometimes we deal in a messy business," he said softly, upending a box of sweepings from the church. "There is always a struggle with evil, a foul and filthy struggle that will continue until Christ's final victory."

Mario adjusted the weight of the wire loops on his shoulder.

"Is that right?" he said with a grin of disdain, and started off toward the van. Father Malcolm's hand gripped his arm.

"Wait," he said softly. "You are here on an investigation of phenomena beyond normal understanding. Your instruments have recorded stresses beyond accounting. You can't have failed to sense the pervasive, inhuman odors, the bone-chilling cold that seems to permeate every nook and crevice of the church. How do *you* explain these things, Mr. Gilbert?"

64

"I observe, Father Malcolm. I measure. I don't label. It takes courage *not* to provide easy explanations. To be able to say, yes, this happened, and this, and this too, and I don't know what it means. Maybe someday I'll know how it all ties up together. But not today. Now now. Now it's pure experience and I record it as best I can. And that's all, Father. No saints. No liturgies. No glib little Trinities."

Smiling, he walked off toward the van.

Father Malcolm did not return to the church until the fire was dead and buried in sand. The smoke of the blackened earth drifted through the hollow, turning the sinking sun to mauve. The shadows disappeared and melded into the deep brown gloom.

Anita ate her dinner behind the temperature systems console. Until things were stabilized, the instruments had to be watched and continually adjusted. The Jesuit was indefatigable, working at his chores of scrubbing and cleaning.

Anita watched him curiously.

"How did you become an exorcist?" she suddenly asked.

Father Malcolm looked at her dark eyes, then shrugged slightly and examined the baseboard rot.

"Every parish has an exorcist," he said modestly. "It's the third of four orders to becoming a priest."

"But you have a special expertise—I mean—aren't exorcists rare and particular people?"

He smiled, enjoying her friendly curiosity. "You've seen too many movies, Miss Wagner." Then, soberly, "I studied. I became a candidate. *Spiritualis imperater*—then in Boston the bishop handed me a book—instructed me—the words and the methods, you understand— That's all it was."

"Have you ever performed an exorcism before?"

"Yes. An old woman. I assisted, really. And it went quite well."

Anita found the subject esoteric, fascinating, but was slightly hesitant to pry. Nevertheless, she felt on comfortable terms with the inward-looking, quiet Jesuit.

"Is it—like magic—?" she asked. "Secret formulas? Sacred words?"

Father Malcolm laughed pleasantly, without ridicule. "The actual procedure has been fixed since the third century, and is often used. For example, in consecrating holy water, there is a ritual exorcism of evil."

"Is it really so simple?" Anita asked.

Father Malcolm moved to the next area, ripped the baseboard from the wall, and dipped the mop into the bucket of water. Then he stopped.

"No, Miss Wagner. It is never simple." He paused, fashioning his thoughts into words. "A successful exorcism depends on the officiating priest. His faith. His power."

Anita nodded. The church was pleasantly quiet. Several of the consoles hummed. The river beyond the church burbled in a low voice. Mario entered carrying a case of video tapes.

"Did you know that there is speculation that Lovell himself had been exorcised?" Father Malcolm volunteered.

Mario put down the tapes and sat down on an optical components trunk.

"I never ran across that," he admitted.

"According to the letters from Lovell—"

"Wait a minute. You have letters of Bernard Lovell?"

"I purchased them from the family. He wrote infrequently to his sister in Charlestown. In one letter he refers to an *imperfect cure.* Now, at first I assumed this was a reference to his limp. Lovell had suffered a mild attack of poliomyelitis and walked with a slight limp. It was only in the last few years, rereading those lines, seeing how circumspectly and unnaturally he phrased the sentences, that another possibility became stronger."

Father Malcolm walked back to them. His face was transformed by enthusiasm, fear, and a strange anxiety.

"You see, in the Catholic Church, no man who has ever been possessed, for whatever period of time, may become a priest."

"Even if cured?" Anita asked.

"Yes."

Anita looked perplexed.

"You must understand the *wiliness* of the foe," the Jesuit insisted. "It would be so characteristic to allow the impression of a cure and then later—return—"

"So you think Lovell was, in effect, an agent of the devil?" Mario asked.

"It is my firm conviction."

A great weight of sadness seemed to descend upon the Jesuit. The shadows now seemed darker, merged with the distant walls, like a theater of the night void, and the Jesuit's voice came deeply out of his own suffering.

"Many people, I suppose, would say that Lovell suffered a nervous breakdown. Induced by isolation, a sense of failure, and physical fatigue. And perhaps it does begin with fatigue. Exhaustion. A certain bitterness against the archdiocese for abandoning him. All this, of course, he cannot admit to himself. He throws himself into further devotion, further church improvements, but it only increases his isolation and fatigue. Then there comes what the Church Fathers call an aridity of the soul. The soul is devoid of consolation. It cannot pray."

"Go on," Anita said softly.

Father Malcolm turned back from the window. Behind his head hung dead fluffs of floated milkweed, spiked on dead black limbs.

"A state of disgust sets in. Disgust with spiritual matters. Disgust with the physical effort of prayer. Disgust with the mission of the Church. The body is worn and the mind exhausted by long, ardent, fruitless supplication. The loneliness erodes the man's personality. A malaise, a melancholy, captures the priest. This, Miss Wagner, is called the dark night of the senses."

Anita nodded slowly, encouraging, unable to escape the timbre of risk in the Jesuit's voice.

"What happens then?" she asked quietly.

"He loses his bearings. He is disoriented. He has no foundation in his soul. He enters what the Church Fathers named the dark night of the spirit."

"Yes."

"It is at this point that a man who has chosen to serve God is at his most vulnerable. And Lovell—I deeply believe that Lovell—was entered at that point. He was physically entered and gave up his will to Satan."

Mario whistled.

"Just like that?" he asked.

"Yes."

Mario shook his head incredulously, turned and began testing the video tape components. The Jesuit took his silence as reproof.

In the darkness, Anita felt that Mario had wounded him. She approached the Jesuit and asked gently, "Why did you buy the letters of Bernard Lovell?"

"To learn everything I could about this church. You see, my uncle was Father James Farrell Malcolm."

"The name is not familiar to us."

"I thought everyone knew. Certainly, if you've researched the church—"

67

"We researched it for six months," Mario said quickly. "There was never a mention of that name."

Father Malcolm smiled painfully. "Then the diocesan archives have remained secret." There was a brief impasse. "He, too, was a Jesuit. A Renaissance scholar. A well-known figure in Boston. He came to Golgotha Falls in 1978."

"Why?"

"For the same reason I am here."

"Exorcism."

Father Malcolm nodded. His face had grown extraordinarily tense. Frustration and bitterness formed tears in his eyes.

"But he died here," Father Malcolm said. "In this church. During the exorcism."

Anita stared at the Jesuit.

"But why the curtain of secrecy?" she demanded.

Father Malcolm found his tongue blocked and his thoughts blank in front of the attractive woman. At last, he spoke.

"T-the Jesuit who assisted him reported that my uncle began to stutter . . . began to hallucinate. At the height of the mass, he began mispronouncing the litany—giving it obscene connotations. . . . A-at that point . . . the assistant blacked out—"

"Please go on," Anita softly encouraged.

Father Malcolm turned to her with a peculiar, almost hostile expression.

"W-when the assistant regained consciousness, he . . . he observed my . . . my uncle . . . James Farrell Malcolm, in . . . in copulation—with . . ." A terrible laughter suddenly broke from the priest. It was utterly without warmth. The strong face looked like a death's head in the black windows. The laugh died instantly. His eyes were hollowed, deep-lined in shame. ". . . with a farm animal—"

Dramatically, the Jesuit pointed at the empty predella where once the altar had been. "Right there!" he exclaimed bitterly.

A chill grew in the church. It was a wet river chill from the clay banks. The cold humidity dripped down the interior walls. Mario looked around. The sound of water dripping echoed through the church. It had not been there the night before, and now it irritated him. The priest irritated him. The complexities of setting up the equipment had become far more difficult than he had envisaged, and that irritated him.

"What makes you think you're any different?" Mario asked brutally.

68

Father Malcolm paled. "What do you mean?"

"Well, Bernard Lovell and then your uncle. Two priests. One performs necrophilia and the other bestiality."

Trembling, the Jesuit leaned forward, hands folded in front of him.

"You're right. That's how he works at Golgotha Falls," Father Malcolm said. "That's the nerve on which he plays."

"The nerve on which *who* plays?" Mario demanded brusquely.

"Satan, Mr. Gilbert," Father Malcolm replied simply.

A burst of harsh laughter escaped from Mario's lips. "Satan?" he shouted. "Cherubim! Seraphim! Dominations, Virtues, Powers, and Principalities! This goddamn church is like a bullfight arena to you priests."

"Indeed, Mario," the Jesuit agreed. "It is a dark, evil-infested road a priest travels down—filled with so many traps, so many ways to overcome him."

Mario dropped a clipboard on the components box. The slap broke the mood.

"What overcomes priests," Mario flung back, "is what's been fermenting in their souls since Saint Paul got the bright idea of celibacy."

"That's outrageous," Father Malcolm protested. "My uncle was a refined man, who found many outlets—"

"But not the natural one."

"There are other expressions of love than the genital."

"Really? Tell me about it." He turned to Anita. "I had ten years of going to confession. You know what they ask you, Anita? 'Did you touch yourself? Did you touch anybody else? Did anybody touch you? Where? How? What did it feel like?' That's what they're dying to know. What did it feel like. And when they're not asking about it, they're trying to find out with their saintly hands."

The Jesuit blanched.

Mario caught the cautionary glance from Anita. For several seconds, he worked clumsily at the tape device. His eyes were black and moist with suppressed rage.

"Look at that rock on which Peter built," Mario said quietly. "Pick it up and look under it and see what crawls there. Celibacy. The entire Church is built contrary to nature."

The Jesuit rose, brushing back his blond hair. To Anita, his revelation had made him a visibly older man, one who had tasted the unsubtle alloy of degradation in the church.

"Is it contrary to nature, Anita?" he said softly. "I don't know any more. The Church is changing—slowly—surely—"

The Jesuit went to the church door. Anita gestured to Mario to apologize, but Mario shook his head.

"I'm sorry if we spoke without respect," she said. "We have some strong feelings about this, too."

"God allows us the truth to overcome our feelings," Father Malcolm said.

He nodded a good night and walked to the rectory.

Mario and Anita went to the van. Mario opened a bottle of wine and began drinking.

"He just pissed me to high heaven," Mario said. "That holiness is like a fingernail on a blackboard to me."

Anita held her silence. She undressed. Mario, nude, studied the seismograph charts. They also revealed the slight stress that had appeared behind the priest.

He put the charts on the shelf, turned off the lantern, and lay beside Anita. He chuckled.

"What's so funny?"

"Father Malcolm's uncle. I hope the farm animal was of consenting age."

"Mario. It was a tragedy. Nothing to laugh about."

But Mario's chuckle was infectious.

Anita felt his arm around her shoulder, the hand on her breast.

Through the side windows, they saw the stars ranged in a dense confusion of constellations. The fields were cold, and the stalks creaked and rubbed in the quick breezes. Dead branches stroked the van. Mario got on his knees.

"Hey," she whispered. "What are you doing?"

"I'm a farm animal."

She tried to push the massive shoulders away, trying not to laugh.

"You were a farm animal last night."

"I like being a farm animal."

Her nipples hardened. She could not push him away. Her laughter began coming through clenched teeth. She pressed Mario down, down into the softness that dominated her. Suddenly, like birds flying out of branches, her body jerked rhythmically and her full cries escaped into the darkness.

It had come so fast, it caught her by surprise. The perspiration dampened her hair and plastered it down onto her forehead. In a state of soft exhaustion she smiled and winced. Mario had entered her.

70

She played her slender fingers across the arched back. She stroked the thick, curly hair. Mario's shoulder muscles tensed, the buttocks strained. Abruptly, he groaned. The heavy body shook, and then shook more slowly.

At the climax of his passion Anita imagined, not the powerful, dark hunger in her arms, but inexplicably, the pale, hesitant face of the Jesuit in the church.

Slowly Mario rolled to her side. He looked up at her as through a heavy dream.

"Is everything all right?" he murmured.

"Everything was wonderful," she assured him, smiling.

As Mario slept, snoring softly, one hand on her shoulder, Anita looked up at the stars through the tiny skylight in the roof of the van. What had brought the Jesuit here? she wondered. Something confused, psychopathological? Or a strange beauty, a spiritual hunger that lived and breathed at Golgotha Falls?

Anita looked fondly at the form of the sleeping male nude. So much strength, so much weakness.

Mario slept in a dark, amoral universe that knew no shame, a brief respite from his deep anxieties. The child emerged in Mario's sleeping face. Trusting, innocent, and vulnerable. In the daytime work, and in the sex of the night, that child was suppressed by the force of his brutal, driving energy.

Anita felt, in his arms, like a wild bird nesting on a dark, storm-tossed ocean.

But was it enough anymore, the extraordinary liberation of the senses? The delicate Anita, the refined child of upstate New York society, the careful writer of science, wanted a quiet place to soar, to seek her own nature. But what indeed was that nature?

Thoughts of a different ecology flowed pleasantly in Anita's memories. She drifted toward a broad expanse of undulating fields that surrounded a white Colonial home. It was Seven Oaks, her family home for three generations. And in her imagination she was riding Tredegar, the slender chestnut Arabian from the long, low-roofed stable.

Seven Oaks was built around a seventeenth-century house that now contained the living room, a sagging roof, and an enormous iron fireplace. Cabinets of china were illumined by small lights. The paintings on the wall were from the French school, and beyond the billiard room was a small indoor swimming pool.

It was Christmas when Mario first visited Seven Oaks. Hedda was working the entire day with the goose and cakes in the kitchen. Mrs. Wagner served sherry in front of the firelight as the snow fell, fell with a purity remembered from the innocence of Anita's childhood.

Mario sat deliberately with his motorcycle boots on the delicately embroidered footstool, answering Mrs. Wagner in grunts and monosyllables. Anita acknowledged to herself that the holidays were moving toward catastrophe. To Mrs. Wagner's polite conversation about modern writers, many of whom she knew personally, or about painting, Mario returned a blank and hostile silence. Only when Anita and Mrs. Wagner reminisced about Anita's father did Mario stir.

Anita's father had been a stockbroker before the fatal airplane crash. Mario was interested in the stock market. Mario was then a fervent Marxist and saw signs of conspiracy in every motion of bonds, corporate tax benefits, and the portfolios of the rich. A few vulgar comments from Mario broke the mood of delicacy, loss, and nostalgia.

Nor was it any better when Mario strode out toward the stables with Anita. The vast expanse of snow-whitened land, the farmers working the farm for a tax loss, the elegant Arabian horses were all, to Mario, signs of a class that had lost its integrity and lived in the past. In every luxury he saw the epitaph of a hundred victims of poverty, the street, drugs and violence.

Nor had Mario missed the significance of the look that passed from Mrs. Wagner to Anita. The look said *boor* and *ill-mannered* and *crude*.

Mario learned to ride in a single afternoon. He was a natural athlete. He also despised Mrs. Wagner's pity and willed himself not to appear foolish in the older woman's eyes.

Despite his surface cynicism, Mario was overawed by Seven Oaks. He knew beyond doubt that Anita came from a life he had never suspected existed. Mrs. Wagner had an integrity of her own, and Mario was vaguely frightened by its assurance.

The guests at the Christmas dinner, in their expensive but casual elegance, the jeweled women, the men in soft open-collared shirts, gradually realized that the brooding young man in Anita's corner was smoldering with a violence they had never had to confront. Mario was drinking too much. The effort of using the correct fork and knife bothered him. The chatter about the choirs of the local churches, the New Year's sleigh ride with horses under the moonlight, made him tense.

"Sleigh rides?" he muttered. "What do you think life is, a perpetual picnic?"

The conversation dwindled to silence.

"You could feed an entire orphanage on what it costs to run your pampered assholes over the snow!"

Anita, blushing deeply, put a hand on his arm. It was too late. Mario shook it off.

"You live in a fiction!" he said, weaving to his feet, pointing at the nearest of the elaborately coiffed women who stared back, shocked, fingers intertwined in a string of pearls. "And everything you have, sleighs and horses, jewels, tax shelters—one day they're going to be taken by people who have had to live in reality!"

Embarrassed at their stares, humiliated, drunk, and still furious, Mario lurched from the deep reddish glow of the exquisite dining room with its illumined china cabinets toward the kitchen, slipped, and then stumbled out into the snow.

The company avoided looking at Anita, and toyed with their food. Anita, throwing her linen napkin onto her plate, ran out after Mario.

He stumbled angrily through the snow toward the silhouette of the estate's farmhouse under the stars and then stopped. A deep, decisive chasm separated him from the landscape.

"It's me or them," he whispered, sensing her behind him.

He turned. In his eyes was a look either of longing and of loss of a childhood he had never had, or of rage, she could not tell which.

"If I lived to be a hundred," he insisted, "I would never fit in with them. Or your mother. Or with that part of you."

He took her shivering shoulders in his strong hands, looking deeply into her face.

"Don't you understand?" he said desperately. "You've got to choose now, Anita."

Anita stared at the hostile, yet vulnerable face and saw instantly that Mario was right. Seven Oaks would never fit into his epistemology. He would never see, never feel, the life that had formed her and which flowed in her still. Mario couldn't bear its superiority to his own miserable origins.

Anita lay against the warm beating heart.

"It's you, Mario," she whispered. "Always you."

"Anita," Mario whispered, half asleep.

She drifted back into his embrace, softer now, his great and naked need enfolding her with tenderness.

73

They did not make love again, but merely lay close and listened to the breeze through the valley.

"Anita," Mario whispered, holding her close, in a curious mixture of pride and affection.

Yet again the mystery of the Jesuit's mission tantalized Anita. Even as she lay with Mario her mind was free. Until she felt divided into two different, equal halves.

The Siloam, restless and deep, moved high on clay banks.

Father Malcolm was emptied by the long confession to the parapsychologists, but it left him agitated. Mario was antagonistic. Anita knew little of Catholicism. Sighing, he turned his attention to the preparation of the coming exorcism.

He examined the silver chalice in its case lined with blue velvet. It reflected his haggard face and the panoply of stars beyond the rectory window. In a separate compartment was the silver dish, the paten, on which would rest the blessed Body of Christ, the Host itself. Then he examined the humeral veil, an embroidered linen that protected the paten from his human hands. It was immaculate. It was reassuring.

In another case was the lavabo, the golden bowl to catch water after the ablution. In cloth wrapping was the censer and capsules of incense grains. In a heavy vessel was the Gregorian water, and chrism, and holy water. All these Bishop Lyons had blessed and given him after the investiture.

Other boxes, tall black silhouettes, held the other implements of exorcism.

A silhouette moved along the edge of the graveyard. It was the parapsychologist, Gilbert. Naked, he urinated luxuriously into the weeds and then went back into the van.

Again, suddenly, a vision of the Potomac flashed into Father Malcolm's reverie, and a hotel with a white balustrade. On the balcony, he sat in an agony of silent expectation, the blood drumming in his ears. On the white bedspread, a woman's dark green hat.

Returning to the rectory, Father Malcolm knelt to pray. When his mind felt somewhat assuaged, he lay down on his rough mattress, pulled the blanket over his naked body, and fell into a troubled sleep.

CHAPTER FIVE

MARIO AWOKE suddenly at four and quietly made his way into the church. The instruments hummed softly. It was reassuring to Mario. Neither the seismograph nor the laser camera tape showed any disturbances, but he felt relaxed and confident among his electronics. It was what he had been made for. The church was otherwise empty, expectant. He nudged the black cables against the wall.

He flicked off the viewing lamp of the seismograph. Then, as he was about to leave—

"Jesus Christ—"

Against the north wall, fluttering like a trapped butterfly, was an aureole of blue light.

It drifted slowly, undulating, dipping down toward the floor.

Mario raised an arm and played it over the moving light. There was no shadow. The light had fine interior striations of blue-white form, and suddenly it flickered and was gone.

The temperature system confirmed a drop of nearly five degrees on the north wall.

It had had the appearance of having come in from the exterior, Mario thought. Exterior not to this space but to this time. The way it flipped as it disappeared implied a geometry of an estranged order.

Mario kept vigil in the dark, empty church. Each sound, each bird call, each crackling of branches over the rectory jarred his nerves. But after two hours, there were no more signs. He turned to the seismograph at the north wall, flicked it on, and went to the van.

Anita slept, her arm thrown back, her black hair across one breast, the deep sleep of the sexually fulfilled. He woke her.

"Luminescence," he whispered. "About two hours ago."

Anita fumbled awake, pulled on trousers and a plaid flannel shirt over her nude body, and then her heavy work boots.

"Exterior?" she asked.

"Interior. North wall. Full form, metamorphosing."

"Low color temperature?"

"No. Blue."

Anita rolled a power cable from the generator and led Mario, who carried a heavy black camera, down to the church.

It was an infrared camera, called a thermovision. At its heart was a Dewar flask containing liquid nitrogen. The camera had seven f-stops and manual focusing, and it resolved temperature discrepancies of less than two-tenths of a degree Celsius.

Mario set the camera at the north wall. By the time Anita connected the braided cables, the east was breaking with a dull ocher light. The mist from the river dripped steadily into the church and formed pools on the floor.

On the thermovision screen, the church architecture appeared a mass of Van Dyke browns and dull umbers.

Father Malcolm came into the church, surprised to see them up so early. In his hand was a bucket of patching plaster and a knife.

"Another camera, Mario?"

"We had a luminescence this morning at four-fifteen."

The Jesuit followed the direction of Mario's gaze and the thermovision unit. The north wall was utterly devoid of marks. But in the church the tension was unmistakable.

"I suppose you were asleep," Mario said.

"Actually, I was praying."

"Well, your prayers must have worked. Something came."

The Jesuit ignored the sarcasm. He began to fill in the badly eroded pillars.

"The eyes of faith," he said, "will see what your cameras will never record."

"Come here, Father Malcolm. This is what I see."

The Jesuit walked behind the thermovision. Against the dull browns was a soft pink flare.

"What is that pink?" Father Malcolm asked.

"The heat of Anita's body."

Father Malcolm saw, in the screen, a nearly transparent figure, with the extension of arms in front, making notes.

Mario adjusted the f-stop ring. The colors grew brighter. Father Malcolm saw the bright skull, the black holes of the nose and eyes. Clothes were not visible. Red flared softly from the heat of her navel, armpits, and breasts.

"Extraordinary," he conceded.

"The days of Tarot cards are long gone, Father Malcolm."

"Indeed."

Father Malcolm found himself staring at the image of the figure, faintly humanoid, and the heat that emanated from where her legs joined. Embarrassed, he turned away.

"With instruments like these," Mario said, "we can reach into areas never before accessible to observation."

"It can come to no good, Mr. Gilbert," the Jesuit said finally. "Man goes too fast. Too far. And he does not always know what he is doing."

"X-rays and microsurgery," Mario countered. "You call those evil?"

"Napalm and atomic weapons, Mr. Gilbert. Are those good?"

Mario shrugged.

"It's the politicians who order weapons and use them. You can't blame somebody like Einstein for seeking out the nature of matter and energy."

Father Malcolm now lifted the bucket in the vestibule. His hands were coated with dried spackle, and his shirt was flecked with it. Even his blond eyebrows and broad forehead were dotted with it.

"I've often thought," Father Malcolm said, "that before tech-

77

nology is applied to our ambitions—there must first be a development toward spiritual humility."

"Maybe. I can't wait."

"No. I can see that."

The Jesuit began applying the doughy white spackle in holes and cracks at the altar base. It made the configurations in the thermovision develop into a riot of maroon, orange, and viridian, as the warm flesh and cold spackle knife crossed past the lens. Mario smiled wryly, flicked off the camera and left the church.

Anita, who had been listening to the two men, now spoke.

"Tell me something, Father Malcolm. Suppose these disturbances do have some kind of spiritual dimension. Why wouldn't it be the defiled dead? I mean, they were grossly violated, maybe right here on the church floor, sawed up, and their limbs grafted in various grotesque postures. Who's to say it's not revenge they're after?"

Father Malcolm did not answer but continued to apply the putty mixture quickly and smoothly down the cracked base.

"That's what Golgotha Falls thinks is going on," Anita persisted.

The priest turned. "They are wrong," he said simply. "There is no return to earth. Judgment of souls is instantaneous and irrevocable."

"What does that mean?"

"For Lovell, damnation means the separation from God and the consciousness of that abandonment. For the dead of this church, if they were legitimately absolved of their sins, they need not fear the second death, which is the suffering of the soul in hell."

"What about your uncle?" Anita asked.

Father Malcolm glanced at her. She seemed not to be sarcastic and had lost even the tough professional edge. She was simply curious.

"I can only pray that he was allowed to see his degradation before he died. That he prayed for forgiveness." He put down the putty knife and approached her. His eyes were bright. "You see, I believe that Christ, in His incarnation as man, suffered the doubt, the alienation, the abysmal horror of annihilation. It was the dark night of the soul that he endured on Golgotha's cross. The same as Bernard Lovell. The same as my uncle. The same as every person must go through at some moment. Only, being Christ, He triumphed over that withering, obscene, encroaching mental anarchy, and thus redeemed us all by our belief in that sacrifice."

He swallowed. He saw her listening. His eyes traversed the ruins above and around them.

"In this church," he stated, "two men in Christ met their dark night and failed. Tomorrow it will be my time to enter it."

Anita was visibly moved. Softly she said, "So Mario was right. This church *is* your arena."

The Jesuit moved to within inches of her lovely face. She could feel his breath on her cheeks.

"Yes, Anita," he whispered. "Tomorrow I will do combat with Christ's most potent adversary." His eyes burned; his face was taut with purpose. *"I must not fail."*

Mario strode down the aisle carrying a videotape recorder.

"Well, isn't this a cozy scene," he muttered.

Anita laughed suddenly, her face flushed.

Confused, the Jesuit stepped away from her. She seemed to snap back to Mario's obdurate skepticism. Had he overestimated her? Was she simply probing him for scientific purposes? Her expression was beyond defining. Father Malcolm realized that he had no experience by which to decipher a woman's manner.

He felt totally lost in Anita's presence.

In the heavy darkness that filed into the valley, the fireflies zipped through the brambles. They spread out in waves from the river in fanning motions, surrounding the church.

The atmosphere was filled with a fine-filtered grit that descended upon the church, seeped into the van, and settled over the rectory. Golgotha Falls was darkened under it. The Siloam smoothed into a viscous black swell.

It was nearly midnight when Father Malcolm came from the church. His trousers and shirt were streaked with dirt. His arms were matted in thick putty and plaster. He thought he saw a light in the van and went quickly up the path.

Suddenly, he stopped.

"Mario," he heard Anita's whisper inside, "not yet—oh—not yet—"

There was a heavy sound, bodies moving, and the stertorous breathing of a large man.

"Oh—yes—Mario—yes, yes. Now! Now!"

The van jerked spasmodically—and the brambles, rising like thorns, suddenly looked like hands clutching upward at the blackening valley air.

The Jesuit turned quickly. In the hurried motion, his ankle was trapped in the sudden embrace of Mario's coiled cables in the grass. With a sudden uprushing of earth and air, the Jesuit felt his body slam down hard into the brambles and cables.

He heard his heart pumping. Absurdly tangled in the thistles, he saw the van door open. It was Mario, naked, glaring, holding a tire iron.

"Who's there?" he demanded.

"Mario—it's me—"

The Jesuit struggled to his feet. He brushed his knees free of the dirt.

Mario laughed without anger.

"What do you want, Father Malcolm? You didn't come to bless the act of love, did you?"

Father Malcolm blushed so deeply Mario saw it in the dark.

"I wondered if you could help me with the altar."

"Altar?"

"I have a new one in the rectory. But it's heavy. And we haven't much time."

Mario glanced back at Anita, who was in the far end of the van, holding the sleeping bag quilt in front of her.

He put on his trousers, and barefoot and bare-chested, followed Father Malcolm along the south wall. The edge of the graveyard was a frenzy of small, flying insects that knocked against them in small clouds.

"What's the big hurry, Father Malcolm?"

"Tomorrow is Sunday."

"So?"

"A church must be consecrated on a Sunday."

The Gothic windows were darker than the cloud-illuminated fields. Mario barely perceived his instruments among the boxes the Jesuit had brought in.

At the rectory, Father Malcolm stood at the door. He saw the red marks along Mario's chest and back. It looked as though he had been raked by claws.

"What's the matter?" Mario asked.

"Nothing. Excuse me. Be careful of the rectory floor. There are nails."

A fat white candle, burned down to its base, illuminated the interior. The Jesuit's tunics hung in the small hall. On the kitchen table were accessory pieces of the vestment. Mario recognized the heavy black cloth burse, which would be worn over the shoulder to contain the Host before it was consecrated. A crucifix had been slanted against the wall. The rectory was fetid not only from the rotting apples under the floorboards, but also from human sweat.

In the vast distance, a low growl of thunder died in the unseen hills.

Through the windows, Mario saw the undersides of heavy clouds flicker brightly, a broad heat lightning below the horizon.

Father Malcolm took a protective blanket from a heavy walnut altar support. The front of the support was inscribed with the name of Christ, IHS, and inlaid with walnut counter-tiles.

"That's the altar?"

"It's the altar base. We will assemble the altar in the church."

Father Malcolm gestured for Mario to lift one end. It weighed nearly a hundred pounds and was shaped awkwardly, the top smaller than the bottom. They wrestled it over the rectory floor, then down the south path, sweating heavily, though the wind was rising, cool and dry.

The church was extraordinarily black inside; the air, like ether, suffocating.

Again they maneuvered the altar base, working it down to the single-step dais. Slowly, they lowered it, teeth gritted and faces trembling. Mario leaned on it, catching his breath.

Already the Jesuit had bolted two tall crucifixes onto the walls, expressionist Christs extended on the armatures of gilded crosses.

Various vials and stoppered vessels were arranged on the floor for the exorcism, and twelve shallow candle holders.

Near the altar, waiting for the linens, was the ornate tabernacle, water and wine cruets, and golden candles in a slender box near a gilded candelabrum. There was also a cardboard box with the altar lamp inside, the ruby-red front glass and the brass chains gleaming.

Where Father Malcolm had nailed fresh planks crudely but effectively, making a shallow platform, they lowered the altar support. Father Malcolm worked the support so that it was centered. Then he lovingly stroked the sides.

"You see?" he said. "The altar will be in contact through the floor to the earth. So it will mediate between God and man."

The altar was so much heavier that they took tiny steps, hefting it in through the door. When they set it down on the support grooves, the massive stone and wood table slid easily into place.

The priest examined the four support points to the altar.

"The contact must never be broken," he said quickly.

"Why not?"

"If contact is broken, even for a second, between altar and the support, the altar will have lost its consecration."

Father Malcolm now unfolded several white linens from a large black leather pouch. He stripped off the protective blanket and carefully placed the front linen, the antependium, over the altar. The antependium carried the embroidered Alpha and Omega, which flashed in the darkness.

Before it covered the altar, Mario glimpsed the naked, flecked stone. It was slightly sloped, slightly recessed. It was the distant descendant, Mario knew, of altar stones that were fluted to carry off blood of animal sacrifices.

Father Malcolm lovingly placed the rear linen piece, the pall, in place. Then from the floor he lifted the ornate tabernacle and set it on the altar.

"Are any of these things consecrated?" Mario asked.

"What? No. Not yet. There are some items in the rectory. But the altar, like the church and graveyard, is still profane."

The seismograph, when Mario glanced at it, showed tremors along the north wall.

"Mario—"

Surprised at the tone of voice, Mario turned to look at the Jesuit, whose face was extraordinarily pale.

"What's the matter?"

"The altar lamp—I can't lift it out of the case—"

Confused, Mario walked over to the wooden case. The tangle of brass chain lay looped over a small, rotund lamp with a ruby-red glass in front of the wick.

"It's only lightweight brass," Mario said. "What's the problem?"

"Please— If you could—"

Mario reached for the altar lamp, experienced a residual heaviness, extraordinary, as though something incredibly powerful pulled back on it. Mario felt it through his hands. The resistance slowly gave way, and Mario lifted it to his chest, the way a weight lifter cradles 150 pounds of iron. Slowly, the brass lamp lightened all the more, and then it tinkled normally in Mario's hands.

The seismograph showed no more tremors.

"Thank you—" Father Malcolm said nervously, mopping his forehead, where perspiration glistened. He looked strangely at Mario, as though afraid.

"You asked me if there was anything consecrated in this church? I was wrong. There is one thing."

"What?"

"*I* am consecrated."

The thermovision showed the temperature falling rapidly as the Siloam chilled in the night air. Yet the atmosphere within the church was fetid, hot and annihilating, like a coal fire.

Father Malcolm looked uncertainly around the interior. The consoles running smoothly on their own power made the only sound. The crickets suddenly had ceased, as though something had entered the valley.

The priest covered the altar linen with the protective blanket. With Mario's help, he bolted the altar lamp so that it hung on a curved chain of brass links over the altar.

The altar lamp began to tremble over the unconsecrated altar. Gradually, it grew still.

"I am going into the rectory now," Father Malcolm said. "To meditate and to pray."

He looked as though he wanted to say much more. Only there was no more time. Something had begun. His eyes were bright with a strange fear and a tic appeared at the corner of his mouth.

"Will you come get me after dawn?" he asked.

"Yes."

"Thank you, Mario."

Nervously, the Jesuit looked around the church. The vials, boxes, and utensils were laid out with maximum efficiency. He went over the exorcism in his mind, satisfied everything was in its place.

They walked out the door into the chill. Father Malcolm locked the church door and handed Mario the key.

"Keep this," Father Malcolm instructed him. "When I tell you tomorrow, use it to open the door."

Mystified, Mario nodded, putting the key into his pocket.

"Also, I must ask you not to enter the church tonight."

It was an order, not a request.

"Not even to check your equipment," Father Malcolm said.

"All right."

Father Malcolm looked back at the closed door. The moonlight was weak, and slanted down over the weathered wood.

"Perhaps your instruments will bring us luck," he said, smiling. "Good night, Mario."

"Good night, Father Malcolm."

Mario watched Father Malcolm walk past the graveyard, head down, to prepare for the exorcism.

Mario found Anita at the van, staring intently out beyond the bog.

Mario stopped short. "What's the matter?"

Anita pointed out at the graveyard. The pebbles in the ragweed were trembling, rolling forward like Mexican jumping beans.

"Undifferentiated RSPK," she said softly. "It's been going on ever since you brought that altar into the church."

The pebbles rolled in waves, crisscrossing, making a bonelike rattling noise when they touched. Then they sifted back into the dust.

"Do you think it's the priest?" she asked.

Mario slumped, rubbing his face, fighting the weariness. "Well, he's certainly catalyzed things since he arrived. I think his own emotional troubles are being projected." Mario slipped his leather jacket over his bare shoulders. "Anyway, the worse off he is, the better for us. Tomorrow's little exercise ought to keep our needles jumping."

For the first time since she'd known him, his quickness, his mental agility, his calculating acumen deviated fundamentally from what she felt. There was a harshness in Mario's thinking that masqueraded as charm. She wondered if that harshness blinded him, if it made him pursue the wrong theory out of misplaced stubbornness.

Mario held up his hand.

"What is it?" she asked.

They listened. The Jesuit's voice traveled from the rectory over the dry mounds of rubble. It was a voice in full vigor, laid bare in an awful nakedness. Anita felt it enter her heart.

"Enemy of the human race—source of death—robber of life— root of evil—seducer of men—serpent of filth—why do you resist?— you know that Christ the Lord has destroyed your plan—"

The rest was lost as the Siloam, driven to a frenzy by the sudden circling of the southerly wind, drove up over the clay banks and soaked into the church's foundations.

"What is he doing?" Anita whispered.

Mario grinned without warmth. "He's invoking Satan."

84

In the rectory, the darkness appeared to flow out from the glass-less windows, as though it was the source of night. The church, too, despite the red monitor lights of the instruments, poured darkness out along the windowsills.

"But that's—that's black magic," she objected.

"Only if improperly used. According to Catholic doctrine, all these disturbances are merely reflections of their master, Satan. So, like any good priest, he has to invoke the original evil in order to expel it."

"For which he needs Jesus Christ."

Mario grinned.

"You catch on fast, my love. That's what it's all about tonight."

They watched the fields and the church, but the southerly wind had stabilized. The Jesuit's voice continued in a monotonous whisper.

"Poor bastard doesn't know who or what could be an agent of the Antichrist," Mario said with sympathy. "The pebbles. The Siloam. Might even be you."

Anita turned. Mario was smiling, but the smile was ambiguous and the eyes were hard.

"What?" she asked.

"You could be an agent of the Antichrist. Without your knowing it."

"Bullshit."

"I've seen him looking at you."

"Now what the hell is that supposed to mean?"

Mario shrugged, turned away, and plucked a stalk of yellowed grass. He stuck it between his front teeth.

"You're triggering something off in him, Anita."

"That's absurd."

"Maybe. Maybe not. He may be a priest, but he was a man first."

"I really find this distasteful, Mario."

"Since when is Anita Wagner a prude?"

Anita said nothing, though the anger in her eyes was enough to make Mario turn away.

"Go down and take a look," he suggested. "See the Catholic Church in action."

"I'd rather not disturb his privacy."

"I'd say as a scientist it's your duty to observe the crucial participant. Particularly in a case of psychoprojection."

Anita caught an edge of sarcasm in Mario's voice. What was he accusing her of? As often happened when Mario needled her, she

85

did precisely as she felt. She walked through the nettles of the rectory path and peered into the window.

The candle was nearly out. White paraffin dripped onto the floor. In the darkness she could see his crucifix slanted on the table, the outstretched arms of Christ glinting toward her in the heat lightning rising from the ridge. Anita smelled the fragrance of incense. Then, like a whispering breeze, came Father Malcolm's intense, barely audible prayer. It reminded her of the subjects she and Mario had studied under the influence of trances.

Father Malcolm knelt, facing the crucifix, lost in a world foreign to her.

So this is what a man's soul looks like, Anita thought. Hands and arms soiled with flecks of dirt, tiny blood scratches on the forearms, the dust tracked in rivulets down his cheeks. The blond hair was matted and unkempt. The eyes were closed. Anita backed against the windowsill. Could Mario be right? Could a woman appear, to a praying priest, as an agent of the ultimate enemy?

Father Malcolm grew silent. He seemed to be waiting. In fact, she knew he was waiting. They were all waiting. If Mario was right, the priest would become the vehicle of their most intense study of psychoprojection. But now, as she looked at the man kneeling on the filthy floor, it occurred to Anita that the priest was just as likely to be the object, even the victim, of the paranormal, and not its psychic cause.

The Jesuit stared fixedly out past the crucifix at the bands of lightning dancing among the clouds. There was an extraordinary intimacy, and it included her. There seemed to be such a thing as soul, and it lent an exceptional sense of peace and waiting to that tired room.

Anita felt its purifying effect. It was chaste as the Siloam, she thought. Intricate and delicate as the lovely night clouds. Deep as the Golgotha Falls well.

It was a dimension of herself growing again.

At that moment on the ridge road, a Ford pickup truck rumbled by. The grizzled driver leaned from the cab and shook a fist at her.

"You'll die, you fools!" came the shout. "All of you!"

86

C H A P T E R
S I X

THE SILENCE of the night was inexplicable. Though the Siloam moved, brushing dead branches into the banks, there was no sound. It was lividly black and gleaming, like a dream, and white moths fluttered up from the bog in vague contours of light.

In the rectory, on his knees, Father Malcolm waited. The final barriers of pride had been destroyed and yet he was not emptied. Formless guilts rose into his mind, were purified, and disappeared. Memories of pettiness, of anger, of ambition burned clean in the fervent devotion.

The groping ego clung to its memories, but the prayer lifted them away and made him unified, sanctified.

A stormy day in the Atlantic when he was twelve and had hit his brother Ian with a sailing spar. The organ booming in Saint Patrick's Cathedral in New York and him hating the sound and fearing death.

The subconscious memories disentangled themselves.

The childhood carpet, an angry father, and Uncle James who was a Jesuit, rotund and jocular, half bald and smiling. Uncle James explaining the Society of Jesus. The gold ring. The cross at the lapel. That complicated man, who had also loved art and sensual beauty, the volumes of the Renaissance, the idealized women in luxurious gardens, painted for the Medici princes.

A stick among the garden rocks, and on the stick two snakes curled, twisted in copulation. Uncle James pointed out the snakes, explained the sexual division of male and female, and went on among the daisies with a certain sadness. For the passions were lovely, he said, but they drew man away from his natural form of love, the spiritual.

But there were other memories. A long hotel with a white balustrade. Below the second floor, the steamy Potomac. Walking along the path among the willows was a woman in a green hat. It was his mirror image, he thought, watching from his bedroom balcony. As Plato wrote, a single nature had been divided into two, the male and the female, and Eamon needed the fulfillment of that union as much as salvation.

Her name was Elizabeth Albers, and she taught at Georgetown University, in the Department of Moral History. Their seminars extended through two terms. In the course of that time, they sensed their mutual respect. By the late summer, it turned to deep affection. By fall, Malcolm knew he had come to a crucial crossroads in his life, and he agonized over his options. There were but two: marriage to Elizabeth, or marriage to the church.

Malcolm lost weight, his studies foundered, and the Jesuits counseled him to break off the relationship. He refused, and stayed one week with the Albers family in Norfolk. That failed to provide an answer. Their plans for marriage foundered; he returned to the seminary, and threw himself into scholarship.

During that period, he visited a psychoanalyst. They discussed his idealization of his uncle and the Society of Jesus. They examined religion as a sublimation of manly love. At the end of the semester, he graduated with honors.

Elizabeth's letter remained unopened, an icon of their love. While going through the preparations for initiation into the Society, he suffered a nervous relapse and returned to Boston. There he found solace in the mementos of his uncle, all his voyages to Venice, his erudite writings, until the horror at Golgotha Falls.

Another letter came from Norfolk. This time he answered. The loneliness of his future spread before him like a chasm. He asked to be suspended as a candidate for the Society. He met Elizabeth on a humid, steamy day on the Potomac. It was at the Cavern's Inn, an expensive resort frequented by congressmen and their mistresses, a fact he discovered after booking his room.

He watched her come down the willow path. In tweeds, with the dark green hat, she was stylish in a way that intimidated him.

When supper was served on the balcony, he suddenly told her he had changed his mind. He had reapplied for candidacy. There was no life for him outside the Church. Elizabeth did not eat her supper, and his tasted like sawdust.

"Why didn't you write the first time?" she asked. "I needed you. You needed me. Where was the harm in that?"

The word "need" was so ambiguous, he forced himself to look at the brilliant sunset over the Potomac.

"I was afraid," he said.

"Why are you so afraid of yourself?" she asked. "Eamon, is it love that you're afraid of?"

Unable to speak, terribly ashamed, he could only stare mutely at the river.

"It's—the physical expression of love," he finally said softly. "It is that I fear."

He turned. To his surprise, nothing angered her, nothing made her ashamed of him.

"And yet it would be the seal of our souls," she said gently. "And where would be the shame in that?"

"None," he admitted. "None at all."

Her green hat lay on the white bedspread. It was a symbol of her, her sophistication, her vulnerability. He was longing for love, he had lived all his life in love's absence, and she was waiting for him.

"None," he said again.

It was dawn when he jerked awake. The linen on the cold supper table was moist with dew. Seated on the sofa, Elizabeth rested against his chest, her white hand on his shoulder. Her pulse beat gently in her pale throat. Her lips moved and she was half awake and dreaming. He realized that he had been praying through the night, praying and sleeping and praying again, fighting every ravaged fiber of his paralyzed body.

Her breasts suddenly pressed against him. With a motion as natural as caressing an infant, she had reached behind his neck to hold him.

He moved to gently push her back. But when his hands held her shoulder, they pulled her forward instead and he closed his eyes and grew dizzy in an intoxication that frightened him.

"Oh, Eamon," she whispered, crying. "Don't deny me. For in denying me, you deny yourself."

In the full light of morning, they received an elegant breakfast. The leering bellboy, confused by the green hat on an undisturbed white bedspread, served cinnamon toast, omelette, and coffee with a silver service. But Eamon felt dead now, and he knew it. Elizabeth's eyes were bleak as he escorted her back through the hotel lobby. She embraced him suddenly and then was gone, taking the Amtrak back to Norfolk.

That was what precipitated the second, and ruinous breakdown. Somehow, after another suspension, he was able to focus on continuing his uncle's work, and on Golgotha Falls. He passed from candidacy to the Society of Jesus, but the victory remained singularly hollow.

As though to compensate for the suspensions, as though to test the remnants of his ties to Elizabeth, he began the long campaign to consecrate the fallen church at Golgotha Falls.

The Jesuit examined his conscience to see whether he coveted glory in bringing the church back into sanctity. He admitted that he did, and prayed that Christ relieve him of that burden. He examined his heart to see whether there was not a trace of revenge in his need to purify the church, a revenge for the obscene defilement of his uncle. He conceded there was, and prayed to be relieved of that burden as well.

But it wasn't enough. Something lurked below these confessions. The success of the exorcism, he knew, depended on rooting it out. So he prayed that the dizzying happiness of being so close to woman also be removed from him, that the momentary pleasure he had known in Georgetown be expunged from his soul, that Christ strengthen him against his vulnerability.

Slowly he began to dress.

First he stripped off the trousers and flannel shirt, the briefs and shoes and socks. Using the cold water in the basin, he scrubbed his forearms, face, chest, and legs, soaping out the grit and paint. He lathered his hair and rinsed. He dried himself vigorously.

From a nail protruding over the hall, he took the tunics of his office, wrapped in white cloth. He slipped on the alb trimmed in lace, reaching to his knees.

"Make me white, O Lord, and cleanse my heart that, made white by the blood of the lamb, I may be able to serve You."

He tied the white tunic with the tasseled cincture.

The black shoes were gleaming in the predawn gray light, and the black ridged biretta fit comfortably on his blond hair. The red chasuble was thick, brocaded, and stiff. The stole fit comfortably, reassuringly, behind his neck, embroidered with the archaic name of Christ.

Strange, he thought. It was almost exactly a year since he had spent the night with Elizabeth.

Moving out of his reverie, he saw Mario staring in disbelief at the doorway.

"You look great, Father Malcolm. Unrecognizable."

Indeed, the Jesuit was transformed. The gold and silver of the cross at his neck, the gold stitching in the chasuble, the white tracery of the alb made him a visible representative of the Church.

The Jesuit took a long pole from behind the armoire. He had wrapped it in a clean sheet. As he unrolled the silver pole, Mario saw it was topped by a small, heavy, ornate silver crucifix. He held himself erect, the crucifix before him.

"The silver case, Mario," he said in a different voice. "Bring it to the graveyard."

Mario reached under the cobwebs of the wall and hoisted a heavy case to his chest. The Jesuit walked steadily out into the open air. He was a magnificent figure in the crimson chasuble, like a creature from another planet. He went slowly as though testing the earth, but Mario knew he was simply concentrating, focusing on the struggle ahead.

The scent of decayed leaves and rotted fruit reminded Mario of the demented Lovell. Now the impassioned, barely repressed Jesuit before him was another of those priests whose missions border on the maniacal. It was an intuition by Mario, an observation of the tell-tale flickers at the eyes, the nervous fingers that belied the outward control. Mario knew priests. Their platitudes like ivy-covered snake pits of unconquerable ids. Maybe, just maybe, he thought, this priest, with emotions similar to Lovell's, could really aid their research.

In any case, the Jesuit was already sending out waves of fear and

91

belief that Mario detected almost palpably in the sultry, sunless morning.

At the graveyard path, Anita stood. She wore blue jeans and a white blouse trimmed in light blue.

"Good morning, Father," she said kindly. "Were you able to sleep?"

The Jesuit did not answer, but pointed to the ground. Mario laid the case at his feet.

"Please hold the crucifix," he said to Mario, "but do not let it touch ground."

As Mario held the heavy pole, the Jesuit knelt down and opened the case. He pulled from the velvet linings the censer, brass and ornate with a fine mesh of interlocking design. In the plate of the censer, he dropped a small pile of resin grains. Then he lit them with a silver wick. The incense billowed up around his head.

In the second compartment of the case was a stoppered chalice.

"Mario, I will need you to hold the holy water."

Mario stared at him, blinking. The idea was vaguely indecent, considering his apostasy.

"Do you expect *me* to be your altar boy?" Mario whispered.

The Jesuit turned to him. His face was stern, the lines deepened, the eyes almost hollow from pain.

"Mario, in the name of anything you love and hold sacred—"

Mario licked his lips. He looked at Anita, and with a repressed expression of distaste, lifted the chalice of holy water.

"Thank you, Mario."

With the holy water chalice was the aspergill, the brush used to flick out the droplets. It all came back to Mario. The endless hours in the chapel, the nuns with their busy feet, the doctrine pounded daily into young heads. Father Pronteus. As he held the offensive chalice, he looked bitterly into the graveyard.

At least, he thought, the instruments were recording everything.

The Jesuit glanced over his shoulder at the black glassless windows of the church. For a long time, he stared. Then he looked out over the graveyard.

Father Malcolm raised the silver crucifix high. With a bold step, he entered the half acre of nettles and fungus-ruined tombstones.

"I abjure you, ancient Serpent," he called out, "by Him who has power to send you to hell, depart from the ground consecrated in the bosom of Christ!"

Mario watched the Jesuit's eyes close, as though the older man summoned the power to continue. Work yourself into a frenzy, he thought. I need results.

"Let evil have no more power over this ground! Let the peace of Christ the Redeemer send its saving grace to this ground!"

The Jesuit swung the censer in the pattern of the cross. Then Mario held the censer as the Jesuit flicked holy water at the dirt.

"Follow me, Mario," he said gently. "Nothing will happen to you."

Out of the corner of his eye, Mario saw Anita discreetly photographing the proceedings.

Father Malcolm plunged into the chest-high weeds, pushing the silver crucifix high in front of him, and repeated the procedure at each of the graves, frequently making the sign of the cross with the edge of his palm. At the fifth grave, that of the missing twin, he intoned, "Repel, O Lord, the power of evil! Dissolve the fallacies of its plots! May the unholy tempter take flight! May this earth be protected by the sign of Your name!"

Again the Jesuit made the sign of the cross. He paused. A chill ran up Mario's back. The clouds above were massing.

It took over an hour and then Father Malcolm sanctified the entire perimeter of the graveyard. When they came back to Anita, he was pale and trembling.

"Are you all right, Father?" she asked.

"The fifth grave . . . I felt something pulling—something nauseating—unspeakably foul—"

The Jesuit wiped the sweat from his neck with a handkerchief. He brushed the red mites from his alb.

"The bell tower now," he said. "Mario, get the ladder."

Mario stared at him, rooted, uncomprehending. The Jesuit turned back to him angrily.

"The bell must be sanctified, too!" he shouted.

Mario put the censer in the case. Then he followed Father Malcolm to the north wall. Overhead, the massed clouds circulated down into the valley.

"Quickly, Mario—"

Mario leaned the gray, weather-beaten ladder against the steeple wall. The Jesuit carried a vial in his hand.

"Father, that ladder won't hold us—"

But the Jesuit belonged to another realm. His eyes glistened and his lips were taut. Mario followed.

They climbed to the roof and held on to the steeple base. The steeple itself swayed in the strong breeze. Below, the entire system of fields ruffled from the crossed currents of the rapidly gusting wind.

The vertigo reeled through Mario's ears and made him nauseous. Normally, he did not suffer from vertigo.

"Fasten this rope to the bell, Mario," the Jesuit said. "The bell must ring again."

Opening his eyes, Mario felt the landscape tilt again. He saw Anita, arms folded, looking up. Everything was unstable. He grabbed hold of the steeple supports.

"Be strong, man!" the Jesuit hissed.

It was such a strange thing to say. Mario stared at him. He wondered if the Jesuit were insane. Finally, he grabbed the end of the rope and worked it through the eye of the bell loop. To his amazement, the massive ridged iron bell, bearing the date of a Philadelphia foundry of 1886, swung loose and free after nearly a century of being crammed into the support.

Father Malcolm unstoppered the vial. Using his fingers, he anointed the bell inside and out.

Abruptly, the stopper was flung from his hand, twirled, and flew spinning into the Siloam. He grabbed Mario's hand.

"He is angry, Mario," he whispered. "Do not be afraid."

Father Malcolm made the sign of the cross over the quarter ton of iron.

"In the name of the Father, the Son, and the Holy Ghost," he said into the wind, "let this bell abjure every evil power and ministration over the land! Let the ancient evil hear its sound and flee it! For it signals the Redemption of our Lord Jesus Christ!"

Now Mario knew where the vertigo came from. The litanies, the Catholic passion in his ear, shouted by a believing priest, brought back his old dreams, so long reviled, of service to the Church.

Storm clouds now rolled through the birch woods. Barrels and bits of branches flew down the streets of Golgotha Falls. In them Mario saw an analogue of the chaos threatening to blow through his brain. When Mario came down the ladder, he felt the tug of the wind at his legs like hands, sucking him back toward the archaic fears and mythologies of the orphanage.

Anita steadied the ladder.

"The priest is completely charged," Mario said sardonically, hiding his torment. "Just wonderful."

But when Father Malcolm stepped down beside her, she saw only the tired, drawn face of a deeply sensitive man.

The Jesuit turned at a sound. Pebbles flew randomly out from the clay banks. The flat stones rattled against the Church foundations. He smiled grimly and led them to the locked door.

Mario held the censer. To Anita, he gave a pewter vessel that contained Gregorian water. The mixture of holy water, salt, wine, and ash was surprisingly heavy in her hand.

Father Malcolm lifted the crucifix.

"Look on the Church of Eternal Sorrows," he said loudly. "A church assaulted by the cunning power of the unclean spirit."

The name of the church was too appropriate, Mario thought. With unerring accuracy, the Catholic Church spotted its mysticisms in the places of neglect.

The Jesuit spoke intimately to the church that had killed his uncle and festered in his thoughts. In some way, it had become an extension of himself. And now, at long last, he had come to defeat the evil within himself and within the church.

"The ancient enemy surrounds the church," he said louder, "and infects the land with misery."

Suddenly, he angrily flicked droplets of Gregorian water at the door. It mingled with the distilled rainwater dribbling past the iron lock.

"Repel, O Lord, the power of evil! Let the unholy one take flight by the sign of Thy name!"

Raising the crucifix, he slowly, grandly, made the gesture of the cross.

He relaxed, watched the droplets of Gregorian water sparkle in the cloudy light and then, in spite of himself, smiled.

"Good," he confided. "Very good. Let us lustrate the church."

The Jesuit went to the corner and again spattered it with Gregorian water.

"In the name of the Judge of the living and the dead!" he proclaimed. "In the name of the Creator! In the name of the Archangel Michael who threw you down into hell! Depart the Church of Eternal Sorrows! Be defeated by the sign of the cross!"

The nausea hit Mario again, squarely in the solar plexus. Like a gravitation field, the litanies were pulling him back into preverbal levels of psychic dependence on the authority of Father Pronteus. He who had so deeply betrayed him.

Mario peered into the windows. The instruments were humming smoothly, the thermovision aimed generally at the altar. The nausea faded. These were the instruments of his own mind, his liberty, his

95

defiance. He felt better. The old bitterness once again sharpened his brain.

The Jesuit handed the Gregorian water to Anita. The wind now whipped her blouse back, revealing the soft, swelling contours within. The Jesuit quickly turned away from her, insensated the clapboards and moved to a spot about ten paces further along the south wall. The red robe flapped like a great crimson bird in the wind. Once again, he took the Gregorian water from Anita.

"In the name of the Judge of the living and the dead!" he repeated. "In the name of the Creator!"

Anita's vague shadow in the cloudlight, falling against the church wall, undulated among the clapboards and the shapes were metamorphic.

The compulsion to turn and see Anita was like a physical torment. Father Malcolm's body trembled, his mind searched for clues. Instead, he flicked the Gregorian droplets at the sliding, unsatisfied shadow.

Out of the corner of his eye, the Jesuit saw that the rain, not yet heavy, had already made the rectory path a living tongue of mud. A gray morass, indistinguishable from the clay banks, sucked at the church foundations.

A dead bird floated around and around in a silent, thick eddy.

Avoiding Anita, he reached back for the vessel.

"Please, Anita. The Gregorian water."

"I've been thinking, Father Malcolm. I could put this to better use."

"What use?"

"I could use it to lubricate myself."

Paralyzed, the Jesuit dared not look. He knew it couldn't be real, that he was hallucinating, still he could not look at her. Along the bottom of the church, the red-brown dirt oozed like soft feces.

Father Malcolm softly intoned the Eighty-sixth Psalm.

> *"Give ear, O Lord, unto my prayer;*
> *and attend to the voice of my supplications.*
> *In the day of trouble I will call upon Thee:*
> *for Thou wilt answer me."*

"It would be my holy douche," Anita's sultry voice insisted.

The Jesuit whirled, his face pale and contorted.

The image *was* Anita's, but infested with evil, unholy. Her tongue

96

flicked rapidly left and right. Her eyes were preternaturally bright and the white teeth bit the moist red tongue.

She smiled a lascivious smile.

"Made you look, didn't I?" the hallucinatory image purred.

Father Malcolm shuddered. It was as though a spike had been driven into him. His eyes filled with tears of rage.

A crack of thunder, like a gunshot, sounded through the valley.

When he turned for the Gregorian water, he saw that Anita again appeared normal, and solicitous, yet he held the crucifix between her and himself.

The Jesuit trembled and swayed in delirium. Mario went to him—grabbed his arm to steady him.

"Father Malcolm," he said gently, "are you all right?"

"Tricks, Mario. Just tricks. I've encountered them before."

The Jesuit pushed past Mario, and the rain flew off the ends of the crucifix in the wind.

"*Mario!*" Anita gasped, pointing.

On the church door, where the Gregorian water had been flicked, scorch marks had eaten into the wood.

Psychic projection, Mario instantly thought. *But so real. So very real. What other horrors will the man's brain spew out once he gets into the church?*

The Jesuit rushed to the door.

"I exorcise you, unclean spirit!" he roared into the driving wind and rain. "Be now uprooted and expelled from the house of God!"

The red chasuble was stained along the bottom by mud. Father Malcolm stood staring at the door, pummeled by the storm.

"Give way to our Lord, Jesus Christ!" he demanded. "Give way to the God who abides in this church!"

The rain came now steadily, cold and hard, making the incense sputter and fume. Then the Jesuit turned from the door and looked around at the bending trees and at the graveyard. Finally, cautiously, he was satisfied.

Slowly, he stepped through the mud, threw the brambles away with the base of the crucifix pole, and addressed the door.

"In the name of the Father, the Son, and the Holy Spirit," he declared, "I enjoin the Church of Eternal Sorrows. Receive the righteous and the holy!"

With one knock of the base of the crucifix pole, he sent a shock rattling into the vestibule. He struck a second time. Then he struck a third time.

He nodded to Mario.

Mario leaned forward to unlock the door. The iron tumblers had jammed. He braced his legs and put all his strength into turning and violently the lock gave way. The door slowly swung inward.

A black, corrosive air leaked out. Mario fell back, coughing.

The Jesuit, horrified, raised the crucifix.

Slowly, he stepped into the vestibule. At the near wall was a heavy wooden box. The Jesuit held the crucifix high in front of them and gestured toward the box.

"The stoppered chalice," he whispered. "Bring it to me."

The Jesuit took it and poured the shimmering holy water into the gleaming basin.

From deep within the church came a low, trembling groan, an obscene murmur of gratification.

It was dark everywhere but the vestibule. The Jesuit advanced toward the interior, but paused. From the church came a stench of corpses and a demented giggle. It was the sound of furtive, hastened delight, a perverted breathing.

"Satan is here," Father Malcolm murmured. "And sensible to us all."

They stepped inside. It was dry, warm, and utterly still, like being in a recently shut-off furnace where the black oils still clung to the walls. Mario saw that the instruments were running smoothly. Whatever the Jesuit was going through, he reflected, its external manifestations were going directly onto film plates, videotapes, and the slowly rolling drums.

"Look on the cross of the Lord!" Father Malcolm proclaimed. "In the name of Jesus Christ through the intercession of the Immaculate Virgin, the blessed apostles Peter and Paul and all the saints of heaven, upon the authority of our office, we undertake the expulsion of diabolic infestation!"

A green slime dribbled over the front of the vestment. Father Malcolm took a white handkerchief from a hidden pocket and wiped it away. Mario looked up. From invisibly tiny strands of silk, a half dozen green caterpillars twirled slowly, slowly in the breeze.

The Jesuit paused. He heard his uncle's voice.

"—yes—yes—Eamon—when you worship—a donkey is good—is good—is good—but a goat—is best—is best—is best—"

Father Malcolm recognized the slightly breathless Boston accent. The church receded into silence.

"He's in good form today," Father Malcolm said, knowingly.

The Jesuit then clenched his jaw, raised the crucifix, and stepped into the blackness.

"May God rise up," he called. "May His enemies be dissipated."

Something slowly glowed along the north and south walls. The two crucifixes. The Jesuit's knees buckled.

The Christs, moments before resplendent and gold, now appeared deformed, humpbacked and tumored; the legs and faces were eaten by scabs, asymmetrical, scourged.

Milk dripped from their loincloths.

"Oh, no—" Father Malcolm moaned. "Such desecration—"

The Jesuit struggled to his feet, glanced at Mario and Anita, but they seemed not to notice.

Anita slipped toward the thermovision. She panned the camera slightly to include the priest. Vibrating swirls of viridian rose from Father Malcolm's biretta and the crucifix, still cold from the rain.

Father Malcolm's face tensed. The perspiration mingled freely with the rainwater running down his neck. He held the crucifix high.

"Cease to injure this church!" he shouted. "Go, Satan! Be humiliated! For God so commands thee!"

In the bishop's throne, the raised wooden platform with its small circular stair that overlooked the altar, in full ocher and crimson vestments, reclined the shaggy-headed, full-horned form of a goat.

The goat's tongue, abrasive and pink, showed itself to the Jesuit.

He dashed droplets of holy water against the bishop's throne.

"Be defeated, ancient Serpent!" he called. "The Mother of God the Virgin Mary commands you! The blood of the martyrs commands you! Be uprooted and exorcised from the house of God!"

There was a sibilant, silly echo.

"—God—pod—mod—fod—lod—rod—tod—"

Then the echo was gone. The Jesuit, in his agony, did not notice that Anita and Mario had slipped behind the instruments to monitor him.

The temperature gauge showed a ten-degree drop.

The Jesuit listened. There was only the diminishing rain thudding into the ground outside.

"Be defeated, all enemies of the cross!" he called defiantly.

The provocation went unanswered. Exorcisms have ebbs and flows. The Jesuit felt the momentary recession of the malevolent presence, as though it had retreated for reinforcements.

"We'd better move very quickly now," the Jesuit whispered, and

99

hurried to the nearest wall, the wall where the laser camera was stationed. In his left hand, he held the vial of chrism. With that mixture of holy water and balsam, he inscribed a cross against the wall.

He took the censer from the floor and insensated the inscribed cross.

Twelve places the Jesuit inscribed a chrism cross, twelve times dedicated the church to God, and at each place around the church left a burning candle to signal the presence of sanctity.

The twelve tall gold candles, set in shallow pewter bowls, dispersed the gloom along the walls.

The Jesuit was perspiring heavily. He traced a St. Andrew's Cross on the floor near the altar using sand and ash. On the beam of the cross, he inscribed the Latin and Greek alphabets.

Father Malcolm looked around the church. The candles flared in the occasional breeze from the exterior, but burned strong and confidently. Anita changed the tape in the thermovision.

The grounds and the walls, exterior and interior, had been made sacred. Mario felt the same claustrophobia he once had felt in the orphanage.

The Jesuit reached into a black trunk and pulled out the altar linens. He spread the appendium so that the ocher Alpha and Omega faced the front. The top linen, immaculate and smooth, covered the limestone, and at the rear the pall. He began flicking Gregorian water liberally, lustrating the base and floor around the altar.

With a strong voice, he chanted the Forty-fourth Psalm.

"Thou hast saved us from our enemies
and hast put to shame those that hated us.
In God we exult all the day and
praise His name forever."

It was as though the Psalm itself, written over two thousand years ago by David, were now present at the altar. It worked its will through the obedience of the living Jesuit.

On the altar linen, Father Malcolm chrismed five spots. Then he burned the resin grains of incense on the altar. He chrismed the four points where the altar stone was in contact with its base. Only when he had done that did he relax. Slowly, he turned.

Anita wore a dark green hat and waited, accusingly, like a Rembrandt in the chiaroscuro of the edge of the church.

"So," Father Malcolm murmured despondently. "He is still here. He wishes to work through you. So be it. I am prepared."

Father Malcolm did not turn, but began to prepare the altar for the Eucharist.

"I waited for you, Eamon," the soft voice said. "I wrote to you twice. You never answered."

From the tabernacle, he laid out the chalice with its white wine mixed with a drop of water, and the silver dish for the Host. He lit the five golden candles in the short candelabrum, and the reflections off the lavabo and silver chalice and plate reassured him.

He raised the silver wick to light the red lamp hanging overhead.

"I needed you," came the vulnerable voice. "You needed me. Where was the harm in that?"

He drew down the long-handled wick, trembling.

"Why are you so afraid of yourself?" said the uncannily accurate voice. "Eamon, is it love that you're afraid of?"

The answer he knew too well. Scarcely a day had gone by without that final scene appearing in some form to his conscious mind. He caught himself framing that answer, and reached again for the red glass of the brass lamp.

"And yet, it would be the seal of our souls," she said. "And where would be the shame in that?"

The Jesuit now knew the correct answer. It had been worked out in seven months of prayer, guidance, and stern discipline. The temptation to respond was so overwhelming he closed his eyes. He called on Christ and the scene of the hotel evaporated and he was acutely aware of the glittering instruments of the Eucharist before him. A third time, he raised the silver wick.

"Eamon—"

He did not know if the sound were real or hallucinated. He quickly reasoned that Anita would not call him by his first name.

"In denying me, you deny yourself."

The words had a hideous second meaning. It was the Serpent's potent insight. It was the accusation that imperfection remained, that the Jesuit belonged to the base order of his own nature.

Father Malcolm withdrew the silver wick from the unlit altar lamp and began the litany of the saints; the strong voice filled the church, and his face was flushed in the heat of the candles.

A sensuous, dreamy atmosphere began circulating over the Eucharist utensils. Father Malcolm resisted, took off the biretta in two fingers and laid it on the altar. He knelt, kissed the altar, crossed himself, and rose.

He unfolded the heavy linen called the corporal, exposing the Host. As he did so, he glanced at Anita. The *real* Anita, standing solicitously by at the thermovision.

Their eyes met. A kind of strength flowed between them. It was inexpressible and the Jesuit turned away. He dipped his thumb and forefinger into a tiny trickle of water he was obliged to pour for himself and the runoff collected in the reflective lavabo.

A great sadness came over the Jesuit, the sadness of his loneliness, the long suffering of comfortless living.

Father Malcolm understood where the emotion originated. He recited the Psalms following the ablution and it went away. Once again, there was a clarity of logic in the celebration of the sacrament.

Then, as he reached the point of consecration, the invocation that turned the wafer and wine into the actual and abiding presence of Christ, he felt the dreamy, sensual warmth come back to the altar.

He felt the pressure of Elizabeth's breasts against his chest and the intoxication of her perfume, felt the urgent, hesitant pressure of her fingers against the back of his neck.

He repeated the Psalms.

Suddenly, to his surprise, he saw Anita beyond the altar. There was concern in her eyes and she seemed afraid, yet determined to speak.

"What— What is it?—" he stammered.

"Father Malcolm—" she said gently. "Are you hallucinating?"

"He has so many tricks, Anita."

The Jesuit mopped the sweat in the circles of his eyes. The church was extraordinarily warm.

"Please go back," he said. "I cannot interrupt the Eucharist."

Anita looked back and the Jesuit saw that she was getting some kind of signal from Mario. She approached the altar.

"I beg you not to be angry with me, Father Malcolm," she said. "But I know why you are hallucinating."

"Why?"

"The contradictions of your sexual nature," she said. "They assert themselves in this kind of tension."

The Jesuit stared at her, studied her. Once again, her image was in Satan's grip. He longed for assistance. The body and mind were ravaged by the sensual storms, and yet he felt himself slipping away from the Eucharist.

"The Church has made you obsessed," she said gently. "It has corrupted the natural desire to worship and serve."

Father Malcolm realized he had been tricked into dialogue with the Evil One. Once in, it would be like pulling oneself from the quicksand to break it off. The ancient Serpent had words whose logic bore in with an unfathomable charisma, and were unanswerable.

"What is the Church so jealous of?" she spat angrily.

"Please, I—"

"It has turned your own nature into a viper's nest of forbidden and perverted thoughts!"

"Not true— I beg you—"

The wine and the host, unconsecrated, remained on the altar, untouched.

"Of course it's true!" she said, eyes blazing. "And you fell for it, hook, line, and sinker!"

Fumbling, the Jesuit turned and tried to begin the O Salutaris Hosta, the beginning of the consecration.

"And why?" she demanded. "So you can hurl your sublimated demands into praise of the Church? Is that what you gave up happiness for, Eamon?"

Father Malcolm vigorously shook his head, but the image of Anita did not go away. The rain-wet blouse shone as she came forward. With one hand, she cupped a breast.

"Look! It's nothing!" she said. "It's a piece of flesh!"

Stuttering through the O Salutaris Hosta, the Jesuit felt himself growing faint in the warm, red heat.

"Now look at you," she said contemptuously. "You want it more than salvation itself."

He began again the O Salutaris Hosta, focusing, the brain picking out the Latin by rote, and tried to project himself into the flavor and meaning of each word. He slowed, then stumbled badly.

Anita smiled. She was moving rhythmically, pumping against the base of the altar. Her eyes closed, but before they did, the pupils rolled in pleasure.

"Stop it— Stop it— I beg you—"

"I'm not finished."

"By the power of the Archangel Michael who sent you to—"

Anita laughed, showing the clean, white, perfect teeth.

"Watch," she said. "Watch my face."

The angular, lovely, pale face smoothed, grew taut, then the brows furrowed and the eyes stuttered shut as her whole body shook and shook again. Gradually, the nostrils ceased to flare. The perspiration beaded her forehead. She caught her breath and the torment evaporated from her features. In its place was a satisfied relaxation.

"See?" she said, her voice quavering from the orgasm. "That's all it is."

Father Malcolm launched into the Tantum Ergo. By the mystery of the Eucharist, the wafer and wine were undergoing transubstantiation into the body and blood of Christ.

There was a kind of visual snap. Anita was gone. The Jesuit turned. She was monitoring the sound recording system, looking at him, very worried.

"Should I get a doctor?" she whispered.

"No. I think he's come out of it," Mario replied.

The Jesuit studied Anita's face and form in the shadowy area of the wall. He seemed to recognize her, as though coming out of a trance.

"It's all right, my friends," he whispered hoarsely. "It was quite bad, but—everything is all right now—Thank you—"

Mario sat down again at the thermovision screen. The concern on their faces had been painful to see. The Jesuit continued the Tantum Ergo. The disturbing heat was gone and he clearly heard, behind him, the drip-dripping of the rain.

"I think it was just too warm for him," he heard Mario whisper.

"Perhaps you should help him."

"Good idea."

The Jesuit, as he intoned the Latin, heard Mario's chair scrape and the heavy boots walk along the wall behind him. He heard a hissing sound. The Tantum Ergo faded into silence.

Mario was urinating on the candles set on the floor.

The Jesuit, as in a nightmare, saw the heavy leather jacket, the slightly stooped knees, the heavily pink and uncircumcised penis and the stream of urine dousing the struggling flame.

Horrified, he turned back and completed the Tantum Ergo.

"I'll show you a real trick," he heard Mario say.

A morbid repulsion shuddered through the Jesuit. What had happened to Lovell and to his uncle was happening to him.

In order to snap back to reality, he looked for Mario and Anita at the instruments. They were not there. Out of the corner of his eye, he saw Anita before him.

Anita was on the floor on hands and knees. She was naked. So was

Mario. Mario penetrated from behind, knees bent out along her flanks as he stood. In deep, rhythmic movement, he eased into her.

Anita tensed, bit her lips, then relaxed and giggled.

"Not at all easy," Mario bragged, stepping away, the heavy penis soft and bouncing as he moved.

"She's all yours," he invited.

The Jesuit gasped and reached to place the Host in the lunette of the monstrance.

"I hardly think this is the time or place for raising the Host," Mario said angrily.

Indeed, the pornography was so thick in the church, the Jesuit felt it like salt on his lips. It was precisely in the midst of such defilement that the Eucharist was needed to assert the domination of Christ. The Jesuit raised the monstrance and blessed the church.

Anita spat on the church floor.

"Here's your Host," she said.

Anita stared directly into the Jesuit's eyes. The bantering tone was gone. She spoke with an authority that chilled him, for it came out of his own deepest nature.

"It's the Host," she said evenly, "for a man who hates God."

The Jesuit felt a galvanic current slither through him. He dared not think, dared not pause, but rushed into the holiest aspect of the Eucharist, the sacrificial offering, the *Unde et memores* of the Amamnesis.

He was defenseless now. There was no strength anywhere. He felt darkness close over him. Christ did not answer and the bitterness of his frustrations, the agonizing breakdowns, the obdurate Church hierarchy that merited his anger floated in his mouth and ears and filled his throat with choking, oily liquid.

He was sinking and he knew it. For he knew now what had really lain, untouchable, beneath the final barriers of the personality during the night vigil. It was unspeakably foul. He tasted it in all its annihilating poison, for it had existed secretly in his own nature.

It was called the hatred against God who denies man his happiness on earth.

His fingers felt as though they belonged to a distant, dying animal. The rage overpowered him, made the hands tremble in confusion and anguish. Father Malcolm groped for the Host to commingle it with the wine to complete the Eucharist.

"Yes," Mario's voice commented bitterly. "You work now for us!"

The fingers paused. Should he stop, and deny a mass celebrated by the Serpent? Or was that a trick, designed to prevent a sacred mass from its completion?

The sweat poured down around the Jesuit's eyes, bathing his vision in tears of sweet horror.

He was forgetting the words. Christ was utterly absent. Still, from the depths of his heart, the Jesuit called on Christ for a clue, a signal of any kind.

"I told you not to deny me, you bastard," Anita hissed.

Christ seemed closer, or was that, too, a trick? Was it a deceiving Presence?

"You brought atheism into the church," Mario said, leaning forward. "You know science is atheism." Mario looked slyly at Father Malcolm. "You *wanted* to be tempted, didn't you?"

Feverishly, Father Malcolm groped for the wafer, but he could not find it in the glittering confusion on the altar linens.

Father Malcolm turned away from the apse. Behind him, Mario stood, eyes closed in pleasure, pressing Anita's obedient face into his moving pubic shadows. He moaned deliciously.

"Watch my face, Father Malcolm."

"No— I forbid it—" he gasped, turning away.

"Forbid it?" Mario laughed, behind the altar, holding a gentleman's vest. "You've been imagining it for three days."

"What's that— Where did you get that vest—"

"A certain James Farrell Malcolm. Alas, he has no need of it where he is now."

Anita giggled. Mario used the vest to wipe the sweat from his legs, then his genitals. He tossed the vest contemptuously into the corner.

Father Malcolm crossed himself, felt cramps cross through his legs, and his heart seemed ready to stop. With all his strength, he peered back at the consoles.

To his inestimable relief and reassurance, Mario and Anita, fully clothed, concerned, adjusting the instruments, sat quietly in the darkness.

Dreamlike, Father Malcolm groped for the Host. He found it. But his arms were as heavy as the altar lamp the previous night. The Jesuit felt the sick drug of hypnotic delusion.

Suddenly, Anita approached the altar.

"I need a towel. Do you mind?" she said, reaching for the altar appendium.

"No— No—" he gasped, and moved back.

At the last instant, he caught himself and remembered not to leave the lustrated area. Anita's smile suddenly froze.

"Almost," she hissed hoarsely.

Father Malcolm desperately held the wafer over the blessed wine. A piece crumbled, fell, twirling, and like a mouth's breath, a furnace of red heat flared through him over the altar.

"My God—" he cried.

Vaguely, near-fainting, clutching his breast, he spied the long black pole with the silver wick. His arms were leaden weights as he grabbed the pole and tried to light the wick. But each time Anita's sultry breath blew it out. Her tinkling laughter echoed through his brain. Finally, by shielding the wick with his body, he managed to ignite the small white flame.

"You'll never light the lamp," taunted Anita from the periphery of the lustrated area.

Struggling to his feet, the battered Jesuit held the pole up to the altar lamp. The pole swayed, snakelike, each time the white flame approached the lamp. Three times, he brought the wick to the altar lamp and three times he was repulsed by a tyrannical force.

"Fuck off, priest!" screamed Mario.

Suddenly, the pole flew from the Jesuit's hand.

"Jesus, Mary and Joseph—!" Father Malcolm cried as he grabbed his temples and pitched forward, crumpling to the ground. Fleetingly, he saw the silver chalice of the Blood of Christ topple and the wine stain the immaculate linen. The Host faltered against the tabernacle, the candelabrum tumbled down, and a black ocean of oblivion poured into him.

Mario was lifting him, urging him to his feet. Anita daubed at the slit of blood trickling from his forehead. He fought his way free of them.

"Leave me!" he said hoarsely.

"Father Malcolm," Mario insisted. "Let me help you!"

"I order you—to depart—!"

"It's us," Anita said gently. "No more hallucinations."

Hesitantly, stiffly, he suffered her to daub again at the bruised forehead.

Then he pushed her away.

"Did I complete the mass?" he demanded.

"Everything," Mario assured him. "We got everything on tape."

The candles on the floor burned brightly at the stations of the chrismed anointment. Father Malcolm turned to examine the floor behind the altar. There was no evidence of anyone having acted improperly there.

"I felt the most awful sensations—*inside my body*—"

"Fear no evil," Mario said, trying to joke, "for my instruments and logbooks shall comfort thee."

"*Mario*—" Anita shouted.

The shout paralyzed both the Jesuit and Mario.

"What is it?"

"You'd better come here, Mario," she said, looking at the thermovision screen.

Mario quickly walked to the unit. The camera had been pointed toward the altar. There was something on the screen. The Jesuit fought his way between them. At the side of the altar, arms extended, the viridian figure of a crucified man hung suspended in the air. Adjusting the aperture and focus made a clearer picture of the fading figure. In addition to the arm extensions on both sides of the central torso, and the twin extensions leading downward, there was a gash in its right side.

Mario stared. Psychic projection? It had to be. But why did he feel so sick, looking at it?

Anita studied the figuration, unwilling to commit herself. Objectivity was everything. But surely it had been expelled out of the nervous volatility of the priest. Or summoned by him from the exterior.

Mario, sweating badly, stared through his morbid distaste at the pure image of his most extraordinary success.

The Jesuit looked up at the altar. There was only the soiled linen, the lavabo fallen to the floor, and paraffin faintly smoking on the appendium. In the air around, there was absolutely nothing else.

The image faded very slowly. By adjusting the f-stop ring, Mario kept it visible for several more seconds. At the side of the camera, the recording tape ran smoothly. The Jesuit looked around the quiet church.

The darkness was utterly gone. The breaking clouds of the afternoon showed blue skies and bird calls echoed through the refreshed valley.

In the camera, the afterimage on the screen faded to a uniform view of the church interior.

"Mario," Father Malcolm said in a quavering voice.

Mario rubbed his eyes and stared, blinking, at the convex screen.

108

"What is it?"

"The altar lamp."

Overhead, the ruby-red glass of the altar lamp, the symbol of Christ's presence, burned in a clear, quiet splendor.

The Jesuit stepped forward insistently, his face pale and frightened.

"*I didn't light it!*"

C H A P T E R
S E V E N

FATHER MALCOLM, his eyes fixed reverently on the lamp overhead, poised between doubt and ecstasy, pointed at the ruby glow in the frontal glass.

"Christ has won," he whispered.

Anita placed a hand on Mario's arm. In the silence, the altar lamp radiated points of reflection on the Jesuit's chasuble, on them, and over their cameras.

"It didn't light itself," Mario muttered.

Father Malcolm turned, emphatic.

"I didn't light it, Mario!"

Mario punched a silver button at the base of the thermovision monitor.

"There's one way to find out," he said.

The black videotape glowed in a reddish band as it flashed in reverse, reflecting the altar lamp. Father Malcolm felt himself drawn toward the screen, magnetically, without breathing. A confusion of crimson flares and a black cross moved down the church aisle in jerked motions. To Father Malcolm, it resembled a soul in purgatory.

Mario played the tape forward at normal speed.

The Jesuit's chasuble was clearly defined, a dark silhouette against the heated convections rising from the joints of his body and at the face. The Jesuit held up the long, black pole of the silver wick. To Mario, it looked like a picture of medieval monks, a heretical fire-service in the caves of Sicily.

"What is that wick?" Mario asked. "What actually lights it?"

"It's flint against steel."

At the tip of the black pole now appeared a white point as the Jesuit lighted it.

Father Malcolm teetered, the pole dipped and struggled, but the lamp remained hard and dark.

"Now do you believe me, Mario?" he whispered. "He was too strong for me then."

Mario set the tape into motion again. Twice more, Father Malcolm raised the silver pole with its wick, and twice more he grappled as with an unseen force. Twice more the lamp remained unlit.

Mario stopped the tape. Bioluminescence, like most forms of psychic luminescence, is cold. Even when red or orange in hue, upon measurement they are barely above room temperature. But he could feel the light of the altar lamp above him warm his face from fifteen feet away.

"Father Malcolm— What was going through your mind when you were trying to light the lamp?"

The Jesuit glared at Mario as though grossly insulted.

"Please, Father Malcolm," Anita said quietly, understanding the drift of Mario's question. "It's important."

Father Malcolm looked at her, his face flushed, and then he turned back to Mario.

"Fantasies," he murmured.

"What kind?" Anita asked.

"Sexual," he whispered.

Mario punched the button and the tape began to inch forward. At times, the convections rose to obscure the lamp, but each time when the view was clear again, the lamp was as before, hard and dark.

Then the figure of the Jesuit threw the pole away. His arms went for his head. Then the camera followed his figure collapsing toward the church floor. The camera swung wildly, corrected itself, and showed the altar area.

The lamp now had a white point of heat within, and from it streamed an ocher grid of undisturbed heat radiance.

"It was a burning heat that I suddenly felt," Father Malcolm said. "As soon as it hit me, I knew what it was. I looked up and the lamp was lit. It glorified me."

Mario reversed the tape until the Jesuit was standing. Then he inched it forward by hand. In the screen, Father Malcolm began reaching for his temples.

Anita's finger pointed out the crimson wave of heat that illuminated the Jesuit's back.

Inch by inch, the figure crumpled and the camera jerked down after him. With each frame, the altar lamp, cold and hard, drifted up toward the top frame line. When the lamp was pushed half out of the frame, a white point of light appeared in the spout of its oil basin.

An ocher radiance began to spill from the shape of the lamp.

Anita knew from the experiments of Dodge and Tippet at Duke that an emotionally hysterical subject could induce momentary suggestibility in receptive persons. But the thermovision had no feelings. It was utterly objective. And now the lamp was hot and the combustion was a chemical union of oil and oxygen. Pyrokinetic combustions had rarely been recorded so unambiguously from a subject undergoing deep stress.

Mario saw Anita's face, and knew her mind was racing through the collective data of previous studies and experiments, trying to find a place for what had happened.

Impulsively, aggressively, Mario pulled his chair toward the lamp.

"What are you doing?" Father Malcolm demanded.

"I'm going to look at the lamp, of course."

Father Malcolm came closer, taking hold of Mario's arm.

"Don't do that, Mario."

"Why not?"

"It's a holy object."

Mario shook off the Jesuit's hands and stepped onto the chair. He peered into the ruby glass. The flame within burned so tranquilly it was like a blue and yellow cone. He opened the small ruby-glass door.

"Mario—no—" Father Malcolm whispered.

The glass door was sharp and cut into Mario's hand, which he ignored in his excitement.

Mario sniffed around the lamp. It was not a petrochemical. He passed his fingers through the flame. It was cool, efficient. The kind of lamp that would have been used eons ago in the Mediterranean.

"What does it burn?"

"Sanctified oil."

Mario smiled. "Ah. Sanctified. That makes all the difference."

From the articles by LaCade at Baton Rouge, Anita knew that very few liquids could self-combust, even in the strongest field of psychic turbulence. She knew the Russian experiments with mediums and volatile liquids had utterly failed. She began to have an uneasy sensation that something altogether different had occurred.

As Mario stepped down from the chair, he pulled a handkerchief from his pocket to stop the bleeding where the glass door had cut him.

He looked up. Father Malcolm had set the thermovision into forward. The screen's glow flared over the Jesuit's hypnotized face, the metamorphic glow of the last moments of documentation.

Slowly coruscating, the viridian figure of the crucified man hung near the hard outlines of the altar. Emblem of the mystery generated out of the Eucharist, it glowed defiantly with subtle deep greens and browns.

Father Malcolm sank slowly to his knees.

"Do Thy grant me judgment, humility, and purity to discern Thy will and be the vessel of Thy grace. Grant me the strength to do Thy bidding, the clear sight to perceive Thy purpose."

Mario studied the kneeling Jesuit. Father Malcolm was praying toward the altar, but it was the cruciform image on the thermovision that had driven him to his knees. He seemed to have abandoned himself to it totally, and a curious sense of relief showed on his face.

Anita indicated to Mario that they leave him to his prayers. The voice of the priest followed them, fading sonorously as they walked toward the van.

It was not yet sunset, but already the skies over Golgotha Falls were deep and ragged purple. The storm had broken the old log-jam at the mouth of the bog, and the Siloam was pouring into the spongy morass, breaking it up, sweeping it down into the valley.

113

Beyond the Volkswagen, several children watched them apprehensively. They were strangely still, like woodland creatures caught in an unnatural light.

Over the roofs of Golgotha Falls rose the thunderclouds, rimmed in violet hues, gilded by the sinking sun below. The roofs of the town shimmered in pools of gold.

"Everything looks different," she whispered.

Mario looked at the cemetery. Some of the milkweed had blossomed from the rain. The tombstones dripped with rainwater, glittered in mauve and crimson from the dying sun. Even the birch forest above seemed abnormally white, touched by the freak incandescence of the sun so soon after the storm.

"What's happened, Mario?" she asked.

"The rainstorm. Swept all the dust out of the air."

Anita stared at Mario in amazement. At a time like this, with a stunning success at their fingertips, his infuriating objectivity rankled her to the core.

"What about the pictures?" she demanded.

"I . . . I don't know. I have to think about it."

Anita maintained her calm. "A self-combusting oil lamp, and a cruciform that looks suspiciously like Jesus on the cross. All firmly preserved on three-quarter-inch tape. What's to think about?"

Mario turned from her. Anita's face softened, her voice lost its bite. "Mario, please . . . After all these years, we've *finally* got something definitive!"

Mario said nothing. Anita moved around to face him. There was a terrible dark antipathy in his eyes. He sank slowly against the wall of the church, rubbing his face with his hands.

"What's wrong, Mario?"

"I don't even remember *taking* those pictures," he groaned. "I don't know what happened." He looked up at her. "Didn't you feel it?" he asked, stupefied.

"Feel what?"

"Anita—I—I could hardly hang on to the camera . . . When the priest went down—"

She stared at him, uncomprehending.

"I didn't feel anything!"

Mario closed his eyes and tried to collect himself.

"All right," he said. "Maybe I was just emotionally involved in the experiment. A kind of sympathetic response."

At 4:37, the moment of the priest's collapse, the instant of the

114

spontaneous illumination of the overhead lamp, Mario had felt, from the groin upward into the solar plexus, a shudder go through him. It pulsed, then died out. It was like a mild electric current. Or an incomplete orgasm.

Now he felt a slight fever rising. It might be due, he thought, to the long hours, the damp miasma of the clay grounds.

Anita touched him gently on the cheek. He smiled and stood up. They heard the soft litany filter through the church. It seemed vaguely in harmony with the peculiar light qualities of the rain-dripping valley.

"I'm beat. Would you go in there and monitor the instruments?" he asked gently.

"All right."

Mario stepped through the sucking mud toward the van. The children did not scatter.

As he stepped into the van, pushing away a black metal case, he sensed the children peering inward, under his arms.

"Is Jesus in the church?" a boy with glasses asked.

"What? What the hell are you talking about?"

"Where will the devil go now?" asked a shy girl.

"Back where he belongs. In people's imaginations."

"The devil will come back," a child called.

"He'll suck out your soul," yelled another.

Mario pulled the door shut.

In the church, Anita replaced the drum of graph paper in the seismograph, watching the Jesuit clean the floor around the altar.

Father Malcolm put the vessels back into their boxes. The chalice and paten he carefully put into the tabernacle. The monstrance and humeral veil he gently lay beside the altar. Anita saw that his hands shook more and more, until he suddenly clutched them to his chest.

Gently, Father Malcolm was crying.

Anita went to him and took his arm. He shivered violently, deliriously happy and yet totally drained by the terror of his experience.

"Father Malcolm," she whispered, "you need rest now."

"Oh, Anita . . . Faith comes . . . That it should come through me—"

"Yes. The exorcism was successful. But God needs you to rest now."

Anita tried to coax the Jesuit from the altar. Gradually, he allowed himself to be led up the aisle. He looked again around the walls, now tinged with the ruby of the lamp. Then he went through the vestibule.

The dying sun gilded the top of the holy water font through the open door.

Outside, over the roofs of Golgotha Falls, a double rainbow arched into the dark ridges on either side. High among new cirrus clouds were the evening stars.

"Like a river of light, He moves through us all."

Father Malcolm turned, and saw Anita, half in the shadow.

"Anita, do you feel the presence of Christ?"

"Something has happened, Father Malcolm. But I don't know what."

"Christ lives, Anita. Through you, as well as through me."

Anita smiled. "I wouldn't know about that, Father. We rely on data. Statistics. Correlations. Our theories have to be proven. Our experiments have to be replicated by others."

"God is the source of all our proofs, Anita. Doesn't this church now prove it?"

"Well, I'm not sure Mario would agree."

"Have you given your soul unto Mario?"

Anita suddenly saw the pain in Father Malcolm's face. It was the pain of separation from her.

"The soul," he said softly, "has needs. Just like the body. Just like the mind. You ignore those needs at great peril, Anita."

"I understand you, Father. I appreciate everything that you say. But it's so very foreign to my thinking."

"But you *will* think about it, Anita. Look around you. Feel. Learn to receive."

"I will, Father. Good night."

Mario couldn't sleep. At two in the morning, he returned to the church. Sitting before the thermovision, he played back the tape on the screen. There it was, the palpable image, vaguely cruciform in shape. Anita was, of course, right. What they had here was truly immense. Everything they had worked for, struggled for, fought for these past seven pitiless years would finally pay off. And it was all worth it, all the hard times and battered pride, the ignoble years that stretched out behind him like a tattered carpet.

Mario studied the image of the thermovision. The incredible

image. Projected, spewed out, emanated from a believer nearly sick with his belief. A palpable image. Not to another mind, but to the heat-seeking thermovision. For the first time, an image fixed in materials that could be shown to the entire world. Or at least that part of it willing to look with an open mind.

Ideas of an address to the Harvard committee on the sciences came to Mario.

Anita would have to work up a psychiatric profile and history on the Jesuit. From abnormal psychology, Mario would move into the Kirlian studies. Kirlian photography recorded different light patterns from meditating yogis than from normal subjects. Also, schizophrenic subjects transmitted altered electrochemical signals compared to normal subjects. There were studies of charisma, its influence on emotions, and studies of telepathy, or thought transference between two minds.

But never, in discrete imagery, the replication of a subject's psychic obsession.

First the priest, Lovell, and then the Jesuit's uncle. Disturbed, highly libidinous individuals who broke apart in their self-destructive dementia. Around the church, the collective imaginations of the natives of Golgotha Valley. Frightened, interpreting the luminescences, obsessed with the church, all adding their emotional energy. Perhaps the geology of the church itself, its strange placement in the clay hollow by the blue river, fissured granitic foundations that had frightened even the Algonquin shamans. All together, a rich psychic humus, a bell jar of volatile gases, into which the third priest, Eamon Malcolm, entered. And by the extraordinary power of his belief and his doubt fired some kind of spark. That spark, that psychic crisis, was now rendered as an image by the very heat of his own repressed thoughts.

Mario shook his head in wonderment.

Golgotha Falls. This sickly, obnoxious site, ill-smelling and morally repellent, was revealing treasures the like of which he had never dared dream.

Meditating on his knees, facing the crucifix, Father Malcolm felt the flush of excitement on his own cheeks. The emotion was overwhelming.

Yet what had happened? That the heat had come into him was beyond question. It came at his back like a whirlwind and then entered, filled the chest walls, and spread rapidly to the brain, and only then did he feel it pass into his limbs. Was this, Father Malcolm wondered, what the old Church Fathers called the "fire of God"? Or was it a diabolic simulacrum of that ecstatic wind?

And how to know the signs? That he was inhabited even now he knew. The interior of the body no longer his own, a fever not his own, and the mind was fueled on an exotic potency he had never known. Were they signs of diabolic infestation, the augury of arrogance and corruption? Or were they inward metamorphoses that proclaimed the presence of Christ?

A worthless, twice-broken, heavy-hearted Jesuit in the wilderness of a poor valley at an abandoned church. Was this the kind of target easily struck by Satan? Or was it precisely the empty vessel that Christ filled at the extreme instant of need?

For surely he was not himself any longer. He served somebody. And it was a lovely, exalted feeling that transfigured him. Dared he trust that image on the scientists' machine? Could Christ in any form be caught in mere mechanical screens? Was not science anti-Christ, a system of atheists? Whoever he served, His emblem was in the extraordinary colored visions of the scientists' thermovision.

Father Malcolm did not fall asleep so much as he passed into increasingly visual doubts, until they became dreams, ravishing dreams of a surpassing loveliness that led him toward the dawn.

Anita sat in the van, notebooks on her knees. Through the partially open rear door she saw the Church of Eternal Sorrows. It rose now like a diadem from the dark valley floor. Its steeple gleamed in the rising moon, pure and radiant. A phallic symbol, according to Mario. A yearning toward God, according to the Roman Catholic Church.

Anita looked from the church to the shelf that held the kerosene lamp. A photograph lay against the base of the lamp. It was Mrs. Wagner. Anita's mother dressed in handsome country tweeds, a face youthful for its years, with crow's feet from smiling and a gracious sense of propriety. The face seemed to look down on Anita with an edge of sadness, reflecting on the distance that had grown between her and her daughter.

Mrs. Wagner detested Mario. To her, he was boorish, unkempt, violent, and foreign. It was not that she did not see what Anita found in him. That was all too apparent. Liberty. Sexual liberty. There was something about Mario, even when he was trying to be intellectual, that reminded Mrs. Wagner of an animal. But Anita had drifted into Mario's orbit, demanding her rights as a sexual being.

The gravitational pull toward Mario puzzled even Anita. She tried to recall her father, but all she remembered was a shadowy, sincere man who died before she was seven. Scenes came to her: after her father's death, a series of men coming to visit her mother. Gracious men, wealthy men, discreet and ambitious men. Even Dean Harvey Osborne. But the child Anita detected in them not substance but a strange absence of virility.

Mrs. Wagner probably detected the same thing. In any event, she never remarried.

The memories flooded back, stimulated by the extraordinary events of the exorcism.

For the exorcism seemed to have broken Mario's hold upon Anita. That gravitational field, that emotional drive of Mario's, suddenly lost its intense hold. Oddly, Mario's sexual liberation was repressive. It repressed the more intuitive, delicate dimension of Anita's emotions.

She recalled the winters at Seven Oaks. Snowshoes down to an iced-over creek behind the stables. Autumn leaves frozen there from the previous autumn, embedded in the bubbles and crystalline outlines of the ice. In that loneliness she had found a tranquility.

It was a slow unfolding of life, a sensuality without sex. An intelligence without aggressive intellectuality. It was a kind of listening and sharing of a humble heart. Father Malcolm would have understood.

It was not innocence that was reborn in Anita. That had long since been left behind in an irretrievable girlhood. But something rare and permanent had happened: an awakening beyond the sexual. A kind of quickening of the spiritual imagination, that owes much to the sensual but soars above it as the dove soars above milk-white, moonlit clouds.

Anita raised herself on one elbow. The church still glowed, from the moonlight, and seemed to answer the birch woods above her. A new echo, a new system of rhythms was alive in Golgotha Valley, as different from what transpired before as the major key is from the minor.

Something had happened that day, something rare, even miraculous. Or was it all deception?

C H A P T E R
E I G H T

SOMETHING RUSTLED at the crucifix. Slow at first, moving inward at the window, the apple petals moved in the sunlight, drifting down onto Father Malcolm's mattress.

He threw the blanket from his body, then felt the pain of stiff muscles. Slowly he massaged them and rose from the bed. In the doorway he saw a rabbit regard him sagely, then hop back down the step.

From its hanger the red chasuble hung in the slanting sun. The mud at the hem had caked, dried, and finally fallen in the night as gray powder to the floor. The biretta was also cloaked in the gray powder. The alb, thrown onto a battered chair, was yellow with sweat and grit.

Father Malcolm carried the chasuble into the Oldsmobile. Then he took the biretta and the shoes. The sun was excessively bright outside the rectory. Not only was the apple tree in brilliant bloom, catching the morning, but two pear trees on the north side of the church had also bloomed after the hard rain.

The Church of Eternal Sorrows rose, bright now and undefiled, the brightest object in the valley. Inside, Mario could be seen keeping vigil over his instruments, haggard from lack of sleep.

As the Jesuit prepared his morning coffee, he looked through the window. Two small, dark birds hopped among the boughs. One of them carried twigs in its beak. Father Malcolm saw a rudimentary nest in the dark crotch among the petals. Father Malcolm slowly drank the coffee.

It had been, in Christian terminology, an ecstatic experience. Mario would call it a physical outbreak. In any case, it was gone now. There was only a sensation of immanence, of being on the threshold either of glory or annihilation.

Now it was a matter of making a report to the bishop. Father Malcolm looked moodily into the grounds floating in his cup. A bee circled lazily around his hand.

It had come as a revelation to him that Christ might have chosen to work through him, even in a single rite. It was something he had never believed, not for one moment, in all the years of his preparation.

For a priest, he believed, especially a Jesuit, can achieve sophistication of intellect, even a sense of style, without ever confronting the final question: Am I worthy of Christ?

His family had placed its hopes on an eldest brother, Ian, meant for the priesthood. When Ian was killed Eamon took his place. Eamon was clever, he imitated well, and he was terrified of failing, so he won scholarships. But the family always knew that in Eamon there was a subtle lack. At the core a strange emptiness where there should have been vitality.

Elizabeth had stirred that emptiness to where it resembled the storms of manhood. But it was somehow a facsimile. Eamon always knew that he would survive in Christ and in Christ only, or perish in His absence.

Now, quite simply, and in all humility, Father Malcolm knew that by joining the Society of Jesus he had been ultimately, fabulously rewarded.

He put on his shoes, standing in the doorway. The cemetery had not escaped the effects of the rain. It blossomed with wild currants, strawberry and black raspberry. Monarch butterflies lingered on the rectory roof. Sweet lilacs hung down over the quick-flowing Siloam.

Eden again, he thought, marveling, and explored the tall grass, shielding his eyes from the morning sun.

Everywhere the valley floor was radiant in tall plants that caught the gold of the sunlight, and milkweed floating in the air bobbed like globes of brilliance. Even the town of Golgotha Falls, washed clean by the rain, was altered. Glittering white gingerbread and clapboard were dominated by bright red Victorian roofs.

A boot rustled in the apple boughs. Father Malcolm looked up. It belonged to a young, unshaven farmer, cradling a rifle. The man's eyes were bloodshot, but he seemed happy.

"Good morning, Father," he said bashfully.

"Well, good heavens, what are you doing up there?"

"We was protecting you."

"From what?"

"From Satan."

Father Malcolm grinned.

"I appreciate your thought. I truly do. But you know that Satan isn't scared away by bullets."

"Maybe not. But we was going to give him what noise we could."

The young man, about twenty-five, slipped down to the ground. Two other farmers, older, in blue denim overalls and filthy caps, cradled rifles in their arms and came from behind the rectory.

"We want you to come with us now, Father," said the oldest farmer.

"But I'm on my way to Boston."

The older farmer, eyes deep brown with red in the corners, gently approached him.

"You'll want to see what we've got to show you, Father."

There was sincerity in the old man's eyes, tinged with fright. Father Malcolm's curiosity was piqued.

"All right," he agreed. "Lead on."

Together they trudged up the plowed hill. They came to a gray, weather-beaten shack adjacent to a barn. A fat woman in an apron and five children watched from the farmhouse.

The old farmer indicated for Father Malcolm to enter the barn. It was so dark the Jesuit saw only the dim red after-globe of the bright Golgotha Falls sun. Then, gradually, he made out horizontal boards, some straw, and, nestled deep in fetid straw, a new-born calf.

"Look on it, Father," said the old farmer, pleading more than commanding. Father Malcolm knelt down. The calf was only hours old, the hide still moist, the knees absurdly knobby and the eyes pink.

"She looks fine to me."

The old farmer hunched down beside him, tipping back his grime-smeared hat.

"She's perfect, Father," he said.

Father Malcolm studied the bewildered men. They stood around him, their rifles loose in their hands. Now the fat woman and the children crowded into the shack.

"We ain't had a natural calf since before my father was born," the farmer confided. "We have to purchase our livestock from Dowson's Repentance."

"I see. And this one?"

"Born this morning. And just perfect."

Father Malcolm stroked the tiny beast. The heavy red tongue lolled against its muzzle. He could not help but smile. The farmer stood up.

"Better come with us, Father," he said.

Father Malcolm followed the men through the side door. One of the farmers closed it so the woman and the children could not see. The others grabbed long-poled shovels and manure forks and began digging at the shady earth.

Father Malcolm blanched.

As the earth was scraped away by the forks, grinning, knob-headed, mutant calves appeared. The forelegs were knotted up, some had mouths where the ears should have been. One had no legs at all but a series of flippers along the matted hide.

"We know who done this to us," the oldest farmer said. "But what happened this morning?"

Father Malcolm swallowed, watching the men shove earth back over the partially decomposed cadavers.

"I am not empowered to answer that," he admitted. "That is why I must go to Boston."

The farmers exchanged glances.

"You going to come back?"

"Most certainly. I belong now to Golgotha Falls."

The oldest farmer nodded. They went back into the gray shack. Father Malcolm noted that, although their clothes were filthy and their hands grimy since dawn, they now washed their hands under a cold tap.

Silent, they escorted him back to the rectory. As they got halfway down the slope the young farmer stopped him with a hand against the chest.

"You don't understand, Father," he said. "There was no sign that she was carrying a calf."

"Oh, well. These things are not always—"

"We talked to everybody in this here valley. And nobody knows what to make of it."

The old farmer stepped closer.

"Who is it done this?" he asked. "If it's Satan's work I'll slit this animal's throat . . . !"

"Please. Wait until I return from Boston."

Sullenly, they watched him descend, tracking mud, toward the church. His forehead was furrowed, thinking of the meaning of the healthy newborn calf. Was this, like the flourishing valley, a further sign of God's immanence, or was it an event inspired by the darker powers? Had the exorcism truly been successful? What was the significance of these signs? Father Malcolm had secretly hoped to have left behind the universe of symbols, portents, and secretly whispered hopes and fears. Now he was not so certain. Like the farmer, he too would have to wait for the answer.

Beside the Volkswagen stood an orange minibus. On its side, in black stenciled letters, were the words *Haverford County Medical Services*. Anita was speaking intently with two men, holding a clipboard in her arm. Father Malcolm went to the church door. Then he stopped, watching.

The men were particularly interested in the cemetery. They pointed, argued, then listened. After some more discussion, they shook hands with Anita, pointed again at the tombstones, got into the minibus and drove slowly out of the valley.

Father Malcolm looked at the cemetery. Among the rich currants and strawberries bloomed the single rose on the fifth grave.

Anita came down the path. She wore a yellow cotton blouse that showed the pale shoulders underneath. She was some kind of sister to him, absurdly, undeniably, Father Malcolm thought. Anita handed him her clipboard.

"What's this?" he asked.

"Reports," she said. "Reactions to the exorcism."

Father Malcolm squinted down at her neat, tiny handwriting, organized carefully on single sheets of paper.

Miss Kenny had died, peacefully, at 4:38. She had stretched out her arms on the bed, and she began to sing. Her eyes were suddenly mild, as though she had glimpsed something extraordinarily beautiful. Her sister stopped the clock at 4:38, the family custom. She noted only that at the moment of death the sun had broken out, traveling like a swath of golden light down Canaan Street toward the church.

Father Malcolm looked at Anita.

"Read the next one," she said.

At that moment, Fred Waller, the mechanic, heard his name being called by Miss Kenny's sister. He had been awakened by the traveling swath of sunlight. So just as his name was called he saw, before the receding thunderclouds, the sun hit the Church of the Eternal Sorrows with full force. Then he heard the Jesuit scream.

It was the opposite of the day he had seen his father die, Waller asserted carefully. On that day, at the hospital, he had sensed something, maybe the soul, leave his father, and even before the doctor came into the room he knew the man was dead. This time something had come *into* the valley and it had hit the church.

"There's more," Anita said. "George Finster, the tavern keeper, arose to close the window from the storm. Then the sun came down Canaan Street. At that moment a bottle of wine exploded."

Father Malcolm studied the obviously sincere face. He flipped through the rest of the reports. Most of them recorded a reaction to the traveling light, a sense of well-being, a sudden lifting of a burden out of the atmosphere.

"In parapsychology, things like this have occurred," she added. "But never so quickly, never so strongly around a single event."

Instead of offering the Church's explanation, which he felt Anita was probing for, something to lend cohesion to the collective reaction to the exorcism, Father Malcolm looked back at the dust where the orange minibus had been.

"Who were those men?" he asked.

"From the home for the elderly. At the west end of Golgotha Valley."

"What did they want?"

Anita gestured to the cemetery and the single heavy rose. The rose glistened, silky in the summer light. The graveyard was a profusion of tiny berries and wildflowers, but the rose now dominated, like the altar lamp in the church.

"There were two separate remissions of disease," Anita said. "Leukemia and tuberculosis. Both patients had hallucinated the rose in our cemetery."

The Jesuit's eyes moved to the cemetery.

The rose bobbed, hung, and bobbed again in the warm breeze.

"What does it mean, Father?" she asked. "In Catholic terminology, what would be your explanation?"

"God's love performs miracles so that man's despair may be turned to faith. There can be no other possibility, Anita."

For an instant he felt loath to leave her side, to go into the church, feeling a residue of the pain that had assailed him yesterday. But when he did it was even more radiant than the exterior valley.

The vestibule bore the footprints in dried clay, sediment from the storm. But the ceiling shimmered with circles of light, like silvery auroras, reflected from the holy water.

Father Malcolm dipped his fingers into the font, genuflected, and murmured a short, silent prayer.

When he went into the main church interior he was overcome by the brilliance within. The sun shining down through the peach blossoms transmitted the brightness of the morning over the entire floor. The walls glowed from the grace of morning.

Father Malcolm turned and saw Mario for the first time. A coffee can of cigarette butts bore mute testament to his fanatical night-long labor. Wires, note cards, pliers, soldering spool, pencils, and all manner of screws and bolts surrounded the viewing screen of the thermovision.

Father Malcolm turned away.

The altar was immaculate. The walls bore no evidence of stain. Even the St. Andrew's Cross on the floor, its ash and sand, had not been disturbed by Mario's heavy boots. Above, the gentle light of the altar lamp cast tiny points of reflection everywhere.

Father Malcolm knelt again, made the sign of the cross, and kissed the altar as he rose.

Whatever had come to the valley, he thought, had invaded them all. Nothing could be the same again. Faith worked through its sentient beings, even the aggressive parapsychologists and their sophisticated instruments.

Father Malcolm gazed deeply at the image generated by the tape cassette fluctuations of random ions.

"I understand that you're going to Boston to make a full report to the bishop," Mario said, smiling. "Lots of luck. I think you'll find that he keeps a strict monopoly on miraculous doings."

For a while Father Malcolm could not respond. It had not occurred to him that Bishop Lyons might not respond wholeheartedly to the revelation at Golgotha Falls.

"Tell me something, Mario," he said, sadly. "Why did you choose parapsychology?"

"It was the ultimate challenge. Also, I was particularly good at it."

"Parapsychology deals in absolute natures, does it not? In realities beyond our normal modes of perception, beyond our habitual cognitive frameworks?"

"Yes."

"It embraces all phenomena in a field of theory. Its nature permeates every aspect of physical and intelligent reality. Does it not?"

"Spit it out, Father."

"Tell me, Mario. What is parapsychology for you but a substitute for the Church? An all-embracing, absolute, mysterious—"

"Oh, Christ," Mario sighed. "You make me sick."

"You've made it your mistress, Mario . . . a mistress who will never reveal her nature to you—deliberately."

"Shut up."

Father Malcolm sank back against the pillar. The cruciform on the thermovision seemed to pin him against the wooden column.

"Mario," he said calmly, "without parapsychology, you would be in a state of despair."

"Listen to him, Anita. You want to listen to a Jesuit debater when he gets wound up?"

Anita had entered the church and was quietly observing the two men. Now the Jesuit turned to her, seeking her understanding.

"A materialist, an atheist, a fatalist," Father Malcolm said, "is always in despair. He has lost God and therefore himself. The devotion to, in this case, parapsychology is no more than a kind of crying out, an expression of need for what he has lost—his future, transcendence. . . ."

Mario ground out his cigarette and dumped it into the can.

"If despair is the condition of honest men," he said, "I accept it."

"No, Mario—"

"Let me tell you something. If Jesus Christ himself came to this valley I would not be as scared as you are now. Because I live according to the truth as I know it and do what I have to do to dig a few inches of clear, sane space for myself in this crapped-up world!"

"Is that your motivation?"

Mario dropped his pencil on the table in anger.

"I never sold out to the Church!" he exclaimed. "I never sold out to the university! And if despair is the price, I gladly pay it!"

Father Malcolm stirred himself from the pillar. He felt Anita's eyes following him. The brilliance of the valley outside infused him with subtle confidence. He turned to Mario.

"Your god is electronics, Mario," he said quietly. "Restricted to wires and recorders. But my God is a summation of all things possible. God is He in whom all things are possible. Therefore it is I who have survived in a living condition."

Father Malcolm took a last look at the computer screen. Then he went outside toward the Oldsmobile.

"He's going to make a fool of himself," Mario warned. "Sucker thinks he's John the Baptist."

Anita ran after Father Malcolm. She caught up to him as he dropped a cardboard box onto the rear seat and put his hand on the door. He paused, seeing her.

"Are you so sure you're doing the right thing?" she asked.

"We'll soon know, Anita."

"Remember—Boston is not Golgotha Falls. What we think of here as a focus of the paranormal—a revelation—to them it's just . . ."

Father Malcolm smiled, putting a hand on her shoulder.

"I know what you're saying. Revelations and miraculous interventions are anathema to the cosmopolitan powers of the Roman Church." He withdrew his hand. "And yet, are not these things at the very heart of the Catholic faith? In Boston. In the Vatican. In the entire world."

With a trembling hand he indicated the blossoming pear tree, the wild and ecstatic irises, and the scintillating white of the reclaimed church. "Who can ignore such proofs as these?"

"Yes, of course," she said. "Still there are many forms of the paranormal, and perhaps this does not mean what you think it does."

Father Malcolm turned on the ignition. The Oldsmobile roared into life, a barely visible fume of blue smoke vented from its muffler.

"You want to protect me from the hardened hearts of the bishop and his secretaries," he said knowingly. "You fear I shall make a fool of myself. Perhaps you're right. Still I must communicate my findings to the bishop, and let him determine their meaning."

He shifted gears. The brake was on, and the Oldsmobile groaned powerfully against its restraints. He sobered only slightly, seeing the worry on Anita's face.

"Do not let your heart be shut away by your science," he advised her. "Let this church and this valley speak to you. It is a testament full of signs, if you will only have the courage to read them."

In gentle dismay, seeing that nothing would stop him, Anita stepped from the Oldsmobile.

"May God be with you, Anita," he said with sincerity.

"And with you, Father."

The Oldsmobile leaped out from its ruts. Father Malcolm waved gaily, nearly struck a dense stand of brush, laughed seeing her laugh too, and then the black car lumbered up onto the loop of the road.

Anita waved back, but her anxiety had returned. The valley was beautiful, the Jesuit's faith a contagious source of confidence. Where did the anxiety come from?

Mario watched the Oldsmobile carry a cloud of dust with it, through the field, until it hit the only road and then disappeared into the birch woods on the ridge. Anita came back into the church.

"Mario," she said softly.

"Yes?"

"What's going on?"

"Going on?" Mario muttered, his attention focused on the thermo-vision console.

"Yes," Anita snapped, "with this church, this town, *me*! What the hell is happening?"

Mario shrugged. "I think you've caught the refraction of Malcolm's belief. The man's a powerful psychic transmitter. That and your own suggestibility."

Unsatisfied, Anita walked down the aisle and stopped under the red altar lamp.

"What about that?" she asked.

"Come off it, Anita. We've had experience with pyrokinesis. The priest was completely charged and it self-combusted. And we've got the tapes to prove it." His certainty irritated her. She walked to the Gothic window and leaned against the sill. The sunlight was warm on her face and the air was redolent of the apple blossoms. The rose bobbed peacefully over the fifth grave.

"What came into the valley, Mario?"

"Four months of drought. Growth cycle fucked up and blocked. Then the rains came. Everything blooms. Four months late."

Anita turned angrily.

"What about the leukemia remission, damn you!" she said. "There was a woman dying of tuberculosis and today she's singing!"

Mario said nothing for a while, pretending to be absorbed in the computer.

"I haven't been to the old folks' home," he said defensively. "I don't know what really happened."

Anita walked down the side aisle, finger idly trailing along the wall where the Jesuit had chrismed it. She stood at the vestibule, looking down at the glittering surface of the holy water.

"Listen, babe," Mario said, sounding worried. "When a place becomes this suggestive, a lot of things start getting real persuasive. So don't let the priest get to you. Okay?"

"I think I can handle it, Mario."

From the northern skies came a V-formation of dark birds, flying effortlessly over the autumnal foliage at the top of the north ridge. As the formation entered Golgotha Valley, individual birds began losing position. The V lost its shape. Confused, the flock circled erratically and came down among the fruit trees beside the church.

Anita looked down. Spiderwebs glistened on the stones of the church path. Old webs were still covered in clay dust, radiating evenly from the inner circles, uniform, articulated lattices. Near the marks made by Father Malcolm's shoes were new webs, still incomplete. Anita watched a long time.

The webs were anarchic cruciform patterns.

Within the church the tiny, discrete motions of Mario working at the thermovision made soft and sensuous ruby shadows over the floor, so pervasive was the glow of the kindled altar lamp above him. Mario studied the cruciform image on the tape, playing and replaying it a dozen times.

A subtle, irremediable change had come over him.

The days of being the campus weirdo, tolerated because of Anita, were over. Levitating yogis, Tarot cards, palm-reading, medium-led seances would never again be tied onto his coattails. The thermovision glowed brightly, source of his scientific justification. The gentlemen of Harvard could jeer, conspire, evade—and they would—

but they could *not*, in the final analysis, refute the image on the thermovision.

Nor, Mario realized with a deep delight, could the Catholic Church.

He laughed aloud. Images of the obdurate Dean Osborne, sarcastic bishops, flowed through his mind. He would show them the thermovision tapes. And their smug faces would fall. A need to destroy the hypocrites made Mario tingle with anticipation.

What if something went wrong? What if the thermovision didn't convince? No. It had to. The days of living in an intellectual backwater, in dread doubts and self-questioning, scarcely concealed by a sardonic facade, must surely, at long last be over. Surely now, within weeks, even days, respectability was at hand.

Still, Mario was apprehensive. Too much was at stake. Failure now meant consignment to science's dustbin of the ludicrous.

Because psychic projections do not die entirely, but fade with almost infinite slowness, the image in the thermovision screen was still faintly visible. Was there not some way of enhancing it? Mario knew that in a laboratory it was possible to augment an image by bathing it in a controlled electromagnetic frequency, the so-called "signature" frequency.

Mario suspected that a frequency proximate to that of the blue luminescences would separate the image from background interference. It had worked in the laboratory with far vaguer projections. Perhaps it would work in the church. Transforming the church into a laboratory appealed to Mario's sense of the ironic.

In the van were light stands, floodlights, and filters through the blue spectrum. Quickly Mario ran to it and began hauling out the equipment. The priest was gone. The church, he realized with dread and excitement, was his.

CHAPTER
NINE

THE OLDSMOBILE crossed the Charles. The north face of the urban sprawl glinted in the western twilight. Already the lights were on in the shadows of the alleys, and freighters at the wharves were faintly illumined by deck lights. Over the longshoremen's tenement rose the great cathedral, massive and brooding like an artificial cliff.

Through the twisted roads, bumping over broken stone, the Oldsmobile bounced into narrow neighborhoods already lost in the night.

Father Malcolm parked behind a Chinese restaurant. A figure in the kitchen doorway eyed him suspiciously, then opened the screen door and threw soapy water into the lot. As Father Malcolm stepped out of the car, he noticed the fog carrying the orange lights of Boston in and around the hills.

Walking up the stone pathway to the bishop's residence, he suddenly saw the brilliant white of the apple boughs at the rectory door. The contrast could not have been more profound. Alley cats screamed and leaped noisily from garbage cans as he approached the ornately carved doors.

Somewhere inside was the sound of a typewriter. Far away, in the dense city, came the echo of a police siren. Father Malcolm felt trapped in the misery of the world.

He raised his hand once, and again, and then finally pushed the doorbell. The typing ceased.

When the door opened, a slender priest in black cassock looked out at him, examining, appraising, superior and disdainful. Father Malcolm, self-conscious, his mouth dry, brushed down his unkempt hair and realized his trousers and shirt were stained with the clay of Golgotha Falls.

The slender priest waited.

"I must see His Grace," Father Malcolm said uncertainly.

The priest shook his head.

"Bishop Lyons has retired. But if you come after ten o'clock tomorrow, you can make an appointment with his appointments secretary."

"It is a matter of great urgency."

"Yes?"

"I am sorry for the late hour. I am sorry for my appearance. But something has happened that has great implications for the archdiocese."

The priest raised a single eyebrow.

Father Malcolm stepped inside. A curved walnut staircase led to the upper chambers, past framed engravings and a portrait of His Holiness, the Sicilian Baldoni, now the newly invested Pope Francis Xavier. The priest gestured to a hard wooden bench and walked down the corridor. Throughout the wood-paneled interior soft red lamps glowed, and a small golden crucifix hung over the priest's desk and typewriter.

Father Malcolm, restless, peered around at two other antique desks under leaded-glass windows. Volumes bound in red leather, codices, and black-bound appointment catalogues were filed under the cherrywood panels.

Footsteps came back up the corridor. The slender priest introduced an older one whose rank was uncertain and retired smoothly to his desk. Sounds of typing filled the paneled lobby.

The older priest sat next to Father Malcolm, uncomfortably close.

"What purpose brings you to this residence?" he asked softly, his gray eyebrows heavy over darting black eyes.

"What purpose?" Father Malcolm said. "How can I begin to say? I must speak directly with His Grace."

"But, you see, he has retired."

"Please tell His Grace that Father Eamon Malcolm has returned from Golgotha Falls. Tell him that something extraordinary has occurred. Tell him that only His Grace is equipped to deal with it now."

The elderly priest, offended by the unkempt black coat over the clay-stained, burr-infested shirt, sighed. He rose, then leaned subtly forward.

"Be aware, Father Malcolm, that your cause had better justify this breach."

"As I have witnessed Christ, I assure you that it does."

The religious affirmation made no impression on the hawk-nosed man. Against his better judgment, the priest went up the curved staircase, past the Pope's portrait, glaring at Father Malcolm.

Father Malcolm buried his chin on his folded hands, then blew on the fingers, which were bone-chilling cold. He stood, paced the green carpet, and tried to distract himself. Outside the cross-paned windows, he saw vague figures walking in the fog, a kaleidoscope of human forms, lost and insecure, in an urban hell.

The slender priest picked up the telephone, which had rung. With a smooth, cheerful voice, he began handling the call. Father Malcolm walked past the desk. As in a dark dream, impelled by a motor force, not of his own volition, more floating than walking, he saw the Pope's picture advance, the curved stairwell straighten. He was noiselessly ascending the steps.

Nervously, Father Malcolm scanned the gray eyes of the Sicilian Pope. The eyes seemed to regard him as well. A long-time organizer and trouble-shooter for the Vatican's secretary of state, Baldoni, the man who became Pontiff, never lost his Sicilian origins. It was rumored that his mother's rosary still hung over his bed in the Borgia Apartments. Francis Xavier had been a manual laborer in the fields of Sicily, and his edicts were replete with that imagery.

In that last five years, the millennialist movement had gained strength and force within the Vatican. In response to the fervor spreading throughout Latin America, Asia, and Africa, the cardinals urged Francis Xavier to prepare the Church for its ultimate purpose: the end of history in the second incarnation of Jesus Christ.

Francis Xavier was known to be a staunch believer in the millennialist doctrine. Father Malcolm had always ignored the millennialists' charisma, but now he was unnerved. The events in Golgotha Valley took on a meaning that made him dizzy.

To have been the vessel of Christ, he felt, to have been used in wresting back to God a defiled church—an inexpressible and radiant destiny—but the Pope's eyes stared down now and challenged his courage, his deeper hope, until the room began swimming—

He climbed the stairs as though deep underwater and saw a long corridor with plush red carpeting. A crucifix gleamed dimly in the walnut panels. The lights of Boston threw vague latticeworks of shadow at his feet. At the corridor's end burned a small desk lamp. There the elderly priest conferred with a young Jesuit.

The elderly priest looked up, still leaning against the tiny desk at the bishop's partially opened door, clearly shocked at Father Malcolm's approach. Behind him, several amber lamps glistened over antique red upholstered chairs in the bedroom.

"Do you realize your position here, Father Malcolm!" the priest whispered sternly.

The Jesuit rose and smiled at Father Malcolm.

"His Grace begs that you see his appointments secretary tomorrow morning."

In the bedchamber, there was the clearing of a throat. Father Malcolm found his way politely but firmly blocked by the other two men. There was a rustle of clothes inside as though a heavyset man shifted his weight on one of the antique chairs. Father Malcolm glimpsed the edge of the bed, an oaken four-poster, and engravings on the wall.

"Tomorrow may be too late!" Father Malcolm stated.

The Jesuit smiled again, an oily smile, but not without politeness.

"Exactly what *is* your problem, Father Malcolm?" he demanded, frustrated.

"I have seen that which ought not be seen," Father Malcolm said, examining their faces.

The Jesuit frowned, trying to maintain the illusion of a smile.

"I fail to understand you, Father," he said kindly, "but as you know, these matters are always screened before they come to His Grace's attention."

The elderly priest looked at Father Malcolm with growing hostility.

Father Malcolm watched them, the refined, tough lineaments of character in their faces. They knew the labyrinths of the archdiocese. They understood access to His Grace, which they guarded jealously. They were both sophisticated intellectuals. Their imaginations could never grasp Golgotha Falls.

"Do return, Father Malcolm," the hawk-nosed priest said, "before you have done your cause irrevocable harm."

Physically only inches from them, less than two feet from the open door, Father Malcolm strained to look inside. At a writing desk, fully dressed, white-haired and massive, Bishop Edward Lyons sealed a letter and pressed the wax with his ring.

As the bishop turned, he saw Father Malcolm in the door. His black eyes squinted, more surprised than outraged at the intrusion. His leonine head rested on a heavy, assured neck, with a body almost too large for the delicate French furniture under him.

Suddenly, Father Malcolm burst between the priest and the Jesuit, ran into the bedchamber, and fell at the bishop's feet.

"See here, Father Malcolm!" the Jesuit expostulated.

Angrily, the elderly priest strode into the bedchamber after Father Malcolm.

"Your Grace," whispered Father Malcolm, kissing the ring on the right hand. "Don't be angry with me. For what I have seen will surely rock the Church!"

Bishop Lyons, discomfited, stirred in the chair. After a while, he withdrew his right hand and with it signaled the priest and the Jesuit to leave.

"Malcolm, Malcolm . . ." the bishop gently scolded. "Impetuous and rash as ever."

Wearily, Bishop Lyons pointed to an adjacent curved-arm chair. Father Malcolm, white-faced with fear, sat on its edge.

"I have returned from Golgotha Falls, Your Grace."

The bishop was silent. He turned back to the correspondence on the desk, studied the pages, and, thinking through the intricacies, furrowed his massive brow and rubbed his forehead. He looked up, almost as though surprised to see Father Malcolm still there.

"And is that sufficient cause to justify this breach of protocol?"

Father Malcolm swallowed. Against the bishop's craggy, indomitable face, all thought flew out like crazed sparrows, leaving a hollow shell, an empty, confused Jesuit who had lost his moorings.

"Well?"

"I have felt the presence of Christ," Father Malcolm said weakly.

Bishop Lyons sank back into the antique chair, regarding Father Malcolm as though the Jesuit were insane.

"You must always feel the presence of Christ," the bishop said.

Father Malcolm leaned forward.

"In my body, Your Grace. At the conclusion of the exorcism. At the most solemn moment of the mass."

A wave of annoyance passed over Bishop Lyons' face.

"Father Malcolm, this is not the sort of issue to bring before me in this manner."

"And exterior to myself."

Distantly, the heavy chimes of an old clock bonged. Father Malcolm sensed the Jesuit in front of the door, listening at the desk. Perhaps the elderly priest was there, too. Father Malcolm felt chasms opening all around him.

Bishop Lyons looked back at the correspondence, tried to focus on its subtle contradictions and insinuations, but it was impossible now. Angrily, he swept it away and turned to the Jesuit.

"I performed the exorcism, as you instructed—" Father Malcolm stated.

"Yes."

"And it was successful."

"Good."

"But during the climax, when the issue was truly joined, and there were the most terrifying hallucinations—of a sexual nature—"

The bishop's eyes narrowed.

"As I commingled the consecrated Host in the chalice, there came into me a burning wind. It invaded me, Your Grace, inhabited me, and I lost consciousness."

"I see."

"And when I came to, the altar lamp was self-ignited."

"Obviously, in your disturbance you forgot having lighted it."

"No."

Bishop Lyons smiled, frustrated. "Good heavens, Father Malcolm. How can you be so sure?"

"Because I have studied the tapes."

Bishop Lyons rose and closed the door of the bedchamber more firmly. He padded back on soft slippers. Then he sat beside Father Malcolm and leaned forward, so closely that the Jesuit smelled the delicate cologne on the burly neck.

"What tapes do you refer to, Father?"

Father Malcolm felt his face go hot. He wiped his forehead with a white handkerchief and carefully folded it.

"Some videotapes have been made," he said.

"Of an exorcism? I instructed you to use discretion."

"I needed assistance. They were already there."

"*Who* was there?"

Father Malcolm carefully put the handkerchief back into the pocket of his worn black coat. He was suddenly afraid.

"Scientists, Your Grace. From Harvard."

Bishop Lyons visibly relaxed.

"We have excellent relations with Harvard. Including the tele-communications department."

Father Malcolm shook his head vigorously.

"Parapsychologists," he forced out.

Bishop Lyons regarded him as though an irreparable division existed now between them.

"They monitored the exorcism, Your Grace."

Bishop Lyons looked down at his own slippers, leaning on the arm rests, shaking his massive head.

"Father, I should never have received this kind of news from you."

"I tried to restrain them."

"But you let them photograph everything!" the bishop said angrily.

Father Malcolm had no response. Bishop Lyons rubbed his neck, massaging tired muscles, and grimaced.

"Every priest, every church, is a door that Satan tries to enter," the bishop said. "And you have opened the door to the atheists of science."

"Please listen to me, Your Grace."

Father Malcolm struggled to find the words to enter the bishop's mind.

"Their specialized cameras have caught a likeness of the Crucifixion."

Bishop Lyons stared at him. Then he burst into a loud coughing fit. Desperately, he ripped a linen handkerchief from his pocket, waved his hand furiously, then slowly, eyes watering, regained composure.

"You shall abjure this image as a profanation of God," the bishop said. "And you shall expel these parapsychologists from the church."

Father Malcolm stood up.

"The valley, Your Grace . . . The valley is blooming as though it were spring. Lilacs and dogwood. Apple blossoms. Peach blossoms. Lilies and marigold all through the town."

Bishop Lyons regarded him with a fascinated distaste. Father Malcolm stepped even closer.

"The livestock have returned to health," he said quickly, "for the first time in years."

"Indeed."

"It happened the morning after the exorcism."

The bishop waved an impatient hand.

"And you are an expert in animal husbandry—?"

"Your Grace. There have been two remissions of serious disease! Both dreamed of the rose in the churchyard—a rose that has not bloomed in living memory!"

"Father—"

"But this morning, it bloomed!"

The bishop backed away.

"Help me, Your Grace," Father Malcolm said softly. "Might not these signs . . . be portents of a time our Church has long awaited . . . ?"

"Signs are deceptive. Satan mimics the signs of Christ. Do not be seduced." Bishop Lyons glared at him angrily. "You have erred in coming here like this, Father Malcolm. And you have given your church to the unsanctified!"

"But I have felt . . . in myself . . . that these signs . . . might be the signs of revelation!"

"Revelation? Ah. Yes. So *this* is your message to me? You've determined these signs herald the Second Coming of Our Blessed Savior. That He has selected this troubled church in Golgotha Falls as His portal of reentry!"

Barely controlling his anger, Bishop Lyons rubbed his hands, over and over. "Let me tell you something, Father Malcolm, about this apocalyptic vision that sets your brain afire. It will be no joyful affair! Its precursors will be thunders, lightnings, great earthquakes, plagues of locust, famines . . . Translated into modern nuclear terms, it could well mean holocaust, the end of life on earth."

"Or the *beginning* of life, Your Grace," Malcolm added simply. " 'And I saw heaven opened, and beheld a white horse,' " he recited, " 'and he that sat upon it was called faithful and true, and he laid hold on the old Serpent which is Satan, and bound him for a thousand years. And on both sides of the river was the tree of life, yielding its fruits for the healing of nations. And divine teaching came to mankind.' ''

Bishop Lyons paced the floor, looked at Father Malcolm, then paced some more. When he stopped, his face had become benign, almost paternal.

"Eamon," he said gently. "Christ will come when He will come. It is not for us to hunt for signs."

"But surely this is no ordinary transformation!"

The bishop maintained his benign smile, though obviously irritated. He put his hands on the Jesuit's shoulders.

"Is it the pale rider on a horse that you've actually *seen*, Eamon, holding the balance to weigh souls?" he asked gently. "Or the moon red with blood? Locusts with the faces of men? Have you seen the beast of seven heads and ten horns? Have you heard people speak in tongues? A language in perfect rhythm, rolling cadences never heard on earth, not known even to the person uttering them, a sweet and ecstatic language unknown to man, such as appeared for the first time in the holy Pentecost? Have you heard this language, Eamon?"

Father Malcolm stammered. "N-No—not that—but—"

"Have you seen the seven angels and the seven vials of the last plagues? Have you, Eamon? For *these* are the signs of apocalypse. Not what you've mentioned. Not pretty peach trees. Not pretty little calves."

"B-But—perhaps—anticipatory signs—for I experienced them in myself and in the church and in the valley!"

Bishop Lyons took him by the arm and drew him to the leaded glass window. Down below, the orange fog crept into the black channels of the bay, and traffic lights pushed up the lonely hills.

"How many souls out there are consecrated unto Christ?" he asked. "Look on the real world, Father Malcolm. It is corrupt with hatred and vile in its ambition!"

"But our mission—"

"Our mission is to refurbish and replenish the Church before we can prepare men's hearts for the final act of history."

Bishop Lyons strode back into the room. He picked up a thick dossier from his desk. Father Malcolm saw many like it on adjacent rosewood bookshelves.

"Do you know what this is?" demanded the bishop.

"Your Grace, please—"

140

"The papal itinerary to Quebec, Eamon. In three days, the Nuncio, Cardinal Bellocchi, is coming. And do you know why?"

Father Malcolm shook his head, abjectly miserable.

"Because in one week, His Holiness Francis Xavier is going to Quebec on a pilgrimage!"

Bishop Lyons advanced slowly, red-faced, toward Father Malcolm.

"Why is His Holiness going to Quebec?" the Bishop whispered. "Why am I going to meet him? Why are the cardinals and bishops of the continent going to Quebec in one week?"

Father Malcolm swallowed hard. Bishop Lyons stepped even closer. The benign smile reappeared. He spoke to Father Malcolm as to a child.

"Because the world is a world of sin and corruption, Eamon. Men do not know God. It is a cynical and bitter world, a world where the Antichrist dwells and flourishes. The Pontiff goes where he must to tame the world, Eamon. To leaven it unto Christ. Hamlet by hamlet. City by city. Country by country."

The bishop returned to his desk and thumped the dossier back onto its surface. The sheer weight of labor involved in the Nuncio's imminent arrival seemed to bear down on him.

"And that means hard work, Eamon," he said slowly. "Cold, sober organization."

Bishop Lyons turned, smiling gently, almost friendly now.

"By maintaining our discipline, our mental fortitude, Eamon," he said softly, "we overthrow the presumptuous mimicry of Satan."

"Yes, Your Grace."

Bishop Lyons padded forward on loose slippers and put his hands on Father Malcolm's shoulders.

"Be content, my son. You have cleansed a church and restored it to God. To attempt more would be to invite the sin of pride."

Father Malcolm felt tears of rage well, but he meekly nodded. The bishop held out the ringed hand. Father Malcolm knelt and kissed it.

"In all probability," the bishop said, "the church was never possessed in the first place, but suffered from a negative parishioner flow."

Shocked, Father Malcolm stared at the ring. Then he rose and crossed the carpeted chamber, face burning. Evidently the bishop had pressed a button, for the door opened and the elderly priest stood there, trying not to smile.

Father Malcolm turned back, but Bishop Lyons was already seated at the desk, absorbed in his correspondence. Father Malcolm allowed himself to be escorted down the stairs.

The portrait of Baldoni, the Sicilian Pope, seemed to observe them all the way to the ground floor.

"Will you be seeing the appointments secretary in the morning?" asked the elderly priest.

"No. Thank you."

"Good evening, Father Malcolm."

"Good evening."

Stepping down into the cold fog, he felt chilled, and trembled, and his shoes echoed over the damp stone.

On the Oldsmobile was a note telling him the lot was reserved for customers of the restaurant. Father Malcolm crumpled it and threw it onto the asphalt.

When he got into the Oldsmobile, the starter motor was stuck. A sickly grating of non-ignition came back from the dashboard. Father Malcolm leaned against the driver's wheel, gazed at the small plastic statuette of Christ on the dashboard.

"Give me strength," he prayed. "Dear God in heaven, give me strength, for I have none."

Father Malcolm stepped from the Oldsmobile. He jammed the gear into second and then rocked the car. When he got back behind the wheel, it started. He backed into the narrow alley. He wiped the tears from his eyes.

He drove over the suspension bridge perched high over the black, moving bay. The orange lights of the wharf gleamed far below. Neon flickered at the underbelly of the clouds. The world was multiple, he realized, and it ran on money and exploited illusions. The Roman Catholic Church had been born in the turbulence of a disintegrating empire, across the ocean, across almost two thousand years. Father Malcolm wondered if the Church, even with the advent of its new Pope, could survive the proliferation of indifference.

It was past midnight when Father Malcolm crested the south ridge of Golgotha Falls. Instantly, there was a warmth and the fragrance of peach and lilac from below. He stopped the Oldsmobile.

The Church of Eternal Sorrows was lighted bright blue like a lunar Roman candle. Cables led through the tall grass and a generator somewhere rumbled. Icy blue light encapsulated the church, throwing dense shadows outward in all directions, even under the steeple. If the red altar lamp was still on, it was utterly dominated by the strange blue lights, for Father Malcolm saw only the ghostly transfiguration of the once serene church.

Furious, he got out of the automobile and slammed the door. Now he noticed, shielding his eyes, smelling the acrid heat of the blue lamps inside the church, several men and women from the town.

"They caught it!" shouted a farmer. "They caught it!"

"Caught what?" Father Malcolm stammered, stumbling past the crowd.

Inside, he saw through the Gothic windows, Mario and Anita hovered in front of the thermovision screen. A vague nausea turned to a more precise terror. He ran into the church.

"What is going on here?" he bellowed over the din of the green generator, shaking and fuming under the windows.

Mario wore his brown leather jacket, very nervous, very excited, nostrils flaring, sweat beading the back of his neck and even glinting in his short, curly hair. Anita turned first, and Father Malcolm saw in her face a mixture of shame and excitement.

A stench of gasoline from the generator filled the church. Over the altar the red lamp looked purple, almost black, certainly unnatural in the arena of tall, blue focused lamps. It was sickly inside; Mario's flesh looked like a theatrical cadaver.

"This is a holy church!" Father Malcolm roared, stepping forward.

"It's my laboratory!" Mario shouted back.

Father Malcolm stepped over the cables. Suddenly, through the space between Anita and Mario, he saw a defined, faintly fluctuating and cobalt-colored version of the cruciform image. Father Malcolm's face went pale, so pale it turned nearly blue under the nearby lamps. Mario, seeing that shocked face, burst out laughing.

"It's the residue," Mario gloated. "Psychic projections don't die."

Father Malcolm gazed at Mario, confused, the din shrieking in his ears.

"What?" he said, lips trembling. "What are you talking about?"

Instead of answering, Mario snapped off the thermovision play-back, and with movements so deft Father Malcolm thought he was watching a magician at work, plucked the videotapes from the camera and slipped it into a plastic cassette.

Anita came forward very slowly. Father Malcolm was still staring at the dark thermovision screen. He felt as though the church had been grossly, vilely violated.

"We got terrific pictures, Father," she said gently, "we're taking the tapes to Harvard."

"No, Mario," Father Malcolm muttered. "I am under an injunction of discretion. From the bishop."

Mario grinned, showing perfect white teeth. The eyes, however, were malicious.

"I don't recognize the authority of bishops," Mario sneered.

Father Malcolm stepped closer to Mario.

"Mario," he whispered, shocked, "you cannot show such an image to the world. It comes from my priestly mission. It would be a profanation."

Mario saw that the Jesuit was frightened. Not that the bishop had instructed him to keep things discreet and out of the newspapers. No. Something far more awesome. The Jesuit believed in that image. The way pilgrims believed in the Shroud of Turin, or in the stigmata of thousands of crucifixes in scores of ignorant, believing countrysides.

"I need an extension!" Mario said heatedly. "I need time! I need money! The faculty wants proof! Well, now I've got it. They can't refuse me."

Father Malcolm was reaching out to the cassette in Mario's hand.

"Mario," he pleaded, "this image belongs here. In this church."

Mario stared disdainfully at Father Malcolm.

"It's a psychic projection," he said coolly. "We publish these images all the time. In journals. In newspapers, if we can. Why not?"

As he turned to go, he found Father Malcolm's hands gripped his leather sleeve.

"No," Father Malcolm said slowly. "I cannot allow you."

Mario laughed, pulling his sleeve away.

"Say it, Father," he taunted. "Say what you think this image is."

Father Malcolm turned to Anita as though for help. But she only looked away again, unable to halt Mario's determination. Father Malcolm felt Mario turning him around again.

"You don't believe in psychic projection, do you?" Mario shouted. *"You really think this is Jesus Christ!"*

"Give me the tape, Mario!"

"Go to hell, priest."

Father Malcolm moved to the arena of the blue lamps. One by one, he sent them crashing onto the church floor. The bulbs were so hot behind the cobalt coating that they exploded, sending heated slivers over the Jesuit's legs.

"I shall not go to hell," he said decisively. "Nor shall this church."

Father Malcolm strode across the center of the church and began casting down the hot lamps there.

Suddenly, Mario's bulk crashed into him and a beefy forearm pinned the Jesuit's throat to the church wall.

"You bastard," Mario hissed, eyes demoniac with rage. The Jesuit felt specks of red invade his vision, and breath came with difficulty. Vaguely, he saw Mario brandishing the tape cassette in front of his face.

"Look on this tape, priest!" Mario yelled, inches from the Jesuit's face. "I've taken the measure and shape of your belief! I've sealed it in a magnetic ribbon! Men swore by these images once. They'll swear by them again, but not in your churches! In universities, in scientific institutes! Wherever free men gather in liberty to analyze the nature of man and his universe!"

Mario released his pressure. The Jesuit crumpled slightly but did not fall, merely rubbing his bruised throat.

"You are a vain, egotistical fool," Father Malcolm shouted, suddenly breaking Mario's grip. Circling around to the altar, eyes on Mario, rubbing his throat, he looked like a wolf dispossessed. Then his eyes fastened upon the altar, saw that it had been moved. For an instant, there was no sound but the rumbling of the generator. In the ghastly blue-white light, his hands and face looked like marble.

"What have you done?" he said softly.

"Oh, that. One of the lights got caught in the cables and fell."

Father Malcolm reached under the linen. The contact between the altar and its base was shifted.

"*YOU'VE BROKEN ITS CONTACT!*" Father Malcolm roared.

"*I NEEDED THE SPACE!*"

Father Malcolm pointed a trembling finger at Mario.

"I know who you are," he said.

"What the hell does that mean?"

"I know who you work for!"

Father Malcolm advanced steadily under the altar lamp. He seized the videotapes and slides. Mario was suddenly all over him. The visual material clattered over the floor.

Father Malcolm reached for the computer. Horrified, Mario leaped on him.

Anita ran forward, but Mario shook her off. The Jesuit struggled forward, scattering electrodes and circuitry plates.

Mario grabbed the priest's blond hair in one hand. With the other, he slapped the livid cheeks, again and again. The Jesuit's hands uselessly tried to protect his face. His lips spattered with blood. Mario held the man's head, pushed and pulled the Jesuit clear down the aisle to the vestibule, slapping him with resounding cracks.

"Mario!" Anita yelled.

Mario shook the priest like a rag doll and threw him into the vestibule. Father Malcolm crashed against the holy water font, tried to hang on to it, and collapsed.

Mario watched, a savage glint in his eyes.

"Don't you every try that again," he whispered.

"Father Malcolm—" Anita cried.

She ran past Mario and knelt beside the Jesuit as he moaned in humiliation and physical pain.

"Leave the bastard alone," Mario said.

"Mario, get out of here!" Anita ordered harshly.

"I'm not leaving my equipment while he's here."

"Don't worry about your equipment. I'm staying!"

Mario stared at her. She was still holding the body of the Jesuit, who was trying to pull himself upright. A grim, awful realization went through Mario.

"With *him*?" he asked slowly.

Father Malcolm daubed at his nostrils. Crimson leaked down on his fingers. Involuntarily, horrified, he looked down at the holy water. The surface there contained great spreading stains of red.

Father Malcolm crossed himself weakly.

"I'm not leaving you here," Mario insisted.

"I'm not going to Harvard with you, or anywhere with you," Anita said softly, resolutely, her eyes filling with tears. "Mario, you've gone completely manic. This church has gotten to you! You've been changed by something you can't control!"

The memory flashed into Mario's brain. The invading shudder at the exorcism's climax. A sense that it was more than a sympathetic muscular spasm.

"Crap!"

Anita looked hard at Mario.

"I'm staying, Mario."

"When I met you," he said coldly, "you had the best scientific mind I'd ever met. Like some dancing computer, Anita. I never dreamed you could go soft. Not after all you taught me."

"I'm not demanding anything from you, Mario, but common human decency!"

146

Mario, outraged, fumbled for words.

"You've fallen for his blood of the lamb epistemology!" he yelled. "You never lost your discipline before! What the hell has happened to you?"

Anita turned from him.

"Leave us alone, Mario," she said.

Mario hesitated, then put the tape into a satchel containing other videotapes and slide boxes. An indefinable mixture of pain, anguish, and outright anger passed over his face. It was not the first time they had fought and split. It was the worst.

"Will you be here when I come back?" he asked.

"I told you, I'll watch the equipment."

He glared at her, found nothing more to say, then looked down at the dazed Jesuit.

"Father," Mario said.

"Leave him alone, Mario."

"You're a lucky man, Father. She's really quite nice."

Father Malcolm looked up, confused. Mario winked conspiratorially, and leaned forward.

"Like dipping it in warm honey."

"You bastard," Anita hissed.

Mario laughed crudely, then turned and charged out of the church into the dark. Soon, the echo of the Volkswagen floated over the valley.

Anita helped Father Malcolm to his feet.

"Are you all right?" she asked.

"Yes, yes."

"I want to apologize for Mario, Father. He likes to hurt when he's angry."

Father Malcolm said nothing.

The generator ran out of gasoline. The rumble growled in a deeper tone, gasped, coughed, and finally died. Alone together, Father Malcolm and Anita saw the lights within the church begin to fade. Orange, and then red, and finally, like an infinitely bloody sunset, the lights cooled and extinguished. Only the gentle altar lamp illumined the interior, calm and imperturbable.

A rising wind disturbed the birch woods. Milkweed floated restlessly past them at the church door.

"Blood has been spilled—the altar profaned," he said softly. "There is much to atone for. I had better perform a vigil."

"Tonight?"

147

"Yes. And every night until it's cleansed."

"All by yourself, Father?" she asked.

"I am in no danger," he said. "The church and its grounds are sanctified."

Nevertheless, the rising wind shook the birch trees, swayed the bushes across the river and rippled in the distant farms. Only in the compound of the church and its consecrated ground was it still.

The rose in the cemetery hung still, heavy, looking black as dried blood in the night.

Father Malcolm pulled a cardboard box from the north wall. From it he took long white candles and fit them into the candleholders behind the altar.

Anita scooped the broken glass into a crate, using a file folder. The gasoline stench was nearly gone. She picked up the fallen light stands and pushed them against the wall.

In the computer image, silent and flickering, was the crucified shape. The interference had returned now the lights were gone. Anita could make out its ambiguous, rounded volumes.

Father Malcolm cleared the area around the altar. She watched. He sank to his knees, crossed himself, and composed himself.

The rising wind buffeted the adjacent fields. Anita anxiously paced the floor. The ions in the atmosphere wreaked havoc with the computer, throwing random arcs of flux through the image, obliterating it.

"Are you sure you'll be all right, Father?"

"Yes, Anita. You may sleep in the rectory, if you wish."

After a while, Anita went through the vestibule and into the night. She was still angry at Mario, and dragged the sleeping bag toward the rectory, wondering what devil had gotten into him.

She suddenly stopped, appalled. The metaphor, though unconscious, was too apt for comfort. A chill swept through her as the sonorous litany of Father Malcolm, the devil's adversary, echoed through the Church of Eternal Sorrows.

CHAPTER
TEN

MARIO LAY on the bed in his tiny laboratory. A fever had somehow lodged in his throat. Everything sounded as though he was hearing it underwater. His heart raced, beating against his chest wall. What the hell is going on? he wondered. I'm thirty-eight years old and in perfect health. Am I having a stroke?

Outside the laboratory a man operated a power floor polisher. An aged black whom Mario had befriended years ago, the man had provided him with access to the building during the campus strikes. Mario reflected fondly on those days. In Dean Osborne's office handling a megaphone. Tear gas down through the Yard. Everything was so easy then. It was like floating downriver. None of these complications.

Golgotha Falls dominated Mario. It breathed somehow in his liver like a live virus. It seemed to pound through the blood in his head. He was so close, so damn close to the ultimate nature of psychic projection.

Groggily he took more aspirin, some Contac, and seltzer water. When he flushed the toilet at the side of the lab, he thought the noise would tear his head off. Under the table of slides, videotapes, and catalogued photographs were barbells of cast iron. He rolled them away with his foot and examined the material.

Three cartridges of color slides, most of which were well exposed, the rest at least good enough for documentary work. The valley of Golgotha Falls, its altered season, the Siloam before and after the exorcism, the rose bush in the cemetery, and the interior of the church as they had first seen it, cluttered with rotted women's clothing and fallen debris. Developed in Boston on a rush order, for which Mario wrote a check that was not, so far as he knew, good.

Two brown plastic cases of videotapes. One transferred from the laser camera, showing architectural stress behind the Jesuit. The other, where Mario's fingers lovingly rested, were the thermovision cassettes of the exorcism itself, including the first viridian suspended image in a cruciform structure, and the halogen-enhanced image.

Large glossy photographs had been blown up from details Anita had taken of their equipment, the consecration of the cemetery showing the dead rose bush, and comparative photos showing the difference in ecology between Golgotha Falls and all its neighboring valleys.

In addition he had a rough chart, on graph paper, of the precise times of sound events and seismic variations. He doubted the subcommittee wanted to get that detailed. The important thing was that they be enthused about the project and convinced it was a mere matter of months before the shield was ripped away from the image residing beside the altar and its true nature identified.

He pored through five pages of neatly typed lecture. There were a couple of marginal notes to stress the Algonquin angle, since one of the faculty was from anthropology. The rest was tight as a Ph.D.'s asshole on dissertation defense day.

Something was wrong with his body. There was a coldness in the pit of his stomach, an unnatural coldness. It came upward from his groin in slow pulses.

Mario wore his tweed jacket. He brushed his unruly thick hair back. The slim black tie was ten years old, but suddenly back in fashion. He knew he looked damned good. It was irrelevant to science, but subtly important in public addresses. Mario had extended the invitation to the entire faculty committee and the *Crimson* and four New England newspapers. He had ordered wine and cheese for seventy and hoped that at least ten might show.

"Well," he muttered. "Freud, Nietzsche, and Gilbert, or do I wash out completely? Once and for all."

He gathered the material, clutched it against his side and left the laboratory.

"Good luck," said the black at the floor polisher.

"Thanks, old friend. I'll damn well need it."

Through the glass door Mario pushed his way into a bush-lined pathway under the campus lights. So close to success, he had never felt himself so nervous. He felt nearly faint, dry-mouthed. For an instant he was disoriented. He tried to tell himself there would be other projects, were this to fail, but he knew this was the watershed.

As he walked past the library he reflected that Anita would have been a great asset at a function like this. He depended on her social graces, her family clout with the faculty. Well, she could stew in Golgotha Falls with the litanies of a loony.

Suddenly he had the profound sensation that he was not really at Harvard at all. Instead he was at Golgotha Falls. It was as though he had become pure spirit, bodiless, among the night lights. Then the feeling passed.

He ran up the cement steps into the lecture building and skipped up two floors to Room 220. His heart sank. Next to the black sign with movable white letters that read:

> *An Assault on the Fourth Dimension*
> *Frontiers of the Paranormal: An Investigation of the Limits of Physical Science at Golgotha Falls*

were nearly one hundred faculty, graduate students, and several hard-bitten types, among whom he recognized the science editor of *The New York Times*.

Before they greeted him he turned wildly to the men's room because he knew he was going to vomit. Instead, the science editor approached and extended his hand.

"A biochemist in nucleic acids, the recipient of the Bollington

Prize, gave his acceptance speech tonight. We heard you were giving a lecture. Decided to stick around after the sherry. Hope you don't mind."

"I'm flattered beyond describing."

Mario hoped his voice came out natural. The science editor smiled coldly and walked away into the crowd. Several reporters, having followed the more notable faculty, crowded around a white cloth-covered table on which the refreshments looked meager indeed.

Dean Osborne emerged from the loud confusion of voices greeting one another.

"Where's Anita?" he asked.

"She's home with the kids."

"You haven't split up, have you?"

"Listen. Can all these people fit inside?"

"Sure. They don't perspire much."

Mario counted the crowd roughly. There were over a hundred. After the acceptance speech of the biochemist, he would have his first real chance of rising to that level of credibility. Or drowning forever, judged mediocre once and for all. Hugging his material, recognizing a few of the graduate physicists and shaking hands, Mario pushed into the lecture hall.

It was all too real now. The green sliding chalkboards. The overhead projector at his disposal. A secretary's handwritten chalk script bearing his name and the title of the lecture. Twelve rows of plush brown chairs leading down to the lectern. Video cameras for in-house documentation.

It was everything he had waited for. Mario sensed the bright radiance of the fluorescent lights overhead, a kind of visual analogue to the panic that flourished in his nerves, yet he thrived on it. It was better than speed. Mario went to the projection booth.

An elderly man waited there, received the slide cartridges, then the videotapes, with Mario's instructions. At the overhead projector he switched the mirror plate so it could throw a reasonable facsimile of the glossies onto a sparkling screen. Mario stepped behind the lectern and leaned toward the microphone.

"Ready. Ready. Golgotha Falls," he intoned.

The elderly man adjusted the sound intake and signaled that he was ready.

Mario's eyes swept the empty, waiting seats, depersonalized and yet intoxicatingly hostile. All those mentalities, he reflected. Confused, resistant, prejudiced, untrained, or hypocritical. He had to penetrate each and every one. He had to fuck those minds and seed them with the idea of Golgotha Falls.

"Okay," he said into the microphone. "Let the bulls in."

The faculty came in first, in blocks, wearing suits. They naturally took the first rows and seated themselves with ease. Graduate students came next, both the short-haired ambitious types anxious to know what the latest venture was and long-haired, slovenly refugees of a past era looking to find anything at all to do. Several women came in together, pert, smart, and subtly aggressive, holding icy smiles and chatting with feigned irrelevance. Barracudas all, Mario thought.

After ten minutes the elderly man turned the rheostat and the house dimmed. A glow from the roof permitted the taking of notes. Several of the women used pen lights.

"The kind of biochemistry that was just explained at least partially to you in the Bollington lecture," Mario began, "is an example of the extraordinary diversity of contemporary physical science. It has gained that diversity and that unprecedented expertise through series after series of shocks to its basic and most prized assumptions. Since the development of the experimental model, roughly during the Renaissance, assumption after assumption has had to be expelled in the face of sheer documentary and experimental data. Perhaps no assumption has been more deeply held until now than the materiality of temporal events."

Mario sipped from the glass of water on the edge of the lectern. The audience was engaged, with him, even rooting for him. They were not immune to ideas.

"Until now," he continued boldly, "any occurrence of immateriality was confined to the experience commonly called religious. In fact, religion may be said to be nothing more than an organized control over the experience of the immaterial."

Now the audience sensed the undertone of attack in the lecture and began to settle in, taking the measure of Mario's intellect.

"The project at Golgotha Falls was an experimental model designed to test the ability of modern technology to crack that borderline between the material and the immaterial. In so doing, our notions of that borderline have received the kind of shock that alters the development of future method and experimentation."

The audience sensed now the high risk Mario put into the presentation. For a lecturer not on the tenure track to put grandiloquent claims to his research was a breach of university etiquette. That privilege was reserved for those who had received honorary chairs or national or international prizes. But the audience was game, and willing to give Mario the shot.

Indeed, there was a rapt quiet in the lecture hall.

"Could we project the large photographs, please?" he asked, sipping more water, checking his notes.

The lights dimmed further. Men rustled in their chairs. Reporters bent over for the light of aisle lamps. Gradually it calmed.

Behind Mario the sparkling screen lowered to the appropriate height. He could not see the person who fed the first photograph into the apparatus, but saw only the brightly illuminated hands and arms. He turned to face the screen.

Spreading nearly ten feet across was a picture of Anita in a foamy bathtub.

Nervous laughter began, died, then swelled as the audience realized Mario had taken the wrong batch of glossies.

Mario felt sparks shooting at the sides of his vision.

"The next photograph!" he said.

Giggles continued, and men's voices circulated through the room, causing women's laughter.

The next photograph showed Anita coyly sitting at the foot of Mario's bed, knees apart, hand decorously placed, nude.

There was more laughter, but it was slightly nervous.

"I didn't take those pictures!" Mario yelled, and ran to the edge of the stage.

He saw a frightened undergraduate, trying to earn a minimum wage as an audiovisual operator.

"Show the next one, damn it!" Mario said.

There were more pictures. They showed Anita in a variety of poses. With a variety of household utensils. They were not coy. They were hard-core pornography and full of genital shots. The audience was shocked.

Mario jumped down beside the projector. He grabbed the photographs and stared at them. They showed the cemetery at Golgotha Falls, the church, and the neighboring valleys.

"I'm fucked," Mario whispered. "What the hell is going on?"

The audiovisual operator backed away, terrified he had lost his job.

Mario violently signaled to the elderly operator in the booth behind the audience. By using his hands the operator asked whether to project the video or slides. Mario pointed his finger at the slides.

Mario climbed back onto the stage. He drank long and hard from the glass of water.

"That isn't the kind of shock I had in mind," he said. "I apologize completely. In all humility, I did not take those photographs. I am as completely repulsed by their puerility as are you. Please accept my most sincere apology."

The audience wavered, and settled restlessly into the plush of their chairs. They were making up their collective mind whether they had been insulted.

"It *was* your associate, or should I say your mistress," came Osborne's chilly voice.

Mario had the clammy sensation, at the back of his neck, that Osborne had somehow sabotaged the lecture. A violent rage flew upward before his eyes, so violent he knew that if it was true he would hunt the dean down and physically rend him.

"The slides, please," Mario said.

The screen shifted upward, to take into account the larger projection format. A raucous cough broke out in the middle rows. The first slide, by mistake, was blinding white light. People hid their eyes. Then came the second slide.

It showed a chameleon, the kind of white chameleon that had scuttled across the grounds at Golgotha Falls.

Mario looked at his notes. He did not remember taking the slide and he could not now recall the purpose of the image.

"Some of the local wildlife," he said lamely. "Could we have the next image, please?"

This time two chameleons on what seemed to be the church floor.

Mystified, Mario stepped out from behind the lectern to see the entire projected image. The audience realized his puzzlement. Whatever was going on was morbidly fascinating. Mario raised his hand, indicating the next slide.

The two chameleons were now much closer, one at the tail of the other.

The next slide showed them mating, pressed belly to belly, with a slight froth of seminal slime visible at the rear of the female.

The science editor of *The New York Times* excused himself to those around him and walked out.

Mario turned to face the projection booth.

"What the hell is this?" he demanded. "I didn't take those slides!"

The elderly operator angrily held up the slide cartridge. It was unmistakably Mario's.

"Go to the end! Take one of the last slides!"

It showed the rectum of a goat.

Several women giggled. Several others left ostentatiously. The reporters had stopped trying to take notes. A few of the senior members of the faculty waited patiently, but the junior members were outraged.

"What is this shit, Gilbert?" one of them asked plaintively.

"I didn't take these—"

"Well, somebody did."

"J-Just a minute . . . P-Please don't go—!" he pleaded.

Mario held up his arms, trying to still the angry and ribald conversations, trying to keep people in their seats. The lights went on.

"I d-don't know any more than you what's going on," he said, fighting tears. "It's uh weal nightmare—"

The tongue was getting thick. The fever was growing. He felt as though he was floating.

"The—thermovision—real good—" he stuttered.

Shocked, concerned, yet strangely fascinated, the audience was transfixed by the catastrophe of a junior lecturer losing his career before their eyes. Even when the lights went down their eyes were as much fixed on Mario as on the screen.

"Thermo-thermowision—it's Christ—we caught it—we caught it—"

Mario grabbed his throat, trying to work free the spasmodic pulses of the muscles at the base of his tongue.

"Oh, God—it's got me—!"

On the screen the thermovision showed, in inverted colors, a horse galloping across deep grass, chasing a man. In horrified silence the audience saw the horse trap the man against a clapboard wall, leap high, and strike with its front hooves. There was a splash of crimson and an intake of breath in the audience. Repeatedly the horse reared high and came down, full force, on the dying man's skull. Bits of brains splashed up against the wall. The eyeballs were ground into ruined sockets. The blood flowed over the hooves even in the air, and when they came down again there was less and less of a recognizable face. Only the arms fibrillated in nervous convulsions.

It was undeniably, revoltingly, sickeningly real. Women made their way quickly to the exit. Even Dean Osborne went white. The reporters, hardened as they were, sat paralyzed by the utter viciousness of the moving image.

"No—no—" Mario stuttered. "I d-d-didn't—thermo—wermo—

not mine—it followed me here—s-s-sick—s-s-sick—prick—prick—lick—"

Mario's tongue moved thickly, protruding from his mouth in a grotesque of the human face.

"Greba—greba—wallsa—d-d-doonda—makoftoo—m-m-mam-malia —yes—yes—yes—sweet Jesus—m-m-mary—togood—yeldaw—rallow —rallow—d-d-doonda—"

Several of the men stood, unable to decide what to do.

"P-p-p-rick—a—lick—s-s-sick sick—"

A young man from the sociology department leaped to the stage, trying to restrain Mario.

Mario battered at him with both fists in rage and frustration, eyes bulging, drooling.

"It's epilepsy," the sociologist announced. "Could I have some help, please?"

Several more men climbed with difficulty onto the stage. They seemed afraid of the wildly kicking Mario, trying to tear himself loose from their grasp as though he were drowning in the ocean.

Mario saw their faces, their alien, blanched faces, come for him. It was the annihilation he had always feared. A man's persona, the façade of the self-made man cannot endure certain assaults. Now it was caving in, and the brute animal rage was all that was left.

In the fever Mario saw the thermovision, still running. As the men wrestled him down to the floor, as he choked on his own tongue, felt the bulging muscles constrict at his throat, he saw the black stallion with bloody feet bounding across the thick grass gloriously.

"F-fitalta—magaserata—perima—hed—barestra—" Mario heard from a thousand miles away.

"It's not epilepsy," said the sociologist.

"Whatever it is, it's got him good."

On the screen a white mare leaped furiously over the brush, saliva falling, pursued by those bloody hooves.

Mario reached incoherently for that screened image, as though to ward off an icon, as though to preserve a lucidity that he was losing forever.

"Gerosma—J-J-J-es—theralpy—o—theralpy—now—perima—ima —ima."

Mario did not feel the hands he saw pin him to the podium floor. Even the panic around him barely entered the fiery storm that had invaded his brain. There was only the ambiguous, suspended image of a cosmos that had suddenly disowned him.

"Gentlemen," said the sociologist, in awe, "he's speaking in tongues."

On the glittering screen, distorted and elongated but all too clear, the long erectile penis of the horse flared out in crimson heat. On its hind legs it rose, a beast driven and yet triumphant, and the mare, trapped in the high brush, turned in wild-eyed fear.

"G-G-G-Gerosma—meta—laffa—now—"

"Anyway, so much for parapsychology," muttered a reporter.

Mario felt himself falling into the substructure of his personality. It was a psyche with a trick door, a weak foundation. He floundered in the primitive origins of soulless life, where rape and violation of being were the natural order, cruelty the mode of existence.

At the bottom of the basement was complete blackness.

CHAPTER
ELEVEN

FATHER MALCOLM remained steadfast at his vigil inside the Church of Eternal Sorrows. It had been three days of solitary meditation and prayer.

Anita brought him water and fruit and cheese, which he accepted absentmindedly. Sometimes he knelt in a mild trance and so she left the plate and cup at his side. He looked to be in no pain, but something was unresolved. He had lost so much weight he looked hollow at the eyes.

Anita watched over him as he meditated. From time to time she adjusted the instruments, replaced the videotapes, or put fresh graph paper in the seismograph. The church interior was completely stabilized. The computer image showed the familiar, subtly iridescent, ambiguous cruciform shape.

People had begun to gather, during the day and into the night, on the slopes around the church.

At times Father Malcolm sang, and the plainchant tenor floated intimately among the pink and white blossoms. Sometimes the evensong was taken up by those watching. Sometimes the voices twirled unaccompanied through the irises and lilacs.

The red altar lamp burned steadily, casting a delicate sheen on the Jesuit's slightly thinning blond hair below.

Around Golgotha Valley the plowed fields were covered in shoots and the dry, cool wind blew tiny buds across the hard ground. The ridges deepened into russet-colored autumnal foliage. An agricultural expert from the Haverford County Farmers' Union came down in his green pickup truck to investigate the scintillating blooming plants of Golgotha Valley. Tests of the soil showed a low alkali content, and almost no breakup of the top layers. The nutrient level was unusually high for New England.

Anita gathered testimony of other anomalous occurrences.

From Dowson's Repentance at the west end of Golgotha Valley the two remission cases were discharged from the clinic for the elderly. Subsequent blood counts in the leukemia showed slight fluctuation and then stabilization just within the proper range. The tuberculosis patient, an eighty-seven-year-old farmer named Henry "Hank" Edmondson, returned to his room in the house of his family on a knoll overlooking the dead town of Kidron. In their interviews with Anita they both told her they visualized clearly the rose hanging from its bush in the cemetery of the Church of Eternal Sorrows.

Both were anxious to visit the church.

Harvey Timms, aged eight, was deaf from birth, but he perceived rumbling deformations along the inmost of the ear bones in the ear canal. On Sunday afternoon he was in the kitchen of his home, taking lessons from the speech therapist from Dowson's Repentance. The therapist held Harvey's fingers against his throat, inducing him to make vocables. Harvey suddenly turned away and became impatient.

It took half an hour through sign language to understand that the rumblings had suddenly grown defined. They were low-pitched rumblings with a metallic echo. Medical examination in Dowson's Repentance showed no softening of the inner ear tissues. But coming home past Golgotha Falls, Harvey suddenly shrieked with delight.

The Jesuit had been ringing the bell at the Church of Eternal Sorrows.

Anita lay on her sleeping bag in the rectory. Outside the window the apple petals hovered, brushed against the crucifix, and beyond the fields the ridges steamed with soft traveling vapors. Mario would be back soon, she realized. The frayed fibers of their relationship would either reknit or sever.

Mario had created a role for himself, aggressive, sexual, and almost frighteningly charming. But in the last two years, the role had trapped him. It seemed to him more important to humiliate Dean Osborne than to prepare a watertight case around the project.

Father Malcolm represented a threat to Mario, not just because of his Catholicism, not just because of the home for wayward boys, but because Father Malcolm represented a level of personality development Mario had refused. Anita had taken Mario to the threshold of that level, to the interconnections of society and their immutable, mysterious operations, but Mario took one look at a world without physical risk, without the vigor of antagonism, unmediated by sex, and he became disgusted and withdrew.

Anita fell into a light dream, a dream that had come to her three nights in succession. In that dream, a man of shadows came up a long path to the rectory door. He came from beyond the grave. He seemed to take off a hat and brush his hair back. He wanted to speak gently with her, saw that she might be asleep, and gradually he grew transparent, until Anita saw the church clearly through him.

Then the dream faded. She was awake. She knew who the man was. It was the last memory she had of her father, the night he left for the airport. He had come into her bedroom, peered under the delicate canopied four-poster bed and mistakenly thought she was asleep. Rather than wake her he merely smiled, turned and left. She never saw him again. The airplane lost altitude out of Boston and ditched in the freezing Atlantic.

Anita listened carefully to Father Malcolm's quiet, melodic voice.

According to the principles of the experimenter-effect, Mario's absence and her presence might alter any of the findings in the instruments. For the subject of a study responds, semiconsciously, to the wishes and feelings of those near him. And what, semiconsciously, was she telling Father Malcolm now that Mario was gone?

Did Anita believe in God? Did she earnestly desire to see Him? To find such undeniable proof of His existence that she need never be troubled by agnostic doubts again?

Or would she feel satisfied with a kind of Heisenberg principle of uncertainty? Perhaps there was a zone in which powerful emotions, suggestibility, and the paranormal intersected, and became detectable at different times in different guises.

The one connection in common, she realized, was love. Repressed love. Yearning love. Ethereal and sublimated love. Love of an ideal. Fear of love. The binding power of man's ultimate need and ultimate weakness, love.

Father Malcolm's voice broke suddenly into a strangulated cry.

"Anita—"

Anita sat up abruptly. She dressed quickly and went to the church window. Father Malcolm still knelt on the floor, his hands composed on his lap. But his head was bowed at an angle, the face grimaced in agony.

She ran into the church.

"Father—"

He seemed aware of her, but unable to turn. She walked down the aisle to see his face. His nostrils were flared, as though the church had an insufficiency of oxygen. His eyes showed white where the lids were partly raised.

She leaned forward and touched his cheek.

"Are you all right, Father?" she whispered.

Suddenly, the lids flew open. The eyes were rolled back. Then slowly, he regained the power of focus. He saw Anita. He tried to smile and then squeezed her hand in his.

"Everything is good, Anita," he whispered.

"I'm glad."

"Kneel, Anita!"

Slowly she knelt at his side, hands on her thighs, and it seemed to comfort him.

Father Malcolm lowered his head again, crossed himself, and listened. His head shook vigorously in a denial. His lips began moving. Anita leaned forward, but could not make out the words.

"Pray, Anita," he suddenly rasped, in pain.

Confused, Anita tried to keep him from falling.

"Please, Father, I—"

"*Pray!*"

Anita, feeling a terrible tension, folded her hands together. Then it was not so terrible, assuming the posture of prayer. It was like a posture of encouragement during group therapy. Or psychic concentration during yoga. Nevertheless, she felt in her guilt that some kind of irreparable divide was forming between her and Mario.

A diminished candle fell, toppled slowly to the floor, in front of them. The paraffin kept burning, glowed brighter, against their faces.

Father Malcolm prayed for the victims of the priest Bernard Lovell. He prayed for the missing twin. He implored that Christ's mercy restore them from their mutilation.

Father Malcolm prayed for Bernard Lovell. He prayed for the love that was abused in the dead man's heart.

Father Malcolm prayed for James Farrell Malcolm. He offered himself as witness to the man's character, the soul with neither pride nor envy. He begged that the last cataclysm of perversion not erase a lifetime of obedience to Christ.

The Siloam sang sweetly, careening among rocks once hidden by the accumulated silt and debris of a half century. Anita opened her eyes. The altar was bright under the candles. The walls of the church seemed to radiate their light rather than reflect it.

Father Malcolm prayed for Mario, that the anger in him be purged and he be restored to Christ. Father Malcolm prayed for the woman at his side, that the child within reawaken to the mercy of an infinite God.

Father Malcolm prayed for the bishop, who had angered him by his indifference.

The Jesuit perceived that, as mediator between earth and heaven, he remained impure. He silently questioned himself.

How were you angry at His Grace?

I was enraged by his spiritual blindness.

You set yourself up as his equal.

In doing so, I became unworthy.

Your pride was insulted.

I felt grievously humiliated.

Enunciate your fantasies.

In my sinful pride, I entertained the fantasy that Christ had ordained for me a role among men. I imagined myself sought after by greater men than I. I went so far as to daydream of an audience with the Holy Father in Rome.

These are infantile fantasies.

In having them, I became unworthy.

Anita lowered her head. The lateness of the hour, the absence of Mario, the torment of the priest next to her had changed her sense of events. There was no rush anymore. She was on a kind of bedrock in which life allowed just enough time for the soul to accomplish what it set out to do.

In the restful atmosphere of the red ambient light, for no reason that she could rationally analyze, she softly began to cry.

Father Malcolm prayed for his father, in all his inadequacies. Father Malcolm prayed for his mother, the timid, frightened woman who never achieved an identity.

He prayed for the soul of his dead brother Ian.

And do you pray unequivocally for your brother Ian?

I revere his memory.

And yet you hated him.

For his goodness.

How could you?

Faith, grace, even in its smallest whisper, was an intolerable and long struggle for me. For Ian, it was a natural gift.

These jealousies are infantile.

I pray unequivocally for Christ's forgiveness.

Anita gently wiped her eyes. She had not had a good cry in a long time. Life with Mario was not conducive to that sort of thing.

"Do not be afraid, Anita," Father Malcolm said. "Give your heart to God."

Father Malcolm prayed for the urban masses, lost in forces they neither controlled nor understood. He prayed for the poor of Golgotha Valley, pawns in the war between good and evil. He continued to silently question himself.

Is your love for Christ absolute?

It is.

Is there no resentment in your heart?

I have accepted the abandonment of the world.

Would you do as Christ commanded?

Suddenly, the voice was no longer his. It was a voice that knew him too well. Father Malcolm sensed a density in the air before him and was afraid to look.

"Anita," Father Malcolm said.

"I'm here, Father."

The Jesuit knew he was safe within the confines of the church and its sanctified grounds. Yet he had to mediate between the souls on earth and God in heaven, through the doctrine and implements of the Church. Now he felt the questioner nibbling, nibbling at his consciousness.

I would do whatsoever Christ commanded.

164

Without reservation?
I would not hold back.
If Christ commands you to go?
I would go.
If Christ commands you to stay?
I would stay.
Then deny Him.

Father Malcolm doubled over in an agony of disbelief. He dared not open his eyes, for he heard vague rustling. The voice waited, not his own voice.

I—I could not—
Must you not experience abandonment?
I am too weak. I am afraid.
Did not Christ experience abandonment in His death agony?
I am not Christ.
You are His echo on earth.

Father Malcolm writhed in pain, holding his head. The mental stress of the paradox was unendurable. Druglike, the red glow of the air permeated his eyes even when the lids were closed.

Anita opened her eyes. Father Malcolm trembled like a poisoned dog. She wiped his forehead with the handkerchief. He leaned heavily against her.

In the computer screen, the flux had obliterated the cruciform shape.

Trembling, teeth chattering, Father Malcolm swayed in Anita's arms in an agony of disbelieving doubt.

He who lit the lamp commands you.
"No—" he murmured aloud.
"Father—it's me—Anita—"
He who brought signs into the valley commands you.
"No!" Father Malcolm called, vigorously shaking his head.
You must pass into that shadow of darkness.
"Never!"
"Please . . . Father—"

In a paroxsym of anguish, Father Malcolm doubled up, writhed away from her, unable to open his eyes.

Do you not believe that Christ will accept you on the other side?

Father Malcolm covered his ears, as though to stop out the sound. But there was no sound. Anita put her hands on his rigid shoulders, tears in her eyes.

"Father Malcolm—it is nearly dawn—please end the vigil—"

Then deny Him.

"No."

Deny Him.

"Never."

Your obedience is false pride. Deny Him.

"Though my soul know God no longer, I shall not!"

Suddenly, a rooster crowed deep in the north slopes of Golgotha Valley. It was like a peal of raucous laughter. The echo rebounded in the church, throwing the needle of the sound system back and forth.

Father Malcolm's face twitched. He pushed himself feebly from Anita, confused.

"Father—are you all right?"

He seemed to focus on her, still disoriented.

"Yes, I—"

A second time, the rooster crowed, lusty, virile.

Father Malcolm looked around the church. It was evenly lit by the imperturbable red lamp. He turned to Anita, surprised at the tears in her eyes.

"You were almost unconscious," she admitted.

A third time the rooster crowed.

"Unlike Saint Peter, I did not deny Christ," he said weakly, trying to smile.

He regained his full awareness.

"Anita—it was so strangely logical . . . My brain locked on me . . . I couldn't think . . . All I could do was refuse—"

"But the vigil is over now."

"Yes. I have come through."

She watched him carefully as he half knelt, half held himself up from the floor, trying to comprehend what had happened.

"I was so close—to a presence—and yet I could not think—nothing was coherent—"

"You had dissociated."

"Yes. Perhaps. I did feel dissolved. Afraid. Did I fail?"

He gazed at her anxiously.

"Look!" she said. "Look at your church! Let that be your testimony!"

A glimmer of golden air stirred at the apse window, the announcement of dawn in Golgotha Valley.

"Love moves so powerfully," he said in amazement. "It is absolute. Its commands are absolute."

Troubled, he wiped his hands on his cassock and bit his lips.

"Christ is love," he said, brows furrowed. "Any movement away from Christ is a motion that contradicts love."

He looked into Anita's blurred eyes.

"Do you see?" he asked passionately. "Christ is acceptance. Only a man standing outside of Christ can understand the notion of separation. So naturally, I was bound in that paradox!"

Overjoyed, Father Malcolm hugged Anita.

"For I am, truly, in Christ. And to deny Him to prove my love to Him—it is a concept that cannot exist in my mind!"

Anita wiped her own eyes, so contagious was Father Malcolm's joy.

"And you, too," he suggested gently, seeing her face. "You have learned something tonight, too?"

Father Malcolm thought of his three-day ordeal, the physical deprivation, the unbearable concentration. He had rent apart his own Christian conscience, ruthlessly, his own Grand Inquisitor, and found himself worthy of the immanence that moved like the river in Golgotha Valley. He saw the transformation, like petals blossoming, of the young woman, who by his assistance had found the secret of unabashed sincerity. Father Malcolm felt proud. It was not, he felt, in the circumstances a major sin.

But it was enough.

Impulsively, he bent forward and kissed her forehead. Anita blushed. She squeezed his forearm.

A second time, slower, his shadow crossing over her face, he kissed her delicately where the black hair swept up from her forehead.

She smiled gently, passing her hand across his cheek.

A tremor passed through him. She felt it and put her hands against his chest to comfort him, to look at his face, and felt the wild erratic pounding of his heart.

Suddenly she understood. She, for whom bodily expression of gratitude and affection had long ago ceased to be a matter of shyness, suddenly realized that the same gesture had unlocked something unstable in the priest. She became frightened. Not for herself, but for him.

Even you could be an agent of the Antichrist for him, Mario had teased.

"Anita—" he choked, warning her, pleading with her against his own nature.

"Don't be frightened, Father."

167

But the words had a horrible second meaning that intoxicated the already disoriented priest.

In his arms was woman, archetype of earthly happiness, analogue to his own desperate loneliness. The same that had lain against his chest on the balcony over the sultry Potomac at night. Father Malcolm's hot-running blood had a sudden wisdom of its own, a knowledge that repudiated all his years of discretion and training.

Anita instantly understood what was happening. She tried to push him gently away, but his embrace grew incredibly strong.

"Father—no—no—"

In his nostrils was the warm feminine scent, breaking down all barriers. His skin grew warm, feverish, as he breathed faster, and felt himself changing, needing, metamorphosing below the waist.

His right hand pressed under her shirt even as he held her, and it sought her breast. Anita arched her back, pushing away at him, but he could not be denied. His mouth clumsily pressed at hers, his hands pinned her head, his tongue penetrated her lips.

Anita violently tore from his face, her brain reeling with fear for him, desperately aware that she had unknowingly exploded something in his nature.

And something far more disturbing: in that touch of rough tongue on hers, a hot and passionate thrill that ran through her body like an electric current.

Anita stumbled from his grasping embrace and saw the church behind him filled with a blood-red light. She quickly looked up at the altar lamp. It flickered over their heads, dying, and suddenly was black and cold. Father Malcolm also stared at it, shocked out of his delirium, white-faced and hollow-eyed.

"*Oh—Anita—*" he roared in disbelief. "*He has made you his whore!*"

She pulled herself away, circled behind the altar. The Jesuit, fumbling frantically, reached for the altar to pull himself up. Instead, the altar linen came down in his hands, and the tabernacle toppled and crashed, sending the chalice and silver paten careening over the floor.

"Oh—dear God—no!" he bellowed, cradling the fallen linens.

Anita kept circling away, further into the apse.

"Anita!"

Father Malcolm grabbed the silver wick by the altar. He slammed a chair in front of the altar and tried to mount it, but some force made the pole weave wildly in his arms, and only an oily smoke drifted down over the Jesuit.

"ANITA!"

Father Malcolm suddenly whirled as though thrown, sending the silver wick end-over-end into the south wall.

"*LIGHT THE LAMP!*" he roared, doubled over in pain.

Cautiously, Anita stepped onto the chair. She brought matches from her shirt pocket, where the buttons had been torn by Father Malcolm. She struck a match. A long, deliberate breath behind her blew it out.

Very slowly, she turned.

"Don't turn around!" Father Malcolm called.

She struck a second match and quickly inserted it into the lamp. Behind her, she heard heavy motions, as of a hairy body, and the stinking splash of volumes of urine at the door.

"By the Blood of the Savior, Jesus Christ, by the intercession of Mary, Mother of God, by the apostles and saints of heaven, we abjure thee and thy foul horror to the deepest pits of hell—"

Father Malcolm's voice broke off abruptly.

Anita held the flame steady. The bright cone of light seemed to run around the lip of the oil basin spout like tiny mice. Then it caught. Warmth spread upward against her face, unpleasantly. The flame held, sickly yellow, exuding a stinking incense.

That's better, she heard a different voice utter. *That's better.*

Anita turned slowly.

The church was still. Father Malcolm lay quiet, trembling, on the floor below. In the thermovision screen sat the likeness of a goat in bishop's miter, bloodied head cocked, and a tilted black crucifix against the savage knees.

A deep rumble of contented laughter echoed and rebounded throughout the Church of Eternal Sorrows.

CHAPTER
TWELVE

THE CAMBRIDGE Municipal Hospital was ill-lit by sloped skylights partially blocked by dirt and debris from the frosty night and the rainy morning. Mario sat on a bed in the eighth ward, wearing a white cotton robe, idly riffling through an old Sunday *New York Times*. From time to time footsteps came to the ward, then receded. How long had he been in this room, he wondered. Two days? Three? After the debacle in the lecture hall, time had ceased to exist as a calculable entity.

Outside it was raining. A vicious, thudding rain. The patient in the adjacent bed, a paunchy gentleman with extraordinarily pink skin, kept moaning and rubbing a shaven chest soon due for the surgeon's scalpel.

Mario turned over the pages of the science section. Two graduate students at MIT had replicated the retinal fibers of a newt's eye. A mathemetician at Berkeley had refined the model for the emission of energy from astronomical black holes. A Marxist historian of science had proved that Darwin's theory of evolution reflected the class needs of a Victorian society.

Mario dazedly studied the articles, seeking clues to the ages of the men involved. Of late, he had become obsessed with the ages of those making their marks. Mario was now pushing past the moment when the best scientists hit their peak. Golgotha Falls was his watershed. It could still be his watershed, he felt, if only he could sort out what had taken place in that lecture hall.

A man in a business suit came into the room. It was Professor Hendricks of the physics department.

"Mario, how are you feeling?" Hendricks said.

Mario attempted a smile, gestured toward a blue plastic chair at the bedside. Hendricks, a handsome man in his early fifties, lean, with white at his temples, sat down stiffly.

"Okay, I guess, Professor," Mario said.

By the way Hendricks had recoiled on seeing him, Mario figured he was still pale as a sheet. The man in the adjacent bed groaned. Hendricks leaned forward.

"You gave us one hell of a scare, Mario," he said. "What happened?"

Mario folded the science section of the newspaper, laid it on the tiny cabinet near the wall. He turned back to the intelligent gray eyes of the physicist Hendricks and folded his hands on his stomach.

"What do *you* think happened?" Mario asked.

"You've got me. The lecture hall was in pandemonium. I thought you had an epileptic fit."

"I mean, what did you see? On the screen?"

Hendricks looked at Mario, puzzled.

"Same thing as everyone else."

"What? Tell me, Professor Hendricks. It's important."

Hendricks rubbed his chin. It was a gesture of embarrassment. Mario waited impatiently.

"Well, there were some pictures of a naked woman—your companion, somebody said—some lizards—and a godawful piece of film —a wild horse stomping some helpless bastard to death. Jesus, it was terrible . . ." Hendricks gazed levelly at Mario.

"What the hell got into you? Pulling a stunt like that after all you'd put into the project."

Instead of answering, Mario leaned back against the doubled pillows.

"Are you *sure* that's what you saw?" he asked after a long while.

"Of course I'm sure, no mistaking something like.that."

"Would you sign an affidavit to that effect?"

"What?"

"If I needed it, would you sign an affidavit?"

"Of course. Why not?"

Mario relaxed a bit more. Color was coming slowly into his cheeks. Hendricks did not know if it was health or a fever.

"Do you remember who else was in the audience?"

Hendricks shrugged.

"Some of the physics faculty."

"Wasn't there some function just before the lecture?"

"Right. The Bollington Prize. Sure. There'd be a roster of names. A list of invited guests. Most of them stayed around to hear you."

"I need that list," Mario said. "I need affidavits from all of them."

"Why?"

"Because it's one of the most distinguished groups ever assembled for a lecture."

Hendricks was baffled. A long-time supporter of Mario, once Mario's professor before the student riots, Hendricks found his former teaching assistant had hardened over the years.

"I don't follow you at all," he said softly.

Mario rose to his elbows. The patient behind them groaned. Mario bent closer to Hendricks.

"Because they all saw what you and I saw," Mario whispered heatedly.

"Of course they did. So what?"

Mario came even closer, making sure no one else overheard him.

"*Those images were not on my slides or my tapes*," he hissed.

Hendricks looked down at the floor, discomfited. Mario gripped the older man's arm.

"Understand what I'm saying? Those images did not come from my tapes!"

Hendricks looked away. A nurse came to feed the adjacent patient a red capsule from a paper cup. She left on soft rubber-soled shoes. Hendricks watched where she had gone.

"You don't believe me," Mario said.

"I'd have to see the slides and tapes, Mario." Hendricks looked back at Mario's distraught face. "Where *are* they?" he asked, his face blank, signifying the absolute control he kept over his feelings.

Mario shook his head. "I figure they're still in the projection booth."

Hendricks stood up. "Well, I'm not sure what I hope to see on them," he admitted. "What you're saying is it was some kind of . . . what? . . . mass—"

"Hallucination. That's it exactly, Professor Hendricks. That's why I need those affidavits."

Hendricks nodded sympathetically. They shook hands. "Get some rest," he said gently. "You look very tired. When you're feeling better, get the tapes and come see me. Okay, Mario?"

"Sure. And thanks for dropping by." Mario collapsed back onto the pillow. He was weaker than he had imagined. Of course Hendricks couldn't believe what he had told him. He'd simply have to show him, face him with the evidence on the tapes. Mario sighed, mechanically picked up the newspaper. As he turned the political pages, a section he rarely read, an article caught his attention.

A secretary to the Vatican financial office had been implicated in arrangements with Sicilian and Brazilian mobsters. There was a photograph of the cardinal involved, resplendent in ebony buttons and pectoral cross, holding his wide-brimmed hat in front of his face like a common criminal. Mario carefully ripped out the photograph. It summed up all the splendor, all the duplicity of that institution.

The Church had an infinite talent for survival, despite its scandals, its heresies, its mercenaries and illegitimate Popes. What was its secret? How did it suck up generation after generation of sons for its medieval and arcane mysteries? Where did its energy come from?

Mario was certain it came from repression. The id was subtly but inexorably metamorphosed with guilt, strange ideas of sexuality, and a host of neo-Freudian nightmares. Only one outlet was provided: reverence to Church authority. It was like hypnotism. A priest became a dreamer, and his images of salvation were but the measure of the id's excruciating agony.

Even a normal man, in solitary confinement, will hallucinate and grow dependent on his delusions.

In isolation, pressurized beyond the normal psychic bounds, an id like Eamon Malcolm's broke out and cast a materialized image of its self-contradictions and pain.

Mario watched the rain pushing veils of wet dirt down the slanted skylight. He barely noticed the man in the adjacent bed being wheeled away for surgery. Instead, he tried to focus on Eamon Malcolm.

Golgotha Falls, its peculiar terrain, its collective fears, its isolation, had twisted Bernard K. Lovell into a necrophiliac. Next it had cracked James Farrell Malcolm and turned him into a bestialist. But Eamon Malcolm, high-strung and highly educated, an idealist in a crude world, had suffered the most incomprehensible fate of all: he had metamorphosed into one of the most remarkable psychic transmitters ever known.

Incredible as it seemed, he had cast his dream net of psychic obsessions over a distance of one hundred miles onto a hundred unsuspecting and sophisticated observers. Was it even remotely possible? If so, why? The images that had been manifest at the lecture were easily decipherable: dreamlike visions of lust and rage. The hostility and the abnormal sexuality appeared in Freudian, that is, disguised form. The stallion assaulting the fleeing man was most likely a metaphor for sexual jealousy and hatred of Mario.

It was a silent psychic scream of pain.

Eamon Malcolm was no doubt unconscious of all this. To him, it was still a moral battle between Christ and Satan, fought through his own unworthy mind and body.

Two unsettling questions were left: Why such violent imagery in the lecture hall? Why not the cruciform shape, symbol of his salvation? Classically, the priest's id should continue to sublimate its hostility into benign imagery.

Unless something had changed in Golgotha Falls.

Another question: were there other potential victims of the priest's unconscious projections?

For the first time, Mario began to feel that Anita might be in danger.

Mario slipped from the hospital bed and reached for his dress shirt on a hook. It was still smeared where he had been wrestled to the auditorium floor.

Dr. Cummins, a young physician, came into the ward.

"Are you leaving, Mr. Gilbert?"

Mario, buttoning his shirt, looked at him. It was an elegant face.

The kind bred for generations on the estates of Long Island or Cape Cod, the private school education and impeccable diction, the kind Mario loathed.

"I've got to retrieve something and get the hell out of here," Mario said.

Dr. Cummins was younger than Mario. Taken aback by Mario's tone of voice, he grew flustered and looked down at his clipboard.

"There was some question of a brain scan for epilepsy."

"I haven't got epilepsy," Mario said, slipping into his dress trousers. Unaccountably, they were striped with mud. Probably fell from the stretcher on the way out of the auditorium. All he remembered now was chaos and shooting red streaks in his vision.

"Mr. Gilbert," Dr. Cummins said, leaning forward slightly, "we think you are suffering from a form of hysteria. You are overworked and overmotivated about your project. You buckled emotionally."

Mario glared at him.

"Is that your diagnosis?" he asked. "I had a breakdown?"

Dr. Cummins licked his lips nervously.

"You were taken screaming and incoherent from a lecture," he said earnestly. "The next time might be even worse."

"What next time?"

"Hallucinations. Violence. It could burst into a real epilepsy for all we know."

"There's nothing wrong with me."

Fully dressed, Mario tried to push past the doctor.

"You are advised to break off your project," Dr. Cummins said, blocking the way. "I'll give you tranquilizers. And we recommend psychotherapy."

Mario looked at him balefully. For an instant, Dr. Cummins thought Mario would throw a punch and he backed off.

"It has nothing to do with my psyche," Mario said. "It's a kind of experience you don't know anything about."

Mario pushed past Dr. Cummins toward the door.

"Showing pornographic materials to a Harvard audience is hardly the behavior of a rational man!" Dr. Cummins shouted.

Mario turned angrily at the door. "We're dealing with irrational phenomena here, Doctor! But *you* wouldn't understand!"

Mario left quickly down the corridor.

Dr. Cummins shouted after him, "At least have the decency to sign out!"

Mario went into the blue elevator. The doors closed and took him down to the ground floor.

It took fifteen minutes to run, slipping through mud and wet hedges, across to the campus.

The projection room of the auditorium was locked. Angrily, Mario rattled the doorknob. Down below were crumpled papers and chalked handwriting on the blackboards.

Mario pounded on the door and kicked it with frustration.

The elderly man came into the auditorium, carrying slide boxes and sheets of paper in his arms.

"Didn't expect to see you again," he muttered, fumbling for the key on a steel link chain at his belt.

"I need my slides. My tapes," Mario said eagerly, brushing the water out of his curled hair.

The projectionist opened the door and carefully set the slides on a table next to twin interlocked projectors.

"Visual material from old lectures are on that bottom shelf," he said.

Mario shoved the slide boxes around on the bottom shelf.

"They're not here," he said.

"Well, check inside the boxes. Sometimes things get mislabeled."

Mario plucked out the initial slides of several lecture programs. Engineering: hydraulic systems. Chemistry: polymers and chain structures. Metallurgy: metal fatigue. And a series from the architectural department: E. R. Robson and the London Board Schools.

"*They're not here!*" Mario yelled.

"Well, maybe they got mixed up with today's lectures."

Mario looked at the shelves next to the twin projectors. All the slide boxes were clearly labeled in other people's handwriting. In any case, there were no plastic cassettes of the thermovision tapes or slide boxes.

At that moment, the undergraduate audiovisual assistant, the one who had worked the projector at the lecture, entered pushing a trolley of acetate diagrams.

Mario bounded up to him and seized his jacket lapels.

"Where are they?" Mario demanded, inches from the boy's face.

"Where are what?"

"My slides. My photographs and tapes."

Mario shoved him painfully against the wall. The undergraduate winced, his temples throbbing in fear.

"I never touched them," he protested.

"Then who did?"

"The campus police."

Mario very slowly eased back from the boy.

"The campus cops?" Mario said incredulously.

"Well, it *was* pornography."

Mario stared at the undergraduate with loathing, then stepped over the crumpling acetate sheets on the floor, and went quickly down the stairs.

It was raining harder. A driving, malicious rain beating over his head and shoulders. Mud oozed from hedges, and umbrellas all over campus were being bent backward. A chill invaded him now. It did not ease when he entered the basement of the campus police department.

Electric lights hung from the tall ceilings. Echoes wound through the cement corridors. On the walls were photostats of FBI-wanted terrorists.

Campus police would remember him well. Three times they had dragged him screaming from occupying the president's office. Twice, without warrants, they had searched his apartment for subversive material. It was two decades ago. But nobody forgot, not deep down.

When Mario entered the corridor leading to the captain's office, he recognized the lurid lighting, the slick and moldy smell of varnished furniture and wall damp, the endless tedium and melancholy of officers who secretly hated the intellectual life and once had hated him.

The captain, a man in his mid-fifties with wrinkled eyelines and sharp gray eyes, received Mario right away. It was clear from his smirk that he knew what had happened at the lecture. He swiveled in his wooden chair, looking at the forlorn, dripping figure in front of him.

"I'd love to nail you on a vice charge, Gilbert," he grinned. "But nobody filed a complaint."

"I've come for my tapes. Campus cops were in the projection booth, and they took them. A witness saw them."

The captain raised an eyebrow, then pressed the button of the intercom. Soon a campus policeman came in and the two engaged in a whispered discussion. Mario had seen the charade before.

"They're not in lost-and-found," the captain said. "And we don't have 'em in our headquarters."

177

The tone of voice was final, flat and metallic. The captain rose and escorted Mario to the door.

"I'll sue you if I have to," Mario said quietly. "You know I will."

The captain grinned and opened the door. "Fine, Gilbert. You just go do that."

Mario left sullenly. He felt the captain and the policeman watching after him with barely contained humor.

Mario ran into the cold, pounding rain, into the sciences building, and down the long muddy corridor to Anita's laboratory.

A new padlock glinted on the door.

Mario rattled it, but the padlock held firm. He ran to their stockroom and it, too, had a shining new padlock bolting the door into place.

There were no windows to the parapsychology laboratory. There was no access through the physics department. It was an unheated cubicle that Dean Osborne had given Anita years ago, gradually transformed into a dense experimental chamber.

Finally, Mario smashed at the padlock with a heavy red fire extinguisher, and chips of wood cracked and splintered onto the floor.

"It's no use, Mario," he heard behind him. "Dean Osborne has closed you down."

Breathing hard, still holding the extinguisher, Mario turned and saw Henry, the black janitor, mopping the mud from the corridor.

"Dean Osborne?" he said, barely audible.

Henry nodded, avoiding Mario's eyes.

"After the lecture, he took everything out of your laboratory. Then he padlocked it. There was cops here and everything. I thought you'd killed somebody."

Mario sagged bleakly against the door.

"He can't do that. The project—my class—it's authorized until the end of the semester."

"He done it."

Mario looked up slowly. Nervous, Henry edged away, sloshing the mop into the far corners of the hall.

"What about my slides?" Mario whispered. "My tapes?"

Henry shrugged but avoided Mario's glare.

"Better speak to Dean Osborne about them."

Mario continued to stare at him. Then he pushed himself from the wall, rubbed the rain from his face, and breathed heavily into his fists.

A shudder ran through Mario's back. Henry watched him go

across the quad, then slowly up the white stone steps to the administration offices.

Mario walked up the poorly lit corridor, heels echoing, to the pebbled glass of the door window that read: *Sciences Administration, Dean Harvey Osborne.*

Mario opened the door. A soft whirr and clacking of electric typewriters ceased. The door closed behind him. Under an annoyingly blinking fluorescent light, the receptionist looked up, startled.

"Mario Gilbert," she smiled. "I thought you were in the hospital."

Mario bent forward onto the desk, leaning on both straight arms.

"I want to see Dean Osborne," he said coldly.

Her smile faded. She spoke into the intercom. There was a whispered conversation. Then she gestured to a straight-backed, leather-covered chair under the wall clock.

"Please be seated," she said.

As he sat there, dripping water into a puddle on the floor, he surveyed the bulletins stapled to a cork board, wire baskets of memoranda, the pigeonholes where faculty collected their mail. Where once a fireplace had been built, but was now boarded over, a scrolled, heavy safe with steel locks stood.

"Is that where my slides and tapes are?" Mario asked.

The receptionist stopped typing.

"You'd better speak to Dean Osborne about that," she said, and resumed her work.

After twenty minutes, Dean Osborne's door opened. A woman in her mid-forties, brunette and worried, emerged. Mario figured her for some mother pleading that her son not be kicked out of basic chemistry. Dean Osborne's door closed.

Then a skinny man with an unlit pipe barged past Mario and, unannounced, went into the dean's office.

Twenty-five minutes passed. Though it was only a little past noon, the rainy sky had turned the day to a dim twilight.

An odd thought struck Mario: If Dean Osborne refused him his tapes, if the lecture went down as a debacle, ridiculed and unexamined, the results of the experiment at Golgotha Falls would never reach the outside world. Mario began to pace the area between the safe and faculty letter boxes.

"Sooner or later, he's going to see me," Mario said slowly. "Tell him that."

The receptionist spoke a second time into the intercom. The

skinny man with the unlit pipe came by, nodded and smiled, and went into the corridor.

"You may go in now."

Mario headed toward the closed oak door, where gold letters spelled out Osborne's name. On both sides, on the paneled walls, were portraits in oils of former deans and eminent Harvard alumni. The entire series of rooms, receptionist, mail room, and two secretaries' rooms, fell silent as Mario walked by.

When Mario opened the door, Dean Osborne was examining several papers against the waning light from the window.

Mario closed the door behind him and sat in the chair in front of the massive desk.

Dean Osborne frowned, initialed something on the two pages, then added a note at the bottom. It finally pleased him. He pressed a button. The receptionist came in, took the pages from him, and left. Dean Osborne swiveled to face Mario.

"Mario," he said amiably. "You no longer exist at Harvard."

Dean Osborne shoved a tabloid across the varnished desk top.

> Psychic Researcher Falls to Evil Influence
>
> Mario Gilbert, a parapsychologist and lecturer at Harvard University, fell Thursday night to the evil influences of his own research. A lecture about the raising of wandering spirits in a remote north Massachusetts church turned to pandemonium when the young scientist fell screaming to the floor.
>
> Witnesses described his tongue as "swollen black" and others described him as "speaking in tongues" while in a "diabolic fit."
>
> The incident occurred shortly after the presentation of pornographic slides taken at the project.

Mario dropped the tabloid into the wastebasket.

"I need my tapes and slides," he said.

Dean Osborne shook his head.

"University property."

"I made them, for Christ's sake."

"On Harvard equipment. For a Harvard project. Presented at Harvard. You know the rules."

Mario rubbed his lips as though a foul taste had settled there. He leaned forward.

"I've got to have them," he said softly.

"Why?"

"Because what is on those slides is not what you and one hundred other people saw."

Dean Osborne's face twitched. The austere façade of the scion of a distinguished New England family was cracking. In its place appeared a flushed and angry man personally humiliated, even threatened, by a debacle he had sponsored.

"What I saw was *filth!*"

"I know you did. But it's not on the visual material."

Dean Osborne swiveled away, trying to control his temper. Mario saw the vein pulse in the dean's neck. Gradually he swiveled back, polite, chilly, and courteous as usual.

"What manner of nonsense are you presenting to me, Gilbert?" he asked.

Mario leaned forward to the desk, fingers jabbing the blotter for emphasis.

"Mass hallucination."

Dean Osborne stared at him for a long time.

"It was a telepathic transmission of imagery!" Mario said enthusiastically. "From a source over one hundred miles away! And I can prove it if you'd only give me the slides!"

Dean Osborne shook his head. There was a look of disbelief in the older man's face. Disbelief in Mario's preposterous claims. Disbelief that he himself could have gotten caught in such a web of insanity. He did not know what to say.

"Dean Osborne," Mario continued rapidly, "I have found a most extraordinary individual at Golgotha Falls. A Jesuit."

The dean winced.

"A very intelligent man," Mario went on. "But emotionally disturbed. Far more disturbed than even he understands."

"That makes two of you."

Mario took a deep breath, ignoring the dean's sarcasm.

"The Jesuit, unconsciously, is the source of that imagery."

Dean Osborne licked his lips. Mario realized the man had grown pale. An involvement with the Catholic Church only deepened the dean's administrative embarrassment.

"*That's* it?" Dean Osborne said, voice quivering. "This is the scientific breakthrough you bring me? This is what justifies making an ass of me in front of the press and our most distinguished faculty?"

Mario retreated to the back of his chair.

"I've already captured an image of one of his psychic obsessions," he said defiantly.

Dean Osborne's head jerked back.

"When? Where?" he challenged.

"On the videotape."

"Mario, that videotape showed nothing but a horse battering the life out of some poor farmer!"

"*Go and look!*" Mario shouted.

Instead, Dean Osborne swiveled in alternate directions, then drummed his fingers on the massive arms of his chair. Mario was making him lose his temper. Dean Osborne felt a certain vulgarity rise inexorably inside him.

"What damn psychic obsession?" he asked.

"Christ. I recorded it at the climax of an exorcism. It's an undeniable image of the cruciform shape!"

Dean Osborne had been involved in many disputes, met many men he disliked. But none had the power that Mario had for disturbing his equanimity. Something about the aggressive face made Dean Osborne want to smash it. Some deeper antagonism than an administrative humiliation brought out a deplorable lack of manners in the distinguished professor.

"Do you know what I think?" Dean Osborne asked.

"What?"

"That it's all bullshit. And you are insane."

Mario, furious, pounded a fist on the desk top.

"Go look at the visual materials!" he demanded. "Unless you're afraid," he added with sudden recognition.

Angrily, Dean Osborne stood up.

"Did you see those portraits out there as you entered?" he said quickly. "Eminent men. Substantial men. Men who have shaped our very thought. Men who have created our modern world. Nobel Prize winners. Deans of great universities. Men who split atoms and invented space travel."

"They had their detractors, too."

"Perhaps. But they didn't traffic with sick priests, and dilapidated churches, and—and—mass hallucinations—"

"It's the truth."

"It's intellectually repugnant!" Dean Osborne said. "Mario, you are a has-been revolutionary, a perpetual student who got derailed in mid–identity crisis by old ladies at seances!"

Mario rose, tears in his eyes.

"You bastard," he whispered. "Give me my tapes and slides!"

Dean Osborne sat heavily in his seat. He dumped tobacco ash into the wastebasket, over the crumpled tabloid. As far as he was concerned, Mario Gilbert did not exist.

Mario leaped forward and pounded both fists on the desk top.

"You can't shut down an experiment because you don't believe in its premise!" he shouted.

"Get out."

"You participated in one of the most sensational events in the history of the paranormal and you won't even examine the evidence!"

"GET OUT!"

Mario's head snapped back at the bellow. The dean's face was livid. Gone was all the gentlemanly politeness. Pure rage was left.

"Even if it were true," he whispered hoarsely, "I would close you down. These psychic abnormalities repulse me, as they would every serious scientist."

Mario backed toward the door, his eyes filled with tears of frustration and rage.

"Send Hendricks to Golgotha Falls," he pleaded.

"No."

"Come yourself. It's a different world out there."

"No."

Dean Osborne hunched over the desk, pointing the pipe stem at Mario. "Your world deals with tea leaves and embroidered pillows. Sitar music and joss sticks. And that's fine. If that's what you want to do. But you can't do it here."

"Why not?"

"Because it isn't science!"

Mario, defeated, turned toward the door.

"I protected you for years. On Anita's account. Well, I can't do it anymore. Not with crap like you're spewing. And sensational articles like this."

Mario opened the door.

"I want that equipment, Gilbert!" Osborne called after him. "Bring it in by the end of the week."

Mario turned sharply.

"A *week?*"

"That's right. Your project is canceled. The cameras cost a fortune. So bring them in."

"But I'm in the middle of a viable experiment!"

"Then rent your own equipment," Dean Osborne said coolly. "Harvard needs it back."

Mario stared at him, wide-eyed at the absolute antagonism directed at him.

"In perfect condition," Dean Osborne added. "I'll send the campus police in a week if I have to."

Mario slammed the door so hard the oil portrait of Dean Osborne's predecessor tilted on its wall.

The dean rose and straightened the painting. He deeply regretted having lost his temper. It had lowered him to Mario's level. Loss of dignity was unforgivable. Gradually the austere orderliness of the office, its calm reassurance, restored his tranquility.

And a pang of guilt. For Mario Gilbert's personal tragedy was that he had been protected long after everybody else got the message that parapsychology was being closed down all over the country. It was Dean Osborne who had shielded the laboratory. And not for scientific reasons. Personal reasons involving Anita's mother.

Dean Osborne peered out through slightly parted blinds. Mario crossed the Yard toward muddy streets. It looked almost as though the young man were crying. Dean Osborne let the blinds snap shut.

Mario was not only going to die academically, he was going to die alone. Dean Osborne had a strong premonition that things were changing between Anita and Mario. Otherwise it would have been Anita in the office arguing for the visual materials, and he would have found it nearly impossible to refuse her. Their splitting up would be the only positive outcome of the wretched Golgotha Falls project.

But the guilt did not die. Maybe he owed Mario a look at the slides.

Dean Osborne walked from his office to the steel safe. It was Friday. The staff had left early. He twirled the tumblers and the massive stubby door slid open.

Payroll checks. Legal drafts for an endowment. A piece of fiber optics shared between physics and biochemistry. On the highest shelf, a carton labeled *Golgotha Falls* containing three boxes of slides and two tape cassettes.

It was uncanny, the sheer driving force of curiosity. He had felt nothing like it since he himself had been a graduate student attending the lectures of the great B. F. Skinner and a whole new universe seemed to be opening for him personally. Dean Osborne perspired freely. If a man's obsession *could* be recorded, even vaguely, suggestively, what extraordinary implications for the psychological sciences!

The emulsion of the slide gleamed almost green. Blue veils of reflections shimmered on the cassettes. Dean Osborne stared, hypnotized, his face trembling.

It was a fraud. Such ideas did not belong in a well-run administration. Mario was a crude showman, and Dean Osborne was damned if he was going to fall for any tricks. The screaming match had unpleasantly excited the dean's imagination. But it didn't work. Dean Osborne regained control of himself and slammed the steel door shut.

The evidence was swallowed up in the safe's darkness. The tumblers clicked. Mario Gilbert did not exist. Golgotha Falls remained shut off from the world.

CHAPTER
THIRTEEN

From the ridge of Golgotha Valley a screen of rain squalls all but obscured the town.

The clay banks crumbled into the swollen, swift Siloam, rising over the land and eroding the substructure of the church. The heavy rains flooded the cellars, disgorged iron tools and heavy glass jars from the days of Bernard Lovell. Bare iron of the old church gate was visible where mud washed away at the head of the church path.

Mario stood on the crest of the valley, peering down its length with a pair of binoculars, face nearly hidden by his yellow oilskin rain hood.

The flowers and blossoms of the trees seemed blasted away, dried and withered, curled and sodden; the ground littered with a black, tarry fruit fallen from the branches.

As the earth soaked in the rain, as the Siloam worked into the soft and porous earth, the graveyard was rising and sinking, and the tombstones were now irregularly tilted like broken teeth.

There was no sign of Anita.

The Jesuit's Oldsmobile was gone. Even from the heights, Mario could see where the big car had sped wildly through the underbrush, gouging erratic ruts across the fields.

Rising from the eerie mass of blowing, bending, shrieking, rain-water-spraying brambles and dead trees, the main structure of the Church of Eternal Sorrows stood inviolate. Thick, brown layers of smoke curled around it, snakelike, from pyres in the valley.

All through the valley farms, small brown pillars of smoke rose, then abruptly flattened in the rain and wind, spread down onto the fields, toward the white church.

What had happened? Mario wondered, as he threaded his way through crushed brambles, dead vines, and thorn bushes. Visibility was terrible on the ridge. Fog and swirling rain mixed in conflicting gusts over the dripping, hollow birch woods. Mario put the binoculars back into his raincoat pocket and got into the Volkswagen.

The van spun its wheels in the mud. Brown streaks smeared the panels and the grill. Great clumps of mud clung to the bumpers. When Mario crossed down into the valley, there was no fog or rain, only a metallic, low cloud cover.

The church was sealed within its valley, curtained from the neighboring valleys.

Mario parked the Volkswagen at the loop of the road, on firmer soil.

As he trod down, his boots left sucking gouges in the soil. The withered blossoms and dead, brown irises had drifted over the rocks and slimy clay, as though victims on some kind of battlefield.

"Anita!" Mario yelled, cupping his hands around his mouth.

He stumbled. At his boots the rain and shifting earth had disgorged remnants of the women's clothing and the deformed crucifix, once burned and then buried. All that was left of Christ's image was a long leg and a molten, grimaced face.

"*ANITA!*"

There was no response. The streets of Golgotha Falls were deserted. Only the dogs roamed there, backs hunched, tails low between their legs.

Dead birds, victims of an altered migratory instinct, now littered the base of the bell steeple.

187

Mario pulled a red plastic flashlight from his raincoat pocket and stepped over warped bits of iron toward the church.

As he stood in the dank vestibule, he played the yellow beam slowly down the interior.

In the dark twilight, glinting when struck by the flashlight beam, were twelve cruciform shapes on the walls: Father Malcolm's chrismed consecration.

The altar lamp gave off a sickly ocher light that flickered weakly onto the floor and walls. Mario walked down the aisle and shined the light into the altar lamp. A heavy black floss hung down from it, making it look almost genital. There was an odor of creosote.

In the apse the seismograph drum continued feebly to turn, though the paper had long come to an end, and the inked pen kept inscribing more lines on an already dense and unreadable black mess.

"*ANITA!*"he called.

An echo took up the name, transformed it, and sent it reverberating through the rafters.

—*ni-ta ni-ta . . . ni-ta . . .*

It was a slurred echo. Was it Mario's voice?

"*ANITA!*"

—*ni-ta . . . ni . . . ta . . .*

A lugubrious, doleful mockery of his call.

Mario walked past the seismograph. The sound recording system was weakly on, the battery light low and flickering.

The laser camera stood, leaning backward against a wall. Blue mold grew up its cables, glittering under Mario's flashlight beam.

. . . ni . . . ta . . . ni . . . ta . . .

An echo now without an initial sound? Or had he called again?

Mario swept the ceiling with the flashlight beam. Where the rainwater had broken through, the black floss hung down in clumps.

The flashlight beam struck the thermovision. A cross had been inscribed in its light coating of dust. Upside down.

Mario strode over the littered floor toward the thermovision camera. His boots crushed berrylike fruits and broken glass. A heavy, oily tar leaked from the broken fruits, and smelled of the creosote.

Quickly, he flicked on the thermovision. The batteries were still operative. The viewing lens showed the interior architecture, cold and stable, with convection currents of colder winds from outside.

When Mario flipped the toggle switch to *tape*, the attached video screen showed only the same dark, brooding interior. The tape was frozen at its last image, having run to the end of its spool. Mario switched the tape into reverse. A melange of varicolored images glittered on the screen.

Mario flicked the switch. The tape stopped.

A squealing sound caused Mario to play the flashlight beam around the church. On the altar linen, popping in and out of the flashlight beam, tiny mice ran in and out of the tabernacle.

"ANITA!"

Came the soft, diminuendo echo.

... ita ... ita ... whore ... whore ...

Mario's eyes gravitated to the thermovision. It was inching very slowly backward of its own volition, pushing different visualizations onto the screen.

Mario put his beam on the convex screen. The tape inched in reverse, toward a violent flux, and a slow flicker of maroon. Mario flicked off the flashlight. In the dark church the imagery came sharper, highly defined, unmistakable.

The coils of form resolved into an image: a shaggy beastlike form on a chair, head cocked, and a black crucifix across its knees.

Mario instantly punched the silver button, freezing the image.

"Oh, Jesus," he murmured, sitting very slowly, staring.

Mario played the videotape backward and forward. The images of the beast appeared for only a few frames, about as long as the cruciform shape had lasted.

The beast seemed cognizant, mocking, grinning insolently.

Mario abruptly left the church.

He slogged through the thistles blown against the church foundation, pushing toward the rectory.

On the rectory floor was Anita's sleeping bag. It was ripped by tiny claws, the stuffing floated through the kitchen, and bits of canvas were scattered over the table, sills, and chairs.

"ANITA!" Mario roared.

There was no answer. Only the smoke-filled wind. Mario stepped over broken branches at the rectory threshold and stomped into the kitchen. The Jesuit's mattress was a nest of small willow snakes, curled and snuggled into the molded canvas for warmth.

The aspergill, used to dash holy water from its vial, lay on the floor, broken by panicked feet. Everywhere the kitchen dishes, towels, and food packages had been tossed, as though someone had fled in hysteria through the rectory toward the waiting Oldsmobile.

When Mario looked out the kitchen window at the ruts and

ripped segments of underbrush left by the escaping Oldsmobile, he saw the vial of holy water, the vial of sacramental oil, and bits of the wooden container, scattered in the grass and mud.

Mario crossed through the rectory, back onto the south path of the church.

In the darkness, he saw the silhouettes of farmers dragging an object to a smoky pyre. It did not take long to realize what it was: a dead newborn calf, hideously deformed. With stern, passionless faces, the farmers heaved the mutant onto the fire and watched it burn. Several carried shotguns and looked anxiously over their shoulders.

As Mario passed the church windows, he saw the image of the beast, back-illuminated in the thermovision screen. By a trick of the angle it seemed to regard him as he walked.

Mario stumbled toward Canaan Street. A small fire burned there, too. A dead puppy was being carried by the legs up the street. The tavern owner heaved it with a gloved hand into the flames. Then Mario saw the dog in the firelight; its face was not a dog's face, but something bestial.

Anita stood with a cigarette in her fingers, watching Mario, at the door of the dilapidated billiard hall.

Mario stared at her, dumbfounded.

"Anita, what the hell's going on?"

Anita looked back at him with dark, hollow eyes, unwilling or unable to speak.

Mario crossed Canaan Street, past the flaming pyre. The rainwater dripped from his curled hair. The smoke particles had begrimed his face and the seams of the yellow raincoat.

"The priest is gone," she said slowly.

Mario blinked at her, face ruddy in the firelight.

"I *know* the priest is gone!" he shouted angrily. "His car is gone! The church is a mess! The cameras are covered with mold! What the hell happened?"

Anita's eyes gazed blankly back at him.

Mario studied her closely, realized how much she had changed. All her idealism seemed charred.

"Anita—" he said, still angry, but softer, "why did you let the equipment go to hell?"

"Because nothing on earth will make me go back into that church."

Mario, surprised at the metallic flatness of the voice, simply stared at her.

"Why?" he asked.

The shock of something vile registered in her face, unnerved him. All she did was turn slowly and go inside the billiard hall.

Mario followed her. It was deserted. Silent. Vague reddish light moved through the windows from the bonfires on Canaan Street. It smelled of damp, of dust, of the rotted beige curtains at the windows.

Anita's clothes and pieces of curtain for a bed lay now under steps that led into darkness. On the crumpled shirt used for a pillow glinted the black revolver.

"Speak to me, Anita," he whispered gently. "What's happened in Golgotha Falls?"

It was a naked, confused question. He sat down warily on the edge of the billiard table, eyes following her every motion.

"What happened to the altar light? What changed?"

Anita leaned against the steps. She watched him for a long time. In that brief period apart, they had both experienced events that now made them strangers.

Then, in a voice devoid of inflection, almost childlike, she spoke.

"It was the last night of the vigil. A terrible ordeal. I knelt with him. To give him encouragement. As he prayed, the church warmed. It was the soft, red glow from the altar lamp. We could see it with our eyes closed."

She paused, eyes wide, reliving each terrible moment that had followed.

"It was about dawn," she continued in the flat, hollow voice. "We had been through a lot together. He was in terrible mental pain."

Anita sank slowly onto a wooden box by the ancient Coke machine.

The shadows etched at her eyes, as though boring into her face. Mario pulled a string and a tiny electric bulb over the table flickered on. It made Anita's skin look strangely cadaverous.

"He grew delirious," she went on. "I tried to bring him out of it. Finally, he seemed to believe that everything had gone well. We prayed together."

Anita stood up from the Coke box and paced the area in front of the curtained windows.

"Then . . . something happened," she said in a broken voice. "Our affection—"

"*Affection?*"

"Turned to something else. He tried to make love to me."

Mario stared at her, incredulous.

"Eamon Malcolm? Christ, that confirms it all. Oh, Jesus."

Mario stood at the billiard table, nervously rattling the ceramic balls down the length of the green felt.

"He touched me. He put his hands under my blouse. We kissed."

Mario gazed at her, then savagely threw a handful of the balls clacking crazily over the table. He turned on her.

"Well, did you fuck?" he demanded.

She made no answer. He leaned, outraged, across the table.

"Well—?" he shouted.

"No. We didn't make love."

Mario struck at the leather cups under the pockets. The rotted material gave way. Several balls fell onto his boots. The others careened across the floor and into the far darkness. He rubbed his hands into his matted, curled hair.

Anita moved closer to him. She leaned forward. She took his shoulders and slowly turned him toward her. Gone was the flat, metallic voice and the hollow shell of a face. She was searching his face, demanding attention, warm and alive again.

"Something left him," she said softly.

"What? Besides his virginity?"

"Like a bird. Without wings. I felt it go out of him."

"I do not understand what you're saying."

Her slender, pale hands gently drew him back to her.

"It was his being, his self—his soul," she said. "Call it what you want. It went out of him and left him empty."

"Is that when the beast's image appeared?"

Anita drew back.

"Then you've seen it! Yes! It was at that very moment that the beast entered the church!"

Anita recalled the moment with a shudder. Father Malcolm's jaw had dropped, his eyes darkened in horror, and simultaneously she saw the cold, dark lamp over the altar. Something broke in him.

"Mario," she said slowly, "do you remember the studies of people dying? Witnesses at the instant of death often see something leave them, something wingless, formless, but perceptible."

"Eamon Malcolm is still alive."

"No. Partially, maybe. But not under his own will. Mario, he lost his soul."

"Since when do we believe in souls?"

The sarcasm had no effect on Anita. She drew back from him, as adamant as he. She leaned against the far wall and in a distant, cool voice said, "Your theory of psychic projection is wrong, Mario."

This was the confrontation. It was not just an alternate hypothesis. It was a refutation of Mario, his reliance on equipment, and his almost inhuman need to destroy in order to find. The storm had been brewing for a long time, and now it had come.

"What the hell are you talking about?" he demanded.

But Anita had the coolness of the days when he had first met her in the physics computer room. She was intuitive. There was a grace in her thinking, a reaching beyond the empirical, that put his teeth on edge. And now she was setting it, firmly and forever, between them.

"That cruciform image, Mario," she said, enunciating clearly. "It was no projection. It was a *presence*."

Mario felt his face go hot, in anger, in disbelief. Their break was complete. Very slowly he swung his legs while sitting on the green felt. He continued to look away from her, out the window at Canaan Street. He did not want her to see his face. For he felt an abyss of self-doubt opening in front of him.

"That bestial image," Anita said, increasingly assured, "is no projection either."

It felt like drowning on dry land. Mario flipped a cube of blue cue chalk against the far wall in feigned indifference. Since the campus rebellions had gone bust Mario had clung to science for refuge against his enormous insecurity. Subtly he had begun clinging to Anita. Golgotha Falls had split them like living wood from dead.

What could he make of the project without Anita? Was his own future, his own life, worth a damn at all anymore? The worst was the almost physical pressure of impending chaos already crowding his brain.

"What is it, then?" he asked casually.

"The Antichrist."

Mario picked up another cube of chalk and angrily threw it at the door. An infantile, monumental rage was building within him.

"Why, Anita?" he asked quietly. "Why the Antichrist? Why Golgotha Falls? There must be a thousand more important places than this scabrous hole."

"It's the priests, Mario. He feeds on the priests."

"Then he must be well fed by now," he said. "He's had three."

"They were only steppingstones. He wants more. I think he's after bigger game."

Mario could hardly credit what he was hearing.

"This is your idea of *science,* Anita?" he stuttered. "The Antichrist recruiting priests? Is that what you believe in now?"

"It's what animates the church."

Mario jumped to the floor. He pointed a trembling finger at her.

"Listen, I was in a lecture hall with over a hundred faculty and reporters when Eamon Malcolm projected onto all of us. Every foul, sick emotion he keeps bottled up in that God-fearing Christ-worshiping psyche of his. Nobody saw our slides! Nobody saw our tapes! It came out pornography!"

Anita stared at him in shock.

"A mass hallucination!" he shouted. "Naked bodies and a horse bashing some poor fucker to death! It was a complete debacle!"

Mario slumped on the table again, defeated.

"I felt like a tongue," he added softly. "A big, fat, bloated tongue. Somebody else was trying to speak through me. Somebody else was showering us with Freudian pictograms. They took me screaming from the auditorium, Anita. We're mud at Harvard. Dean Osborne has closed us down. Class, laboratory, project. Everything. One week to return the equipment."

Anita absorbed the news slowly. She came around the table to embrace him, but, ashamed, he moved away.

"The priest," Mario said slowly, "is a psychic killer. And I'm his target."

"You're wrong, Mario."

He looked at her pitifully.

"All the nights he spent in that vigil, Anita," he said, "all that holy praying and moaning and desiring your ass. That's the time he was transmitting, into me—and into that whole auditorium—"

Anita leaned against the Coke machine. In a strange way, it was a relief to have the project canceled.

"You're fishing," she said. "The priest is a victim. Like you. Like me. Like everybody in Golgotha Falls."

Mario paced, agitated and angry.

"That cruciform shape—that bestial shape—" he insisted "—are like the images that assaulted my lecture—those are Freudian dream images of his own sickness—"

"A shaggy, horned beast?" Anita countered. "Come off it, Mario! What does that represent?"

"His uncle. His own lust. Or the bishop. He was deeply dependent on the bishop. It's a malevolent metaphor of the bishop!"

"Why so malevolent?"

"HOW THE HELL SHOULD I KNOW? *HE'S* THE SICKIE! NOT ME!"

Mario slammed the cue rack in the corner with his boot, and it shattered into sharp pieces, disgorging rusty nails.

"Maybe he was pissed at the bishop. You know how it works in the unconscious. The psyche gets its revenge."

Mario tried to calm himself. Several times he turned to Anita. Each time she stood her ground, obdurately, unconvinced, staring back at him.

"Face it, Anita," he said unpleasantly. "You got pretty involved with Eamon Malcolm."

"He was screaming in agony. Of course I tried to help."

"That's not what I meant."

Mario sat near her on the closest edge of the table.

"He was a father figure to you, Anita," he said coolly. "Your own father died in an airplane crash before you even reached puberty. Add to that remnants of guilt, living freely with me. You needed a safe harbor to work out your own Oedipal problems. That's why he is charismatic to you. That's why you adopted his mythology."

Anita folded her arms and turned away from him.

"It's so easy, isn't it?" she said. "Sooner or later, everything gets back to sex."

"That's where idealization starts. For you and for him."

She shook her head very slowly.

"I don't know what's made you like that, Mario. Freud has his place in our science. Instruments have their place. But Freud and instruments lead into a blind alley if you don't keep your options open."

"The priest has seduced you, Anita. He's fucked your head if not your body."

Anita retreated under the vulgarity.

"To be a real scientist, Mario, you have to be more than a technician. You have to know when to trust yourself, when to leap beyond the instruments and grasp intuitively at the phenomena. And I know what I've experienced and I know it's real."

Mario ignored her. He became very nervous, rubbing his hands. Anita saw that she had already slipped from his consciousness.

"Otherwise it looks like science, Mario," she continued. "But it isn't."

Mario, stung, turned to look at her.

"What is it?" he asked.

"A vendetta of some kind, masquerading as science."

For a long time they looked into each other's eyes, as though they had passed from lovers to enemies by some unknowable alchemy. Mario turned away and peeked out the window at the dying embers of Canaan Street.

"What are you going to do?" she asked.

"Fix the cameras. Keep going. There's nothing else I can do."

"Without the priest?"

"He'll come back," Mario murmured. "He's got to. I've got one week to replicate the evidence on those tapes."

"If there is a God," Anita said softly, "He won't let Eamon Malcolm come back."

Mario picked up his leather jacket from the table. He looked at Anita.

She had one of the most analytical minds he had ever known. Now she had tumbled into the mythology of a schizophrenic priest. Suggestion? Physical attraction? What did they share? What had really happened at Friday sunrise?

Why did Anita stay at Golgotha Falls if she was afraid of the church? Was she waiting for Eamon Malcolm?

Mario zipped his jacket.

When he stepped out into Canaan Street, the vapor, struck by the moon, floated like translucent fingers down the sidewalks. Ahead, on the ridges, the rain squalls were blowing inward, sending long and lacy fingers of wet fog down over the tombstones.

Mario stepped into the church. The beast's image flickered vaguely in the thermovision screen, lord of all it surveyed. Overhead the altar lamp glowed pallidly.

He cleaned two sensors with a chamois and inserted them into the altar lamp. He adjusted the threshold of the sound system: small, high-frequency sibilant sounds were passing through the church.

. . . ni . . . ta . . . ni . . . ta . . .

Mario seized the earphones. The echoes were being recorded. And he had the beast's image. Could it convince Osborne?

No. It wouldn't. Who was to say how Mario had produced the tapes? Mario needed to correlate the formation of images and echoes with violent physical and emotional changes in the priest. The evidence had to be that tight.

A wave of depression surged through him. What if the Jesuit did not come back? Eamon Malcolm was spewing out visions from the raw libido itself, but Mario needed skin receptors, sensors braided into the man's hair across the temples, body thermometers. It had to be correlated. Osborne would accept nothing less.

It was vaguely like the campus unrest. As the risks increased, so did Mario's determination. He would get those images, though he destroy the priest in the process.

And, just as in the days of unrest, the awful specter of utter failure swam all about him.

What the hell did Osborne—or any authority—need from him? His guts? Served on a silver platter? Here. Take it. It's my body, my soul, everything I'm made of. Now, is it acceptable? Can I keep my laboratory?

Mario spat angrily on the floor.

What if he brought Osborne the trussed and wriggling form of Christ? What would the granite old New Englander say? He doesn't belong in my kind of science. Get Him out of my office. Crucify Him again!

Mario laughed out loud, a bitter laugh, with tears of rage in his eyes.

C-crucify Him . . . C-crucify Him . . . C-crucify Him . . .

The blasphemy died among the dark corners of the church.

Mario's bitter smile faded with an infinite slowness.

He had said nothing out loud.

C-crucify . . . C-crucify . . . C-crucify . . .

The echo persisted deep down at the threshold of human hearing, a hissing threnody, steady and aggressive, like insects in a summer field.

Mario put down the earphones and stared, transfixed, at the beast's image grinning back to him.

What had Anita said?

"He feeds on priests."

A terrible uncertainty swept through Mario. Could his theory be rubbish?

"He's after bigger game."

Mario stood up defiantly.

"What bigger game?" he shouted aloud, derisively, defensively at the image. "The fucking bishop? Pope Francis Xavier?"

Mario chortled nastily, but the terrible chill of the church invaded him and robbed him of confidence.

"Jesus Christ Himself?" Mario yelled.

. . . Christ . . . Ch . . . rist . . . ist . . . st . . . t . . .

C H A P T E R
F O U R T E E N

BISHOP LYONS sat in an oakwood chair, in the bishop's miter, head slightly cocked, and a long crucifix over his knees.

He was in the grip of a déjà vu. In his own antechamber, he felt suddenly like a figure in a dream. His palms grew moist. A kind of invisible light, a resistant yet immaterial force, attended the motions of his hands and feet.

It had stalked him since the morning, and now it surrounded and observed him.

The bishop calmed himself. Suddenly, bustling figures came through the corridors.

"His Eminence has arrived," whispered a Franciscan.

Bishop Lyons looked up, still pale.

"Cardinal Bellocchi? The Nuncio?" he murmured.

"The delegation has received him at the door."

Bishop Lyons sighed and rose from the scrolled, massive chair. The psychic disturbances were gone. He surveyed the corridors full of priests, the Jesuit secretaries and the Franciscans, the many antique desks with ornate telephones, the dossiers with gilded bindings; and the power of his high office reassured him.

"Are you not well?" asked the Franciscan, guiding the bishop's elbow.

"It's just the excitement of the moment."

Bishop Lyons then led a trio of Franciscans down the carpeted corridors past floral arrangements and under brilliant chandeliers to the massive oak doors.

The bishop paused. The Nuncio was an unknown quantity to him. Aptly named, Bellocchi was both eyes and ears for His Holiness, ferreting out the characters of men for the Quebec conclave. The Nuncio was an old warhorse of the Roman *curia,* but he was also deeply enamored of Francis Xavier. And lately, Francis Xavier had sent him on curious missions.

When the bishop stepped onto the flagstone of the porch, arms extended in brotherly greeting, a radiance of azure skies and brilliant autumn leaves momentarily blinded him. The Nuncio, troubleshooter to North America, papal delegate to Quebec, was a short, swarthy man, resplendent in crimson robe, crimson slippers, and crimson skullcap. The October sunlight exploded over the heavy pectoral cross.

"It is our great honor to welcome you in Christ's name," Bishop Lyons said grandly, kissing the Nuncio's ring.

"In Christ's name," the Nuncio answered, smiling.

Trailing robes, the two men ascended the stone steps toward the oak doors held open by awed Franciscans.

"Was your flight difficult?" asked the bishop, extending a hand, a gesture for the Nuncio to enter the episcopal residence.

"I slept badly," Cardinal Bellocchi said, examining the chandeliers and walnut crossbeams of the ceiling.

"Indeed?"

Cardinal Bellocchi turned to the bishop and smiled.

"I dreamed I was a soldier," he said, gold-tipped teeth glinting, surveying the bishop astutely. "Carrying out a secret mission."

"A secret mission, Your Eminence?"

"Yes. And I did not know what it was."

The Italian accent was melodious, faintly scholarly. Bishop Lyons extended his hand toward the corridor that led to the garden and the luncheon; the Nuncio followed, robes sweeping audibly over the carpets.

The Nuncio spoke by indirection, by subtle metaphor, probing and measuring the man in front of him. Bishop Lyons felt uneasy, since he himself was a practical man, a man of well-kept accounts, obedient councilors, and a smooth-running board of diocesan administrators.

As they walked past the stained-glass windows, the standing priests, a coterie of blushing nuns from the kitchen staff, an aura of pomp radiated from Cardinal Bellocchi, transforming the residence into something suddenly almost palatial.

Flowers everywhere decorated the courtyard. Huge glass bowls of imported fruits sat on white-linen-covered tables. The sunlight sent crinkles of light in ovals through the crystal tableware, and black-cassocked priests, bustling among the water pitchers and napkins, ceased when the cardinal stepped down onto the stone of the court-yard.

"I hope Your Eminence will take pleasure in our modest luncheon," Bishop Lyons said, gesturing toward a single table with two chairs softened by mauve appliqué pillows.

The Nuncio sat slowly, using his hands to move the robe, the chair itself handled behind him by a priest.

"An army travels on its stomach," Cardinal Bellocchi said, admiring the glittering china and crystal place settings, "and so does the Vatican."

Bishop Lyons sat opposite the cardinal. The adjacent tables filled with the bishop's assistants and the cardinal's delegation, many of whom did not speak English but merely smiled at their hosts. Light conversation rose among the flowers as the first of the many decanters of wine was poured. The bishop admired the suave ease with which the Nuncio handled himself. The kind of Vatican functions and state dinners to which the Italian must be privy made the bishop envious.

The Nuncio was studying the bishop closely.

"How goes Christ's work?" Cardinal Bellocchi asked.

"I believe our records are in excellent order, Your Eminence, and are ready for examination."

"You mean, the archdiocese is efficiently administered?"

Bishop Lyons beamed, but tried to remain modest.

"It is a well-oiled machine," he replied. "If I may be permitted that expression."

The Nuncio abruptly dipped his spoon into the asparagus soup and then slurped it noisily.

"That's it?" he asked. "A well-oiled machine?"

Bishop Lyons felt a hot flush crawling up his neck and into his face. He was aware the conversation at the nearest table had stopped. An unreasonable panic threatened.

"Surely that is the function of administration," the bishop protested.

The Nuncio grunted, allowed a priest to remove the soup bowl, and dried his lips with the linen napkin.

Over the courtyard, the autumn birds hopped among the black branches, flashes of green and indigo feathers through the dry yellow leaves and rustling twigs.

Cardinal Bellocchi grinned.

"Do you see the bird with the green throat?" he asked, pointing to the oak tree over the courtyard wall.

Bishop Lyons turned with difficulty and strained his neck, looking.

"Yes, Your Eminence."

"Look how busy he is. So full of anxiety. He hops around as though the Evil One is watching him."

Bishop Lyons looked into the brilliant leaves, confused. When he looked back at the Nuncio, the Italian's dark and piercing eyes were trained on him. Somehow, the bishop understood that he was already a known quantity to Cardinal Bellocchi.

"In such a manner have you been busy," Cardinal Bellocchi observed. "Preparing your records for me."

Bishop Lyons managed a smile. "Certainly, I have not been observed by the Evil One," he replied.

The Nuncio said nothing. The main course was set before them, beef in wine sauce and artichokes in seasoned butter. Behind the Nuncio, animated conversations had broken out among the Italians and the bishop's Jesuits and Franciscans. A flash of blue shot through the leaves overhead, two birds tumbling in mutual flight. Cardinal Bellocchi watched, delighted.

"Have you ever seen birds take flight, either in joy or out of a sense of danger?" he asked.

"Many times."

"Sometimes hundreds and hundreds of birds, in a single instant, less than a second even, will rise like a cloud toward the sun. It is like a burst. Suddenly, they are in the air, disciplined and in formation."

"It is a marvel of nature," the bishop agreed.

"How do you think they communicate with one another so fast? How does the leader express his perception of danger?" the Nuncio asked. "Is it telepathy?"

"I hardly think so."

The main course dishes were cleared away. It had grown slightly chilly despite the brilliance of the sunshine.

"You do not believe in telepathy?" the Nuncio inquired.

"No."

"His Holiness does."

Bishop Lyons's smile faded instantly.

"Our Holy Father is a great fancier of birds," the Nuncio continued, "as is well known. He has formed theories as to their behavior." The Nuncio drank water from a crystal glass. "Of course, doctrinally, there is no authority for believing in telepathy."

"None."

"Nevertheless, Francis Xavier has experienced it during his priesthood."

"I was not aware of that, Your Eminence."

"His Holiness is a Sicilian," the Nuncio said, smiling, "once the peasant Baldoni. And in Sicily, faith is like a hot breeze in the vineyards. Men live in it, move against it, all the days of their lives."

"But, of course—"

"The Second Incarnation of Jesus Christ is no fairy tale to such men," Cardinal Bellocchi interrupted. "They listen. They look for signs."

A long silence went by.

"Such men move in passionate faith," Cardinal Bellocchi continued. "Such men are vulnerable targets."

"Targets?" Bishop Lyons asked. "Of whom?"

Cardinal Bellocchi's dark eyes became even darker.

"Of ancient enemies," he said, rising.

Instantly, both delegations were on their feet. Bishop Lyons led Cardinal Bellocchi back into the soft, brown corridors, where skylights overhead threw rectangular brilliances at their feet. Far ahead, the bishop heard his staff preparing the conference room, laying dossiers in place, pouring water into glasses, and arranging the walnut chairs around the long table.

"The Vatican is making preparations," confided the Nuncio.

"Preparations?"

"For an Ecumenical Council. On the subject of the Second Incarnation."

Bishop Lyons was so shocked he nearly stopped. Cardinal Bellocchi inserted his hand into the crook of the bishop's elbow and kept him walking smoothly.

That the papal troubleshooter should confide one of the great political secrets of the Vatican sent the bishop's mind whirling. Was the Nuncio an opponent of Francis Xavier? Had he perceived in the bishop of Boston a pragmatic ally?

"If I could only tell you," Cardinal Bellocchi whispered, "what has been going on the last few weeks inside the Vatican."

Bishop Lyons, still stunned by the news, only shook his head. Once an Ecumenical Council was opened, there was no control over events, doctrinally or structurally.

"Is such a thing wise?" Bishop Lyons stammered. "Even politically? How much support can His Holiness have?"

"All the support he needs," Cardinal Bellocchi said with a dry bitterness. "The Holy Ghost."

Impending political battles rose into the bishop's mind. All the connections to North American bishops and cardinals revolved among his calculations.

The déjà vu returned.

Bishop Lyons grew visibly pale, felt himself a vague and dream-like figure in a powerful dream. Several Franciscans in the corridors noticed the whitening of his face, the darting, frightened eyes. The bishop stumbled.

Suddenly, the déjà vu, the disorientation, became palpable as a shadow leaped from a darkened side corridor.

Bishop Lyons whirled in confusion as a priest's figure crashed into the entourage and sank to his knees clutching at the crimson robes of Cardinal Bellocchi.

Cardinal Bellocchi, stammering in confusion, tried to raise the distraught priest to his feet. But Father Malcolm only sank lower, burying his face in the crimson hem, as though trying to find a hiding place among the holy men.

"In Christ's name, protect me!" Father Malcolm cried out.

"But, of course, my son—"

"The church—my church—is defiled through my body!"

203

Uncomprehending, Cardinal Bellocchi placed his ringed finger against the Jesuit's cheek, which felt alternately fevered and chilled.

"*Christ has been defeated!*" Father Malcolm shouted to Cardinal Bellocchi. "*Through me!*"

Cardinal Bellocchi paled but did not retreat. Several Franciscans crossed themselves. The turmoil was so acute that three Jesuits moved to carry the lunatic away but were resisted by the Franciscans.

"Such a thing is not possible!" yelled a young Franciscan angrily.

"The lamp lit by Christ reeks of corruption!" Father Malcolm retorted, rising and finding himself tangled in protective arms and cassocks.

"The image of the goathead dominates the church and mocks us all!" Father Malcolm shouted.

Bishop Lyons's angry hand whirled Father Malcolm around. "What image?" he demanded, the veins of his face extended in anger.

Father Malcolm gazed at the bishop with a peculiar mixture of savage anger and helpless pleading.

"The image of Him who now dominates the church! Because of you! I needed help! And you wouldn't give it to me!"

Bishop Lyons, paralyzed by the effrontery, flushed deeply red, pushed very close to Father Malcolm, whispering.

"Do you even know where you are now, Eamon Malcolm?" he rasped. "Do you realize that this is Cardinal Bellocchi, the papal Nuncio?"

Father Malcolm defiantly threw off the bishop's hands. He pointed an accusing finger at the bishop.

"*The stigmata of the Antichrist,*" he said with a horrified conviction, "*flourish in the church you ignored!*"

Bishop Lyons, taken aback by the vehemence of the denunciation, humiliated in front of the Nuncio, then did a very curious thing. He looked down one darkened corridor and then, craning his neck, looked down the other, as if in fear of being secretly observed.

Cardinal Bellocchi stepped firmly in front of Father Malcolm and held high the glittering pectoral cross from his own robes.

"Do you affirm that Jesus Christ is the true Son of Our Lord God and that Francis Xavier is His vicar on earth?"

Father Malcolm pulled away, back into the restraining arms.

"I cannot affirm," he muttered weakly. "He has taken my soul away."

"And yet you have escaped to holy men," observed the cardinal.

"To warn you all," Father Malcolm said, rising, *"Christ has been evicted from Golgotha Falls!"*

Several Franciscans held their hands over their ears against the blasphemy.

"Affirm," ordered Cardinal Bellocchi, pushing the crucifix up to Father Malcolm's face.

"I affirm," he said hoarsely, both dominated and mesmerized by the gold, glinting sculpture of Christ in His agony.

"Kiss in obedience," Cardinal Bellocchi said.

The Franciscans wrestled Father Malcolm toward the heavy sculpted cross on a gold chain. Father Malcolm seemed to turn his head slightly away, then slowly his pursed lips touched the cool gold. Tears ran freely, abruptly, down his cheeks.

"I have been running from Satan," Father Malcolm wept, "since dawn."

"Let Christ now be your refuge."

Disoriented, Father Malcolm found himself looking on the shocked and curious faces. Then he was stumbling down corridors, past floral arrangements and stained-glass windows. Though his feet functioned, two Franciscans escorted him under both arms into the depths of the episcopal residence. At the threshold of the bishop's chapel, in the incense and soft candle glow near the confessional booth, he fainted into the arms of the two Franciscans.

In the corridor, profoundly shocked, Cardinal Bellocchi stood with the bishop.

"Where is this church?" the Nuncio demanded.

"North of here, in the town of Golgotha Falls. It has ceased to function these many years due to a dwindling parish and . . ."

Cardinal Bellocchi's eyes narrowed. "And . . ."

"And a terrible tragedy that befell the original priest, Father Bernard Lovell."

"I will want to know all the details of this tragedy," the Nuncio said.

"Yes, Your Eminence. The records have been kept."

Cardinal Bellocchi gazed dolefully down the corridor, along the path of the departed Jesuit.

"This is an excellent young man," the Nuncio continued. "Why did you send him alone to danger?"

"He seemed to strong," the bishop apologized. "His faith was so very passionate."

The Nuncio glared at him.

"Of course," he said savagely. "Such men are the most vulnerable targets."

Bishop Lyons swallowed heavily under the Nuncio's rebuke. "I shall close the church immediately," he promised. "And the Jesuit will confess and be absolved. Indeed, I shall have him guarded for his own safety in the seminary."

The Nuncio eyed the bishop with great disappointment.

"Your well-oiled machine," he said sternly, "was your own fantasy!"

After the conference, preparing the agenda for the Quebec pastoral visit in the next week, the Nuncio left for a meeting of lay Catholics in Baltimore. Bishop Lyons retained the extraordinary impression of being simultaneously the cardinal's political ally and his spiritual enemy.

Disturbed, the bishop went to the chapel. There he was told that the Jesuit had collapsed prior to confession and had been taken to the seminary dormitory where he was asleep.

That evening, Bishop Lyons dined alone, served by a silent valet.

The archives of the diocese were closed to everyone except the episcopal authority and several secretaries of the staff. In the green metal filing bins and wooden boxes were correspondence and edicts since 1745. It was a long, drafty chamber under the residence, lit now with hanging electric bulbs, like a morgue. In those archives, Bishop Lyons had once searched for and found the file of the psychopathic priest Bernard K. Lovell.

Lovell was a graceless, poorly educated, crippled boy, son of a barrel-maker and undistinguished by scholarly ambition. The correspondence revealed a mediocre personality fueled by bitterness, not love or a sense of mission.

The archives concealed poorly the abject complicity of the diocese: The abnormal Lovell had been left to die in sin, and the church at Golgotha Falls left to disintegrate, until even the financial records grew scanty.

Why? Because in the dioceses of the Roman Catholic Church existed hundreds, if not thousands, of derelict churches. Unfunded, unsupervised, they were breeding grounds of delusion and blasphemy. There the gullible faithful manufactured images of their own despair and guilt and foisted them on parishioners or, failing that, onto their own frightened imaginations. Golgotha Falls was no different, thought Bishop Lyons.

Except that Bernard Lovell, in his last coherent letter, had used the same phrase as Eamon Malcolm: *Christ was defeated at Golgotha Falls.*

It was not ecclesiastically possible.

Bishop Lyons took a chicken fragment from between his teeth. The archives did report several odd occurrences around the parishes in February 1914. Certain cases of hysteria. Questionable signs of the Second Coming. Rather like those Eamon Malcolm had spoken of.

The case of James Farrell Malcolm made no sense at all. A white-haired Renaissance scholar, connected through his mother's side to several judges and well-placed attorneys, the old man had been a favorite of the Boston literati. His *bon mots* were widely quoted and his expertise on Titian made him one of the board members of the Boston Museum of Art.

The bishop's acute memory plucked out the last letter ever received from James Farrell Malcolm.

> I shall go to the Church of Eternal Sorrows, alone but for Him who always abides with me, and there I shall in nightly vigil and prayer, by the strength of Him who is the source of all our hopes of the Resurrection, give the lie to him who proclaimed that *Christ was defeated at Golgotha Falls.*

That was the hook. Trial of faith. A temptation for every ordained man. Including the Pope, Francis Xavier. How else explain Francis Xavier's famous vigils in the caves of Sicily? But for every saint who comes through confirmed in his faith, hundreds of human wrecks, like Eamon Malcolm, are scattered in confusion and terror.

Was that the ambiguous message of Cardinal Bellocchi? That spiritually they must further His Holiness's predilection toward the mystic, but that politically they must guard and even resist him?

The bishop happily had it figured out at last.

"Bring me writing materials," he instructed his valet. "I wish to prepare two edicts this evening."

Surprised, the valet nevertheless set out blotter, pen, and stationery on the antique desk in the bedchamber.

Two instructions would go immediately, even at this late hour, to the administrative council of the archdiocese: The Church of Eternal Sorrows was to be cut off from the living Church of Rome so that no priest would serve there again.

"We have lost three priests to that nest of snakes," he muttered.

The second instruction was more detailed, and written in a less exalted form: The Church of Eternal Sorrows, being consigned as no-longer-sanctified real estate, would be sold on the open market.

Satisfied with his edicts, Bishop Lyons retired to his evening bath, lowering himself into a steaming tub. The suds filled the porcelain over his body. The tiles dripped with moisture, and so did the copper piping on the walls. Frost formed at the dark windows, making engaging shapes.

"See if the Jesuit has made his confession," the bishop called to his valet.

The valet nodded and pattered out into the corridor.

The Church of Eternal Sorrows would fetch little, Bishop Lyons reflected. It was a depressed market. Perhaps a summer theater group would find the space attractive.

Suddenly, the bishop had an intuition that the church should be razed and the real estate be the sole item for sale. Intuition became conviction and he rose to amend the instructions of sale.

Slipping on his red quilted robe, he felt the déjà vu returned. The Eamon Malcolm affair had assaulted his sensibilities, nearly destroyed his reputation in front of the Nuncio, and now caused a painful ringing in his ears.

Violent chills shuddered through his body. He looked down on his edicts, so carefully composed. His eyes bulged and a sound of profound terror exploded from him. The writing on the edicts was his own, but the sentences now proclaimed a foul and disgusting doggerel poetry in praise of animal husbandry.

Bishop Lyons looked up at the dark window. A shaggy goathead grinned and slowly, very slowly, a bloodlike substance burst from its head and flowed down its shaggy chops.

"G-G-God—!" he screamed.

The bishop choked, his back arched, and suddenly, at the rear and top of his head, he felt the vessels blind him with white pain and the blood, broken free, flowed into his brain with a paralyzing pressure.

Bishop Lyons writhed on the floor, heels dug into the carpet.

The needles of frost penetrated his breathing functions, sadistic and sharp. The lights flared around the frosted window. The bishop raised himself to an elbow.

Take the sacrament, slave of God! he heard in the resonant echo of his own damaged cranial cavity.

The valet ran in, horrified. He knew immediately it must be a stroke, but like none other he had ever witnessed. He put his ear to the bishop's mouth. From the bishop's tortured, urgent throat came the grunt of a lusty animal.

"*Bahhhhhh!*" the bishop bleated. "*Baa-ahhhh!*"

CHAPTER FIFTEEN

THE SICKLY yellow frost, illumined by the moon, shone into the dormitory of the cathedral seminary.

Long shadows flowed from the silhouette sitting beside the window. It was cold when Father Malcolm regained consciousness. As he pulled himself to an elbow, the silhouette stirred.

"Where am I?" he said hoarsely.

"In the bishop's dormitory," said a gentle voice. "You fainted before you could give confession."

Father Malcolm sat at the edge of the lower cot of a bunkbed. Several other bunkbeds lined the walls. At the end of the room was a tiny kitchen range and over it a crucifix.

"Could I have something to drink?" Father Malcolm said, rubbing his neck.

The silhouette at the window, a Franciscan, shuffled toward the kitchen range and boiled water.

The globe of the moon hung motionless when the clouds passed. Father Malcolm leaned against the bunkbed post.

"What time is it?" he asked.

"It is two o'clock in the morning," said the Franciscan, bringing him tea.

The steaming cup was under his nose. Looking up, he saw the priest's solicitous curiosity. Father Malcolm nodded his thanks, took the cup in both hands, and sipped. It burned sweetly down into him, bringing life.

The Franciscan shuffled his chair closer, his cheek illumined by the shaft from the frosted window. His brown eyes continued to bend over him in extreme curiosity.

"What is it like?" he whispered. "To lose one's soul?"

Father Malcolm felt the coldness of the night drain back into him. He drank more tea. Then he held the cup in both hands, staring at the oblique moonlight on the hardwood floor.

"You live in a vacuum," Father Malcolm replied bitterly. "And you have no will."

"No will?"

Father Malcolm shook his head.

"You are anybody's slave. You fear it. You flee it. You beg for Christ. But there is no Christ. Not inside. Not anymore."

Father Malcolm recalled his vigil in the Church of Eternal Sorrows. There had been a premonition, then recognition. He had turned from Anita and the vileness of his own vanity and confusion. He saw the altar lamp, dead and cold. In that one split second, he had called, not on Christ, but on the bishop, in rage. But neither bishop nor Christ had prevented him from rushing out into the cool dawn air, an empty shell, a marionette, fleeing a new Master.

Father Malcolm buried his head in his hands. The first time, at the exorcism, when he felt drowning in fever and hallucination, he had impulsively, naturally, and with all his power called on Christ. It was almost a bodily tension and release. But, in the aftermath of the vigil, he had cursed the bishop, a father figure who had rebuffed him.

Father Malcolm moaned in his own depravity.

The Franciscan tugged at his sleeve. "Did you see *him*?" he asked urgently.

211

"Who?"

"He who opposes the Lord Jesus Christ."

Father Malcolm tipped the cup to his lips though the tea was gone. He felt ravenously hungry. Hungry for warmth, for the semblance of normality.

"I saw his face in every man I passed," Father Malcolm said, shuddering. "And in every town I drove through."

The Franciscan, fascinated, leaned toward him.

"What did he look like, Father?" he asked, trembling in eagerness.

"Like you and like me."

The Franciscan stared at Father Malcolm. "Explain yourself, Father."

"In every face, I saw the evil of greed, ambition, and hypocrisy. I saw that the towns were filled by those who served evil. Behind the eyes of total strangers, I knew who it was looking back at me and grinning."

"But you fled him," the Franciscan said. "You're safe here."

"Am I?"

The Franciscan frowned, then smiled softly, leaned forward, and tapped Father Malcolm's knee casually, intimately.

"Now, when you ran into the residence, and you saw the bishop, did you not see a sanctified face?"

"On the contrary. I perceived duplicity and a hard heart."

The Franciscan drew back, discomfited.

"And what did you think of Cardinal Bellocchi?" he asked testily.

"I was so very disoriented, brother. I hardly recall."

"But surely you have some impression."

"A good man. A hard man. But Christ dwells within him."

The Franciscan relaxed. Father Malcolm shivered violently and pulled a thick, dark blanket over his shoulders.

"In any case," he said, sadly, "the bishop has received his reward."

The Franciscan looked at him blankly.

"What do you mean, Father Malcolm?"

Father Malcolm stared at him, confused. "Isn't it obvious?" he said. "The poor man is close to death."

"As far as I know, Bishop Lyons is in excellent health. In fact, he sent his valet to inquire about you only a few hours ago."

Father Malcolm rubbed his forehead. Disoriented, he then held on to the bunkbed post for support.

"I don't know why I said that," he confessed. "Sometimes ideas come. I don't know from where."

"Well, you were angry at the bishop," surmised the Franciscan.

Father Malcolm closed his eyes.

"I was. I confess it. He let me suffer alone."

"You must confess these angers, Father Malcolm," said the Franciscan in a drier, more efficient tone of voice. "These and all your experiences of the last week."

"Why?"

The Franciscan was bringing a battered night table across the floor. When he set it down in front of Father Malcolm, he opened the drawers and set writing materials on it: ink bottle, fountain pen, green felt blotter, and lovely beige stationery.

"What is this?" Father Malcolm demanded, drawing back.

"Cardinal Bellocchi has instructed that you make a good confession."

"I thought Cardinal Bellocchi had left."

"He will be in Baltimore until the morning. Your confession will be hand-delivered to him."

"But why?"

"Because, as you observed, Christ dwells within him."

Father Malcolm licked his bruised lips. The stationery seemed to glow in the long shafts of the yellow-white moon-glow. The fountain pen glinted. He adjusted the woolen blanket over his shoulders.

"This is irregular," Father Malcolm protested.

"On the contrary," said the Franciscan, "it will be taken by His Eminence directly to the Sacred Apostolic Penitentiary at the Vatican."

Father Malcolm looked up, shocked.

"To Rome? When?"

"Late tomorrow. And that holy tribunal, within its competence, will adjudicate your penance."

Father Malcolm's heart began racing. Despite the chill in the poorly heated dormitory, beads of perspiration broke out on his forehead.

"My penance?" he whispered slowly.

"Let us pray it will not be harsh," said the Franciscan encouragingly. "But it will bring you absolution."

A long silence reigned in the dormitory. Vague and distant clatter of pots and pans from the kitchen came up the corridors, and with it a faint smell of cabbage and soap suds.

Father Malcolm leaned forward, abruptly knocking over the ink bottle.

213

Instantly, the Franciscan was at the table, blotting up the station-ery. From the drawer, he produced a packet of clean paper. He filled the fountain pen, tested it, and handed it to Father Malcolm.

"Write with a contrite heart, Father Malcolm."

Disoriented, Father Malcolm felt the weight of the pen in his fingers. Rome. It gave him courage.

Father Malcolm began.

> In search to perfect myself and restore a defiled church unto our Lord Jesus Christ, I, Father Eamon James Malcolm, of the Society of Jesus, in the archdiocese of Boston, Massachusetts, traveled alone to the Church of Eternal Sorrows at Golgotha Falls.

Father Malcolm felt his teeth chattering. The Franciscan dragged a portable electric heater to his legs. The confession, once begun, developed a peculiar momentum of its own.

It could take hours. Father Malcolm looked up. The Franciscan had infinite patience. He would accompany him all night, if necessary.

Then Father Malcolm had the unmistakable impression that he was not so much protecting him from the exterior world as keeping guard over him like a prisoner.

The guilt of failure rose in his throat like black bile.

The stationery gleamed, though the moon had passed beyond the frame of the window. Father Malcolm reviewed his own handwriting.

> In search to defile myself and wrest an abandoned church from the Lord Jesus Christ, I, Father Eamon James Malcolm, of the Society of Jesus, in the archdiocese of Boston, Massachusetts, traveled alone to the Church of Eternal Sorrows at Golgotha Falls.

Father Malcolm dropped the fountain pen.

"I feel ill," he said hoarsely.

He tried to rise, but the massive hand of the Franciscan pushed him down.

"Continue, Father. And leave nothing out."

Father Malcolm held the sheet of paper, trembling, to the shadowed Franciscan.

"I beg you," he whispered. "Read it."

"We cannot. It is strictly confidential. No one will read it until it arrives at the Vatican."

"But in Christ's name . . . I beg you—"

"Continue, Father," he said sternly. "Though it be painful. The tribunal will interpret it."

Father Malcolm's trembling hand hovered over the stationery. He continued in a seizure of fear, staring at his own moving hand.

> Under authority of the bishop, following the canon and codes of Church rites, I successfully exorcised the Church of Eternal Sorrows and returned it unto Christ.

Father Malcolm sank, eyes closed, against the bedpost. The strain of coherent thought was pulling him apart. Resistance rose everywhere within.

Hesitantly, from the oblique angle, Father Malcolm squinted down at the desk.

> Under authority of the goathead, mimicking the canon and codes of Church rites, I successfully exorcised the Church of Eternal Sorrows from Christ.

A broken, bitter exclamation burst from Eamon Malcolm's bleeding lips.

"Read it!" he shouted, flourishing the paper.

But the Franciscan merely returned the paper and Father Malcolm's hand to the table top. peering into the Jesuit's whitened face.

"Your lips," the Franciscan murmured. "You've bitten them."

Suddenly, Father Malcolm felt the hot blood there. He instantly daubed his lips with a white handkerchief.

"Continue your entire confession," ordered the Franciscan slowly. Then added, "Father."

> And I was rewarded by the signal of His holy presence twofold: by the miraculous lighting of the altar lamp, from no man's hand, and by the miraculous image of His Holy Sorrow on the cross beside the altar.

215

Father Malcolm felt only a cool chill within his limbs as he wrote. His intellect perceived acutely the formation of letters, words, and punctuation. His senses felt caught in a black net. For what he thought and executed in fact did not appear consistent with what he viewed on the paper.

The disorientation was formidable: Which was real, what he wrote or what he thought he read?

Worse: The ordained brother of Christ was unable to help him in any way.

A broken, hoarse laughter, of despairing helplessness and fear, erupted from his mouth as he read:

> And I was rewarded by the signal of his presence twofold: by the obscene mimicry of the altar lamp, lit by no man's hand, and by the sadistic pornography of Christ's writhing death on the cross beside the altar.

The confession continued. It took seven pages. Exhausted, he signaled that it was over. The Franciscan instantly sealed the seven pages into a heavy envelope.

"Good. The bishop will be pleased," said the Franciscan.

"Will he?" Father Malcolm stammered, confused. "Perhaps, if he recovers."

The Franciscan frowned. "That is the second time you have said that."

"Is it?"

The Franciscan pressed a small bell. Footsteps were shortly heard rustling up the corridor. The Franciscan unbolted and unlocked the door.

"Will you go and inquire after the bishop's health?" he whispered to the light-filled crack in the door.

"At this hour?" came the surprised reply.

"As fast as you can, brother."

Father Malcolm watched the door close. Dread and anxiety assailed him. Ahead of him, on the table, the Franciscan was pressing a facsimile of the bishop's seal into red wax on the heavy envelope.

The envelope seemed charged with a subtle life of its own.

Father Malcolm slumped wearily. "I feel as though that confession were written by the very author of sin himself."

"Indeed. It often seems that way."

Father Malcolm felt the hot liquid at his lips. As he daubed away the blood in the dark, he felt the Franciscan watching him closely.

"May I wash myself in the lavatory?" he asked weakly.

"Certainly."

The Franciscan opened the door. Father Malcolm stepped into the tiled corridor. Far away, other corridors led to the exit of the seminary. The Franciscan pulled him in the other direction. Nodding asleep on a chair against the wall was a priest in simple black cassock. Father Malcolm did not remember the corridors of his own seminary being guarded in such a fashion.

The priest jerked awake with a sheepish smile. He nodded at the Franciscan.

Father Malcolm walked into the lavatory. The bright gleaming tiles brilliantly reflected the fluorescent tubes overhead. As he washed his face in refreshing cold water at the porcelain basin, the priest and the Franciscan guarded him at the door.

"It will soon be dawn," said the priest.

"Really?" Father Malcolm said. "I've lost track of time."

"Soon it will be the hour of matins."

Father Malcolm rubbed his face with a rough white terrycloth towel, not quite comprehending.

"We should like you to lead the service, Father Malcolm," said the priest, studying the Jesuit carefully.

"Oh?"

"Are you not pleased to do so?"

Father Malcolm swallowed heavily. Then he rubbed both his hands vigorously.

"It would be an honor."

"And perhaps a bit of a homecoming for you," the Franciscan added compassionately.

Father Malcolm turned back to the mirrors. Acutely self-conscious, he tried to staunch the blood at his lips. The priest and Franciscan watched him carefully.

Then, to his horror, Father Malcolm perceived, in his own image, the Face he had been running from all day. A burning, triumphant glint in his own eyes. In that brief glance, he saw all his own duplicity, vanity, lust, and rage.

Father Malcolm bent before the image of vileness, shuddered, and broke into great sobbing gasps.

Moved, the cassocked priest and Franciscan rushed to his side.

"I was filled as the vessel of Christ!" Father Malcolm said in his degradation. "I ceased to exist but as an extension of His sweet grace! I flowered! I was in ecstasy! And Christ—the sweet peace of pure love—was in my hands and in my breast!" Father Malcolm wiped his tears with the terrycloth towel. "But now Christ has abandoned me! I am impure! It were better had I never been born."

The priest and the Franciscan laid gentle hands on their fallen brother, their lips forming prayers.

Suddenly, Father Malcolm felt a great, inexplicable urgency. He pulled himself free and spun around toward the priest and Franciscan.

"You miserable hypocrites," he whispered hoarsely. "You spend your days in the dust of libraries and carrying tea for a bishop who cannot truly comprehend the mysteries of Christ, and you think you can protect me from evil!"

The Franciscan and the priest backed away, unnerved.

"It is not we who protect you," the Franciscan reminded him, "but the absolution of your penance."

Father Malcolm heard fervent whispers exchanged at the dormitory door. He wound the towel around his fists so hard that the knuckles went white. He came closer to the priest and Franciscan.

"What do you know of religious experience?" he sneered. "What can you even imagine about it? What would you do if the Antichrist came to *you*? *Pray*?"

"But what else?"

A rage at their bookish simplicity, their simpering superiority, blinded Father Malcolm. The very sight of their robe and cassock, the cultivated gentleness of their voices, nauseated him. It was fraud. They were people who could not cope with the real world, or with real religious experience, and sought refuge in the mindless routine of the bishop's seminary.

"That is what *I* did," Father Malcolm hissed. "And Christ was not there!"

The priest swallowed nervously.

"Then you erred in your heart. You were not sincere."

"Oh, yes. Rationalize. Make believe."

"What possible explanation is there otherwise for your fall?" demanded the Franciscan, flushed and angry.

Father Malcolm could not answer. In the silence, he heard footsteps in the distant corridor. It was the messenger returning from the bishop's chamber.

Instead of answering, Father Malcolm pushed past them into the corridor.

The Franciscan grabbed his arm.

"Stop!" he shouted. "You are under our authority—"

Father Malcolm whirled the Franciscan from him, shoving him against the priest, cascading towels from the clothes hamper at the lavatory door.

"I am not under your authority!" he shouted.

The messenger from the bishop's chamber rushed up to the Franciscan and the priest, wild-eyed. They conferred briefly, then, lifting the skirts of their robes, were running down the corridor away from Father Malcolm.

"Christ was defeated at Golgotha Falls!" the Jesuit howled after them in a bitter, broken voice.

As he ran, dodging shadows, Father Malcolm pushed through double doors, past the kitchen. Another cassocked priest rose from his chair at another door. With a terrific yell, Father Malcolm slammed into the priest, sending him sprawling among sacks of potatoes.

Father Malcolm turned in rage and ran down another corridor. He fled through the coal basement and out an exit blindly, sucking frigid night air into bursting lungs.

Father Malcolm stumbled into the bishop's garden.

The lights were on in the bishop's chamber and silhouettes moved against the windows. Father Malcolm had the odd sensation that he was partially responsible. But he did not know why. Indeed, except for the frantic gestures of the silhouettes, there was no way to know that anything unusual had happened.

He walked uncertainly toward the parking lot. The rage within him was gone. The great power of a foreign and controlling presence was gone. He hugged himself, trying to keep warm. Everything was normal again. He got into the Oldsmobile, trying to comprehend what had happened.

Had it happened in a dream? The violence, the blasphemy—it could not be his. There was a power in his body that was independent of him. Suddenly, he became terrified of the cathedral and drove out of the alley. Father Malcolm realized he was driving onto the long bridge over the Charles River, heading north. He was returning to Golgotha Falls.

"Dear God, have mercy on my soul," he whispered.

The steering wheel wrenched sharply to the right, and he drove toward a gap of rail and steel cable in the bridge. A brief flash of Bernard Lovell throwing himself under a transport wagon shot through his brain and Father Malcolm understood: It was to avoid servitude. The Oldsmobile struck a concrete bank hidden under the snow, bounced, and came to a stop.

Father Malcolm struggled to open the door.

"Never," he swore aloud. "Never shall I serve against Christ!"

Slipping over the ice, he ran to the bridge railing. Down below moved the black, frigid, annihilating Charles River.

A bright light paralyzed him. He turned sharply, and saw the red nose and moon-shaped face of a policeman under a blue earmuff hat.

The policeman came closer, putting the flashlight into his leather belt.

"Father," said a Boston Irish brogue. "Are you all right?"

Father Malcolm, unable to answer, stared at the policeman, perceiving in the man's face a mixture of greed, lust, and deception. It was a sickening sensation. Father Malcolm looked away.

Barely visible in the fog, the cathedral loomed like the bulkhead of a great ship going down in the hills to the south.

"Which way were you going, Father, when you skidded on the ice?"

"North."

"Are you far from your parish?"

"Parish?"

"Yes. How many miles?"

The policeman stepped closer. The piggish, glinting eyes seemed demoniac, even sadistic. Father Malcolm knew it was a hallucination. He was looking into the Face of his own evil, the Master who ruled those absent from Christ.

"Are you all right?" the policeman asked again.

"Yes."

The policeman studied the Jesuit's face. It was clear the priest had suffered some kind of psychological trauma, but it was not a result of the accident.

"Maybe you should stay at the cathedral tonight," the policeman suggested. "It's the devil's own night for driving."

"No. Not in the cathedral."

"What's the problem, Father?" he asked gently. "Maybe I can help."

Father Malcolm felt the bruised lip. It tasted like vinegar.

"Have you ever," Father Malcolm asked delicately, "doubted the divinity of Christ?"

The policeman was at a loss. Finally, he deferred to the authority of the Jesuit.

"Never, Father. Not once."

"Then you are a fortunate man."

Father Malcolm involuntarily turned to look at the dark road to the north. An infinite blackness stretched out there, a twisted route into Golgotha Falls.

The policeman clapped him on the shoulder.

"Since you won't go to the cathedral, you might as well go to your parish. Come, I'll help you get your car back onto the highway."

Father Malcolm numbly got into the Oldsmobile. The policeman used the patrol car to nudge the Oldsmobile off the sidewalk and onto the road.

The ignition started instantly.

"Can I do anything else for you?" the patrolman asked cheerily, pulling up beside him.

"Only God can help me," Father Malcolm mumbled.

But the policeman misunderstood. He smiled.

"God bless you, too, Father."

The patrol car moved off.

As though of its own volition, the Oldsmobile began lumbering up the moonstruck ice patches, then into the dark forests toward the north.

An icy chill flowed through Father Malcolm. His body was not his own. He was now afraid. Could Mario Gilbert, being violent, have perceived the buried violence that now ran rampant in him? *Some* psychological force was tearing his personality apart, as a dog shakes an old slipper.

A pale figure stared at him with red eyes.

It was the plastic Christ on the dashboard. The smash into the bridge rails had activated its batteries. Now the features of the Man of Sorrow gazed in sadness at an unfeeling world. The eyes bore into Father Malcolm. Strangely, it had suffered a small injury in the accident. Its back was twisted and humped. The red eyes glinted malevolently. The haggard facial shadows, the striated, dirty beard looked more and more like Christ's opposite, glowing in passages of moonlight through the trees.

With each passage under the trees into moonlight, the figure metamorphosed more and more.

Suddenly, with an inarticulate yell, Father Malcolm rolled down the window and threw the figure out. He heard it bounce, tumble and twirl, cracking on the hard shoulder of the road.

"That's better—much better—" he said, in a voice that sounded strange even to himself. "Christ, have mercy on me!" he whispered.

Fishtailing, pounding onward over the twisting and ice-crossed highway, the Oldsmobile raced toward the cancerous moon high over Golgotha Falls.

C H A P T E R
S I X T E E N

CARDINAL BELLOCCHI crossed the vast spaces of St. Peter's Square.

Over the campaniles and domed churches of Vatican City, a moon of saffron yellow sailed among stars. The sewers had broken, and puddles on the cobblestones shivered in a dusty wind. Far away, a dog howled under the aqueduct. *Carabinieri* patrolled the perimeter of the city within the city of Rome.

The Tiber smelled sluggish and dank. Olive trees within the Vatican gardens were fragrant. Cardinal Bellocchi stepped out of the square, into the columns and shadows, and down the garden pathway, moving toward the Borgia Apartments.

Seven Jesuits followed in close ranks, carrying leather cases from North America. Their shadows passed down the moonstruck marble columns, and fell into the oblivion of the darker shadows of the

Basilica. Cardinal Bellocchi moved faster, as though the ghosts of former enemies pursued through the midnight.

Cardinal Bellocchi's Jesuits, breathing hard, tried to catch up with him at the broad marble steps. They staggered like uncertain vertical shadows in the moon-gilded perspectives of domes, distant fountains, and basilicas. Inside the Borgia Apartments, the Jesuits carried their briefcases down the frescoed corridors, past desks manned by private chamberlains, deeper and deeper, farther from the metropolis of the restless streets.

Cardinal Bellocchi lowered his head, passed down different corridors, past shadowed faces in white cowls, under low-burning lamps, until his footsteps echoed like the Jesuits' on the swirled marble of the papal living quarters.

The Vatican was dark, a place of oblique whispers behind Baroque pillars. Distantly, the midnight bells of Vatican City and Rome began, deep-voiced iron, brass, and melodious steel resonating within seconds of one another in the night.

A superior of the Benedictines came white-faced down the corridor. Cardinal Bellocchi grabbed his elbow.

"He waits for you."

"And?"

The Benedictine removed his arm.

"That's all, Your Eminence. He waits. For you."

The Benedictine left. Cardinal Bellocchi and his Jesuits resumed their rapid march into the interiors.

Of late, His Holiness had undertaken night-long vigils in the minor basilicas of Rome. He prayed at midnight in the dank catacombs, where thigh bones and skulls decorated the vaults of friars and monks long passed unto Christ. Surprise visits had been paid to the Vatican Observatory, where His Holiness displayed an extraordinary expertise on the configuration of the heavenly motions.

Twice in the month, incognito, with a single Jesuit assistant, he had traveled to Boulogne for the midnight mass, and once to his hometown of San Rignazzi in Sicily for services in the abandoned caves there.

Last Friday dawn, it was whispered, the white candles of the papal chapel in the Borgia Apartments had self-ignited, sending sweet fragrance toward the gilded ceiling.

At Friday midnight, two *carabinieri* swore they saluted the silhouette of His Holiness on the balcony of the private chambers. Yet

His Holiness, returning from San Rignazzi, had slept that night at the Castel Gandolfo instead.

Cardinal Bellocchi left his Jesuits holding their leather cases, faces half shadowed, half sallow from the dim lamps at the walls, and pushed toward the inmost antechambers. As he approached the gilt door he felt the pressure of the Pope's imminent presence.

In the antechamber of the Borgia Apartments, Cardinal Bellocchi paused briefly in front of the frescoed landscape, rimmed in exquisite gold leaf, wherein Saint Jerome crushed the rock against his breast in the spiritual wilderness.

Of late, behind the charisma, deeper chasms of Francis Xavier's strange and powerful personality had been revealed. A communication of a nameless dread, insomnia, doubts, and moodiness, and yet nothing deterred or even slowed his headlong rush toward an Ecumenical Council on the subject of the Resurrection.

Under the lighted candles, in a white embroidered chair, sat Francis Xavier.

A white, gold-embroidered robe and slippers set off the handsome figure of the Sicilian. The broad, intelligent forehead, the deep gray eyes now almost black in the candlelight, piercing Cardinal Bellocchi as he entered the private chamber, the knotted, strong hands that gripped the armrest in regal and restless assurance, seemed but the exterior manifestations of the indwelling charisma of the Holy Spirit Itself.

Cardinal Bellocchi knelt and reverently kissed the gold Ring of the Fisherman on Francis Xavier's hand.

"How goes Christ's work?" Francis Xavier asked.

"I planted the seed where I could, Your Holiness. Sometimes the soil was rough."

"The strongest trees grow from rough soil."

Cardinal Bellocchi sat in a plush velvet chair opposite. The Pope's kindly voice belied the deep gravity of the eyes. Francis Xavier looked strengthened, confident, from his recent vigils.

In the corridors beyond his Jesuits, Cardinal Bellocchi heard the personnel of the Vatican carrying leather suitcases, ornate and silvered boxes of personal effects for the great journey to North America.

Francis Xavier heard it, too, and seemed to awaken from a mild dread.

"Our whole endeavor in Quebec," he said, "must be to prepare, as a fundamental mission of the Church, for the Second Incarnation."

"We have a full calendar, Your Holiness—many matters of political and social natures to attend to."

Francis Xavier frowned. Cardinal Bellocchi was his chief obstacle to the Quebec conclave.

"Yes, I know. And so, according to their worth, shall they receive our attention."

"John XXIII," Cardinal Bellocchi insisted, leaning forward, "in calling Vatican II, was also moved by the Holy Spirit. And yet, without prior organization, what really changed? Almost nothing."

A whisper of the night breeze disturbed the candles, and delicate puffs of smoke rose, twisted, and then, smoothed upward from the pure white flame.

"You are a Roman, Cardinal Bellocchi," Francis Xavier said. "You understand the workings of institutions. You understand politicians. But the believing world is not like Rome."

"It is more like Rome than Your Holiness wishes to think."

Francis Xavier settled back against the floral stitchery of the gold and white chair. He shook his head vehemently. Then he leaned forward impulsively. The hands, flexed together in his lap, looked knotted and bony, like a peasant's.

"No. When I go down to San Rignazzi, I visit my relatives. I go back to the old house of my parents, my old friends, the stone church where I was baptized. I walk through the olive groves where my father worked. My uncles and nephews still work there. Do you know what they demand of me?"

"No, Your Holiness."

"They demand: Baldoni—they still call me Baldoni—when? When is Christ coming?"

Francis Xavier remained leaning forward, eyes flashing, hands apart now, gesturing, and he was smiling happily.

"You understand, Cardinal Bellocchi?" he said. "Not *if. When?*"

Cardinal Bellocchi wiped his forehead with a linen handkerchief, briefly glanced at the grit of Rome that left pale impressions there, and put the handkerchief back into his pocket.

Francis Xavier wagged a formidable finger as he grinned.

"And I tell them I don't know when, Cardinal Bellocchi. But it will be soon. *Very soon!*"

Cardinal Bellocchi tried to smile. Francis Xavier jabbed the cardinal's knee for emphasis.

"Because in San Rignazzi, you can *feel* Christ! In the sky, in the rocks, in the stone houses! He is a few minutes away, Bellocchi—you can sense Him in the air you breathe!"

The declaration had no effect on the cardinal. Francis Xavier settled back against the chair. As he studied the Nuncio, he tapped his finger thoughtfully against his lips, and a gentle twinkle came into his eyes.

"I will send you to San Rignazzi," he said. "It will take the Roman cosmopolitanism out of your soul." Francis Xavier flexed his fingers, lacing them together, smiling. "Yes. A year among the hard-working and the poor, Cardinal Bellocchi. It would rekindle your spiritual expectations."

The cardinal was not certain if Francis Xavier was joking. Was a purge being contemplated against the nonmillennialists? Cardinal Bellocchi felt his heart pounding as he tried to picture the catastrophe of a year's banishment to Sicily, among the banality and superstitions of peasants.

Francis Xavier rose slowly from the chair. With an outstretched hand, he indicated for the Nuncio to remain seated. The dark look was in his eyes again.

"Do you remember the circumstances of my election?" he asked.

Surprised by the question, wary, Cardinal Bellocchi watched as Francis Xavier picked up a heavily wrought silver crucifix on an ebony base, elongated and sorrowful, in the tortured, mystic style of the Spanish Hapsburgs.

"Do you?" he repeated.

Cardinal Bellocchi grinned the gold-toothed grin.

"It was a most extraordinary representation of the Holy Spirit," he answered.

Francis Xavier carefully set down the Man of Sorrows and turned away.

"Did it never seem strange to you," he asked, "that the archbishop of Genoa, conveying the message of the Holy Spirit, should do so while being struck by a cerebral hemorrhage?"

"He was well into his nineties, Your Holiness."

Francis Xavier looked out the small, open windows above the candles. Cardinal Bellocchi marveled at the spiritual beauty of the face, a face that moved millions by its unpremeditated spirituality. But it was a lonely face. It was an isolated, melancholy face of late.

"I have had premonitions," Francis Xavier said very quietly. "There have been messages."

Francis Xavier felt more than heard the robes shift and rustle as Cardinal Bellocchi stood and walked toward the candles.

"The Second Incarnation of Christ," Francis Xavier said softly. "I know it in Rome as I know it in San Rignazzi."

"But these signs can be deceptive, Your Holiness."

"The signs have pursued me all my life."

"Holy men, men of passionate faith, are vulnerable to deceitful signs."

Francis Xavier said nothing for a long time. A choir far away massed powerfully in the night breeze, brought a Gregorian chant rising and falling from a chamber beyond the gardens.

"Christ does not deceive," he said.

Cardinal Bellocchi nervously leaned forward, fingers on the velvet cloth cover of the table at the base of the candelabra.

"The time cannot be right," he whispered.

"I have been speaking with Monsignor Tafuri—"

Cardinal Bellocchi's jaw clenched.

"Monsignor Tafuri is an opportunist, Your Holiness!"

"Monsignor Tafuri supervises the archives of the Holy Office," Francis Xavier said, dully. "A rather humble vantage point for ambition, I would think."

"The twentieth century is filled with massacres," Cardinal Bellocchi protested. "Children annihilated by rockets. The creation of artificial embryos. Bizarre religions and drug cults. And the civilized world suffocates in material wealth that gives no meaning. This century, Your Holiness, is not prepared for Christ!"

Francis Xavier smiled secretively.

"These are signs of the Antichrist."

Francis Xavier sat triumphantly on the white embroidered chair. Cardinal Bellocchi paced the carpet, his black shoes treading softly on the crown and keys sewn into the thick pile.

"And the Antichrist," Francis Xavier concluded, "shall be present before the Second Coming!"

Cardinal Bellocchi stared at him, then lowered his head, a sign of acquiescence. Francis Xavier's moods were mercurial. At times such as these, there was no influence possible with him.

The bells of Rome rang out the hour of one o'clock in the morning, a crescendo, then a dying resonance in the cloudy air.

There was a long silence. Francis Xavier relaxed. His eyes fastened on the carpet between them.

"What is this, my dear Nuncio?" he asked gently.

A heavy white envelope, addressed to the Sacred Apostolic Penitentiary of Vatican City, from the cathedral of the metropolitan See of Boston, Massachusetts, lay in a rectangle of pallid moonlight at Francis Xavier's feet.

It had fallen from the dossier case of leather, still on the cardinal's chair.

"A confession," Cardinal Bellocchi said, moving toward it. "I had promised to deliver it."

Francis Xavier gently put his slippered foot on the envelope. It was strangely cool.

"I sent you to North America to prepare my conclave," he teased. "Instead, you work for the Sacred Penitentiary."

Francis Xavier bent down and picked up the weighty envelope. He bounced it slowly in his hand.

"Please," Cardinal Bellocchi pleaded, embarrassed. "Let me deliver it."

"You have," Francis Xavier said, slitting it open with a silver knife. "Are we not the supreme authority of the Sacred Penitentiary?"

Cardinal Bellocchi smoothed his robes while the Pope read, adjusting rimless spectacles onto the bridge of his nose. One by one, he handed the pages to Cardinal Bellocchi.

"Extraordinary," Francis Xavier said. "Have you read this?"

"Of course not."

Francis Xavier slipped his spectacles into his petit point case and put the case under the candles.

"It is not a confession at all," he said worriedly.

With increasing trepidation, Cardinal Bellocchi read the contents of the last page. "It is a testament of a divided soul."

"Christ and Satan. Two voices. One man."

Francis Xavier waited until Cardinal Bellocchi folded the pages together, slipped them back into the envelope, and put the envelope back into his personal dossier leather case.

Francis Xavier was studying him warily.

"How did you come to deliver this letter?" he asked quietly.

"There was an unpleasant incident in the Boston diocese. An American Jesuit—the man threw himself at my feet, screaming for Christ's safety."

"Why?"

Cardinal Bellocchi felt uncomfortable in the long, dark stare from Francis Xavier.

"Why, Cardinal Bellocchi?"

"The Antichrist had driven him from his church."

Francis Xavier flexed his fingers, then leaned forward suddenly.

"Do you know how many priests we have lost in the last month?" he asked in a tense voice. "Do you have any idea what is happening to us?"

Cardinal Bellocchi declined to answer.

"Fleeing churches. Perversions. Heresies. But always—always, Cardinal Bellocchi—after glimpsing signs of the Second Coming!"

"Yes," the Nuncio said lamely. "The man mentioned—signs— in his text—"

Francis Xavier, suddenly moody, stirred restlessly in his chair.

"It is all too clear," he said, "the nature of things."

Abruptly, he stood, extended his hand, and Cardinal Bellocchi was obliged to kneel and kiss the great ring.

"In the morning, we will depart for Quebec," Francis Xavier said. "Present your dossiers to the secretary of state."

"Yes, Your Holiness."

Cardinal Bellocchi walked heavily toward the ornate door. No records, only oral tradition in the Vatican, memorialized the dangers that circulated like hot breezes toward the chair of Saint Peter. The world had no conception of the risks deep inside the Renaissance corridors, behind the resplendent ceremony of Vatican grandeur.

Popes were corrupted by holy passions, deformed into heresies, retarding the mission of the Church for generations.

"It is a grand design, Cardinal Bellocchi," Francis Xavier said gently. "We listen. We go. We are guided by the supernatural."

"Yes, Your Holiness."

In the antechambers, Cardinal Bellocchi, grim-faced, raised his hand and swept his Jesuits out into the corridors with him.

In front of them, waiting for an audience, was Monsignor Tafuri, with five leading millennialists in a semicircle behind him. They looked hollow-eyed, almost vampirish in the pallor of the moonlight now coming through the distant balconies.

"Do you scent your prey, Monsignor?" Cardinal Bellocchi said.

Monsignor Tafuri grinned unctuously.

"His Holiness wishes to hear our counsel."

Cardinal Bellocchi swept forward and his Jesuits made the millennialists split into two halves as they passed.

All the gilt antiques of the courts of Venice and the Bavarian kingdom graced the long corridors. Paintings of the Spanish monarchy and the Christs of Sienna, Florence, and Pisa. The Church grew, in spite of all its difficulties, into the twentieth century.

It did so by its driving faith and its superior organizaton, commanding the beliefs of a billion human beings. It did so not by personal charisma and intrigue, but by the patient accumulation of organizational advantage over the world. Of this, Cardinal Bellocchi was certain.

Within the papal chamber, Francis Xavier remained alone by the half-burned candles, shielding his eyes, supporting his head against his fingers.

A dizziness momentarily disoriented him.

With a grave premonition, Francis Xavier retired to his private chapel. In his hand, he clenched the black wooden rosary given him by his mother on his ordination as a priest in San Rignazzi.

The Duccio gold-leaf Christ shimmered behind twin censers that disgorged fragrant smoke at spiral Baroque pillars. The altar linen was embroidered with the crown and the keys. The tabernacle, studded with rhinestones, glimmered under the massive series of diagonally placed white candles on the altar.

Francis Xavier knelt in prayer.

Gradually, the unpleasant sensation of the American Jesuit's confession faded. Instead came the effulgent expansion from the Duccio Christ, the radiant assurance of the sunlike canopy overhead, and the feeling of wingless, ineffable motions of the Holy Spirit inside his heart.

A gentle tremble of the chandelier tinkled over his head.

The melancholy image of Christ regarded Francis Xavier with the glitter perceptible to few, of which the painted halo was but a metaphor in pigment.

Suddenly, the rosary separated from his fingers, defying gravity. The beads lifted gently and hung suspended in the saffron, incense-heavy air. Slowly, very slowly. Francis Xavier placed his fingers around it again and the black wooden beads resumed weight.

The chapel shimmered in a fluttering, musical dance of gold light.

Soon, Francis Xavier felt, deep within the meditative heart, *Very soon now.*

CHAPTER
SEVENTEEN

IN THE upper woods of the south ridge, overlooking Golgotha Valley, Harvey Timms, the deaf child, clapped his hands over his ears at sunrise and screamed. The screams echoed down to the Siloam and infiltrated the graveyard and the streets of Golgotha Falls.

The grocery clerk said that Harvey Timms heard the devil's laughter of triumph after entering the priest.

The infections of animals passed from the deformed newborn to adult cattle and pigs. Thrown onto the burning pyres, they split down the stomachs from the boiling heat within.

Fred Waller, the mechanic, closed his garage and waited, corpselike, for the dominion of the unsanctified dead.

Miss Kenny, aberrant since the death of her sister, carried a lantern through the side streets of Golgotha Falls, calling in her mouselike high-pitched voice for the strangled and violated twin, Maxwell McAliskey, whose empty grave now was marked by a single withered rose stem.

Only the red calf seemed immune from the general fear. It wandered untended, foraging at the churchyard, its tail docked by superstitious children, its hide bearing the scourge marks of charred wood or sharp branches. At sunrise, its bawling rose into a strange harmony with the fading screams of Harvey Timms.

Hank Edmondson died before his eighty-eighth birthday and was buried in a private family plot outside Kidron. The earth, as it was turned over, disgorged writhing white maggots that slithered away from the shovels. When the tuberculosis had corrupted both his lungs on Friday dawn, his last words were: "The graves shall be opened."

In the tavern, the remark was taken to mean a premonition of death. The tavern owner said it meant something else: The violated graves of the Church of Eternal Sorrows would be opened by unsanctified force.

Men moved in pairs and small groups, waiting, watching the skies, from the sidewalks and the tavern. Only the aged Miss Kenny, calling fitfully among the ruins of the mill and the vacant Victorian houses, disturbed the chill silence of Golgotha Falls.

Mass hysteria, Mario wrote in his notebook. *As a neurotic clings to his illness, the people of Golgotha Valley have clung to the Church of Eternal Sorrows as a focus of their poverty and anxiety. If the priest returns, he will absorb the emotional power of their superstitions.*

Mario's blackouts, symptom of exhaustion, abated after sunrise. Anita smoked cigarettes on the doorstep of the rectory. She was still unwilling to enter the church.

Inside the church, the walls took on the ashen, desolate color of the prewinter sterility of the fields and the clay church grounds.

The only light within was the pale, pulsating yellow altar lamp and the slightly greenish hue of the thermovision image of the beast. Throughout the days and nights. Mario remained at his station, guarding the equipment against the town's hysteria. The black revolver tucked in his belt, he continued to make entries in his notebook.

Eamon Malcolm has disintegrated with his loss of faith. As a result, the raw visual and aural fragments of his libido are being projected

233

like an unstructured dream. Steady flow of image possible if all re-
pression removed. Last vestige of repression: the idea of God. I must
destroy it.

Impatiently, Mario waited for the Jesuit. Just as nervously, Anita
watched from the doorway of the rectory. With each passing hour,
the likelihood of Eamon's return diminished and the dread began
to lift from her mind.

Then, over the squeaking, searching calls of Miss Kenny by the
ruined mill, Mario heard the approaching rumble of a large automobile.

The Oldsmobile topped the ridge like a great wounded bird, one
wheel flapping over the mud, the passenger door scraped and badly
dented, and steam escaped from the radiator.

"Oh, God—no—" Anita whispered.

She ran out to intercept the Oldsmobile.

The Jesuit did not park it as much as let it die, crashing gently
into the bushes by the road loop. He remained sitting, eyes cast down,
haggard, lips twitching.

Very slowly, he looked up as Anita climbed the slope toward him.
It was chilly and she wore a thick red plaid jacket over her white
blouse. The belt buckle and leather boots, in western cut, seemed
oddly out of place against the white church in the gray soil.

He looked down at his shaking hands, then back into her pale face.

"I am heartily sorry," he said quietly, "that I offended you, Anita."

For an instant, she watched him, the unshaven face, the eyes grown
deeper with self-knowledge, the inability to look at her for more
than a second or two.

When she came closer, she saw the bruise of his lips and the torn
dashboard. The passenger window was cracked and the metal below
savagely angled by the collision.

"It's not important now, Father," she said. "There is only one
necessity . . . Get out of Golgotha Falls!"

Instead, he opened the door, pulled himself out of the Oldsmobile,
swayed, and grabbed the open door.

"Free will," he said in despair, "is so often an illusion, Anita." The
cracked lip began slowly bleeding again. "What we do, the thoughts
that move our bodies, our desires—are signals of forces that can tear
the earth apart."

In his eyes, she saw the shattered remnants of the once-proud Jesuit
and in his place was a vastly more complex being, a man come face
to face with his own unfathomable and self-destructive passions.

"This valley is my perimeter, Anita," he said, "until a greater one than myself comes."

"Father, I want to take you to Boston. I want you to have medical advice."

The rain squalls on the ridge flared like a corona over the scrub brush and then fell back on the gray fields. In Golgotha Valley, people of the town and farmers aimlessly wandered the furrowed and dessicated fields.

"This happened through me, Anita," he said softly. "I am rooted here. By work—and prayer—perhaps things will turn right—again—"

But the immensity of the labor to overcome himself and to consecrate the church yet again and to tend the people of Golgotha Valley seemed momentarily to crush his purpose.

"I fled my absolution to come here," he whispered to Anita. "A penance is due to arrive at the cathedral, but I escaped before it could come."

He wiped the thin thread of blood from his lip with his thumb.

"I cannot perform the mass," he said in a broken voice, "but I can restore the church. Work. Pray. Perhaps—I—will be able to leave Golgotha Falls—someday—"

"Let me take you! Now!"

"You would place your very life in danger."

Bitterly, yet subdued, fatalistic, he began walking down the ashen gray slope toward the church.

"Father!" she yelled, running after him.

But he continued marching down, without a contrary will, cognizant of the internal horrors of the church.

"Father!"

Mario, his legs up against the thermovision, where the shaggy beast grinned at the Jesuit, also grinned.

"I knew you'd come back, Father."

Father Malcolm walked slowly through the dirty church. Bits of detritus fallen from the dead peach trees crunched under his shoes. The image of the beast glared at him malevolently. He stopped in front of it, his jaws clenching.

"This is why I had to come back, Mario," he whispered.

Anita came from the vestibule, breathing hard, and stopped at the main part of the church. Mario casually lowered his legs and turned to the Jesuit.

"That's why you came back," he said, pointing at Anita.

Father Malcolm whirled toward Anita, white and trembling.

"The beast appeared the instant you wanted sex with her," Mario said coolly. "It's your own lust. Made into an image. By your brain."

Father Malcolm's jaw worked, clenching over and over, as though deep and bitter rage dominated him now.

Anita walked softly into the main part of the church. Father Malcolm heard each footstep, felt almost palpably the weight of the slender woman over the floor.

"Mario," she said. "He fled his absolution to come back."

"His what?"

"I wrote a confession for Cardinal Bellocchi," Father Malcolm muttered, eyes transfixed by the goathead taunting him silently. "But I—broke out of the cathedral—blindly—it seems that a powerful and arrogant stranger lies within me and corrupts my very thoughts!"

"I'm taking him back," Anita stated.

Mario looked, dismayed, at Anita. Incredibly, she wanted to return the Jesuit to Boston for the fiction of absolution. The last thing Mario needed was to have the priest's superego bolstered by Catholic mythology.

"Why did you flee?" Mario asked. "Why didn't you just walk away?"

"I—I became infested with violence—anger—"

"There must be a reason why you were angry at them."

Father Malcolm looked up, eyes flashing.

"They had no conception of what I had been through!"

Mario smiled softly and walked closer to the Jesuit.

"And what was that?" he asked with a dangerous slowness.

"A religious experience," Father Malcolm said, blinking. "They were bookmen. Library sitters. Toadies to the bishop. Mere administrators. But I—"

Mario suddenly leaned forward and shouted, *"Had a sexual experience!"*

Father Malcolm backed away. He looked, confused, at Anita, at the thermovision screen, at the flickering yellow altar lamp, and vigorously shook his head.

"You despised them for their sexlessness!" Mario said, pursuing him. "She was right there. Available. Willing. Up against you! And it was delicious!"

"Mario—for God's sake—" Anita protested.

But Mario came even closer to the Jesuit.

"That emotional explosion sent sensations and ideas into your brain that scared the shit out of you! That's what you ran from, Father Malcolm! It's what you've run from all your life!"

Father Malcolm, backed against the aisle pillar, gazed back at Mario with repugnance.

"But it followed you to the cathedral!" Mario shouted. "Of course it followed you to the cathedral! Because it's part of you! You'll never escape it!"

A malignant glance came from Father Malcolm, the glance of a cornered man.

Anita watched the sweating Jesuit and Mario, and the strange electricity between them. It was as though their personal antagonism was but the juncture of a far more annihilating confrontation.

"Your own sexuality drove you back to Golgotha Falls!" Mario taunted.

Father Malcolm pointed vigorously to the blue crosses of mold that glittered in twelve places on the walls.

"Is that the work of sex?" he demanded heatedly.

"No."

"Blasphemous mockeries of the Crucifixion . . . The finger of the hand of Evil has been here and inscribed his mark!"

Mario sneered. "You chrismed the walls. The chrism contains moisture. Contains a nutrient. Obviously, mildew will grow on it."

Father Malcolm, checked, turned away in disgust. Suddenly, he gestured at the desolate landscape outside the Gothic window.

"Who has sucked the life out of the valley?" he asked in a strong, assured, yet worried voice.

"It's October. Things get desolate in October."

The Jesuit laughed harshly.

"Ridiculous! You blind yourself like a child!"

"After the drought came rains. Dormant fruit trees blossomed. Now it's cold October. The valley is dead. Why search for Satan in rhythms of nature?"

The linchpin was being worked loose from the Jesuit's brain. Darker, less coherent impulses rose to the surface.

Anita saw him suffer, the trembling of the face that mutely expressed a loss of all moorings. As she took a single step toward him, he feared her and whirled away.

"Who lit the lamp?" he rasped, pointing at the sick, pulsing yellow flame.

For a moment, they watched the tongues of saffron licking out from the oil basin. As the day grew darker, the strength of the lamp increased, and sent its hollow light flickering over the tabernacle, the cameras and instruments, and onto their faces.

"Anita lit it."

Father Malcolm advanced confidently.

"But why is it so sick?" he demanded. "Who makes the red lamp of Christ sick with sin?"

"Anita cracked the red glass while lighting it."

Mario dragged a chair under the lamp, quickly stood on it, and dislodged a wedge of red glass. He held it in his fingers to show the Jesuit. Then he let it crash to the floor. The yellow lamp flared more powerfully over his face.

"And it pulses because it's nearly out of fuel," Mario said, eyes dark in the yellow flicker.

He tapped the oil basin with his fingers, snapping at it, until the empty *ping* ricocheted softly in the darkening church.

"No Satan," Mario said, smiling quietly.

Father Malcolm staggered backward against the altar, clutching at it, but reluctant to touch the holy cloth. The result was that he stumbled down the length of the sacrificial table.

"The lamp was extinguished," the Jesuit shouted, "at the hour of sin!"

"It was the wind," Anita said softly. "The wind changed."

In horror, Father Malcolm looked at Anita. Mario had momentarily seduced her again. The cold, cruel logic of his science let her betray what she had felt the dawn of that Friday. Father Malcolm, unmoored, felt himself groping in the same hallucinatory universe he had fled on the Charles bridge.

Fighting collapse, Father Malcolm felt all the idealism in his early life, his brother Ian, his uncle James Farrell Malcolm, Elizabeth, even Christ Himself, observing his downfall, an irrevocable downfall without mercy or salvation.

His lips bled profusely.

Mario advanced slowly until he was near the Jesuit. Father Malcolm backed away, afraid. Mario gently touched the wounded mouth. The Jesuit's head jerked back in pain.

"I kissed the cardinal's crucifix," he whispered hoarsely, "and my lips bled. As you can see, my very body is tormented by Satan."

Father Malcolm fell on his knees in front of the altar. His lips moved rapidly, and he breathed raspingly. Anita crossed the floor toward him, but Mario roughly caught her by the shoulder and held her back.

The thermovision showed increased crimson flares. Mario knew the Jesuit's resistance was breaking down.

"Mario . . . he's dangerously ill—"

"He's ready to project," Mario whispered, eyes gleaming. "But he's holding back."

"Mario—he's not an animal!"

Mario laughed in her face.

"Of course he's an animal! We're all animals!"

Mario turned back to the Jesuit, who with every failure of concentration threw himself more violently into his prayer.

"What kind of saint do you think you are?" Mario taunted. "There are no saints in this world!"

Father Malcolm paused.

"I do not abjure God," he said quietly.

He turned slowly to Mario, his face drawn.

"Or His saints," he added softly.

Father Malcolm turned back and once again moved his lips in prayer. Mario stepped closer to him.

"Are you trying to be God?" Mario shouted. "Do you think you're Christ?"

"No."

"Who else?" Mario demanded. "Who else in all of history was so damn sacred as you pretend to be?"

Father Malcolm stopped in mid-prayer.

"My brother Ian," he said gently. "Ian was gifted by the grace of God."

"Well, where is this saint now?"

"He's dead. He drowned when he was twelve."

"So your parents beatified him."

Father Malcolm paused.

"My family owed a son to the Church. I was sent to take Ian's place."

"But you hated it."

Father Malcolm, unable to concentrate, let his hands fall. He no longer had defenses.

"Every mass you performed," Mario pointed out, "was in the chains of your dead brother!"

Mario advanced.

"But you're not Ian! You're Eamon Malcolm! Somewhere under that saintly posture lives a real man, and that real man has sexual needs and wants! Let him loose!"

Father Malcolm rubbed his face wearily. He had not slept since his collapse in the cathedral. Somewhere, deep in the subconscious, Mario had struck home. The repressed anger of a foreign being rose in inarticulate rebellion.

"My uncle was a saintly man," he said firmly.

"Yes, and you spent many a fine afternoon on his lap, looking at Renaissance nudes!"

"Mario, your puerility astonishes me!"

But Mario sensed something crumbling in the Jesuit finally. He leaned over the kneeling man.

"Feelings arose that frightened you," Mario said, enunciating with exaggerated care. "So you idealized him. You desexualized him. And yourself!"

Anita tried to pull Mario away, but he roughly shook off her hands.

"*Then* you heard how he died!" Mario shouted. "You found out he was no saint at all!"

The thermovision flared violent crimson, swirled, but formed hybrid shapes and died again into the red flux.

Father Malcolm, unable to pray, stood up angrily and pushed Mario away. Suddenly, in mid-stride toward the vestibule, he extended his right arm. He leaned against the pillar. In terrible moans, his breath escaped him, and his shoulders heaved. Anita heard the awful timbre of a crushed voice, issuing from a broken personality.

"It's true—" Father Malcolm wept hoarsely. "What you say is true! Oh, God!"

Father Malcolm tried to stagger out of the church, away from the twin mockeries of the grinning beast and Mario's insights piercing his vital being.

"What happened to Bernard Lovell—is happening to me—"

"Just abnormal psychology," Mario said, snapping a fresh videotape into the thermovision.

Father Malcolm, coughing, stumbled down the center aisle, his back illuminated by the full force of the yellow lamp. He looked at it in terror. Anita saw that he no longer knew where he was. He groped like a blind man, avoiding, yet transfixed by, the cool lamp that glowed throughout the dark church.

"Lovell . . . Lovell . . . I am Lovell . . ." he muttered.

Anita pushed past Mario.

"I'm getting him out of here," she said defiantly.

"I'm not through with him!"

"Yes, you are."

Mario pointed at the orange, crimson, and white-hot flares in the thermovision screen.

"Not now, Anita! For Christ's sake, he's volatile!"

Anita struggled to put the Jesuit's arm over her shoulder. The warmth of her body made him dizzy.

"I am Lovell," he whispered. "I am James Farrell Malcolm. I am sin incarnate!"

The horrible force of Mario's universe, the aggressive nothingness, penetrated him again and again, and he shuddered repeatedly. Anita's voice dimly rose over the rising chaos.

"Eamon Malcolm is too sick for any experiments!" she pleaded. "I'm driving him back to Boston!"

Suddenly, a barrage of suggestive imagery reared inside the red-orange flux of the thermovision. Anita and Mario turned and saw shapes form and disintegrate.

"This is it!" Mario hissed. "Direct projection! Don't leave me now!"

"It's not worth it, Mario. Nothing is worth it."

She backed away with Father Malcolm. Mario followed her and grabbed her arm painfully.

"I don't know what's happened to you, Anita," he said softly. "Once I'd have given the world for you. But this bastard has changed you—"

"It's you, Mario . . . You've lost all decency—"

She broke away, and again he followed her toward the door and held her back.

"Science makes a sacrifice of us all, damn it!" he said. "I've given my life and half my sanity for this. Don't take it from me now!"

She glared at him. The barrier between them was complete.

"No, Mario," she said. "Love makes sacrifices, too."

Astounded, he watched her. Then a violent corona of energy burst within the thermovision viewfinder, illuminating the walls, reflecting red over the altar linen, glittering on the blue crosses.

Mario stumbled closer to the thermovision, the way a priest stumbles, reverent and fearful, to his image of Christ. In that instant, she guided the distracted priest out of the church.

They were crossing the mounds of rubble, toward the Volkswagen at the end of Canaan Street, when Mario ran out of the church door, looking right and left, brandishing the revolver.

"Come back!" he roared.

Eamon Malcolm turned back toward the stocky figure in the frame of the door, a figure entrapped in an evil so large, so overwhelming, that it warped the very roof and steeple of the church.

A shot rang out.

"Come back!"

Anita pulled and pushed the Jesuit down the street and opened the Volkswagen door.

Eamon's teeth chattered. Premonitions of the catastrophe of death —an unconsecrated, unabsolved death—assailed his soul.

Damnation loped at him in the form of the outraged scientist rushing over the rubble mounds.

"Get in, Father!" Anita hissed.

But she was too late. Mario lunged forward, took hold of the Jesuit's coat, and whirled him from the front seat.

Anita screamed and ran to the other door. Father Malcolm moaned on the ground, covered in dust. He tackled Mario's legs, and Mario brought the butt of the revolver down on the priest's hands.

The engine roared, broken branches shot from the rear wheels, the front end of the van lifted, and as the vehicle moved ahead in a cloud of dust, Mario was thrown in a circle from the open passenger door.

Aiming at the tires, on one knee, Mario pulled the trigger three times. The shots echoed dully in the twilight. Slowly, very slowly, came thrice the mocking answer: The bell tolled gently from the steeple.

"God have pity on you," Father Malcolm moaned.

The van looped around the field and caught the road. Mario put the revolver into his belt. The Jesuit stared at him in disbelief, white-faced and trembling.

The Jesuit crawled away, crablike, toward the town. Mario jerked him up from the ground.

"We're not finished, Father!" he hissed into the priest's ear. "We're going back into that church!"

Dragging the Jesuit after him, Mario savagely threw him inside toward the altar.

The ceiling glittered with a strange light.

Mario walked slowly toward the thermovision. For a long time, he stared into it. Father Malcolm noted Mario's horrified expression.

"What . . . what is it?" he whispered. "*WHAT IS IT?*"

Mario turned the thermovision camera slowly on its hinge.

The Jesuit crawled toward the thermovision screen, stared in shock at the clearly defined image of a skeletal figure, with flesh hanging onto its ribs and forehead, clawed out of the grave's depth, holding high a crucifix.

"It's my death—" he whispered.

Mario sank back against the pillar, fumbling for a cigarette in his shirt pocket.

The videotape recorded the dark, fading image. It was ghastly in its struggle against the holding earth. The skeletal teeth grimaced in effort, thrusting the cross high into the dark air.

"You projected without religion," Mario said, regaining his calm and assurance at the moment of triumph. "No rituals. No litanies. The raw stuff."

Father Malcolm stared dully in despair.

"The image is my penance—" he tried to say.

"It's your depression. Your despair."

The half-decomposed figure bore a striking resemblance to Eamon Malcolm, down to the dark coat and the wisps of blond hair. The agony of the face was unmistakably his own.

"No Christ; no Satan," Mario said coolly, exhaling a cloud of cigarette smoke. "Just your own very human problems."

Father Malcolm slumped in brokenhearted comprehension before the altar. Mario felt sorry for him.

"I believed in the sign of the cross," he groaned.

"A fantasy."

Father Malcolm's head lowered toward the floor.

"I believed the church to be filled with the holy presence."

"Sexual sublimation."

Mario smoked calmly, waiting for the final weight of the truth to enter the priest and claim him. Removing the repressive idea of God had opened the pathway to direct projection. It would cripple the miraculous claims of religion. It would prove where those miracles began. In the unsatisfied drives of sexual beings.

The Jesuit's voice became more and more slurred, drunken, groveling. "Holy—men—believe—signs—"

"Yeah. Well, I'm sorry, Father. It was your own naive nature that believed in the images. It's just psychology. Nothing more."

Mario flicked away the driving, unseen insects from his face. A fever rose into his forehead. He felt the pressure of a mild blackout approach.

Father Malcolm slumped very close to the ground.

"Holy men—will—believe—signs—"

Annoyed, Mario slapped away more of the insects. Sweat rolled down his forehead. The cigarette fell to the floor. He steadied himself against the thermovision.

"What are you moaning about, goddamn it?" he said.

The Jesuit's voice seemed to come from the far walls and rafters of the church.

"As—you—did—"

Mario looked at the sound recording system. In the slightly undulating church, the stability of the machines gave him assurance. The needles gently moved at the priest's voice. Yet the priest's lips were not moving.

"What? What the hell is going on?" Mario shouted.

. . . Evil . . . is the destruction . . . of good . . . in a man. . . .

The words resonated deep within Mario's brain.

The thermovision showed the deep viridian green of the cold church flowing into the figure of the Jesuit, filling it entirely.

"What—? What's happening—?"

Mario backed away, tripped over braided cables, and crashed downward through clipboards, coffee cups, and blank videotapes. The figure on the church floor rose. The Jesuit's blue eyes faded. Deep inside was a glow of pure evil, the red of molten lava. Mario stared at Eamon Malcolm's lips pulled back in a death-head's rictus —a hypnotic amalgam of satanic derision and amusement.

Trembling spasmodically, Mario could not choke forth the scream of terror that welled from the depths of his soul. He stared at the screen, groping desperately for a logical answer. The Jesuit's projection had undoubtedly gotten into his own mind as well as the infrared tape. Worse than the invading fever at the exorcism, stronger than the mass hallucinations at the lecture, Mario felt the full force of an undisguised psychic hatred emanating from the Jesuit.

Through a roaming, unstable haze of warped vision, Mario warily watched Eamon Malcolm at the altar.

. . . Evil . . . Evil . . . Evil . . .

The Jesuit's lips did not move. But the sound system needle moved. The projections were audible.

The Jesuit then deftly sliced a thin bloodline in his palm with a shard of the altar lamp glass. A drop fell into the wine. A second drop he rubbed around the paten until it was thoroughly melded into the ornamental scrollwork.

"You're defiling your own mass, you fool!" Mario stammered weakly.

The figure was lost in its private nightmare. But the nightmare was contagious. Mario felt the room undulate slowly, as the Jesuit rustled down the aisle and washed the bloodied hand in the holy water font in the vestibule. Mario staggered after him, holding on to the pillar.

"Come back, goddamnit!" he shouted, fighting the disorientation. "I'm not through with you!"

The Jesuit glanced at him. It was a glance from a different planet. Malign eyes narrowed at him. In his fist was a black revolver. Mario recognized it as his. Mario backed away.

"*I* am through with you," Eamon said simply.

The disorientation returned in a savage rush, multiplied by panic. Mario edged backward past his instruments. The red glint in the priest's eyes was the color of drops of blood.

. . . Evil . . . is the . . . systematic breakdown of good . . . in a man . . .

Again, the lips did not move. The church echoed sounds thought, not uttered. Eamon followed Mario carefully through the shadows of the instruments.

"We . . . we could use each other—" Mario said lamely, white and shaking.

Eamon grinned knowingly.

"I don't need *you* at all," he said, raising the revolver in both hands.

Mario tripped. Something struck him on the head. It was the thermovision lens. The thermovision was disgorging images. Cruciform shapes, goatheads, and through it all, the skeletal figure desperately raising the crucifix on a mission not of this earth.

A shot rang out. Mario heard the bullet whistle down the Gothic nave.

The seismographic paper unrolled, hiccuping over the church floor.

"Oh, Jesus—" Mario blurted. "My instruments—"

Mario's final defense, his final retreat, collapsed with the sight of instruments in revolt, of science under the power of illusion.

Mario crashed over the sound recording system. The playback was on.

Gerasma—J-J-J-es—theralpy—o—theralpy—now—perima—ima— ima—

It was his own voice, speaking in tongues, on the Harvard auditorium floor.

G-G-G-Gerasma—meta—laffa—now—

"NO!" Mario screamed.

The needle in the temperature recording system moved back and forth, back and forth, lazily swinging, under the control of the Jesuit.

Eamon grinned. A bluish vapor was expelled from his lips. As he raised the revolver a second time, Mario saw that the color of the blue luminescences was the same as the Jesuit's breath.

Objective reality and psychic distortion suddenly fused.

Mario found himself running, running out of the vestibule, sucking in great draughts of chill night air.

"Anita! Anita! Help me!" he yelled, all semblance of rational control gone.

Mario tripped on the church path. In the doorway, Eamon stood. The visage was barely human. It had the malevolence of the goathead. Very slowly, it raised its revolver in a preternatural, steady fist.

"Thank you, sucker! You've done your job well!"

Lightning flashed, the Jesuit's eyes glistened red, and the valley echoed with his savage, resonant laughter as the gun discharged.

CHAPTER
EIGHTEEN

THE VATICAN jet reached a cruising height of 34,000 feet and swung out over the Atlantic Ocean.

In the forward cabin sat six Jesuits, an administrative assistant, and the undersecretary of state for the Vatican. The Jesuits busily typed or wrote at their desks or conversed in whispers. The undersecretary and his assistant penciled notations on the Quebec agenda.

In the rear cabin, two suede chairs were embossed with the crown and keys. On the left sat Cardinal Bellocchio writing paragraphs in the margins of typed documents. He snapped his fingers and a Jesuit came immediately. Soon the clicking of the typewriter filled the air.

In the other chair, Francis Xavier removed his spectacles, rubbing the bridge of the nose, letting his documents down to the desk top.

"Such heavenly perfection," he mused, staring at the clouds tinged pink and orange in the early evening sun-glow. "Such confusion below."

Cardinal Bellocchi smiled. "True, Your Holiness. Our mission is to dispel that confusion."

Francis Xavier sank into a fatigued, somnolent state, at rest and warm in the sunlight piercing the double thickness of the window. Visions from the past came to his mind.

A scene from San Rignazzi: an explosion of black snakes, escaping from white rocks under the olive groves.

It was the afternoon, over forty years ago, that Guido Baldoni, the uncle of Giacomo, scythed in half a nest of vipers in the heat of the sun. The slender, deeply religious peasant screamed and ran into San Rignazzi. Bitten thrice on one leg and twice in the arm, he fell shivering like a dog at the church door. Then he went into deeper convulsions and died with a fire in his brain.

It was the first time Giacomo saw Satan.

Another scene from the sterile, hot land: Giacomo's neighbor, a mother of a priest, wrapped in black rags and throttled in her own sputum, writhing on a mattress of straw. Over the mottled wall at her face moved a winged shadow. Giacomo had seen it before: over his uncle's dead body. When the wings settled on the woman, she stopped breathing.

The bitter struggle to win back territory for Christ was filled with setbacks. In the spiders infesting the sacks of olives, in the death of unbaptised infants, in the rotted trunks of diseased groves, young Giacomo saw the steady advance of Satan in the landscape.

The song of Satan burbled up from the gorges where black rivers sped past twisted dead trees and white rock.

Sun-bleached bones of goats shimmered triumphantly with flies in the hills.

The Vatican jet jolted in a turbulence. Francis Xavier saw Cardinal Bellocchi leaning toward him, gently touching his arm.

"You have slept, Your Holiness."

Francis Xavier rubbed his eyes.

"I dreamed I was a child again in San Rignazzi. The child perceives the evil and the Christlike with pure eyes."

Cardinal Bellocchi smiled. Francis Xavier drifted into a calm, receptive state.

A scene from Bologna seminary: the headstrong Sicilian priest, Giacomo Baldoni, late at night in the sweltering library, trapped by clever Jesuit debaters into a position of heresy.

Returning to San Rignazzi, he saw the winged shadow resting on his father's coat. That midnight, the powerful peasant Luigi Baldoni, rising from bed, began to scream. Spitting blood, he stumbled crashing among kitchen plates, kicking through iron kettles, but the lungs ruptured more swiftly than seemed possible. Giacomo's father fell, stretched halfway into the dusty street of San Rignazzi, over fifty yards from the church.

The winged shadow, as it faded into the opposite alley, looked back at the priest Giacomo with a knowing smile.

"Your Holiness," whispered the assistant to the Pope.

Startled, Francis Xavier opened his eyes. Then, with a gracious smile, he took the sheaf of papers, read through them cursorily, and initialed them. The assistant bowed and took them into the forward cabin.

The Vatican jet bumped gently into dance wisps of cloud and then burst into the maroon sunset glow.

"Is your dear mother still with us?" asked Cardinal Bellocchi, seeing the fingers of Francis Xavier wound around the black rosary.

Francis Xavier smiled.

"Yes. She is eighty-three years old and still works the olive groves. A formidable woman."

Cardinal Bellocchi grinned amicably.

"She was the one who gave me my faith," Francis Xavier confided. "Many years ago."

The cardinal watched the subtly mercurial face of the Pope. Capable of the sweetest gestures and most graceful phrases, he was nonetheless obsessed with the decisive Quebec conclave.

"And you have given that faith to millions," Cardinal Bellocchi observed.

"I am only a priest."

Cardinal Bellocchi chuckled.

"But only the bishop of Rome is infallible," he said gently.

"No one is infallible."

At his first mass, Francis Xavier recalled with chagrin, out of sheer nervousness, the stumbling priest Baldoni spilled consecrated wine on the stone floor of the San Rignazzi church.

"But Your Holiness trusts directly in the Holy Spirit in a manner far closer than the parish priest."

"I am only a priest."

Cardinal Bellocchi appreciated the sincerity of Francis Xavier's humility. It endeared him to the masses who perceived in the Sicilian something nearer a saint than a man.

"It is to you, and to you alone, that the Church and a billion souls look."

"Others watch us, too." A foreboding crept into the Pope's voice.

From Boulogne: In the crypt of the great church, Bishop Baldoni, incognito, prayed on his knees with the other pilgrims, and the torch-lit shadows moved on the stone floor, and he murmured in a state of ecstasy.

It was a night vigil, and he sank into deeper and deeper levels of meditation. Suddenly, a whisper pierced his brain.

Leave this place, for thou shalt be Pope.

Baldoni's heart trembled. Wrapping his black cloak about his shoulders, he exited quickly, climbing through the tangled shoes and legs of the simple French pilgrims. The crypt was dank and infected. In three weeks, seventeen people caught the viral infection. Before the contagion burned itself out, ten were dead.

Was it the message of Christ? Or was it Satan's secret test of his ambition, for which ten souls were lost?

Francis Xavier opened his eyes wide. His fists clenched. He stared out the window at the night clouds.

Suddenly, ink flew up from the bottle of the nearest Jesuit. The fingers of the startled priest dripped with black.

"*Jesu figlio, Maria,*" the Jesuit whispered, and began wiping his hand with a tissue.

The jet droned on, sleepily, bouncing into stormy night clouds.

Then, in rapid succession, all the ink bottles of the eight remaining desks blew their caps. Black fountains spurted and stained the robes, the walls, and the carpet with the Vatican insignia.

The Jesuits stared in amazement at the mess.

"It's the new pressurized ink caps," the undersecretary, a hawk-nosed Florentine intellectual, announced. "The pressure of the cabin has fallen in the storm."

Lightning flashes illumined Jesuits, on hands and knees, cleaning the carpet and chairs with sponges and towels from the lavatory.

Francis Xavier nudged Cardinal Bellocchi and pointed to the cardinal's ink bottle. Instantly, the Nuncio covered it with a white towel. A muffled pop was heard, and a blue-black stain oozed up between the cardinal's ring and middle fingers.

"Mankind was not meant to rise so high toward God," Francis Xavier said softly. "Our proximity has resulted in the signed protest of the Holy Spirit."

Indeed, the spattered filaments of ink on the walls resembled the spidery caligraphy of monastic handwriting.

Cardinal Bellocchi chuckled heartily, grinned at Francis Xavier with affection, and gently deposited the soiled towel and ink bottle in a plastic receptacle under the desk.

The earliest memory: Giacomo's mother, prematurely grayed, explained in the dark, stony house that Christ battled constantly in the skies, in the seas, and in the cities against Satan. By candlelight, she explained to Giacomo, suffering from a child's fever, that when Christ should triumph, the good and the decent would live forever without sickness or pain, in glory and righteousness at Christ's right hand.

In the mild delirium, Giacomo, aged five, promised to become a priest and to be Christ's lieutenant.

When his mother stroked his hair, her forehead creased in worry: she saw the vulnerability in her youngest son's proud gray eyes.

The Vatican jet whined against strong headwinds. In the forward cabin, the Jesuits buckled their seatbelts.

Cardinal Bellocchi pretended to sleep. It was no use. He turned his face. Francis Xavier was deep in thought, reviewing the strange course of events that had accompanied his long rise to the papacy, and that shadowed him even now, on the eve of the Quebec conference.

"The day I was raised to the cardinalcy," he said, "I arrived in Bogotá and celebrated an open-air mass with twenty-seven priests, many of them Indians, and all recently baptized by our missionaries in the mountains."

Francis Xavier turned to the cardinal.

"All twenty-seven were shot in two weeks by the military government. Why? Why did Satan celebrate my cardinalcy with twenty-seven souls?"

Cardinal Bellocchi recognized the melancholy mood returning. He tried to smile encouragingly.

"I hear from Sicily that wax figurines of Your Holiness have been set in the churches with ferns and small flowers. Aged couples have been cured of glaucoma. Surely this is a truer sign."

Francis Xavier gently stroked the black rosary. Its weight, momentarily absent in the papal chapel, now was comforting in his fingers.

All he said was, "The millennium, Cardinal Bellocchi, is coming."

If he slept in the bucking, struggling jet, Francis Xavier was not aware of it. The air simply grew darker and the wind shrieked over the steel wings.

The storm pushed the jet south, and the pilots continually banked back into the howling rain.

A series of explosions startled him into awareness. The amber lights on the walls had gone off, one after the other, in cadenced destruction. The Jesuits stared, disbelieving, at the shards of plastic on the papal insignia of the floor.

Several crossed themselves.

As the lights died away, a curious silence permeated the Vatican jet, despite the sleet smashing over the trembling wings and windows.

Blue luminescences, cold and oval, slid down the leather walls and suede chairs of the forward cabin, hunting, gliding, searching rearward in the chill atmosphere.

The prelates watched as the ovals grew transparent, slithered over the typewriters on desks, across the chest of the undersecretary, and down from the cockpit door.

Francis Xavier raised two fingers of his right hand, signifying the authority of his office.

"It is a sign," he said, "which we do not fear."

The luminiscences glittered at the thick windows and disappeared into the hail and sleet of the night.

The Jesuits exchanged glances and fought their way over the plush carpet to their seats. For a moment, they sat in the dark. The lights began to flicker and glow again. Still, no one was able to work.

The cockpit door opened. The copilot leaned over the under-secretary, who nodded, and the Jesuits watched the copilot return to the cockpit.

"Do not be frightened," Francis Xavier said to Cardinal Bellocchi.

The cockpit door opened again. The copilot gestured animatedly toward the rear cabin. The undersecretary whispered to his assistant, who pulled a small white telephone and directory from the cabinet, and rose heavily from his seat.

Against the sickening, unpredictable drops of altitude, the under-secretary balanced his way toward the Pope through the forward cabin, fighting vertigo.

"Your Holiness," he said in a sudden absence of shrieking wind. "The fuel is no longer sufficient to reach Quebec."

The Jesuits stared panic-stricken at the undersecretary.

"Our radio contact is poor. The copilot is searching for an alter-nate airport in Newfoundland."

"We shall not land in Newfoundland," Francis Xavier replied.

Uncertain what His Holiness meant, the undersecretary looked at Cardinal Bellocchi. The Nuncio gave him no clue.

"I will inform Your Holiness," he said, "of what is happening."

The undersecretary returned to his assistant, who was trying to raise the cathedral of Quebec without success.

The drone of the jet was erratic, banging into blocks of massed air, pushed ever south, and frost now formed a further drag on the white steel wings.

"Our brothers are frightened," Cardinal Bellocchi said.

Whispered panic circulated rapidly in the forward cabin. Despite the undersecretary rapping his pencil and then his knuckles on his desk, the Jesuits gazed at the hail-battered windows and moaned.

The copilot opened the cockpit door. His face was white, and with a dry mouth and cracked lips, he whispered to the undersec-retary.

The undersecretary made his way to the rear cabin door.

"There is no fuel to reach Newfoundland!"

Francis Xavier said nothing.

The undersecretary made his way past the staring Jesuits.

Cardinal Bellocchi nervously fingered his own rosary at his frosted window.

There was a gliding sensation as the jet lost altitude. The winds lessened.

"There, you see?" enthused the undersecretary. "The very storm subsides for His Holiness's safety!"

A massive roar of frigid air knocked the fuselage to an angle. Briefcases, blankets, pillows, and typewriters cascaded around the Jesuits and smashed into broken coffee cups.

The undersecretary and his assistant fumbled desperately through the pages of the spiral-bound Vatican directory. The assistant furiously banged the telephone contact and shouted into the crackling receiver.

The cockpit door opened.

"What is it?" the undersecretary said in a dread voice.

The copilot's voice was drowned out by the storm. With great deliberation, the undersecretary made his way a final time to the papal cabin.

"Boston will take the jet."

A cumulative sigh of relief floated through the forward cabin.

The undersecretary, perceiving a strange response in the Pope and the cardinal, bowed and discreetly retired.

"The letter was from Boston," Francis Xavier said quietly.

"Yes," said Cardinal Bellocchi.

"Perhaps we are answering it."

At that moment, increased activity broke out in the forward cabin. The undersecretary had made contact with the cathedral of Boston.

An American military jet, bearing the star on its stubby wing, and then a second jet, banked through the clouds, wheeled closer, to escort them down to the storm-shattered seaboard of Massachusetts.

All three jets were streaming down now, angling quickly into the dense power of the storm. The radio and telephone crackled with flat American voices.

"I'm afraid a tragedy has occurred," said a Jesuit, suddenly appearing at the rear cabin door.

"Tragedy?" Cardinal Bellocchi asked.

"The bishop of Boston, Bishop Lyons, is in intensive care."

Cardinal Bellocchi's jaw dropped.

"But I was with him only a few days ago!" he protested. "He was in the full vigor of health!"

"A cerebral disorder, Your Eminence. Not a stroke. The cranial cavity is being investigated for a malignancy."

Cardinal Bellocchi crossed himself gently, saying an inaudible prayer for the bishop's recovery. Outside, the wind howled like dogs yelping over the down-angled wings.

"Do not be so frightened, Cardinal Bellocchi," Francis Xavier said softly. "All men are vulnerable."

Cardinal Bellocchi tried to smile.

"I only regret that between birth and death, which is salvation in Christ, so much suffering is reserved for mankind."

"It is the consequence of original sin."

"Indeed."

"Which shall endure until the Second Incarnation of Our Lord Jesus Christ."

An immense clap of lightning bathed the cabins, so intense, so close, it turned the figures of the Jesuits into reverse shadows. For an instant the scene looked like a film negative.

Clouds parted, freighters were visible in the dark waters below, and then, much sooner than Cardinal Bellocchi believed possible, the long lights and concrete runway appeared as the jet floundered heavily downward.

Red revolving lights of fire trucks and ambulances lined the runways.

The military jets swooped up and away as the Vatican jet hit the concrete very fast.

The right wheel strut cracked. Everything was curiously suspended, and then a blast of screeching, protesting metal ripped through the fuselage. The Jesuits covered their ears with their hands.

"*Oh, Dio . . . Dio . . . Jesu . . .*" came the cries.

Cardinal Bellocchi stared, amazed, out the window. The control tower seemed to rotate lazily around them. Flesh turned green and yellow as airport lights flashed past. Foam flowed, buckled, and streamed from fire hoses toward the belly of the jet.

The Vatican jet nose dipped, rose, righted, and with a sickening lurch, as though a steel cable grabbed it from behind, stopped.

"*Oh, Dio . . . Jesu . . .*"

Cardinal Bellocchi vigorously mopped the sweat from his forehead. His heart was fluttering badly, the ventricles skipping pulses. A nervous tic separated his lips into a grotesque facsimile of a grin.

Limousines and police cars raced toward the stricken jet. The entire runway came alive with yellow-garbed crew in the rainstorm running toward the smoking right wheel.

The pilot and copilot emerged from the cockpit, badly shaken, but smiling, holding their thumbs up, and the Jesuits cheered.

"We have arrived, Your Holiness!" Cardinal Bellocchi said.

A strange calm made him turn to the figure in white and gold.

Francis Xavier, the human being he loved more than himself, whose destiny he feared more than his own, said nothing, but the gray eyes were flashing and he was listening.

"Not yet, dear Nuncio," he whispered intensely. "Not yet!"

The doubt, the melancholy, the introspection, were gone. A deep, charismatic assurance flowed almost palpably from Francis Xavier. Cardinal Bellocchi stared in amazement.

Rain squalls battered the airport. Francis Xavier saw the black clouds boiling over the city's lights, and the immensities of rain on the black rolling ocean. The shrieking air screamed in voices of no known language.

Under the crimson flares, the red revolving lights, the streaming mercury floodlamps, men worked in the storm. Their eyes were dark, their uniforms drenched. Francis Xavier saw, in the blistering hard rain on the control tower, a presentiment of the greater storm that would end their tragic burdens.

Image out of the future: A skeleton, with fragments of black coat and wisps of light-colored hair, struggled from the grave, holding high its gold cross.

It was surely a sign.

Francis Xavier stirred restlessly as the wheeled stairs were pushed against the jet and the acting bishop of Boston arrived by black limousine between police lines.

"Not yet, dear Nuncio," he whispered again, eyes deepened by vision beyond the ordinary. "Not yet!"

C H A P T E R
N I N E T E E N

RAIN SQUALLS whirled down the long white Colonial houses of the Cambridge suburbs. The deep green shutters banged in the midnight storm and the street lanterns shook in the fierce rain. Branches rolled and broke apart down the immaculate broad streets.

Anita parked the white van at 355 Bilgaren Avenue. Through the windshield wipers, she looked at Dean Osborne's broad-lawned and ivy-trimmed residence. A chandelier was lighted in the hall and a fireplace reflected through the partially drawn green velvet curtains of a bay window.

She covered her face with her hands. The rain drummed mercilessly on the metal roof. All she saw in her mind was Mario standing at the door of the church, holding the revolver, and then Eamon Malcolm flung from the van to the ground and groveling.

The police could not shut down the experiment. Mario was too far gone for that. He was just crazy enough to use that revolver on them. Who else? Who else in all God's earth could ease Mario away from annihilating the priest? Anita knew, but she knew that by seeking that help, she might be destroying everything she had once been to Mario.

There was no alternative. Anita crossed the street, and a deep, booming thunder echoed down the deserted yards and wet, brown leaves snapped at her face. By the time she reached Dean Osborne's door, her long, black hair was soaked and heavy with the cold rain.

She pressed a pearl-like doorbell, heard nothing, then struck the brass knocker over the nameplate, which read *Osborne*. She struck it again and again. The glass of the upper door brightened, footsteps were audible, and Emily Osborne, the dean's wife, wearing a luxurious silk robe, opened the door cautiously.

"Why, Anita Wagner," she whispered.

"I'm terribly sorry," Anita fumbled. "I know it's late. Is the dean awake?"

"Yes. In the study."

Mrs. Osborne hesitated. In her scrutiny of the younger woman, daughter of an old rival, there was a trace of caution, even suspicion.

Then she smiled artificially and let Anita in.

Anita waited, shivering, dripping water on the Aubusson carpet. The chandelier glittered in a sickly yellow reflection that recalled the altar lamp. Dean Osborne's black umbrella rested in a wooden stand and his galoshes dried on a rubber mat. As the storm whistled through the arbor and garden behind the house, the trees creaked threateningly out on the street.

Mrs. Osborne returned from the study, smiled politely but coldly, and retired to a small den near the kitchen. Dean Osborne, wearing a heavy brown sweater and black slacks, came into the hall.

Immediately he knew that something terrible had driven Anita to his house alone.

"Please," he said, gesturing toward his study.

Anita walked into the large, thickly carpeted room. A tall fireplace burned brightly under a marble mantel and several brass antique clocks soundlessly moved on exquisite miniature gears. Fine etchings, seascapes of the Massachusetts coast, lined the library walls, and a huge Frankenthaler dominated the area behind the black mahogany desk.

Dean Osborne self-consciously watched her. She stood dripping by the doorway.

It was the image of her mother, twenty years earlier, the raven-haired, arrogant beauty that needed no one, nothing, to fulfill its own nature.

But something had changed. Anita was in need now.

"The fire will dry you," he said gently.

She moved hesitantly in front of the leaping yellow flames. They, too, seemed to shed the same sickly pallor of the altar lamp.

"I've come for your help," she said.

Dean Osborne considered. There were things he could not change, even to a personal appeal. He went to the shelf of his library wall, removed two snifters, and poured a small amount of Napoleon brandy into them.

He handed a snifter to Anita.

"I protected Mario for seven years," he said softly. "I can't do it anymore."

"That isn't what I came to see you about."

Dean Osborne raised an eyebrow. He sat down in a black leather chair in front of the fireplace. On the table, in front of the lamp, was a signed group portrait of the genetics team that had developed the DNA model.

"Then what is it, Anita?"

Anita, refusing his gesture to sit in the chair opposite, sipped the brandy. Its heat caught her by surprise. She inhaled, unable to face him yet, staring into the suggestive metamorphoses of the fireplace.

"Mario is breaking down a good and decent man. A Jesuit," she said slowly.

Dean Osborne's face twitched and his eyes seemed to darken against the ruddy glow of the firelight.

"I know. It was one reason why I canceled the project."

Abruptly, she drank the rest of the brandy, shivering.

"The problem, Dean Osborne," she said in a strange, flat voice, "is that Mario is getting results by destroying the priest."

"I don't understand, Anita."

"Mario has achieved direct psychic projection from the man. The same types of images on the tapes you're holding."

"Those images were not projections, Anita. They were some sort of pornography."

"No. Not what you saw. What's on the slides. It's real, Dean Osborne. The real thing."

Guiltily, Dean Osborne shifted his weight in his chair, trying to mask his feelings with a gracious smile. Anita was an enigma to him. A girl too lovely to stay with Mario, an intellect too fine to have gotten sucked into parapsychology. Now she had a secret stubborn obsession.

"I don't believe it," he said flatly.

"One of those images resembles the Crucifixion."

"That's the bill of goods Mario tried to peddle me. I threw him out of my office."

"Well, it's true."

Dean Osborne held his silence. Anita moved slowly from the fireplace, running her finger over the glistening brass clocks, where the internal movements seemed too perfect, too refined, for the unbounded world that Mario had ripped open at Golgotha Falls.

"Friday morning another image appeared on the thermovision screen."

Dean Osborne swallowed heavily. He searched in a carved Florentine box for a cigar. He rummaged among books and papers on his desk for a clipper.

"What kind of image?"

"A satanic image."

Dean Osborne lighted the cigar, and the flare sent shadows up from his eyebrows.

"This priest seems to be some sort of holy conduit between heaven and hell," he commented dryly, flicking ash into the fireplace. He leaned forward, conscious of the woman at the wall, and there was no need to look at her. A curious intimacy, born of conflict and sympathy, united them. Their shadows flew into the study, away from the firelight.

"Look, Anita," he said, irritated. "I saw the images Mario showed at the lecture. They were incoherent. Embarrassing. Pornographic. There was no Christ in them. He claimed we all were hallucinating." He turned to her. "You're not going to tell me you agree with him, are you?" he added.

Her silence, her brooding, restless stare, was an affirmation he found disconcerting. This was the new breed, he reflected. A superior mind that refused to duck under the familiar wiles of femininity. It was will against will, intellect against intellect. It was a violation of the subtler codes Dean Osborne had grown up with.

He felt oddly at a loss. He began thinking fast, trying to determine how to control her.

"I can't protect Mario," he said again. "He's washed up. Through. At least as far as Harvard is concerned."

"It's the priest I want you to protect."

Dean Osborne turned to her again. The dimensions of the woman baffled him. What she had gone through at Golgotha Falls, what she was going through now, he could not begin to understand.

"The priest is one of the finest, truest men I've ever known," she said softly. "Mario is tearing him to pieces."

"I don't see what I can do about it."

She turned to him simply, not pleading, but demanding.

"Drive to Golgotha Falls. Tell Mario you accept his evidence. He doesn't need to destroy the priest any further."

Dean Osborne was gripped by confused and conflicting emotions.

"Tonight," Anita said coldly.

"Tonight? I can't. I won't. It's a gale out there. Anita—"

"The priest is on the edge of irrevocable breakdown."

Dean Osborne clenched his jaw. A natural sense of mercy conflicted with that deep, indestructible hatred of Mario. Bleakly he stared at her, then into the wildly flaring fire.

"Tell Mario I accept his evidence?" he muttered. "Reinstate him? After the humiliation he has caused me? The rank and utter humiliation!"

Anita stepped closer, between the dean and the firelight, her eyes penetrating his defenses.

"As project supervisor, if anything happens to the priest you would be implicated."

Dean Osborne paused, glared at her, and downed the rest of his brandy. He went to the decanter and poured more.

"I'm not going to drive to Golgotha Falls," he said. "That's two hours away and it's a goddamn hurricane out there."

"The priest is dissociating! Disoriented! For all I know, he's already beyond help!"

"Telephone the cathedral. It's their problem."

"I can't call the cathedral."

Surprised, Dean Osborne turned back. "Why not?"

Anita avoided his glance. She was framed against the black bay window, and behind her, moaning, the storm threw leaves and rain glittering into the light.

"He fled his absolution. It may not seem much to us. But to the Church, it's a mortal sin. He'd be disciplined."

Dean Osborne shook his head in confusion.

"Maybe that's what he needs."

"He needs our help. And he needs it tonight."

Dean Osborne walked slowly to his desk and stopped, sipping brandy.

"On one condition," he said quietly.

Anita looked up, warily attuned to the change of his voice.

"What's the condition?" she asked.

"Give up parapsychology."

She stared at him angrily and curiously. He took a step toward her.

"Give it up, Anita. You see what it's done to your priest. You see what a monster it's made of Mario."

"Mario is the most brilliant intellect at Harvard."

"His science is machiavellianism," Dean Osborne stated forcefully. "He plays dictator with other people's minds."

"Yes. He's manipulative. He's violent. He's ill-mannered and offensive. Tonight he tried to shoot the tires out of the van to prevent my coming here."

Dean Osborne, shocked, stared at her, the calm, matter-of-fact way she reported such violence. She was staring at him with a piercing gaze of such beauty, such assurance, that he felt violated by it.

"But he's right about those tapes and slides!"

Dean Osborne turned away, disgusted.

"I don't believe you."

Dean Osborne sat obdurately on his desk. Anita trailed her fingers over the dark, dusty volumes of the library. A strange expression came into her eyes. Walking to a wall switch, she turned on the library lamps, one by one, until a series of amber lights in delicate upturned glass illuminated the massive rows of periodicals, texts, and collected essays.

"Dean Osborne, you were a scientist once."

Astounded, angry, he began to say something, but then let it die. The dust on the books, drifting down from her fingers as she held the volumes in front of the amber light, was excruciatingly eloquent.

"Scientific aptitude is not genetically acquired," he joked feebly.

The distinguished portraits on the wall caught his eye, and he looked guiltily away.

"The desire to know, to understand, never fades," he said, almost as though addressing the portraits and not Anita. "But the drive . . . something inside . . . goes quickly . . ."

Anita picked up a bound volume that occupied a niche by itself. It was Osborne's Ph.D. thesis. Behavioral psychology. Dean Osborne felt a piercing pain in his heart, seeing his old ambition, his once-fiery dream, resting in Anita's lovely hands like a dead piece of antiquity.

"One goes into administration," Dean Osborne said, "to provide opportunities for those who have that drive . . . that insatiable curiosity, that inexorable energy . . ."

Anita turned slowly, still holding the book. In her eyes Dean Osborne read contempt, anger, and, strangely, an infinite compassion.

"Mario *is* such a man," she whispered.

Dean Osborne grimaced.

"All right, I'll make a deal. Go back to Golgotha Falls. See how the priest is doing. If he's as bad as you say, call me. I'll send a private ambulance."

"The priest's sanity is too fragile, Dean Osborne."

"I won't justify Mario. I won't. I won't give him that satisfaction!"

"Dean Osborne, let us look at those slides. If it's pornography I'll renounce parapsychology. But if it's the real thing, then you'll come to Golgotha Falls."

Dean Osborne had turned an ashen gray, loath to make this confrontation with Mario, with his career, with himself.

So many images whirled loose in his mind he became dizzy. His father, his grandfather, both Harvard professors. His uncle Philip, famous for his work on the cyclotron. Images of sedate homes, country estates, scientific conventions. Images of strangers and colleagues, inaudibly saying *failure* as they regarded him with merciless eyes.

Something goes soft after three generations. Some vital impulse is lost to even the most prominent of families. It was Dean Osborne's bad luck to have inherited a destiny too heavy for his nature. Respected and quoted in newspapers, a man of means and influence, he had lived in subtle but constant humiliation among the scientific community. And Anita had reopened the wound tonight.

Dean Osborne recalled the omniverous curiosity, the sheer and immense *desire to know* as he had stared the other evening at Mario's slides.

Was it his destiny, his final humiliation, to be party to Mario Gilbert's success? Or was there something else, a rebirth of the intellect, a rebirth of the spirit inside himself, that waited in the safe?

That waited, possibly, at Golgotha Falls.

There was a muffled noise from the corridor. Mrs. Osborne appeared with a book under her arm.

"I'm going to bed, Harvey," she said. "Will you be long?"

"There's a man dying, Mrs. Osborne," Anita told her.

She raised an eyebrow, coolly and composed, but concerned.

"Is this true, Harvey? What is going on?"

Dean Osborne fretfully paced the floor behind his desk and then threw the remains of his dead cigar into the fireplace. A stroke of lightning turned the trees into livid, fiery blurs outside the window.

"I don't know," he confessed. "I don't *know* what· is going on." His face expressed annoyance. "Look, Emily. I have to go to campus for a short while. Go to bed and I'll be home in half an hour."

Mrs. Osborne glanced at Anita, then back at Dean Osborne.

"The storm warning is for gale winds, Harvey."

He kissed her gently on the forehead.

"Keep the hall light on," he said. "I'll be home soon."

Anita felt her looking as they went into the hall. Mrs. Osborne's aloofness was a mask for neurotic hypersensitivity, and with each flash of lightning she winced.

Dean Osborne smiled wanly and, pulling on galoshes, black raincoat, and umbrella, went out the door with Anita.

The wind turned the umbrella inside out before they got to the van.

In seven minutes, they reached the parking stall behind the sciences administration building. Dean Osborne unlocked the door, and together, dripping rainwater, they went up the marbled stairs. In the far distance, they heard the gurgle of the all-night chemistry retorts and a smell of organic compounds being filtrated by a night experiment.

The office was deserted, and the fluorescent lights made it surrealistically bleak.

Dean Osborne knelt down and turned the tumblers of the safe. His hands trembled, and his heart pounded, and as he swung open the door, he paused, not knowing what he wished to find. Dripping water, he sat at a desk used to collate mimeographed bulletins, and placed the box marked *Golgotha Falls* between himself and Anita.

"Open it," Anita breathed.

With nervous, clumsy fingers, Dean Osborne lifted off the long box top. The slides were too small, too tightly packed to come out easily. He knocked several onto the table top.

The emulsions glittered viridian under the fluorescent lamps.

Dean Osborne picked up a slide at random and held it to the light. The lightning flash silently illumined his tense profile.

He picked up another slide and peered at it. Then another, and another.

"Take a look," he said.

Anita slowly lifted a slide at random up toward the long, white fluorescent tube. She stared at it a long time.

Magnificent, clearly defined, the cruciform shape hung in an ambiguous space of the thermovision flux.

"So," Dean Osborne said in a breaking voice. "Mario's done it."

Anita said nothing.

"He's really, really done it," he repeated, squinting at the slide.

For an instant, she thought he was going to cry. The lips trembled and the face, in a peculiar expression of outrage against fate, against Mario, against the injustice of a brilliance not his own, a mockery of his own youthful ambitions, only slowly composed itself again. He covered his face in his hand and then stared again at the viridian slide.

"Christ," he mumbled.

He gazed at Anita. "Then what happened in the lecture hall," he stammered, "*was* truly a mass delusion."

Dean Osborne dropped the slide. It fell onto the other slides, glittering softly. He stared at them with repulsion.

"The paranormal frightens me," he whispered, abruptly pushing the pile away. "It has no place in this world!"

Anita rose. She stood above him.

"Dean Osborne. A man is dying. Will you help me?"

Dean Osborne nodded slowly, confusedly.

Anita moved toward the door. "Please call Mrs. Osborne. We have to get to Golgotha Falls right now."

Dean Osborne dutifully telephoned, then joined Anita in the dark corridor, turning off the office lights.

Down the corridor she walked while the rain battered the skylights overhead. Dean Osborne caught up with her and together they went quickly down the stairs and out into the parking lot.

Dean Osborne, dripping wet, clung to the dashboard as to life itself as the Volkswagen screeched up the streets of Cambridge, back into the darkness, toward Golgotha Falls.

CHAPTER
TWENTY

WITHIN THE papal jet, Francis Xavier watched the terminal building in dismay. It was very dark. Squalls battered the plate-glass windows of the terminal lounges where faces pressed forward, mesmerized by the spectacle of the gleaming, floodlit papal jet.

"Where?" Cardinal Bellochi muttered nervously, pacing the rear cabin. "Where shall we go now?"

Francis Xavier closed his eyes and leaned against the linen covering his headrest.

"Where Christ sends us," he answered softly.

The rain and sleet drummed overhead. Out on the runway, under umbrellas blown inside-out, the delegation of Bishop James McElroy of Springfield spoke urgently with the undersecretary of state for the Vatican.

In the forward cabin, the Jesuits waited. Some blew on their fingers to warm them. They alternately watched Cardinal Bellocchi and Francis Xavier.

Francis Xavier opened his eyes calmly. A police car rolled past on the runway outside, its lights revolving. Flares and floodlights glittered iridescent in the violence of the storm. Energy seemed to spiral out of a pure, annihilating darkness.

"Have the implements of the mass brought forward," Francis Xavier calmly ordered.

Cardinal Bellocchi raised an eyebrow, then signaled to a Jesuit. The Jesuit came forward and Cardinal Bellocchi whispered into his ear. Dumbfounded, the Jesuit nodded. Two other Jesuits followed him out onto the metal stairs.

The Jesuit ducked into the rain and went rapidly down the pebbled steps to the concrete.

In the cabins of the Vatican jet, no one spoke or moved as the grating sound of luggage compartments opening trembled along the curved walls.

The bishop of Springfield spied three Jesuits, each carrying a heavy walnut box on his shoulder containing the personal religious vestments and articles of the Pontiff's Office. Bishop McElroy, a large and florid-faced man, lumbered after them.

"What is wrong?" Bishop McElroy demanded. "Why is His Holiness waiting inside?"

The Jesuit stared at him, rainwater dripping off both their faces.

"Excuse me," the Jesuit said, pushing past Bishop McElroy.

The Jesuit made his way back into the jet. Once inside, the three heavy containers were laid in the center of the plush carpet. Cold water dripped steadily onto the Vatican insignia. Silent, the Italian watched the slick, glistening water drip, drip . . .

Francis Xavier stood in the forward compartment. The Jesuits turned to him reverently.

"The journey that brought us here is a journey of more than six hours," Francis Xavier said quietly. "But it is a journey that began even before our pontificate."

The Jesuits exchanged glances. Cardinal Bellocchi saw the lips of Francis Xavier tensely drawn, the forehead beaded with perspiration, belying the soft enunciation of words.

"The journey began even before our birth."

Several of the Jesuits swallowed heavily. A few had grown pale in inward terror.

Francis Xavier stepped further into the cabin, embracing them all with his glance.

"It is the journey begun two millennia ago, when Christ pitched battle against Satan," Francis Xavier said slowly. "It is the journey down which the Eternal Church has marched on its holy mission. Brothers in Christ, that which we now embark upon is the longest journey of all."

A dull crash of thunder rolled over the airfield. Red flares and police lights flashed over Francis Xavier's face, making his eyes soft and dark in the shadows.

"My children," he said very gently. "My soldiers. That journey is nearly ended."

Amber lights on the cabin walls flickered as the pilot tried an auxiliary circuit. The filaments flared, burned ruby red, and broke in two.

The Jesuits crossed themselves.

"We shall not be afraid," Francis Xavier concluded. "For our strength is Christ."

A stern fist rapped at the metal door frame.

Cardinal Kennedy of New York, a slender, white-haired man with quick, piercing eyes, stood on the final step. Behind him stood Bishop McElroy and four black-cassocked priests holding umbrellas.

"The airport will be closed for three hours because of the storm," Cardinal Kennedy said quickly to Cardinal Bellocchi. "Also, there will be no departures until the morning."

Bishop McElroy whispered behind Cardinal Kennedy.

"The secret service is worried about the crowds blocking the exits."

Cardinal Bellocchi rubbed the ring on his finger. The mass of faces pressed against the passenger terminal windows disturbed the Nuncio. In their eyes was a dark, anguished appeal. The police cordons on the runways were badly pressured by reporters and television crews wielding portable lights that splayed over the jet door.

"Come to the cathedral," Cardinal Kennedy pleaded. "His Holiness will refresh himself. In the daylight, the weather will clear."

But the cathedral recalled to Cardinal Bellocchi's mind an image of the Jesuit who had thrown himself at Bishop Lyons. Then came the arrogant, supplicating letter to the Apostolic Penitentiary. He left Cardinal Kennedy on the steps and went inside. For several long minutes, he and Francis Xavier whispered together.

"His Holiness will depart from the jet," Cardinal Bellocchi announced.

Three black limousines circled lazily out onto the runway. A great cheer arose as Cardinal Bellocchi descended the metal stairs behind Cardinal Kennedy. Flashes of cameras and brilliant floodlights burned onto the stairway.

The secret servicemen cleared the limousines and stepped back. Reporters' voices were audible, shouting into microphones. Nuns from a Boston convent pressed ecstatically against the police lines.

Then the three Jesuits came down the metal stairs, carrying the three heavy containers. Cardinal Bellocchi directed them into the first limousine.

"Surely the ground crew could deliver His Holiness's luggage!" Cardinal Kennedy whispered.

The roar of the crowd drowned Cardinal Bellocchi's reply. Red-flashing police cars surrounded the limousines. Secret servicemen edged toward the metal stairway. Even the policemen holding back the nuns turned toward the jet aperture, platinum-white in television lights.

The howl of the storm mingled into the shriek of the crowd.

Diminutive, shy, smiling, extending a single arm, Francis Xavier appeared at the doorway, and the white robe and skullcap glittered in the assault of white light.

Under an umbrella held by the Vatican undersecretary of state, Francis Xavier stepped down the ramp into a blaze of flash cameras. A sudden group of prelates, priests, and anxious police surged around the bottom of the steps. Francis Xavier seemed to disappear inside the swelling press of bodies.

In the lead limousine, in front of the three Jesuits with their wooden containers, Bishop McElroy was seated with the chauffeur.

In the second limousine, seated with the undersecretary of state and his administrative assistant, Cardinal Kennedy, much beloved and acknowledging cheers, waved to the crowds.

In the third limousine, equipped with writing table and a white telephone, Francis Xavier sat alone in the rear seat. Cardinal Bellocchi sat in the jump seat. A secret serviceman drove the long, glistening Cadillac.

Hundreds of tiny cameras clicked, miniature plastic cameras held by nuns, airport personnel, and passengers come running from the terminals. Francis Xavier waved gently to them. Television floodlights from the white communications cars wavered over the limousine and blinded him.

Three Boston Municipal Police cars formed the vanguard and led the limousines away from the Vatican jet in a broad semicircle. Four more police cars followed.

Seven motorcycle police cut through the entourage, wheeled, and formed the spearhead in the rain.

In the first limousine, Bishop McElroy looked over his shoulder and, without comprehending, saw the Jesuits jealously guarding their containers. Water dripped from them, slow and ominous. Bishop McElroy reached for a tiny black telephone and contacted the Boston cathedral.

"What do you mean, difficulties?" he thundered. "I tell you, I am in the papal entourage, and we are leaving the airport and are en route to the cathedral!"

Bishop McElroy nestled his jowls into his collar and listened.

"I am aware of His Grace's state of health."

Bishop McElroy's red face turned scarlet with anger. He listened. Then he punched a button at the base of the telephone. Cardinal Kennedy listened gravely in the second limousine.

"Disturbances?" Cardinal Kennedy asked. "What disturbances?"

He listened thoughtfully.

"Since when?" he asked. "Saturday?"

Cardinal Kennedy glanced at his watch and craned his neck to examine the eastern skies. They were still dark and foreboding.

"No," he said, irritated. "I don't know anything about a Jesuit. Well, if Cardinal Bellocchi was there, maybe he does."

Cardinal Bellocchi picked up his white telephone.

"I understand," he said after a while. "Yes. I will speak to His Holiness."

Cardinal Bellocchi put down the receiver. For a long time, he was content to watch the rain slanting down on the freeways. Then he turned and spoke quietly to Francis Xavier.

"There have been disturbing signals at the cathedral," he said gently. "The cathedral staff is badly frightened."

"When did it start?"

"Apparently after the incident I told you about."

"And the priest?"

"Nobody knows where he is."

Francis Xavier looked carefully into the reflective clouds over the wet metropolis.

"Delay our arrival until daylight."

Cardinal Bellocchi nodded. Working with Bishop McElroy and the cathedral staff, he organized a route that would circle through the heavy Catholic suburbs of the North.

By 5:00 A.M., the Boston radio stations had announced that His Holiness had decided to make an impromptu tour of the outlying dioceses before returning to the cathedral.

In the bedchamber of Bishop Lyons's residence, the stricken prelate gazed in mute horror at a television set on the armoire. Images of a skeletal figure alternated with images of the papal entourage winding into the northern suburbs.

The shock of the déjà vu immobilized the bishop. It was a vision of death, he knew, meant for Francis Xavier.

"Absolve . . ." murmured Bishop Lyons.

A Venetian vase shattered on the windowsill, sending fragments of glass onto the carpet.

"Absolve!"

The Gospel on the antique desk fluttered in a sudden breeze. One by one, stirred, the pages slowly advanced, as though an invisible finger traced the litany.

"ABSOLVE!" Bishop Lyons shrieked, face flushed red, neck straining in an arc, veins bulging, back stiff.

The Franciscans gathered closer to the bedside. To ease the bishop's torments, they began to open the vials of holy oils, and commenced the last rites.

It was a blue-gray dawn atmosphere for an eight-year-old boy named Eddie Fremont.

Something was strange. In the kitchen his mother listened to the radio. She bent over it, rapt. Frightened, Eddie rubbed the sleep from his eyes and walked barefoot toward her.

It was confusing to the boy. In his half-dreaming state he heard, or thought he heard, an airplane landing, and thousands of worshipers gathered at the Boston airport. At first Eddie thought his father had been killed in a crash. His mother, however, listened with a calm, serene sense of the miraculous.

She looked at him with an intimate glance, wondering and curious. "The Holy Father has come to Boston," she whispered, awe-struck.

Then neighbors were at the door in raincoats. Without breakfast he was dressed, stuffed into raingear, and driven headlong toward the industrial parking lot beyond the last cul-de-sac. Crowds already milled on the asphalt. The masses of nuns, priests, and parochial students with hastily made banners frightened him.

"Francis Xavier!" chanted the throng.

Suddenly the crowd cheered. Eddie turned. Up the suburban roads came a black limousine preceded and followed by police cars and motorcycles.

The crowd surged forward in expectation and the priests tried ineffectually to maintain a semblance of order. Eddie felt the collective joy come into his heart. The black limousine momentarily ducked out of sight behind a knoll.

In the limousine, Francis Xavier pressed his fingers to his temples.

The vision of the skeletal figure rising burgeoned in his mind.

Dreamlike, Francis Xavier saw the crowds under a sea of umbrellas lining the roads. Mutely, those faces expressed a potent hunger. Francis Xavier had broken from his itinerary, and he moved on an expedition of great risk.

The crowds grew as the entourage circled toward the parking lot of the industrial complex, ablaze with perimeter lights. Cafeteria workers, assembly-line men, mothers with children, several hundred priests and nuns, cheered as the limousines were sighted. But when Francis Xavier examined the faces again, he saw the same dark, spiritual dread.

"Do they sense it?" he whispered. "Do they sense something in their souls?"

Francis Xavier suddenly lowered his face into his hands.

"Cardinal Bellocchi. I have no strength. My knees tremble like an old woman's."

Cardinal Bellocchi grasped Francis Xavier's forearm.

"To him whom the Holy Spirit elects," Cardinal Bellocchi whispered fervently, repeating what he had said the morning of Baldoni's election, "to him the Holy Spirit gives strength."

And just as savagely, Francis Xavier, in a sudden agony of self-doubt, retorted again, "But *is* it the Holy Spirit?"

The déjà vu, with its skeletal figure rising, became unbearable.

"Stop the limousine!"

Francis Xavier stepped unsteadily from the limousine, assisted by his Nuncio.

In the parking lot, an extraordinary cheer shook the ground. Feverishly, Francis Xavier scrambled up a grassy knoll where he was in plain sight of nearly three thousand people. In a gesture transmitted instantaneously throughout the world, the elegant white robes flapping in the wet wind, he spread both arms and blessed the surging crowds.

"Deliver us not into the power of evil!" Francis Xavier prayed. "We feel Thy holy presence, and look for a sign of Thy holy will!"

The workers, sleepy children, and management officials saw the strained, white face on the grassy slope, and something surged through them, something altering, raising their relationship to the material earth.

"Forgive those deceived by false signs!" Francis Xavier thundered. "At the final hour, open their hearts to the mystery of Thy sacred love!"

Francis Xavier lowered his head.

"Give us the power to endure the terrors that shall precede Thy Second Coming," he prayed. "Lead us through the storm into the final harbors of eternal peace."

Many of the crowd had fallen to their knees and, hats in hand, listened, then crossed themselves. Eddie Fremont felt an electric thrill at the sight of the Pontiff and an irrepressible desire to go forward and touch him, to be touched by him, to share that sense of blessing. Eddie was not alone. The entire crowd surged forward and the secret service began to panic.

"They feel it!" Francis Xavier said, raising two fists to his chest in his esctasy. "It is soon! And it is very near!"

The police were pushing the church officials back into the limousine. Police lines were breaking down, and figures darted over the mud to seize and kiss the papal hand.

"Bishop Lyons has slipped into a coma," Cardinal Kennedy said, holding the telephone on its curled extension cord. "His final word was ... 'Absolve' ..."

Francis Xavier anxiously scanned the skies. A leaden dawn was breaking over the metropolis, heavy with the grief of centuries and generations of unfulfilled promises.

"Could it be—the priest he was referring to—?" Francis Xavier wondered aloud, stepping away, watching the northern cloud conformations. Within the boiling gray silhouettes were the winged shadows Francis Xavier had seen over his uncle, over the dying woman, on his father's coat. Francis Xavier gripped his mother's rosary until his knuckles were white.

273

"So long have I sought you," he whispered. "In San Rignazzi. In Boulogne. In the Bolivian mountains. But never, never have I been so close!"

The gloom of the wet fields and forests seemed suddenly animated. Shadows crept closer to the limousines. Francis Xavier felt the chill of an observing power.

"And when I find the snake," he said in Sicilian dialect, "I will cut off its head!"

Cardinal Kennedy touched Francis Xavier's arm.

"The weather has cleared," Cardinal Kennedy said. "We can return to the airport."

"We are not going to the airport."

"But, Your Holiness. The Quebec conference has already been postponed a day!"

"We are answering a summons, Cardinal Kennedy." Francis Xavier turned to Cardinal Bellocchi. "The priest—Eamon Malcolm, I believe—where is his parish?"

"Golgotha Falls, Your Holiness," replied the Nuncio.

Cardinal Kennedy stepped immediately forward.

"It's an isolated church in a poor valley, hours away in that direction," he complained, pointing toward the azure patch beyond the wooded hills where the dark shapes circled in the sky. "It was defiled, then attempts were made to consecrate it again. But all attempts failed."

Cardinal Bellocchi and Francis Xavier exchanged glances.

"Then *we* shall go to Golgotha Falls," said the Pope.

CHAPTER
TWENTY-ONE

MARIO GROPED through dark mud. A stench of moldered stubble and dried blood entered his nostrils. Thistles. Black beetles on his hands and shirt.

... Sucker ...

Gradually he saw again, in the mind's eye made vivid by panic, the Jesuit standing at the church door, revolver in hand. The priest's face was foxlike with a smug malignancy.

... Sucker ...

Why? How had he been used? By whom?

Percussive reports seemed to go off inside his head. The shrubs floundered around him as he flailed up the ridge. His boots dug into the wet clay. The Jesuit's insinuating laughter ricocheted in his imagination.

The first time Eamon Malcolm projected, during the exorcism, a shaft of that energy had struck Mario. The second time Eamon Malcolm projected, Mario had fallen in delirium on the Harvard lecture floor. But this time—the image of the rising dead—was like a firestorm in his head. There was no telling hallucination from reality. All Mario knew was that he had been hit with the full force of an extraordinary and insane rage.

Men's hands grabbed his arms. Mario's boots trailed over the mud.

"What . . . What the hell—?"

Overalled farmers, grim-faced and spattered with mud, were dragging him toward a weatherbeaten barn.

Mario kicked furiously, panicked.

"Let me go, you bastards! What do you think you're doing?"

But the farmers only held harder to his legs and arms, wrestling him, pushing him, carrying him toward the old structure.

"It almost happened when that priest Lovell was here," whispered a farmer with a terrifying bitterness.

"What did? What are you talking about?"

Brutally Mario felt a thistle bush smash into his ribs. The farmers carried him relentlessly over the muddy road. From time to time they looked back, ashen-faced, at the church.

"And it nearly come to pass when that white-haired man come out to Boston," said a younger farmer. "Blessed be God he died before it happened."

"Before *what* happened?"

Mario wrestled against their hold. Then he saw that two farm boys were opening the barn doors. A yawning black void greeted him.

Shouting at his captors, Mario kicked. The strong farmers' hands made him still.

"Then *you* come along," said the first farmer, breathing into Mario's face. "You and this new priest. Oh, *you* two done it all right!"

"What? What are you talking about?"

The farmer seized Mario by the collar, dragging him upward.

"We know who you been working for, mister!"

Then suddenly, Mario was catapulted into darkness. A stench of manure, wet hay, and mud enveloped him. Mario whirled and ran to the door. It was too late. The exterior wooden bar slammed into place.

Mario desperately rattled the door.

A farmer's eye appeared in a knothole.

"Taint nothing left now but to go and be divided," the farmer muttered in a voice of dread and fear.

The voice paralyzed Mario with its undeniable horror. Again he remembered all that Anita had said about what brought the images into the thermovision, the events into the church, and the fear into the Jesuit. Mario pounded on the door.

"Divided into what?" he yelled, comprehending in spite of every fiber of his being.

The twin barrels of a shotgun poked slowly through a crack in the gray timbers.

"Into the righteous and the damned!" came the grim voice.

Mario tumbled backward, over the bales of hay. Voices of the Jesuit, of Anita, of Father Pronteus roared at him through the thunder of the flying heavy-gauge buckshot.

The percussive shots reverberated twice into the dark woods south of Dowson's Repentance, east of Golgotha Valley. Anita slammed on the brakes. A third muffled report reached her ears.

"My God," Anita whispered starkly, "they're coming from Golgotha Falls."

Anita surveyed the valley. Blue fog rolled up from the Siloam and spread out, hugging the fields. It was nearly 6:00 A.M.

The van had outrun the storm. Black clouds raged outward from the coastline toward the sea. Wind gusts still buffeted the oaks and the fields, and barn doors slammed, breaking the eerie silence. Occasionally an owl called and a black form flew with great loops of its wings into the forest.

"It's so desolate," Dean Osborne muttered nervously. "It's what hell must be like."

"That road," Anita said, pointing. "I don't know if the van can get over it."

The asphalt leading into fallen branches was badly rutted. Crevices loomed like chasms under the headlights. Vague fingers of the blue fog drifted over the road from the wetter woods.

Anita started the van. Resolutely she drove into the grit and broken asphalt, the branches snapping under the wheels and flying out from the rear. Dean Osborne instinctively ducked, holding on to the dashboard as he bounced.

The gloom of the predawn light filled the valley with a blanket of stillness.

"Anita," Dean Osborne said.

"Yes?"

"I never believed in God."

Anita did not answer.

"I tried to," he said, assuaging his unease by talking. "I went to church regularly until I was thirteen. I even studied comparative religion in college. But it made no sense to me. Not *logical*. You know what I mean?"

He opened his eyes and turned to her. Anita, intent on the road, wiped away the moisture from the inside of the windshield.

"Did you, Anita?" he asked gently. "Did you ever believe?"

Anita kept her eyes on the dark, wooded path among the ferns.

"I met a man who believed in God," she finally said. "It's changed my mind."

Dean Osborne held on to the dashboard as the van rolled over black branches.

"The Jesuit?"

She nodded.

"Through him I experienced some . . . some kind of force, some kind of love. I felt it in him and now it's in me." She looked at him. "It's like a small captured bird deep inside."

Impressed, his eyes turned back toward the road.

"My wife is not well," he said. "The doctors don't know what's wrong. I've searched again, Anita, for some divine answer. But all I find is a great emptiness."

Anita slowed the van down. She was approaching Golgotha Falls from the north, the far side of the Siloam, having swung around the edge of the valley. The road gradually disappeared into a short morass of hard mud and decayed trunks. She brought the van to a sudden stop.

"What is it?" Dean Osborne asked.

In the glare of the headlights a raccoon stood on its hind legs. The blinding beams froze the animal. Its tiny forelegs wavered, mesmerized.

Anita got out and gently pushed her boot at the raccoon. It stumbled sideways into the ferns. Then it waddled into the dense mushrooms and fallen logs of the blue fog.

Sharp, glistening holly grew along the logs. Red berries were ripe and bright at the center of the leaves.

"Strange," Dean Osborne said as Anita got behind the wheel. "It's not the season for holly."

"I know," Anita said softly.

Puzzled, Dean Osborne looked at her. Then Anita gunned the engine, the Volkswagen shot forward, and they pushed into the cold ultimate dawn unfolding at the far end of Golgotha Valley.

Mario awoke with a piercing pain in his side. His groan filled the blue-gray light of a cloudy dawn. For an instant he had no recollection of where he was or who he was or why he lay in a filthy barn.

Then the nightmare of a Jesuit who was not a Jesuit came back to him, and he remembered.

The farmers were gone. Why hadn't they come into the barn, making sure of killing him, just as they had destroyed a score of deformed calves and lambs? The buckshot had torn out heavy timbers in the rear of the barn, but had gone over his head.

Maybe, Mario realized, they were running out of time.

He pulled himself loose from the straw and manure heap where he lay. He slapped the crud from his shirt and trousers, his eyes searching the upper regions of the hayloft. A solitary window offered a possible avenue of escape.

Mario piled bales over a broken harrow and climbed on top. He reached the sturdy steps of a rickety ladder, swung his weight onto it, and hoisted himself painfully into the loft. From the window he had an unobstructed view of Golgotha Valley.

The fog had lifted. The morning was clear. The farmers and townspeople were nowhere in sight. The church seemed empty. Mario could not see any of his instruments from his angle. Eamon Malcolm was nowhere in sight.

"Sick bastard!" Mario muttered.

A peculiar sound drifted over the south ridge, a droning like a slurred version of bees in flight.

Mario turned, craning his neck. Over the birch woods he saw only the turbulent clouds of the storm far to the east. Birds flew up from the branches. The drone grew louder.

A motorcycle crested the ridge and drove down the looping road.

Astounded, Mario leaned further out the window. The motorcycle glinted in the sun, far away, and the rider wore boots. It was a policeman. Mario ducked back into the barn.

Had Anita sent the police after him? Maybe someone from Golgotha Falls had alerted the police to the danger of Eamon Malcolm?

Slowly he looked again.

A second motorcycle crested the ridge and followed the first down the looping road. Then a third and a fourth policeman entered the valley.

Four cops to pick up—who?

But the policemen stopped at the large loop in the road to confer. They pointed at spots around the church and the town with their gloves. One spoke into a radio. They acted efficiently, quickly, and the motorcycles fanned out to take up stations along Canaan Street.

Had they been summoned by the priest's projective power?

Mario flung bales onto the ground below the window. Grabbing the rope from a pulley he swung down over the bales, then dropped painfully to the ground.

He walked slowly along the grassed slope of the south ridge. Two more motorcycles, then a single one abruptly crested the birch woods. Mario ducked into the shrubs. When they had passed he loped along the hillside, head down, for a better view of the entire town.

A deer, caught in the shadows of interlaced branches, stared at Mario. Where the bony antlers came together on the head a white cruciform glowed, halolike, in the rising sunlight.

"Oh, Christ!" Mario breathed.

He ran furiously toward the top of the ridge. A different kind of drone came, faded, then came stronger through the redolent air. Mario crouched among the thick ferns.

A Boston Municipal Police car sent dust flying as it curved up over the ridge.

Did Anita tell some precinct about his revolver? Still, it seemed unlikely so many police would have come.

A second squad car, skidding slightly on the loose gravel and pebbles, came past the break in the birch woods. Mario watched. The two policemen looked very professional, scanning Golgotha Valley before descending into it.

Mario stood up. *What the hell was going on?*

Behind a third and fourth squad car, glinting in a sun-flecked patch of road, came a black Cadillac limousine bearing the Catholic insignia of the Boston diocese. Mario stumbled out into the road in total confusion. Lamely, he waved his arms.

But the limousine roared relentlessly past. Mario stepped back, coughing in the dust. Three Jesuits in the rear seat stared at him, clutching wooden boxes. Mario stared at the Cadillac.

Had the cathedral sent its Jesuits to reconsecrate the Church of Eternal Sorrows, not realizing the manic powers of Eamon Malcolm, perhaps not suspecting he was even there?

"Go back!" he shouted.

Then he saw in the distance two motorcycle police veer about and head his way. Mario could see the aggressive clamp of their jaws, the hard eyes prepared for violence. He backed quickly down the road.

A second limousine roared around a loop in the road, coming up from the birch shadows.

Cardinal Kennedy, seated in the rear, glared at the figure in the road, the wild matted hair, the scratched face, the fiery eyes. Mario stopped, shocked by the sight of a cardinal in the desolate valley.

Cardinal Kennedy held his hand out the window, slowing down the procession, and gazing nervously at the limousine behind him.

It was then that Mario saw the white and gold papal flags fluttering on each fender of the last Cadillac in the convoy. Within its deepest recess, the visage of Francis Xavier, the Pontiff himself, stared questioningly back into Mario's stricken eyes.

All at once Anita's words came hurtling back at him: *"He feeds on priests . . . he's after bigger game . . . !"* And his own cynical response: *"And who would that be? . . . The bishop? . . . The Pope? . . . Jesus Christ Himself? . . ."*

Anita believed Eamon to be in danger of the Antichrist. Was that what had ultimately possessed him?

Or was it, as Mario still tried to believe, an uncanny power of psychic projection out of the priest?

Could that power have gone beyond Harvard? Into, say, the cathedral of Boston, into the minds of clerics and prelates there? Or further, further than the cathedral, into the very heart of the universal Church, to mesmerize, falsify, and torture with its extraordinary primal rage of personal pain?

Either way, only he knew the danger into which the papal entourage was driving with such blind assurance.

"Go back!" he shouted, waving his arms before the startled Pontiff. A police car moved out of the calvacade, heading for the intruder. The two motorcycles converged on him.

"For Christ's sake get out of here!" Mario yelled, rushing at the Pope's Cadillac and beating his fists against the bullet-proof glass. *"IT'S A TRAP!"*

Instantly the two motor policemen tackled him. They struggled in the dust. Mario kicked, bucked, and threw himself forward, crawling on hands and knees.

"THE PRIEST IS MAD!" Mario shouted.

281

A nightstick crashed down on top of his head. He fell, but did not lose consciousness. The police car stopped beside the Pope's limousine and two more policemen jumped into the clouds of swirling dust, revolvers drawn.

"The priest is—" Mario tried to say, his arms twisted and handcuffed behind his back, legs kicking out into the air.

Two more police dismounted on the crest of the ridge and with revolvers drawn examined the edge of the birch woods for further interlopers.

The chief's squad car drew up to the handcuffed Mario. "Get him in the patrol car!" he grunted from his open window. "Keep a sharp eyes on him!"

Mario felt himself lifted, then thrown bodily into the rear of a car, behind a mesh that separated him from the front seat.

Slowly the limousines moved forward and continued their descent into Golgotha Valley.

"Get out of here!" Mario bellowed, kneeling toward the patrol car window. *"It's a—"*

A rough fist stopped the shout. Mario fell slowly against the glass. He saw dessicated fields below and the dark, shadowy form of the Jesuit inside the church.

"... trap ... God ... stop him ..."

Disgusted, the policeman in the front seat closed the wire barrier. "Loony bastard," he said.

From the squad car's vantage point parked on the ridge, Mario had a mezzanine view of the unfolding drama. Further up the ridge the papal party was congregating, arranging itself for its triumphal entry into the Church of Eternal Sorrows. Below, a steady stream of incoming traffic inched its way toward the throng already gathered before the church.

"Christ," the policeman commented. "Looks like all Boston's come out for this circus."

Mario threw himself forward against the restraining cage. "The Pope . . ." he stammered through gritted teeth. "He's in mortal danger!"

The policeman turned and stared at Mario. "Why?" he asked dryly. "Are there more of you?"

Mario edged closer to the wire. "The Jesuit priest inside the church," he rasped. "He's got a gun!"

The policeman scrutinized the burly figure in the back seat. "Where would he get a gun?"

Mario licked his lips. The police hostility was far more intense than anything he had experienced from the campus cops. These men were accustomed to violence. Mario had the impression they'd be glad to work him over a bit with their nightsticks.

"I—I had a revolver. He stole it."

"You licensed to carry a gun?"

"No—"

The policeman leaned intently toward the wire divider. Flickering shadows of the morning sun passing through trees dappled his face.

"Who are you working for?" he asked tautly. "Some revolutionary group?"

"Goddamn it!" Mario shouted. "I'm trying to tell you the priest in that church is insane! He's capable of psychic projection! He can deform thought! He can make you see Satan!"

The policeman blinked, staring at Mario. Then, without warning, he burst out laughing. He laughed so hard he had to wipe his eyes with a handkerchief. His partner behind the wheel joined in the hilarity.

"Satan!" the policeman gasped, drying his eyes. "Dear God— Satan!" Focusing his red-rimmed eyes on Mario, he shook his head. "You want to see Satan, mister, you don't have to go to Golgotha Falls to find him. We can show you Satan right in our precinct house. We got a man there killed his brother, raped his sister. We got a sweet little lady put strychnine in the milk of schoolchildren. Satan is everywhere you look, buddy!"

Defeated, Mario slumped back in his seat. Miserably he stared at the spectacle below. The Catholic Church, following its nose for exploitation, was transforming the twentieth century's clearest proof of the paranormal into a religious bacchanal.

Mario could take on Harvard, Dean Osborne, Eamon Malcolm. The police of the world. False sentiments and illusions, backed by the almighty Catholic Church. But not all together, in concert. Not handcuffed in the rear cage of a police car, forgotten and disdained by anyone in power.

The bitter residue of complete defeat left salt on Mario's lips.

"All right, you bastards," he whispered. "You've been warned."

C H A P T E R
T W E N T Y - T W O

FRANCIS XAVIER stood on the ridge of Golgotha Valley. The ground below was ashen gray, disturbed by a breeze that shifted the sediment of the clay at the river. Lilies poked up from the slopes and purple irises shimmered on the banks. A smell of smoke curled down through the valley.

In the deepest part of the valley, where the wind-blown dust and ash circled, stood the white clapboard church.

Francis Xavier studied the Church of Eternal Sorrows.

"It's not what I imagined," he murmured. "Not what I expected at all."

Cardinal Bellocchi peered down past the shivering scrub brush and brambles at the edge of the cemetery. A motion at the church door caught his attention. The church's Jesuit sensed he was being observed, and ducked abruptly back inside.

"I don't like it," Cardinal Bellocchi said worriedly.

Crowds had gathered before the church and along Canaan Street. Their faces were filled with an agitated expectancy as the police firmly took up stations around them.

A need appeared in their eyes, something coming from deep within their worn bodies and beaten spirits.

The robes of the Pope filled out in the wind. He rubbed his hands together against the morning chill. "It's a desolate place. As are the caverns of hell, and Christ's tomb."

In the restless ash and fields of the valley encompassing the church Francis Xavier saw a curious mixture of Christ and Satan, life and death, struggling with each other to a bitter, savage end.

The crackle of police car radios and the low commentary of radio and television crews rose with the breeze. A droning murmur came from the crowds who pressed impatiently against the police lines. From the north and the south a steady procession of cars and trucks moved sluggishly into the town, converging on the white church.

Then the church bell tolled; each peal strong, commanding, vibrant. Francis Xavier saw the heads of the crowd jerk in the direction of the white steeple, and with each clang of the iron bell, press forward in a massive phalanx. Police and secret servicemen nervously spread out in a vain effort to contain the hordes.

"Yes," Francis Xavier whispered. "It is here. It is now."

At a signal from Francis Xavier the Jesuits lifted the wooden boxes onto their shoulders and prepared to descend the dusty ridge.

"We are in the living presence of evil," Francis Xavier cautioned. "Trust in Christ and observe the signs of His tormentor."

The Jesuits, pale, hair blown wildly by the increasing dry wind, licked their lips and nodded.

The newsmen could not comprehend why the Pope stayed so long on the ridge, nor why the limousines had stopped there at all.

Bishop McElroy edged back, closer to Francis Xavier. The crowds below were pushing upward against the police lines, and the dark hunger in their eyes looked to him like some barely muted animal rage. Cardinal Kennedy, too, felt an ominous emotional density in the valley.

"Extraordinary. Really extraordinary," spoke the WABC commentator into his microphone. "Francis Xavier, simply by seeking out an isolated parish church, which boasts only a single Jesuit priest, has galvanized Catholics and non-Catholics alike. This valley, like

285

the airport and the suburbs, is filled with an expectancy and hope I have never witnessed before."

Stepping onto the valley floor, Francis Xavier clenched the black rosary tightly.

"Let us begin," Francis Xavier said. The Pope walked into Golgotha Valley.

Steam rose at each step.

Bishop McElroy, astounded, drew back. Cardinal Bellocchi pulled the bishop onward by the crook of the elbow. Behind them came the Jesuits carrying the boxes, and the undersecretary of the papal state and his assistant, dressed in carmine robes and capes.

Cardinal Kennedy fell behind Cardinal Bellocchi. As they walked down along the edge of the cemetery toward the mass of worshipers, an acidic scent assailed his nostrils.

A policeman drinking coffee by his motorcycle in front of the grocery store looked behind him. Canaan Street steamed from the fissures in the old asphalt, rising above stalled cars, trucks, and the crowd.

Francis Xavier advanced toward the Church of Eternal Sorrows, photographed by three television teams.

Two secret servicemen stepped out of the church. All they had found inside was a lone Jesuit preparing the mass and some electronic cables and equipment they assumed belonged to WABC.

Like sheep before the shepherd, farmers, townspeople, and out-of-towners massed before the church door in anticipation of Francis Xavier.

A cameraman for WSBN waited in the rubble mounds for a good shot. A cacophony of competing radio and television commentators jabbered over his head, and the dust swirled up from the boots and shoes of the multitude. At last the head of Francis Xavier came into view, framed against a clear blue sky.

The Pope looked at him through the lens. The cameraman felt a sudden suspension of weight and time. It was his first experience with charisma. Then it was over. His camera swung around as nearly two thousand people, worshipers in total awe of Christ's surrogate on earth, fell back and cleared a path for him and his holy entourage.

From the north a white Volkswagen van raised a cloud of gray dust in the morning sun.

The van screeched to halt at the police roadblock, skidding halfway around on the broken asphalt, sending bits of pavement flying.

Instantly two patrolmen advanced with their hands on their revolvers.

Anita stuck her head out from the driver's side. The van now straddled the road, from which point she could look down the gentle slope toward Golgotha Falls. Steam wavered up from the streets. Police and reporters milled about, and along the rooftops were stationed more police in plain clothes.

In the clay hollow, among the crowds of people massed before the church, she saw the mechanic Fred Waller, the eccentric spinster Miss Kenny, and the grocery store clerk. Then she spotted the carmine cape of a cardinal, his hands folded together, moving majestically through the masses before the church.

Anita stepped out of the van. Why were all those people here? Where was Eamon Malcolm? Where was Mario? Then she saw another prelate, wearing a shimmering white cape and skullcap, appearing in advance of the marching group.

She turned to the approaching patrolman.

"Who are those church officials? Why are they in Golgotha Falls?"

"They're part of the Vatican party," said the first patrolman.

Anita stared at him. "The Vatican party—" her lips formed silently, as she stepped further up the asphalt road.

The patrolman's arm stopped her.

"That's about as far as you go, lady," he said. "The town is filled with all the people it can hold."

She shook off the hand. In the rising gray dust below she saw a familiar figure approach the church door.

"Who is that man?" she said, her voice flat and slow.

"Now who do you *think* he is?" smiled the patrolman.

Anita studied the olive-skinned face under the white skullcap. An aggressive face, a worried face, yet alight with confidence and determination.

Anita looked above at the ridge. There were three parked black limousines, one of which bore the fluttering papal flags on the fenders. Suddenly the presence of so many policemen made an awful, unmistakable sense. Suddenly she knew who the familiar figure was.

Dean Osborne had climbed out of the van and was standing by her side. "What's happening down there?" he asked her.

"I can't believe it," she whispered in shock. The words she had used to warn Mario now assailed her. *"He's collecting priests . . . These are only steppingstones!"*

Suddenly Anita broke away, running toward the church.

"No!" she shouted. "God, NO!"

"What's your problem, lady?"

"You've got to stop him! He mustn't enter that church!"

"Stop the Pope? It's *his* church!"

Through the roseate window, Anita vaguely glimpsed the black form of the Jesuit at the altar. He moved in a stealthy way, reptilian, and not at all like Eamon.

"No, it isn't! It isn't his church at all!"

Francis Xavier clutched the black rosary as he stepped onto the threshold of the church door.

The crowds pressed against the police lines. Many of the police crossed themselves as the Pope knelt on the threshold and kissed the ground. Then, rising, Francis Xavier in a loud voice called, "Where is the priest who brought us here?"

The church door slowly opened.

The figure of Father Eamon Farrell Malcolm humbly knelt in the vestibule. He held out his hand to Francis Xavier, who stepped over the threshold and into the Church of Eternal Sorrows.

Standing in the sunlight, Cardinal Bellocchi dimly saw the face of the Jesuit. It was the face of an unabsolved man. The shadowed eyes were confused, dangerous, and driven by a mute horror.

Eamon reached for the extended hand of Francis Xavier, pursed his lips, and kissed in obedience the gold Ring of the Fisherman.

Cardinal Bellocchi quickly ran toward the church threshold.

"No, Your Holiness!" he shouted. "That priest is not absolved!"

Eamon rose quickly, turning to Cardinal Bellocchi. The Jesuit's eyes narrowed, and a reddish glint came from their depths. A malevolent grin displayed sharp, white teeth, and a black tongue flicked out of the lips.

Cardinal Bellocchi drew back sharply, covering his face in the stench.

"Baldoni's mine!" rasped a strange voice out of the Jesuit. Whereupon the oaken door slammed shut with a resounding reverberation, cutting off Cardinal Bellocchi at the threshold.

Cardinal Bellocchi rapped desperately on the door, then pulled on the handle with all his strength.

"Open the door!" he shouted hoarsely.

"Not until Christ Himself touches the bolt!" came the twisted voice from inside the vestibule.

The Vatican Jesuits lowered their wooden cases and ran to join Cardinal Bellocchi at the door. They pulled at the handle, pounded, tried to jimmy the hinges, but the simple wooden door, glistening in the sunlight of Golgotha Falls, was obdurate.

Cardinal Bellocchi, dismayed, trembling with premonitions of catastrophe, walked weakly back from the door as beyond he heard, "Come, Baldoni," hissed by a voice like an insect's. "Come with me to my altar."

The police and secret servicemen beat against the door furiously. It was no use. The door was closed with a preternatural force.

"Get the axes!" commanded the police chief. "Break it down!"

Two policemen wielding heavy axes strode up to the door and raised them above their heads. At the very first contact of steel against wood a bolt of lightning and a shower of fiery sparks sent the axes flying from their hands and their bodies hurling senseless to the ground. The mob and prelates fanned back in terror.

In despair Cardinal Bellocchi looked through the Gothic window. Francis Xavier, face white in the light of a strange and flickering yellow altar lamp, walked toward a gleaming white altar. The black-cassocked Jesuit, obsequiously bowing and leading the way, led him toward the center of his own unholy domain.

Francis Xavier walked calmly beside Eamon, down the central aisle, examining the face of the Jesuit. In that agonized, arrogant visage there were two souls: one in supplication to be freed, and a second filled with a venomous hatred.

For a long time neither spoke, each taking the measure of the other.

Francis Xavier turned to observe the details of the nineteenth-century church: the modest architecture, the spare pillars and rafters, the straightforward Gothic windows. It had neither the splendor of Rome nor the stone crudeness of San Rignazzi.

The light of day ceased at the windows. Removed from the external world of matter and appearance, the church atmosphere flickered in the light from the yellow altar lamp.

"I would love to have served in such a church," the Pope said softly.

Francis Xavier turned to Eamon. In those eyes he saw, overwhelming the nature of the man within, the ancient power that had tormented him from San Rignazzi to Boulogne to the Vatican. In the abode now of evil's creation, Francis Xavier would either expell the defilement from the Jesuit and his church or suffer himself the excruciating death of the soul.

The struggle was joined. It would be elemental, brutal, and without compromise.

"You fool!" Eamon sneered, lip rising. "It is Satan's church!"

"It shall be made Christ's," Francis Xavier said calmly, and then, addressing Eamon within the body, added, "through you."

But the power twisted Eamon's lips into a hideous grin, revealing the dark tongue and sharp white teeth.

"Look what has come," he shouted triumphantly, "through me!"

Eamon raised an arm, gesturing around the church walls. A grim twilight descended from the rafters. The light level in the church fell. As the gloom deepened it grew cold, and Francis Xavier's breath steamed white. Blue luminescences, like tiny barracudas, glided around the church pillars and fed off the defiled altar. The sickly yellow lamp flared supreme over their heads.

"Don't you realize now who brought you to Golgotha Falls?" Eamon demanded.

"The Holy Spirit."

Eamon laughed, and the blue, parched lips looked almost black under the altar lamp.

"No," he chuckled rudely. "My messengers."

Eamon pointed to the Gothic windows. There, silhouetted against the light of day, clustered the winged shadows. They were the messengers of defilement and death that Francis Xavier had seen at San Rignazzi.

The winged shadows that had led him from the suburbs to the white church swarmed lazily into the church, intimately clustering on Eamon's shoulders, then fading into the dark gloom.

In the cold darkness the ruby tints of Eamon's eyes burned fiercely at Francis Xavier.

"I watched you as a child, Giacomo Baldoni," he whispered with a primordial hatred. "I whispered in your ear in Boulogne."

Francis Xavier recalled the ambiguous, chilling breath that had made him leave the disease-ridden crypt so long ago.

"I chose you as my own," Eamon said. "I followed you throughout your whole career."

Francis Xavier remembered now the deaths of the religious, the recently baptized, the devout priests who had attended his rise toward the chair of Saint Peter.

Eamon stepped closer, his breath foul, his eyes gleaming and derisory.

"When the archbishop of Genoa stumbled over the Sistine Chapel floor, pointing at you, saying, 'It is you, it is you,' who did he see in your eyes?"

"The Holy Spirit."

Eamon showed his teeth in a soundless laugh that hissed into the dead silence of the church.

"It was *me* he saw!" Eamon laughed shrilly. "And he was mightily surprised!"

Francis Xavier smiled softly, looking Eamon directly in the eyes.

"You lost that election," Francis Xavier said gently.

Eamon recoiled. In the simplicity, the unbreakable assurance of Francis Xavier he felt an unbearable obduracy.

"*Who led you to Golgotha Falls?*" Eamon roared, outraged.

"The Holy Spirit."

"*I* led you here!"

Eamon suddenly raised a hand and held it over the black rosary in Francis Xavier's hand. It grew slowly weightless. Francis Xavier, pale, watched it twirl, unheld, in the dark atmosphere of the church.

"Look at your vision of the Resurrection!" Eamon yelled.

Eamon pointed to the thermovision camera on its twisted tripod in the shadows. On the screen Francis Xavier saw a skeletal figure rising, holding a gold crucifix: his vision out of the storm that brought him down in Boston.

"Mimicry," Francis Xavier said calmly, turning back to Eamon. "You mimic the signs of the Holy Spirit. But it was the Holy Spirit that led me here. And for one purpose."

Eamon listened warily. Francis Xavier watched the foxlike face show agonies of hatred, doubt, and a brutal impatience. He also saw, beneath that, the vulnerable and delicate soul of a frightened priest.

"To expel you from the priest's body," Francis Xavier said calmly.

Eamon exhaled a bluish stream of cold vapor, laughing in derision.

"And from his sanctified church," added the Pontiff.

Peals of laughter shook Eamon's body. He raised his arms lovingly toward the unholy altar lamp.

"*My* church!" he roared. "*My* priest!"

The altar lamp swung wildly. Veils of burning oil slipped from the reservoir basin. Small balls of fire scattered, stinking, onto the church floor and around Francis Xavier's feet.

"MY WORLD!"

The tortured laughter of the Jesuit rang out into the hard sunlight of Golgotha Falls. It was a mesmerizing sound. The kneeling crowds before the church clasped their hands before them. Several policemen sank to their knees and removed their caps. The cynics of the television teams also found themselves moved, as within the church the windless atmosphere shook with the demented laughter of the fallen priest.

"Per Dominum nostrum Jesum Christum Filium tuum—"

Cardinal Bellocchi's exquisite voice rose in ascending scales, confident and masculine, leading the priests and the Christians gathered before the church, who signified;

"Qui venturus est judicare vivos et mortuos—"

From within the church the clear voice of Francis Xavier joined the prayer.

"Propitius esto, exaudi nos, Domine—"

Cardinal Kennedy and Bishop McElroy translated in English.

"From all evil, deliver us, O Lord."

"Ab omni peccato, a morte perpetua—"

"From all sin, from everlasting death."

"Per mysterium sanctae Incarnationis tuae—"

"Through the mystery of Thy Holy Incarnation."

The WABC sound recorders registered all.

Then, as if by some innate sense, all heads raised from their prayers and looked upward into the east. Massive, boiling cloud formations moved toward Golgotha Falls.

Anita stood in the cemetery, a sudden wind whipping through her hair. Dean Osborne, standing beside her, loosened his tie and removed his coat.

Anita noticed how pallid his face had turned, how his hands trembled.

"Something extraordinary is happening," he whispered.

Anita scrutinized the eyes grown dark, excited, eager, extraordinarily eager as he scanned the skies, the crowd, the pale and gleaming church.

"I studied mass psychology," he said. "My God, Anita, something unprecedented is going on here!"

292

Anita listened to the chanting emerging from the church and the responses of the throng. She gazed at the uplifted faces, even the children's, suffused with a belief she found stirring.

"Is that all it is?" she asked. "Mass psychology?"

Dean Osborne brushed his hair down against the wind and watched her step away to study the faces of the crowd.

"You can feel it," Dean Osborne maintained. "What these people feel. It charges the air."

Dean Osborne stepped up to Anita and took her elbow.

"Their reality has fused into a collective emotion," he explained. "By God, I recognize it now!"

"*Their* reality?" Anita said gently, looking him directly in the eyes. "Why isn't it—simply—*reality*—?"

Taken aback, Dean Osborne was momentarily stopped. He let go of her arm. Anita turned to the crowds again.

"The ultimate reality . . ." she whispered.

Dean Osborne nervously paced the edge of the cemetery. Fragments of theory, ideas now ten years out of date, surged through his brain. Yet he felt extraordinary in the presence of such a mass phenomenon.

He even felt, though easily resisted, the temptation to kneel and pray with the crowds.

Mario pressed his face against the squad car window. Figures in the cemetery reminded him of Anita and Dean Osborne. Hallucinations? Mario shook his head, trying to clear his mind. When he looked again he was certain it *was* Anita. The beefy body of a policeman blocked his view.

"Nice ass," he commented. "She a buddy of yours?"

"Yes," Mario replied quietly.

"What's her business, blowing up bridges?"

"She's a parapsychologist."

"What the hell is that?"

"A scientific discipline."

"Well, whatever it is," the policeman leered, "I might just enroll in it someday."

But Mario wasn't listening. Had that really been Dean Osborne? What could bring him to the Golgotha Falls site?

Pope Francis Xavier and Eamon became visible through the Gothic window. In the altar light the two seemed caught in a momentary stasis. Mario felt the old sensations of reverence toward the Holy Pontiff rise despite all the years of psychoanalysis and scientific training. In some deep corner of his heart, Mario realized, the Church had indeed sunk its shaft. With a start he saw Francis Xavier suddenly leap forward, grab Eamon's right wrist, and pull it toward him.

"I have come for *you*, Eamon Malcolm!" he whispered, searching for the lost soul within the cagey face.

Eamon tried to shake off Francis Xavier's grip. But the strong hands of the peasant tightened around the wrist. Francis Xavier's deep gray eyes bore into Eamon's.

"Pray with me, Eamon!" Francis Xavier commanded. "Give your soul back to Christ!"

Eamon wrestled against the grip, but to no avail. His nostrils ran with mucus. His bloodshot eyes looked back in mute horror.

Astounded, Francis Xavier saw in Eamon the priest he once must have been. A passion seemed to burn within that knew no bounds. It had no trappings of ecclesiastical power. It flared with a terrifying, vulnerable purity.

"Let me go!" rasped the foreign, obscene voice out of Eamon's lips.

Francis Xavier looked deeper into those blue, supplicating eyes. Suddenly the mission to Golgotha Falls was revealed. The endless incognito visits to grottoes, crypts, and parish churches around the world had had but this as their goal: to find the fierce, eternal flame of faith that had once consumed him so utterly as a boy in San Rignazzi.

"Pray with me, Eamon!" Francis Xavier whispered again. "As a child prays. Without reservation. Your whole heart must believe; you must call for Christ to enter your heart again!"

"I—can't—" Eamon faltered, a cracked human voice rising momentarily from its imprisonment.

Francis Xavier's eyes brightened at having achieved the slight contact with Eamon's inner spirit.

"Then I shall show you how, my son," he said very gently.

Francis Xavier guided Eamon down, down to his knees before the altar. Gently the peasant hands folded Eamon's into the attitude of prayer. Francis Xavier smiled encouragingly.

Suddenly a terrible nausea swept through Eamon and he doubled over. Francis Xavier raised him again.

"Holy Father," Eamon managed to whisper. "I shall surely die."

Francis Xavier, astounded at the intensity of Eamon's torment, recognized a rare and extraordinary gift of faith.

"He who believes in Christ," Francis Xavier said lovingly, "shall never die."

From deep within the confinement of an evil so abhorrent that he longed for death, Eamon saw the gleaming pectoral cross, the immaculate vestments, and the distinguished, dreamlike Sicilian face in the darkness of the church.

Dimly, Eamon understood that he himself had been chosen as the vehicle of a struggle so profound it threatened the earth itself with destruction.

Freely the charisma of Francis Xavier came flowing in, burning away the corrosion, and Eamon dared to rise, spiritually, toward that force.

Francis Xavier folded his hands in prayer and eyed Eamon significantly.

"Say as I do, Eamon," he whispered.

Eamon felt the devil rise within himself. It formed an indomitable wall of vileness, an arrogant, suffocating power, and he began to choke. Eamon closed his eyes and felt himself slipping back into the deep tunnel of imprisonment.

"*Propitius esto, parce nobis, Domine,*" Francis Xavier began.

The words penetrated Eamon like a beacon. With cracked lips, terrified of revenge, Eamon suddenly placed his faith in Francis Xavier.

"From all evil, deliver us, O Lord," Eamon repeated in English.

Visions of white chameleons, bellies trailing blood, assailed him behind closed eyes. The force that imprisoned him sent clouds of insects, vile hallucinations, to plague the devout brain.

In the silence he felt the proximity of Francis Xavier.

"*Ab omni peccato, a morte perpetua,*" Francis Xavier said calmly.

"From all sin, from everlasting death!"

It was a plea from Eamon's heart, so anguished that Francis Xavier opened his eyes and studied the face of the tortured priest. It was a subtle echo of his own desperate wanderings to grottoes and crypts and parish churches.

"*Per mysterium sanctae Incarnationis tuae,*" Francis Xavier continued boldly.

But the devotion was broken. Eamon slipped down, back to the dark well in which he was drowning. On the Jesuit's face once again was the malevolent, triumphant snicker.

Eamon darted out his black tongue and crossed himself with a foul gesture.

"By the—m-m-m-mystery of the holy In-In-In-Incarnation-n-n," he mocked.

Distraught, Francis Xavier closed his eyes, searching again for the meditative strength.

"Per adventum Spiritis Sancti, in die judicii—"

Eamon laughed loudly.

"The D-D-Day of Judgment!" Eamon roared sarcastically. "Where is your fucking Day of Judgment, Baldoni?"

Francis Xavier felt the Jesuit slip away into the vile blackness, a rebuke to himself, and suddenly he realized the risk.

If he, as head of the Roman Catholic Church, could not perform the exorcism due to a flaw in his own spiritual nature, then all was lost.

Blue luminescences swarmed at Francis Xavier's face and vestments, alighting on the gold cross, feeding at long last on the Sicilian.

Eamon came close, confident and arrogant.

"I deceived you with child's tricks, Giacomo Baldoni, playing on your vanity," he hissed.

Francis Xavier groped for some prayer to concentrate on, losing his way, then began stuttering the Litany of Saints.

"Your ceremonials stink of vanity!" Eamon shouted, drowning out the litany. "Your vestments hang heavy with gold!"

Francis Xavier felt the déjà vu. It was like a wave of encompassing darkness. He lost balance, reaching for the defiled altar linen.

"Rome sits on its gold bullion while children starve!" Eamon shrieked. "The Pope runs to grottoes and caves and parish churches, searching for the lost soul of his own religion!"

"Sancte Michaello, ora pro nobis. Sancte Gabriello, ora pro nobis. Sancte Giuseppe, ora pro nobis," Francis Xavier gasped.

"You are lost, Baldoni," Eamon shouted. "Lost under the wealth of two thousand years! Lost under the pomp of your own vanity! Lost under the weight of politicians who betrayed the simplicity of Christ! Lost, Baldoni, like a sheep in the San Rignazzi river gorge!"

... Lost ... Lost ... Lost ... came the mournful echo from the apse.

Eamon smiled disdainfully. He flicked at the gold buttons, the gold pectoral cross on the white vestment. He traced his finger along the gold embroidery of the immaculate white cape.

"Pimp," Eamon whispered. *"Pimp of Christ!"*

Francis Xavier felt a great heat invade his brain. The doubts seeded by the supreme trickster were blossoming into corrosive despair.

"Where is your Second Coming?" Eamon taunted. "Where is your Resurrection?"

Desperately Francis Xavier floundered among the images of San Rignazzi. In that harsh landscape he saw his father, whose body grew stronger with each bad harvest, whose voice in the church sang louder with every death, every illness, every disease of the olive groves. For prayer is a weapon, he had been taught, and it attacks Satan in the very abode of evil: the wavering and despair of the human heart.

Silently Francis Xavier called on his father's faith.

"Sancte Joannes Baptista, ora pro nobis. Omni sancti Angeli et Archangeli, orate pro nobis!"

But the power seeded in Eamon perceived a subtle quality of fear and doubt in Francis Xavier.

Eamon leaned over the crouched form. "You're naked, Baldoni," Eamon whispered. "All your vestments, all your gold, all your Vatican riches cannot assuage your misery now!"

Vague auditory hallucinations stirred behind Francis Xavier.

When he turned to look over his shoulder, he saw to his horror a congregation of deathly waxen figures sitting in the pews, skins varnished in a disfiguring, obscene manner, in old-fashioned Victorian dresses, scraggly hair under shredding bonnets.

Hooves thundered in the aspe. Francis Xavier whirled. A lascivious goat leaped among the shadows, pink tongue flicking wetly, a priest's cassock caught on its horns.

Francis Xavier closed his eyes, trembling, but Eamon's voice continued hot in his ears.

"We are joined this instant, Giacomo Baldoni," he breathed. "From this hour, whatsoever you say, it shall be with my tongue. Whatsoever you decree, it shall be with my signature."

Suddenly there was a subtle stillness behind the altar. Francis Xavier opened his eyes.

He saw his own likeness, resplendent on the Vatican throne, holding the Shepherd's Crook, and the vestments glistened like a thousand stars under the altar lamp. But the smile on the face was twisted. Two ram's horns curled up from under the pontifical miter.

"Dear Christ—" Francis Xavier gasped, shielding his eyes with his arm, his voice rising in an agonized cry, "HELP ME!"

Eddie Fremont wandered alone on the ridge above Golgotha Valley. The praying throng drew him, called him away from the cars, pickup trucks, and station wagons stranded behind the police barricades.

The strange day, the strangest in young Eddie's memory, had begun in the darkness with the radio announcing something extraordinary at the Boston airport. Then came the rumors from neighbors, and the race to the industrial parking lot packed with workers, priests, and nuns. And the strange sense of illumination when the distant Holy Father, a figure in white under the storm clouds, blessed them all.

Now it was 12:30 P.M. and those storm clouds were growing over the desolate valley. And the white church that his mother gazed upon in rapture and prayer was filled with frightening groans and mocking laughter.

Eddie walked deeper into the heart of the birch woods.

Occasional shards of sunlight transformed the tops of the trees into strange shapes. A rabbit—or was it a squirrel—leaped over a fallen log into a gilded patch of mushrooms.

Then the gilded light changed into forms, seven forms, floating densely in the birch grove, sending oblique shafts of silvery luminescence onto the ferns.

Eddie, mesmerized, walked closer, staring at their brilliance, a brilliance of seven metamorphosing quicksilver shapes of light.

A voice drifted down from the vague human shapes. Eddie could not see their eyes, but he knew they were aware of him, looking at him, instructing him.

The voice said: "*Et tu puer Propheta Altissimi vocaberis: praebis enim ante faciem Domini parare vias ejus.*"

Eddie backed away, tripped over a fallen branch, and fell into the soft ferns. Shielding his eyes as he turned his face back toward the figures, he saw that they held seven large jars. They were restless, impatient, yet determined, in a final campaign to communicate to Eddie.

"*Ad dandam scientam salutis plebi ejus, in remissionem peccatorumeoram.*"

Eddie felt their light glowing against his face. He crab-crawled backward over the soft forest ground, then picked himself up and began running.

He ran until he came out of the forest, and down the slope, where a raven-haired woman stood on the edge of the cemetery next to a tall, distinguished gentleman.

Eddie stood, awed, staring first at Anita, then at Dean Osborne.

"I saw angels," Eddie whispered. "Seven. Carrying jars."

Anita nodded, pale and lovely, as though the news in some strange way was not unexpected.

"They spoke to me," the child said to her.

Dean Osborne came close to the boy, laying a firm hand on his shoulder.

"What did they say?" he asked kindly.

Eddie swallowed, then turned cautiously back toward the birch woods. The sunlight played, hovered, metamorphosed on the tree-tops, gilding the branches as the storm clouds rolled in.

"It was a strange language," Eddie said.

But Dean Osborne saw the signs of intelligence in the boy's eyes, and guessed that the mass psychology had engendered some kind of personal vision.

"Tell us," Dean Osborne encouraged.

Eddie found, to his surprise, that the words had pierced his heart and, though in a foreign language, he could now give them utterance in English.

"They said, 'And thou, child, shalt be called the prophet of the Highest, for thou shalt go before the face of the Lord to prepare His ways, to give knowledge of salvation to His people, unto the remission of their sins.' "

Dean Osborne was thunderstruck at the exactness of the biblical quotation.

"I don't even know what it means," Eddie smiled sheepishly.

"It means just what it says," Anita said quietly.

Dean Osborne caught the otherworldly quality of Anita's assurance.

"Go," she said gently to the boy. "Repeat those words to your mother. Tell them to the people at the church."

Eddie nodded, then turned and ran furiously toward the densely packed, praying crowds kneeling before the Church of Eternal Sorrows.

"Come now," Dean Osborne cautioned. "You mustn't get swept up into this belief phenomenon, Anita."

Dean Osborne stopped. The gentle smile on his face slowly froze. He followed Anita's look upward. The massive cloud formations spread in a barely ambiguous cruciform flux he had seen only once before in his life.

On Mario's slides.

Reddish, rolling, and volatile.

"Dean Osborne," Anita whispered. "I think we are coming to the end of history."

Transfixed, Dean Osborne watched the clouds spread, gathering definition.

The metamorphoses of the eastern clouds had also drawn Mario's attention. Shapes of what seemed like animals were embedded in them. Galloping horses. Dull tremors reverberated beneath the squad car.

The policeman up front picked up the mike.

"Riley here. Come in."

"What is it, Riley?" crackled a voice.

"Mild tremors on the ridge here," Riley reported. "Is there blasting going on somewhere?"

"Will check. Over and out."

Mario was intrigued with the boiling forms in the reddish clouds. No doubt reflections. But of what? He looked at the dark forest on the side of the ridge, then the steep incline leading down to the cemetery and the church. The immense cloud buildup seemed to be pressing toward the church from the east.

The darkness of the sky unnerved him. What kind of storm was brewing? The ridge road they were parked on seemed to divide the universe between a darkness too terrible to imagine and an unfolding that also terrified him. What the hell was happening?

The policeman up front rolled down his window. From below were heard the quavering litanies from the crowds, accented by distant thunders, and the horrible laughter emanating from within the church.

Eamon's laughter grew and the echoes did not diminish, until the cacophony boomed among the rafters.

"You chased me, seeking the Second Coming, stinking of the Church's wealth!" Eamon roared. "But it was all a snare, and you fell into it like a pig in a wallow!"

Francis Xavier held the black rosary tightly.

Renata Baldoni, the white-haired Sicilian peasant's wife, had given him a sure faith. A faith that lived intimately with Christ, in a nourishing mercy, as a sapling is nourished by the irrigation of cool waters. The child learned to desire nothing, feel nothing, but the subtle sensations of that vulnerable mercy stirring throughout the world.

It was a musical, devout influence that once had moved him to tears of rapture.

"What are you doing?" Eamon demanded, furious, and yet strangely disquieted.

Francis Xavier had risen from his kneeling position and stood at the side of the altar. Slowly, very slowly, he slipped off the massive gold Ring of the Fisherman and put it on a chair.

"You fool!" Eamon hissed.

But Eamon's face paled, uncertain, watching Francis Xavier warily.

"Even the great trickster can serve Christ when he speaks the truth," Francis Xavier said, untying the gold-embroidered tassels of his cape.

To choose between the grandeur of Rome and the instincts given him by his mother had never been such a painful, divisive dilemma. But it was so now. And Francis Xavier chose.

Francis Xavier folded the white and gold cape and placed it on the chair, lovingly, over the Vatican ring.

"Pimp!" Eamon roared.

The blue luminescences swarmed around Francis Xavier. Unperturbed, he lifted the heavy gold pectoral cross over his head, kissed it, and laid it on the folded cape.

The satin skullcap, embroidered by the Vatican tailors according to centuries-old tradition of pattern, was also placed on the chair.

Eamon retreated, uncertain. The figure before him, divested of its magnificent outer vestments, lost its pomp and grandeur. All that remained was a Sicilian priest.

In the gnarled hand, reflecting the light of the yellow altar lamp, was the simple, black rosary.

"*Roman pimp!*" Eamon shrieked, livid with rage.

Francis Xavier approached the Jesuit. He extended his hands slightly, as though to show himself unarmed, except for the black rosary.

Francis Xavier knelt, crossed himself, and kissed the rosary. He closed his eyes.

"Pray with me, Eamon," he whispered, in startling simplicity.

Deep within, Eamon realized the impossible: The very vulnerability of Francis Xavier, materially and spiritually, would be his only weapon.

Behind them both, sounds of hooves and the airborne stench of foul creatures assailed their senses.

"I, too, have been lost, Eamon," Francis Xavier said. "You and I both. No priest can live without serving Christ with all his soul."

Eamon's lips distorted into a sneer. The winged silhouettes swooped down and fed greedily from the defiled Host and chalice on the altar. Eamon trembled under the impact of Francis Xavier's calm, invading spirituality.

"*You* have shown me this, Eamon."

Eamon raised his hands, covering his ears. Francis Xavier reached out and pulled the hands away. When Eamon looked up, he saw the Sicilian's deep, masculine gray eyes penetrating his.

"Christ has *chosen you* to show me this, Eamon," Francis Xavier insisted.

The church rafters trembled, then subsided. Eamon felt the exquisite vulnerability of Francis Xavier, and it terrified him. For the Sicilian was offering himself as a sacrifice.

"No—Holy Father—" Eamon blurted through clenched teeth. "H-He is too strong for us—"

Francis Xavier held up the black rosary.

"In simplicity is our strength, Eamon."

Eamon felt a piercing pain in his right side, and a throbbing agony in his wrists and feet, and a pounding ache along the crown of his head, mockeries of the Crucifixion.

Francis Xavier's cool hands righted him.

"I'm so afraid, Holy Father—" Eamon stammered, eyes glistening, grasping at the peasant's hands.

Eamon looked deeply into Francis Xavier's eyes. He saw that there, too, a terrible pain resided, and yet the Sicilian was unafraid.

"Be strong, Eamon," Francis Xavier whispered. "For whosoever believeth in Christ with the heart of a child, to him shall Christ come."

Gently, for the second time, Francis Xavier folded Eamon's trembling hands under the altar lamp into the gesture of prayer.

"*Per sanctam Resurrection tuam, libera nos, Domine,*" Francis Xavier began, hushed and confident.

Gaining strength from Francis Xavier's example, Eamon dared a second time to repeat in English.

"Through Thy holy Resurrection deliver us, O Lord."

Francis Xavier continued the litany. Eamon's voice gained strength, then faltered as the ancient power rose more forcefully than before.

Dream images of his dead father, his dead uncle among black vipers, interfered in the litany.

Francis Xavier heard the litany transformed by the church echoes into denunciations of Christ.

But worse were waves of a vile, palpable hatred emanating from Eamon, breaking against him, pounding at his resolve. With each savage thrust the energy stung the skin, and stank, and crept up his arms, searching for his soul.

Francis Xavier smiled softly.

He forced his mind to perceive himself as a child, praying at the wooden bed, with his mother at his side. Then, the waves of fear had dissipated as she showed him how, and now he felt from her a force more indomitable than sin or death.

That simplicity, after all the years, after being raised against his will by his gifts through the Church hierarchy into the very chair of Saint Peter, flowed back like cleansing water.

Francis Xavier paused.

"*Per sanctam Resurrection tuam, libera nos, Domine,*" he said again, softly, with unassailable conviction.

"Through Thy holy Resurrection, deliver us, O Lord!" Eamon cried out with a totality of being that echoed and rebounded in the darkness.

Suddenly waves of putrescence broke against the alb of the Sicilian. Stinging, glittering lights attacked the gnarled hand that held the rosary.

Unafraid, Francis Xavier raised his head to the dark rafters above, and his voice rang out, clear and commanding:

"*Begone, Satan! For Christ is at hand!*"

Rolling westward under red, massive clouds, a great cruciform shape gradually began to form above the skies of Golgotha Valley, accompanied by knifing bolts of lightning and claps of earth-shaking thunder.

A hushed silence spread throughout the huddled throng before the church, cowering beneath the splendid yet fearsome sight approaching from the east.

From the unsanctified church came the strong voice of Francis Xavier.

"*Corpus Domini nostri Jesu Christi custodiat animam tuam in vitam aeternam.*"

Cardinal Bellocchi loudly translated.

"May the Body of Our Lord Jesus Christ preserve thy soul to life everlasting."

Everywhere the windows of Golgotha Falls reflected the great cruciform shape moving steadily in the eastern skies.

"*Laudate Dominum, omnes Gentes: laudate eum, omnes populi,*" reverberated Francis Xavier's voice, clear in the valley.

"Praise the Lord, all ye nations; praise Him, all ye people," Cardinal Kennedy's voice sang out.

The ancient command sent television reporters, cameramen, and sound recorders to their knees. A policeman lowered his head, and began to cry, facing the east.

The cruciform cloud moved over the town of Golgotha Falls. A murmur of dread and expectation flowed down over the kneeling people.

"Mamma, are we going to die?" asked a small girl's voice.

"Pray, Cindy. Pray to God."

In other sections of the crowd fathers cradled their frightened children against their breasts, mouthing half-remembered prayers.

The ground was shaking. As Dean Osborne and Anita moved toward the police barricades they held on to shrubs, on to one another, ducking against the grit blown up by the winds.

Dean Osborne saw that even the hard-bitten policemen were rapt by the religious atmosphere. Over his shoulder he saw the immense arms of the cross-shape, and a defined figure began to form at its center.

How extraordinary, he thought, to perceive and to analyze one's perceptions simultaneously. It was more subjective than anything B. F. Skinner had dared. But pages out of his thesis surfaced in Dean Osborne's mind now, and he suddenly realized how that theme had been there, afraid of the strict authority of the great behavioralist.

Anita walked faster over the stubbled ground. Dean Osborne slowed, staring in amazement at the lightning striking the birch forest of Golgotha Valley. Never had life, curiosity, vitality surged so triumphantly within his breast. The red trails of the swirling clouds blanketed the eastern edge of the town, and fingers of the heated air groped relentlessly toward the police barricades.

In the swirling dust Dean Osborne lost Anita.

"Anita!" he called.

But the winds sucked up his words. The dean stumbled toward the police barricades, arm in front of his eyes, holding on to shrubs against the wind.

"Deo gratias, alleluia, alleluia!" came the voice of Francis Xavier through the maelstrom.

Dean Osborne needed no Catholic priest to translate.

"Praise God!" shouted the people kneeling. "Hallelujah! Hallelujah!"

The shrieking antiphony of the red cruciform shape came whistling through the streets of Golgotha Falls.

"I have seen the vision," Dean Osborne whispered.

The cruciform mass, identical to what had appeared in the thermovision tapes, now hung triumphant over the Church of Eternal Sorrows, bending trees and snapping branches in its force and heat.

On the ridge the two policemen stood beside their squad car, staring in terror at the approaching holocaust. The next moment they were both running for cover in the nearby birch forest.

Caged in the rear of the squad car, Mario shouted hoarsely, "Let me out! Goddamn you bastards—!"

He braced his back against the car door and slammed his boots repeatedly at the opposite window. The shatterproof glass finally crystallized and powdered under the steady assault. Mario painfully squeezed his body out through the narrow window, scratching his face, arms, and legs. He tumbled to the ground, trying to break his fall with his handcuffed hands. Unable to gain his balance, he rolled down the steep embankment. A tree stump brought him to a jarring stop and a flash of white pain shot behind his eyes.

"Anita!" Mario shouted, though his voice was absorbed in the howling winds and rumbling thunder.

"ANITA!"

Wincing in pain, Mario tried desperately to crawl out from the thorny shrub. Dimly he thought he saw a familiar figure groping toward him in the storm.

"ANITA!" he roared.

Anita stopped, turned, to listen in the swirling debris. Was she imagining that naked cry?

"MARIO!"

Battered by the searing storm, Mario began to move, stumbling on his knees, blindly, toward the figure of the woman once his lover.

"ANITA!"

Anita changed direction, bending low into the winds. The pain in the voice was mixed with a peculiar, final kind of hopelessness.

Then, among the debris, the shreds of fabric hurled by the howling winds, between a thorn shrub and the police cars, she saw the brown-jacketed figure, kneeling, unpenitent, unbroken, but confused.

"*Mario*—" she gasped, running in his direction.

Immediately she embraced him, felt him shuddering. His hot, salty tears flowed unashamedly against her face. They had trussed him up like a common criminal and half killed the soul inside.

"Anita," he whispered. "I've been in hell without you!"

Anita pressed his face against her breast, rocking him slowly.

"There will be no more hell, Mario," she said gently in his ear.

Mario looked up slowly. The calm assurance of her voice eradicated the psychic storms of the night before, eradicated even the uncanny fear of the metamorphosing storm, out of which now stumbled a figure with a tattered raincoat. Dean Osborne, handkerchief over mouth, had found Anita and Mario at last. Mario saw the transfigured excitement in the old professor's eyes. Suspiciously, Mario recoiled.

Dean Osborne covered Mario and Anita with his coat, shielding them from the storm.

In the cemetery the mounds of loam, restless, cracked and heaved. Tombstones pushed up from the thistles, bits of Victorian brass and velvet from coffin interiors were disgorged.

"I believe in God," Anita said, staring at the cemetery and at the white church where Francis Xavier and Eamon Malcolm prayed. "I do, without reservation, believe in a God Almighty!"

The clouds burst with a torrent of hail and sleet. The Victorian façades slid into Canaan Street.

Dean Osborne, still shielding Anita and Mario from the storm, saw the timbers crash into the fissures of the asphalt. Dogs howled. The Siloam flowed over its banks, thrashing at the church foundation.

Scientific objectivity tugged at his heart and so did another, inchoate, powerful feeling, leaving him divided, confused, and amazed.

"Could it really be?" he whispered.

Mario struggled to his knees, gazing in disbelief at the soft black loam shifting in the graveyard. Groaning coffins ruptured, emerging from the century-old hold of the earth.

Then it came. A skeletal figure, rising from its Victorian casket, clutched with its bony fingers its gold cross. As the ground buckled, it raised the casket higher, and the skeleton raised the cross higher to the red cruciform shape, tightly clutched in the rigidity of death.

"No!" Mario shouted defiantly. "I don't believe!"

Anita held him closer. "I believe in the power and the grace of that which can never be measured," Anita whispered, lowering her head reverently, at peace with herself.

Dean Osborne licked his lips, frozen in uncertainty.

Mario turned desperately around him, face frozen in a rictus of incomprehension and denial. As though betraying him, the policemen were on their knees. And so were the news teams. Mario whirled to face the insignia of the storm.

"I DON'T BELIEVE IN GOD!" he roared defiantly.

But Anita heard the faltering in that roar. Indeed, the Church, or God, had sunk its shaft deep into Mario's heart.

Then the three—the atheist, the agnostic, and the believer—felt the deepest parts of their personalities drawn inexorably toward that spiraling, sediment-tinted figuration over the church.

It was as though they were all dying and a final, immutable portion of their bodies were rising to the heavens.

The asphalt on Canaan Street crumbled into bluish steam. Cars and trucks tilted, then crashed onto their sides. Balls of sleet bounced upon the earth.

Through it all Anita's face burned with an inner radiance.

"Have mercy, dear Lord," Anita breathed, raising her head, hair blown fiercely back by the roaring agony. *"Have mercy on us all!"*

Anita saw, perfectly defined in the floating cloud above, the Figure bearing wounds in the red apocalypse.

In that instantaneous liberation she felt a sense of soaring, as though flying out through a window, and then, on the brink of the last portals of human knowledge, amidst the wails and cries of the multitudes, all motion ceased.

The storm abated suddenly.

The force stilled, and the stillness was shattering.

Cardinal Bellocchi, Cardinal Kennedy, Bishop McElroy, the Italian Jesuits, the undersecretary of state and his diplomatic assistant, in perfect unison, sang out over and over.

"Benedictus vos omnipotens Deus! Benedictus vos omnipotens Deus!"

Soon two thousand voices took up the chant.

The thunderous litany penetrated Eamon's tortured brain. Weakly his eyes lifted toward the Holy Father.

Francis Xavier lay prostrate before the altar. He had sunk to the final retreat, where hope and decency live, in the fundamental child. And all for Eamon's salvation.

Eamon trembled with a joy he had never felt before, not in all the days of his childhood.

Francis Xavier turned to gaze upon Eamon. His face reflected a loving heart.

"Through Thy holy Resurrection!" Francis Xavier said ambiguously.

Eamon stared at the Pontiff. Francis Xavier's face. The gray eyes, nearly black in that light, brimmed with tears.

Eamon suddenly looked overhead, and understood.

"The lamp—" he breathed. "The lamp of Christ!"

The altar lamp, partially covered by the cracked glass, glowed a deep and holy red.

Through the interior of the church the atmosphere was a warm red, bathing the lazily circulating currents of dust in a gentle radiance.

Francis Xavier rose, arms extended, and stumbled under the lamp.

The vow made so long ago in San Rignazzi was finally, eternally answered.

"We are in the very presence of Jesus Christ, Eamon!" Francis Xavier whispered, his cheeks running freely with tears. "Eamon— do you feel Him?"

Suddenly something sucked down through Eamon's being, a vile, corrosive substance, burning, destroying, leaving him pale and shaking in pain.

"It burns! It burns!" Eamon shrieked, shielding himself from the lamp's glow.

Francis Xavier immediately bent down to pull Eamon's hands away from his eyes.

"Embrace the light, Eamon! Let it enter you! Receive Him Who sent it!"

"I can't! It burns! It burns inside!"

"Yes! Yes! It burns, Eamon! It is the flame of Christ! Let it cleanse you as it has me!"

Eamon twisted on his stomach, trying to crawl away. Then he saw the chair by the central aisle. In it lay the priceless gold ring, the heavy pectoral cross, and the embroidered, immaculate white and gold cape, all embossed with the Vatican insignia.

For him Francis Xavier had shed the last remnant of worldly power, and offered himself, trusting in Christ.

That the Pope should offer his own eternal soul as a sacrifice, to save the unworthiest priest in a desolate valley church, drawn by a mystery Eamon could not comprehend, was overwhelming.

Tears of gratitude suddenly burst from the Jesuit. He turned, kissing the shoes of Francis Xavier.

"Oh, Holy Father," he wept, unashamed. "I have sinned! I have been proud of heart! I have been used as an instrument to mock the divinity of Christ!"

Francis Xavier held Eamon's head in both his assured peasant's hands, raising the Jesuit's face.

"Do you renounce Satan, and all his pomps, and all his works?" Francis Xavier asked.

"I do!"

"Do you believe in Jesus Christ and the remission of sins?"

The red light glowed warmly over them both, uniting them in a bond of extraordinary experience that could have but one answer.

"Yes!"

Francis Xavier gazed fondly at Eamon. The Jesuit, by his torment, had revealed the purity of the believing heart, had galvanized him, even from the gilded magnificence of the chair of Saint Peter, to acknowledge the simplest of all truths: that only he who is a child may walk in the fields of Christ.

The constituent parts of Eamon's conscience fell away. Ian, his uncle, the seminarians, and Elizabeth—all disintegrated and lost their hold on his heart. The loneliness of a child whose hunger for Christ had created fear of others evaporated. Eamon knew finally that his sacrifices for the priesthood were justified.

That was the dual mission of Golgotha Falls.

"Eamon," Francis Xavier intoned, making the sign of the cross over the Jesuit, "I absolve thee!"

The altar lamp trembled. Through the Gothic windows the two transfigured men saw the gathered people, and Anita, Mario, and the policemen and the newsmen on their knees in the late afternoon.

The coastal storm that had inflicted its ravages on Golgotha Falls retreated into the stratosphere as the sun began its slow descent in the west.

The cruciform red cloud, twirling ragged bolts of lightning at its base, rose high above Golgotha Falls with diminishing intensity.

Francis Xavier and Eamon simultaneously lowered their faces, crossed themselves, and felt the radiance of the storm mingle with a sacred hush into the soft ruby of the altar lamp.

"In the name of the Father, the Son, and the Holy Spirit, amen," Francis Xavier concluded.

The cruciform shape, rising still higher in the heavens, slowly dispersed, casting veils of mist over the valley. Doubled rainbows glittered across the afternoon sky.

Anita looked from the red cloud and onto the church. Whatever had passed between Francis Xavier and Eamon Malcolm would remain forever secret. There were domains science could not penetrate, beyond the remotest external signs. And yet, as she looked from the suffused faces of the kneeling priests, one at the head of the Roman Catholic Church and the other at its most humble rank, she knew for certain there was a connection between what had transpired between them and the awesome configuration over the valley.

A sense of someone beside her made Anita turn. Mario, still on his knees, wrists in handcuffs, face and arms bleeding, stared dazedly in shock at the church, his lips stammering.

"G-Gerasima—P-P-P-Pontif-if-if o theralpy—py—Pronteus—oh, God—I'm dead—dead—bed—ted—med—ged—"

Dean Osborne tried to comfort Mario.

"It's all right, Mario," he whispered. "Don't deny what you've seen, what you've felt."

But Mario had been taken past the boundaries of his strength.

Dean Osborne looked mutely at Anita for assistance. She embraced Mario sadly, slowly, yet her heart was as much with the crowd as with Mario.

For the great mass of people had discerned the movement of the two holy men inside the church, and a mighty cheer rose from their collective throats.

Great shafts of sunlight penetrated the breaking clouds, spotlighting the church, and struck the door. Untouched, it glided smoothly open.

Ahead of Anita, living proof for them all, stood the Pope of the Roman Catholic Church, eyes radiant, in his splendid vestments, and beside him the joyous Jesuit, Eamon Malcolm.

EPILOGUE

"The Golgotha Effect" became communications slang for confusion and incompetence.

From the four television crews and two radio teams, eight men and women were fired.

Videotapes of the heavenly apparition showed only a massive cumulus cloud, split into two armatures, rising over the eastern edge of Golgotha Valley. Reporters examining the tapes could not explain the fever and dread and religious awe that had seized them in the paroxsym of that day in October.

Nor did the Boston Municipal Police find a satisfactory explanation for the dereliction of duty of twelve motorcycle patrolmen and five squad car officers.

The secret service refused to discuss the affair with TV reporters, the press, or anyone else.

The videotapes of the church showed fluctuations of color, temperature, and light intensity within the interior, but nothing unexplainable. Sound recordings, though imperfect, revealed a multitude of Gregorian chants and litanies.

An amnesia flowed through the multitudes who had attended Golgotha Falls that day. No one responded to reporters' questions.

Within a year only the photographs and videotapes remained, crammed among others, in the morgues of newspaper offices and the Boston television studios.

Dean Osborne retired from the faculty of Harvard, having received a two-year grant to write a history of the psychological sciences.

He performed the task with erudition and conscientiousness. In the process he reviewed the research of the previous ten years. It filled a deep void. His wife had died after a lingering bout with cancer.

He worked late into the night, sipping sherry, at ease finally under the portraits of his ancestors in the firelight of his study. The desk and bookshelves, and even the carpet and chairs, were filled with the orderly confusion of folios, articles, and reference volumes. Dean Osborne became fascinated with the great epistemological question: what is the difference between what a human being sees and what he *thinks* he sees?

It was a conundrum that would have baffled William James, despite all the great man's research into religious experience.

Often Dean Osborne's sharpened mind drifted from the immediate task and he stared into the firelight. What *had* happened at Golgotha Falls? His training inclined him toward a materialist position, that he had witnessed a mass outpouring of faith that had resulted in a collective delusion.

In fact, his own religious hunger had made him susceptible to the same delusion.

But the dean had too much respect for Anita Wagner, whom he had supported in seeking a position at the University of Pennsylvania, to utterly dismiss the possibility, however remote, that extra-subjective factors might have been operative.

Particularly in the dawn, in the long winter dawn when he awoke and the housekeeper served him coffee and he gazed down the purity of the snow-covered estate toward the clouded sun, particularly then was he mindful of Anita's attitude. For in that quiet hour, that almost timeless, silent hour of perpetual renewal, he felt that, at some level deeper than his research could ever take him, he too had experienced a vision of the Christian apocalypse.

Mario Gilbert committed himself to the psychiatric unit of Boston General Hospital for two months' observation.

In those two months he filled twelve notebooks with observations, theories, and future experimental models. Mario wrote to Dean Osborne, to the president of Harvard, and to the National Science Foundation, demanding to have his laboratory restored. The Harvard Science Faculty rejected his claims and severed him from the university. However, upon the closing down of his department, the tapes, seismographic records, slides, and sound recordings taken from the Church of Eternal Sorrows were returned to him.

Anita visited Mario several times at the hospital. Gradually both realized there was no relationship possible between them anymore.

Released from the hospital, Mario worked on his notebooks, editing them, organizing his theories into a volume titled *Golgotha Falls: An Assault on the Fourth Dimension*. In it, he outlined with scrupulous care the developing power of a sick Jesuit priest to cast imagery into a thermovision tape, into a crowded lecture hall, and finally onto an emotional crowd of newsmen, police, urbanites, semiliterate farmers, and even the highest echelons of the Roman Catholic Church. Mario never submitted the manuscript for publication.

He took a job as an electronics maintenance engineer for the naval shipyards south of Boston. The rage and humiliation of Golgotha Falls gradually subsided. Mario never fought for parapsychology again.

Sometimes, at night, in his small apartment, he thumbed through his notebooks and his boxes of slides and photographs. The handwriting was mainly unreadable. The ideas were random. They hurt his mind. Not a day went by that he did not reflect on that cataclysmic day in October. His only salvation lay in the scientific approach; in developing a legitimate rationale for the unexplainable. The red sediment, he reasoned, blown up by the cyclonic storm winds, had spread into a twin armature as it reached the upper, thinner levels of the atmosphere. The crowd, excited by the ritual and the costumes of the Vatican party, under the suggestiveness of Golgotha Valley, interpreted the natural event as a Christian vision. It was an analysis that satisfied Mario, further abetted by his research that revealed the military had been conducting secret tests of new jet engines in nearby

Falmouth, which explained the shock waves and tremors that undermined the houses on Canaan Street. Then, too, the Siloam, rushing faster after the cloudburst, had eaten away at the clay banks at a quicker rate, weakening the ground, which would also account for the shifting of the old graves in the cemetery and the disintegration of the Victorian buildings adjacent to it.

All these facts, combined with Eamon Malcolm's unique powers of projection, had worked on the crowds, on the policemen, the news teams, Anita, Dean Osborne, Francis Xavier, and, Mario realized to his great chagrin, himself.

Mario chuckled bitterly, swilling down his fourth bottle of beer. Everybody had blacked out.

Francis Xavier probably thought the Incarnation of Christ was at hand.

Mario seized his temples. The pain that pounded through his head always came when he thought about Golgotha Falls.

At such times he reached for his weights and pressed up the old iron on the floor of his tiny room that smelled of sweat. Still the agony did not fade.

What inexpressible trauma could have caused the Jesuit to project the goathead onto the thermovision screen? How and why did he manifest such an image?

Gritting his teeth, nostrils flaring, Mario increased the weights, until the pain of muscles penetrated the pain of mind with a more bearable torment.

Mario paused, blinking, sweating, alone in his perpetual isolation.

The seven angelic figures reported by the eight-year-old boy. His ability to translate Latin into English. The figure rising from the grave, witnessed by no fewer than two thousand people.

Were they indeed precursors to the Resurrection?

Francis Xavier cut short the Quebec conference and reduced it to a conclave of North American cardinals and bishops. He returned to Rome, enthusiastic over the spectacular success of the American vigil. European delegations and Latin American prelates flooded into Rome, filled with the emotions of the impending second millennium. Triumphant and refreshed, Francis Xavier addressed over two hundred thousand of the faithful in St. Peter's Square.

In the evening he received word that his mother, while attempting to rescue her favorite lamb, the one with the single black ear, had stumbled, fallen, and drowned in the raging San Rignazzi River.

Francis Xavier donned the coat and hat of a peasant and returned to San Rignazzi. Alone at her bier, guarded by his relatives and the local parish priest, he prayed deeply and loudly.

Christ's lieutenant he had vowed to be, and Christ's lieutenant he had become. In the primacy of his innocence he had been touched by a destiny that transcended understanding. Yet even as the Church crossed relentlessly toward the third millennium, what had changed?

Satan still battled daily with Christ, in terrains of tormented souls, touched with the bitterness of mortality.

Francis Xavier's fist formed around the worn black rosary. At Golgotha Falls he knew—utterly *knew*, beyond any possibility of doubt—the Second Coming was at hand.

The great insight came from stripping away the vestments of office, and wrestling with Satan embedded in a man of passionate and corrupted faith.

Had it been a salutory warning? That not only he, but the entire Roman Church look to its roots? Look back to its origins in the caves and groves at the dawn of history, when God moved among the generations, as at San Rignazzi?

In the presence of his mother Francis Xavier was reassured. Unafraid, trusting, the very vulnerability and selflessness of her intimate faith had been the fortress against which Satan crumbled. In Golgotha Falls, in the Vatican, and now, back in San Rignazzi.

Gently he performed the last litanies. Francis Xavier blessed her body and her soul. Even though sorrow struck him, remembering her self-sacrifice for him through all the years of poverty, there was a great reassurance: For the Christian, death was but the portal to eternal salvation.

Golgotha Falls had proved that.

It was a clear morning in September at the University of Pennsylvania. Dr. Anita Wagner pointed to the triptych of projected images on the screen behind the lectern.

In the darkened auditorium the cruciform shape, the goathead, and the skeletal figure rising from the grave glittered toward the students.

"The background flux in all three cases is identical," Anita pointed out. "Characteristic of thermovision renderings. The projections themselves are highly defined. It has been conjectured that they were formed by a human mind, not generated in some manner from either the flux, or some other, perhaps discarnate, agency."

Anita turned back to her lecture notes under a tiny lamp. Her black hair was cut short, and gold earrings sent the light flickering over her tweed jacket. She had changed, matured, since Golgotha Falls, into a professional lecturer.

"In the unpublished Gilbert treatise, *Golgotha Falls: An Assault on the Fourth Dimension*, it is stated that the projector of these images was a Jesuit priest," Anita said. "A sophisticated man, well educated, and with a refined, sensitive nature. The projections occurred, Mr. Gilbert believed, during extreme psychological crises. Having been an intimate part of this experiment, I must say that I do not hold with his opinion."

Anita turned toward the enigmatic trio of psychic emblems. They hung resplendent in space, icons of the nonmaterial universe. Captivated, the students stopped taking notes.

"The extraordinary variety and definition of these images," Anita continued, "are a testimony, I believe, to a power and a source beyond the human imagination."

The students studied the three images, which remained somehow unfathomed, hypnotic, and relentlessly foreboding.

"Still, in partial defense of Mr. Gilbert's theory, the paranormal *is* often experienced by people involved in situations of great emotional stress."

The campus bell rang. Students gathered their notebooks and filed noisily toward the doors. The auditorium lights came on slowly, a soft amber, and the projected images faded.

Eamon Malcolm stood alone among the seats. He looked at Anita with a soft despair, a fatalism of time passing.

Anita went quickly down the steps, toward him, paused, and then took his hand in hers.

"What happened to you, Eamon?" she whispered. "I called the cathedral. I checked the newspapers. You just disappeared."

Eamon flushed deeply.

"They put me in a seminary in Vermont," he confessed. "A kind of resting station for troubled Jesuits. Very disciplined."

Eamon smiled nervously. Meeting Anita was a greater shock than he had anticipated. His awkwardness was momentarily relieved when a pimply-faced youth came down from the projection booth with the lecture slides.

When the boy left Eamon felt the impasse return.

"And Mario?" he asked. "Where is he?"

Anita's face grew somber.

"Mario won't answer my letters," she said. "Nobody has heard of him since."

Eamon nodded in sympathy.

"I didn't like Mario," he confessed. "But the man was brilliant. Aggressive, uncouth perhaps, even reckless, but he had his own kind of courage."

Anita sensed Eamon's floundering. She put her hand into the crook of his elbow and escorted him into the autumn sunlight. Eamon paused on the threshold, dazzled by the blazing red and yellow trees.

"Eamon, why didn't you write?" Anita asked. "You could have found where I was through Harvard."

"I was ashamed."

Another class was beginning. Students pushed past them into the auditorium. Eamon and Anita walked onto the asphalt path that led under a canopy of elms.

"After—after that Friday dawn," Eamon confessed, "I thought it best—that is, I felt uneasy about contacting you."

Eamon kept his eyes averted. When he turned to Anita she answered him thoughtfully.

"I never despised you, Eamon," she said. "In fact, it was seeing you through the church window that gave me the strength to survive the storm."

Eamon smiled ironically.

"Anita, what do you believe happened that day?"

Anita's brow furrowed. "I can't say, really. I've thought about it so often. At the time I felt certain that it was a truly religious experience."

"And now?"

"At some level," she said, "in the deepest levels of awareness, there may be no difference between the paranormal and the religious."

Eamon nodded, his voice still troubled.

"I can't talk about this with anyone else," he said. "But these last few months, alone in my cell, working in the gardens, meditating, I've come to the same conclusion."

They walked under an oak that stood bare but defiant under the azure skies. The grass was covered with brown and red leaves. The air was redolent of autumn dust, an invigorating and nostalgic fragrance.

"I was in a kind of tunnel," he said thoughtfully. "It was a cave, until Francis Xavier kept chipping away at the other end. Finally, the light came through and I was freed."

317

Anita took his arm again. Eamon knew he was talking fast now, earnestly, about all those things pent up by nearly a year of hard discipline and enforced silence.

"The extraordinary thing," he said enthusiastically, "was the charisma of Francis Xavier. It was like a field of pure light that came into the church. I was clinically dead, and yet he breathed life into me."

Eamon turned to Anita, looked hard into her eyes.

"Where did Francis Xavier get such a force?"

"From his belief, of course," Anita replied, smiling.

Eamon nodded. He seemed suddenly abstracted. He stopped near the campus rose garden.

"Do you know what my penance is?" he asked. "The penance from the Apostolic Penitentiary? It is to work two years in a hospital as a menial laborer. The lowest of the orderlies."

Eamon shrugged.

"I accept the wisdom of the Church," he said. "Intellectuals need to learn to work with suffering, to channel their emotions, to learn humanity."

The sun glistened on his forehead.

"Anita, the hospital I've been sent to is near Rome."

"Is that unusual?"

"No. But . . . I just can't help thinking that Francis Xavier is behind this penance."

"Why?"

"Because the direction of the Church turned one hundred eighty degrees after Golgotha Falls. There have been purges and realignments. The whole impetus toward rethinking the Second Incarnation is gathering force."

Eamon faltered, then took a deep breath.

"My guess is that Francis Xavier wants to talk to me about Golgotha Falls."

Anita paused.

"Eamon, what about the Church of Eternal Sorrows? What became of it?"

"It's functioning, I hear. Simply and effectively. A Jesuit named Joseph Casper oversees a small parish."

"Strange. After all that happened there, I imagined it would have become a shrine. Another Lourdes."

"Yes, I know what you mean. Mortals have a need for icons and shrines. But I suppose the destiny of that church was never in the hands of mere mortals."

Anita gazed at him, puzzled.

"Then whose?"

"Why, you said it before in your lecture. *'A power and a source far beyond the human imagination.'*"

When they said farewell at the train taking Eamon back to New York, they felt like brother and sister taking leave. Anita's religious instincts, and Eamon's newfound respect for the paranormal, had blossomed in the wake of Golgotha Falls.

"The day will come," Eamon predicted, "when science and religion, matter and spirit, will reveal their unfolding purpose to mankind simultaneously."

"When, Eamon?"

He smiled gently.

"Why, the last day, of course."